p.

DESPERATE DESIRE

She pressed against him, suddenly unafraid. She wanted him and all he could give her. It was proof of her trust. If there had been others before her, she would make him forget every one. If he had ever been with Amelia he would never want to be again.

Panting, he tore his lips from her mouth and buried his face in her neck, kissing her, sending shivers of excitement through her body. When one of his hands closed over her breast, pressed up eagerly by the squeezing corset, her entire body suddenly became electrified. She felt molten inside, weak and mindless. Nothing mattered except that he was touching her. Tightening her arms around his neck, clutching his silky hair, she sought his lips. Desperate for his touch, he obeyed her silent command, grasping both breasts possessively. Then with a groan, he kissed her deeply, tasting her mouth, circling her back with his arms, crushing her to him as if to make her part of him.

Kiss of Gold

Kiss of Gold

FIRST HE TAUGHT HER TO LIVE...
THEN HE TAUGHT HER TO LOVE

SAMANTHA HARTE

Futura

A Troubadour Book

Copyright © 1985 by Samantha Harte

First published in Great Britain in 1988
by Futura Publications, a Division of
Macdonald & Co (Publishers) Ltd
London & Sydney

ISBN 0 7088 3643 7

Reproduced, printed and bound in Great Britain by
Hazell Watson & Viney Limited
Member of BPCC plc
Aylesbury Bucks

Futura Publications
A Division of
Macdonald & Co (Publishers) Ltd
Greater London House
Hampstead Road
London NW1 7QX
A member of Pergamon MCC Publishing Corporation plc

To Bill, for believing in me.
To Laura, Bob and Kathy, for putting up with me.
To Carole, for helping me.

Kiss of Gold

Chapter One

Bethinghamshire, England, 1893

Restively, Daisie turned from the ivy-framed window. Outside, in the garden sagging with pink and white blooms stretched the eager carpet of bright new grass. At last, it was spring. She'd be married in one more month.

Sinking to the rose brocade Queen Anne chair by the narrow window, Daisie set her elbow on the glossy gold of the oak sill and gazed out into the confectionery world.

Marriage. She should be deliriously happy, but when a young lady was betrothed to a lamb like Norwood Poole and wanted to wed a lion, well, the future did not inspire great joy.

Norwood was a darling boy, and of impeccable family. He stood five feet seven inches tall. His wonderfully glossy black curls and fair oval face bespoke intelligence and sensitivity. Daisie's fourteen-year-old sister, Pammie, thought his mustache utterly adult. And he kissed like . . . .

Daisie sighed.

Norwood's family had enough money to allow Daisie's mother and sister, after the wedding to continue to live in the ivy-covered brick cottage with the marvelous, two-storey bay window facing on to Bethinghamshire's sleepy streets. Daisie and

Norwood would be expected to move to Downingwood, the Poole family estate. Norwood's mama and papa, Lord and Lady Poole, had a grand place in Kent — acres and acres given over to the raising of sheep and blood horses and wheat. Already, they were remodeling the "little" seventeen-room cottage behind the manor house as a wedding gift.

Money, Daisie thought, narrowing her eyes until the garden became a blur. She loved this old matron of a house. She loved the garden enclosed by low stone walls and surrounded by grandfatherly black elms. She loved to stroll among the groves of rhododendrons to pick violets, pansies and lilies of the valley. She loved the sweet scent of honeysuckle and lavender that filled the air.

As she unrolled the ribbons that turned her straighter-than-kite-string hair into gossamer, wheat-gold curls, Daisie didn't feel a scrap of happiness. Norwood was about as exciting as cold porridge.

Shaking out her ringlets, she scanned her room, scowling affectionately at the delicate cherrywood four-poster, armoire, bureau and dressing table. The pieces still looked as elegant as they must have seventy years before when her grandmother had bought them. The carpet, draperies, lace coverlet, linens and tatted doilies, however, had been mended so often it seemed scarcely any of the original fabric remained.

Daisie's mother, poor darling, was at the end of her tether, hanging onto the house by sheer charm and the volume of her tears. If only Papa were here . . . .

Feeling a sudden gust of anger, Daisie sprang from the chair and began to tidy her room. Their faithful but aging housemaid, Edna, couldn't serve breakfast, keep fires burning, attend her sundry chores *and* be expected to serve as upstairs chambermaid. Poor old woman, Daisie thought, her heart twisting. It must be difficult serving three destitute females living for the day that Gregory Browning returned from the gold fields of America to pay all the bills and save their social faces.

Casting off her threadbare cotton day gown, Daisie laced herself into her corset. She must look presentable in case Norwood rode over to pay court and remind her that only three weeks remained until "their day."

Though the room wasn't cold, Daisie shivered. How she longed to tell Norwood the truth. She had never loved him. When doing one's duty, shouldn't there be just the slightest possibility of love sprouting in the future? She didn't like contemplating a future as chaste as her past. At least, thought Daisie, gazing wistfully into the long, beveled looking-glass at her hour-glass silhouette, a young woman with apple blossoms riotous outside her bedroom window and glowing on her cheeks didn't like it. If she was to marry money to save her family from ruin, why couldn't salvation take the shape of a tall, handsome man with broad shoulders and a lightning-like smile?

Daisie smoothed her tucked and embroidered lawn blouse into place, fastened the black, six-gore skirt around her tiny waist and hurried down to the morning room.

Her mama looked even more worn with anxiety than the day before.

Daisie leaned over the back of the white wicker chair and kissed Cynthia Browning's rouged cheek. "Did you sleep well?"

Mrs. Browning smiled. "I tried. I shall never get used to your father being away from me. I cannot drop off without the thunder of his snores. A year is long enough to find treasure, don't you think? If only he would write . . . ." She sighed. "Be a good girl and hand me that envelope Edna just brought in. A messenger came with it a moment ago."

Glancing at the pale blue stationery and the elaborate script across it, Daisie tensed. She glanced anxiously at her mother, thinking she sounded melancholy.

"To lovely Miss Daisie Browning," Norwood had written. Daisie looked away, wishing she felt even the slightest bit thrilled at the prospect of marrying him.

"Mama," Daisie began, unwilling to open the envelope. "I feel quite uneasy about all this."

Mrs. Browning looked up. "You look lovely, dear. Norwood never notices that you always wear the same skirt. All the dear boy sees is your sweet face. You have always been the most beautiful child, but since your bethrothal you look somehow older. So very — '' She swallowed and cast her eyes down. "The word *tragic* came to mind," her mother said softly. "You'll forgive me in time, I hope.''

Daisie flew to her mother's side and knelt at her feet. Grasping her mother's soft hands, Daisie shook them a little. "Forgive *you*? You must forgive *me* for being so selfish!''

Glimpsing her mother's sorrow made Daisie momentarily wish she could marry Norwood that very day to ease her mother's suffering. To see this cultured woman reduced to such circumstances — waited on by a single tired servant, clad in a shabby, fading gown and inhabiting a neglected, echoing house— made Daisie think she should marry and be glad of it!

"You deserve some say in the matter," her mother said, her voice tremulous. "When I suggested you consider young Norwood, I was under great pressure. I've regretted it since, but I haven't had the courage to say so.''

"Hush, Mama. Norwood adores me. We'll be happy together. You'll have everything you need. Think of the grandchildren, of all the booties you'll knit and — '' Daisie's voice betrayed her constricted throat. How sad that a nice man like Norwood, who would some day be Lord Poole of Downingwood, should make a girl feel so passionless.

"I *am* thinking of your children, my dear. I've been unforgivably selfish in asking you to marry for our comfort. If I sold this house, Pammie and I could get a cottage in the village and live quite well until your papa comes home.''

"Don't even think it!" Daisie clutched her mother's trembling fingers. Gone were the gold and pearl rings, the richly dark garnet bracelets, the rock-crystal necklace with the garnet pendant, the matched pearl earrings and now even the locket brooch with the fine Italian enameling that had belonged to her great, great grandmother and was to have been hers one day.

Daisie threw back her head and felt her wheat-gold curls dance like whispers against her neck. "I won't let you do it!''

"You'd marry though you don't love that boy — just so I can

go on living here?'' Her mother's eyes grew moist and shone like the sapphires she had once worn. Her shoulders relaxed and she smiled as if relieved to be done with a difficult decision.

"Yes, and gladly, Mama. What I meant before was . . . I . . . er . . . was worried about . . . all the things I don't know. Matronly things, Mama.'' Daisie's cheeks grew hot. "I meant only that.''

"When the time comes, you'll learn. There's no better teacher than love. But I will not condemn you to another kind of poverty while I live here in plenty. I could not be happy. Hush a moment, Daisie. Listen to your foolish old mother. I've decided you should have what I've most treasured in my lifetime. Love.''

Daisie's heart suddenly lifted, and she smiled. "You've found another rich man for me?''

"That will come in good time. Ask Norwood for tea this afternoon. We'll break the news to him as gently as possible. I've known all along you didn't love him.'' Daisie's mother spread a triangle of toast with orange marmalade. Her hand trembled as she brought the toast to her lips.

"I don't understand, Mama.''

"Sh-h-h, I hear Pammie on the stairs. She likes Norwood very much, you know. She's been looking forward to your wedding. She'll be disappointed, but in time she'll be glad. Now that I think of it, Norwood is too young for marriage. When Pammie is seventeen, perhaps she'll find him to her liking.''

Daisie's heart skipped a beat. "I'll marry Norwood. When Papa comes home you'll be here where you belong.''

"I was so lucky to have found your father,'' Mrs. Browning mused as if she hadn't heard a word. "Such a wonderful, generous man. He did all he could for us and, you know, I would have been just as happy had he never done so well that we could move here. If he hadn't, the labor problems and the financial setbacks of these times — such difficult times for everyone — would not have made him so ashamed of failing. I want you to have a great love — like your Papa and I had.''

Daisie shook her head to clear her stinging eyes. "He's coming back, Mama!''

Her mother's gaze was steady. "We've had no letter from him in six months. Before that he wrote regularly.'' She looked aside, blinking. "I think something has happened. He wouldn't keep me wondering like this, otherwise.''

"I won't believe it,'' Daisie exclaimed, pacing restlessly in the confines of the room. Her heart ached with the secret fear now exposed between them. But at the moment her younger sister burst in.

"Believe what?'' Pammie shrilled. "Mama, you promised I could tell Daisie myself!'' Her eyes were huge and blue.

Daisie's cheeks blanched. "We haven't been asked to leave?''

Pammie tossed her gold braids and spun around once. "We're moving into the village! I'm to go to school with my friends instead of having that bag of bones Fennyworth teach me in the musty old nursery. Won't Norwood be surprised? He'll know then that you're not marrying him for his family's money.''

Daisie's mouth dropped open in horror. "Pammie!''

Choking, their mother dropped her toast into her lap. "What a thing to say! Norwood has no reason to think — ''

Pammie jammed her fists into her pinafore pockets. "He does! He once said to me he wished he had more than just money to make Daisie love him. Honestly, Mama, that's what he said. He sees how we're living. He's not stupid!'' Her eyes were accusing.

Daisie's gaze wandered to the window that stood open to the fragrant, sun-filled garden. "I never meant him to think I didn't love him, Mama. I tried very hard.''

"No matter now, Daisie. It's better this way, truly. Especially if he's been dissatisfied as well. We'll take a place in the village and live simply.'' Mrs. Browning worried out a marmalade spot in her skirt, a deep crease between her brows.

"I can't let you sell! Papa will be so angry,'' Daisie cried.

Her mother's eyes were almost gay as she replied, "It's already done. We're moving as soon as . . . well, I had thought you'd be married — But no matter. You and Pammie will share the loft. We'll move as soon as we can."

Daisie's hands clenched into fists. To think that her mother had done this behind her back.

Mrs. Browning's smile changed to a grimace of alarm. "Have you been so very happy here that you cannot bear to leave?"

"You can't mean you *want* to live in the village," Daisie said.

"Yes, indeed, dear. We'll survive quite nicely for a year, or even more. If your papa doesn't write by then — " Abruptly she shut her mouth.

Pammie's voice rose hysterically. "Has something happened to Papa?"

"Not at all, darling! Do calm down. I only meant if we hear nothing we'll send someone after your father. America is a wild place of Indian savages and vast deserts. It's very possible they have no postal service where he is. God only knows how remote this gold field is he's gone to. Come, come, child. Don't cry! Think of the lovely summer ahead, and all your chums and the parties. We'll have money again. You can have a new dress!"

Pammie didn't calm down for some time. Daisie retreated to her room, shaken and stunned. She had never dared think that harm might come to her dear foolish papa. That he might be lost forever in the American wilderness set her heart into a painful uproar of fear and fury.

When Norwood arrived for tea, Daisie still hadn't read his note or even changed her blouse. Hearing his knock, she hurried down to the cluttered drawing room where her mother sat among the fringes and dark carved furniture in the lengthening shadows.

"*Can* you have sold the house when it belonged to Papa?"

Her mother smiled. "Have you never heard of a woman acting on her own in financial matters?"

Daisie felt light-headed. A woman acting on her own . . . .

"Norwood's waiting, dear. I assure you, I'm not at all helpless, though for months I've seemed so. When our Mr. Bedlow—the solicitor, dear—came to me with the offer last month, I decided to act. Now that you're not going to be married, some of the proceeds should go toward something you want. More schooling, perhaps. You must get out in the world if you're to meet that special young man I've dreamed of for you. Perhaps you'd like a London season. This change should bring us our heart's desire. Especially you, Daisie, because you were so willing to sacrifice yourself.''

"You make me sound like a saint, Mama." Daisie squirmed. "We both know I'm not."

Her mother patted her hand. "Go in to Norwood and explain. I'll be sitting here until he leaves — if you need me."

Her mind whirling, Daisie crept down the dark hall to the formal front parlor where Norwood perched on the black velvet divan, hat in hand, his suit coat firmly buttoned over his waistcoat, his tight shirt collar stabbing at his throat. His dark eyes and thick lashes made him look fragile. His glossy curls gleamed.

As she closed the parlor doors and greeted him with a nervous, stammering hello, Daisie remembered the day he had first kissed her. He had proposed on bended knee, kneeling on the red and black carpet, and when she had accepted, he had leaned his elbows on her knees, kissing her hastily, worried lest she think he was taking undue liberties. Now she wanted to run.

As she moved toward him, she whispered, "Did you hear the news, Norwood?"

He rubbed his knees and had trouble meeting her eyes. "Your note said you . . . wanted to see me." His face flushed crimson and his precise, almost school-boyish voice faltered.

Taking a chair near the tea service, Daisie poured, wondering suddenly if they'd sell every stick of furniture and piece of china with the house. A lump of tears lodged in her throat. She looked around, thinking of the home she loved so. To give it all up . . . . All she had to do was marry Norwood.

Briefly eyeing Norwood, tentatively reconsidering, Daisie quickly looked away. She felt nothing for him and was ashamed.

"Are you quite well, Daisie?" Norwood asked, looking concerned.

She shuddered. "Mama has sold this house."

Norwood's cup and saucer began to rattle. "I beg your pardon?"

"We're moving into the village. For economic reasons. Papa's been in America more than a year now. We've heard nothing." Blindly, she stared at her hands. The fear that she was making a grave mistake drained out of her, leaving her limp. She had made the right choice.

"I intended to care for your family," Norwood said, his eyes luminous and large. His slim white fingers trembled. "I didn't consider it a duty, but a privilege."

"I know," Daisie said, struggling to be diplomatic. "You've always been so kind. Truly, I didn't know about this until this morning. Mama made all the arrangements herself—I'm quite unsettled by it."

"How enterprising of her." Norwood looked bewildered.

"I have to confess something," Daisie continued feeling uneasy and restless again, "that I hope won't hurt you too deeply."

He straightened. "Hurt me?"

Curling her hands into fists, Daisie met Norwood's eyes. "I cannot marry you."

He looked blank. Then he set his teacup on the tray, blinked at the empty saucer in his hand and frowned. "Did you get my note this morning?"

"I've been so upset. I . . . . Forgive me, I haven't opened it. Norwood, are you terribly angry? I decided just this afternoon that I can't let Mama set up housekeeping in the village alone. I don't know what she's thinking of. Since Papa went off she hasn't been herself. None of us has. You do understand."

"Only too well," he said, rising and reaching for his hat, which had fallen to the floor. "I admire your honesty." His voice had a suddenly deeper, more masculine ring. He settled his hat on his well-groomed curls. "You'll forgive me if I do not finish my tea." He strode to the door and turned, looking puzzled. "What will you do then, after you've moved?"

"Oh . . . ." Daisie couldn't bring herself to mention a London season or schooling. "I thought I might — " She paused, her heart beating wildly. "Someone should look for Papa."

Norwood looked almost as startled by the idea as Daisie was. After he bade her goodbye and good luck and disappeared out the front door, Daisie sat for a moment, thinking deeply. Why hadn't it occurred to her before? Mama didn't really need her, but Papa might.

She wandered from the parlor and mounted the stairs to her bedroom. She stood looking out her ivy-framed window. The garden looked strangely different, bathed in a glaring kind of sunlight that left her thoughts, motives and desires bared for honest examination. Was she mad? Look for Papa?

Looking lovely and frail, her mother pushed open the bedroom door. "Was he terribly crushed, dear?"

Daisie turned, head high, eyes wide. "I'm going to America, Mama. I'm going to find Papa myself and bring him back home to England where he belongs."

The words hung between them, as alien and impossible as if Daisie had just turned into a neighing horse.

Her mother's face paled, and for a moment Daisie feared she might faint. Then, unexpectedly, Mrs. Browning smiled, sagging against the door frame. "What a little dreamer you are. A young lady cannot travel alone in *England*, much less the American *wilderness!*"

"You said yourself a modern woman can take things into her own hands," Daisie cried.

"Selling a small, debt-ridden property to a solicitor, perhaps. But travel thousands — thousands! — of miles to a gold field? Alone!" Shaking her head, she staggered to a chair. "I believe you've lost your senses!" She plucked a lace-edged hankie from her bosom and patted moisture from her brow and throat.

"I can't have a London season. Norwood would think me horrid. You couldn't hold up your head if I was accused of being fickle. Norwood will think I'm looking for a more agreeable husband. I wouldn't dream of shaming him, not when he let me go without a single reproach. Mama, don't you see? It's what I must do! Why wait another moment? What if Papa needs help now?"

Her mother raised frightened, bewildered eyes, as if, by ignoring her husband's long absence, she could pretend he was only away in London on business. "Oh, Daisie," she whispered, tears brimming. Then her expression darkened. She seemed to believe Daisie might actually go. Getting stiffly to her feet, she looked up in Daisie's determined face. "You're going nowhere but to the village with Pammie and me."

Daisie felt her resolve shrivel in the face of her mother's surprising, unexpected strength, but her shaking hands curled into determined fists. "Until this idea came to me I had no purpose in life other than to marry Norwood. And I didn't want to do that, not wholeheartedly, as I should have."

"Finding your father in a wild foreign country is not your life's purpose! I *forbid* you to go! My dear, you are, as always, too unselfish. If you wish, we can use your share of the money to hire someone to fetch Papa."

"Mama, I've decided. I'm nearly twenty! I'm going." Suddenly, Daisie felt enormously capable and mature.

The set of Mrs. Browning's lips grew firmer. "You have a rash streak, just like your father. If you think I will stand by and let you leave as I let your father leave, and then spend the months waiting for letters that never come . . . . I don't wish to treat you like a child, Daisie, but you're not going. I have enough to worry about. Have a little rest, and forget this wild notion."

Daisie marveled at her mother's hidden strength. But Daisie was strong, too. She lifted her chin and straightened her back. "I *will* go, Mother. I want to go. I must go. If you don't care what's become of Papa, I do!"

Taking a stumbling step backwards, her mother's snapping eyes overflowed with tears. "You're behaving like a child, Daisie."

Daisie shook her head.

"How can you defy me when I am under this terrible strain?" her mother whispered.

"You needn't worry. I'll find Papa, and we'll be completely safe together." Daisie wanted to go into her mother's arms, but a gulf had opened between them. "Trust me, Mother."

"This is hardly a question of trust. You're not going. That is my last word on the subject." When Mrs. Browning failed to stare Daisie down, she turned with a sharp sigh of annoyance and left the room, her back rigidly erect, her head held high. Daisie felt desolate.

She sank slowly down onto her bed. Trembling, she dashed tears from her cheeks. To go to America. . . .

Then an overwhelming burst of excitement filled her. Hugging herself, she threw herself back into the soft embrace of the feather mattress. America! Crowing with delight, she sprang up, ran to the window, and threw up the sash. She leaned out, breathing the sweet, green fragrance of spring and aching with impatience. She would find her father! No one could stop her now that she'd made up her mind. Mr. Bedlow would help her secure passage.

Dancing and whirling, she went from the dresser to the armoire, plucking at her threadbare skirt and mended blouse.

America!

She paused, noticing Norwood's unopened note lying on her bed. Tearing the pale blue envelope open, she unfolded a piece of paper edged in navy and stamped with the Downingwood crest. Reading quickly, she thought for a moment to recapture the security she'd known since the day Norwood proposed. Now her future yawned before her as vast as the Atlantic ocean that separated England from America.

My very dearest Daisie,
I cannot bring myself to say in person what has burdened my heart for many days now. I beg your forgiveness and plead that you will think kindly of me as the summer passes and we do not join as I promised we would.

Daisie blinked and reread the lines. What was he saying? Her face grew hot. Stunned, she sank back onto the bed.

My dear, I find my heart does not convince my head that this marriage is what I truly want. I am afraid that at twenty-three I am not mature enough to handle the responsibility. Can you forgive me, dearest? I do love you, but I would like to put this off. I will explain later.

Your humble servant,
Norwood Poole.

She felt as he had looked in the parlor—blank, empty. He had broken off with her and had come expecting to see her devastated. At the very least, she should have been dismayed. Not only had she been preoccupied, she had broken off with him! They had rejected each other. She felt like laughing, but found herself weeping. Norwood had not loved her after all. Not enough, anyway.

An uncomfortable itch of embarrassment crawled over Daisie's arms. She was a fool. Only that morning she had thought Norwood a bowl of cold porridge, when, indeed, he had been thinking the same of her.

Folding the note, she replaced it carefully in the envelope. Now she really must go to America. Perhaps she would disappear into that vast, mysterious wilderness forever. Suddenly, the idea was not so unappealing.

Chapter Two

Denver, Colorado

The English young lady who arrived in Denver's rail depot five days after leaving New York State was not the most sweet-tempered of travelers. Aching with fatigue, she stood looking at the rugged line of mountains, thirty miles distant, that stretched as far north and south as she could see.

In haughty silence the mountains jutted into the startling blue sky. Though it was late June, pockets of blue-shadowed snow huddled in those lofty crags, silent testimony that there, in the windy heights, summer hadn't yet arrived. Daisie felt humbled by them, wary of them. It was daunting, after coming so far, to find them standing in her path, mutely domineering.

"I can't find no trunks, missie," the black porter called again, hobbling up behind her. Daisie jumped and then wondered how such a stoooped old man could work at a depot hefting trunks she could scarcely drag across the floor.

Sighing, she made a concerted effort to remain civil. To herself she muttered, "I shan't complain. I was the one eager to undertake this journey." She smiled for the old man. "I'll be staying at the Brown Palace Hotel for a few days, or until my trunks are found. Please have them delivered to me when they arrive. I want to leave for Cripple Creek right away." She tipped the man generously, giving her name and repeating the name of the hotel.

Only six days before she had been comfortably situated in upper New York State with a wonderful couple Mr. Bedlow had introduced her to. Brandon and Hilary Arnold had been visiting England when Daisie went to Mr. Bedlow the day after her broken engagement to ask for help with her travel arrangements. The Arnolds had been delighted to have Daisie's company for the Atlantic crossing.

Brandon Arnold had written to hotels in the West asking after Daisie's father, and had received a reply from the Brown Palace in Denver. *"The gentleman you seek — Lord Gregory Browning – resided here until March, leaving as his forwarding address the Cripple Creek post office . . . ."*

"How soon can I leave?" Daisie had asked. She had wept for joy, certain that in a few weeks she'd be sailing home with her papa in tow.

"We can't tell you what to do, surely," Hilary Arnold had said, her gray eyes kind. "But you mustn't go alone. It just isn't done."

"It will be done. By me!" Daisie had said determinedly. "How long does it take to get to Denver? Is there a train?"

Scowling, Brandon Arnold had ignored her question. "Your father is apparently trying to pass himself off as a lord, Daisie. It's a symptom of gold fever, surely. If you find him, he may not want to leave."

"You might reach Denver safely," Hilary added, "but you couldn't go into the mountains —"

"What are a few hills?" Daisie had exclaimed, hugging the woman. "You've assured me that the Indians are docile, and that Denver is no different from New York."

Excitedly, she had repacked her trunks with all the wonderful things Hilary had given her — things Hilary claimed she no longer wore. The nearly new silk, linen and organza blouses, the gabardine and worsted skirts, the underthings and silk stockings, the day gowns and evening gowns, the white kid shoes and the dressing gown of flowered pink and lavender chintz — all were carefully stowed, and the next morning Daisie climbed resolutely into the carriage for the ride to the depot.

On the journey, she wore a rose-pink wool traveling suit with a fitted jacket trimmed with gray braid, and a gored skirt draped up over a saucy bustle. She waved goodbye and turned her face westward.

Now she stood at the foot of those "hills", impatience flooding her veins. Grinning, the porter followed as she moved toward the carriages for hire. "You're a furriner, ain't ya?"

"English," she said, her thoughts less polite than her voice. If, Daisie vowed, one more person told her she was foreign, traveling alone, or pretty for somebody who talked funny, she would give out with a cockney caterwaul that would make them remember this sweet miss for all time.

Lifting her head and squaring her shoulders, Daisie signaled for a carriage and climbed aboard. "Don't forget to find my trunks," she called, settling into the seat with a satisfied sigh.

In spite of her fatigue she couldn't help but marvel that, a mere thirty years earlier this city of the wild west had been nothing but grassy prairie.

The summer sun had baked the streets to a dry, reddish dust. Rising up from the rocky, weedy prairie was the pungent fragrance of sage grass. The sparkling sky was a deep, rich turquoise. As she rolled into the city she saw delicate cottonwoods bordering the creek and dark, lush evergreens lining the streets. The city's brick buildings rose four and five stories. Rows of high, narrow, arched windows bore signs advertising dry goods stores, lawyers, dentists, assayers, land offices, and newspaper offices. Electrical fixtures mounted on tall, ornate iron lampposts flooded the streets with light as bright as day. There had certainly been nothing like it in Bethinghamshire.

Up and down those wide streets clattered horse-drawn and electric-powered trolleys. Along the wooden sidewalks walked every sort of person, from gaudily dressed ladies of questionable virtue to frockcoated gentlemen and Indians wearing blankets.

The hotel proved more than adequate. Many of the guests

crowding the vast and magnificent lobby seemed every bit as grand as the grandest lords and ladies of England. Daisie's room contained a sturdy oak bedstead, a carved dresser with a tilting oval mirror, a round clawfoot table with two chairs and rich green wallpaper with matching cut-velvet draperies.

From her third-floor window she gaped a long while at those tantalizing Rocky Mountains — misty gray, slate blue, dreamy lavender — now silhouetted against a dazzling orange and pink sunset. They were waiting, beckoning.

Her heart thrilled to think she had survived this astounding journey. Hat boxes in tow, she had thrown herself aboard that first chugging, hissing, impatient beast of a train. That evening, after making her connection to Pennsylvania, she had missed supper.

All the next day she smiled patiently at gawking children in beribboned straw hats and ignored brawny, cigar-puffing gentlemen, who tipped their hats to her anyway and looked her over in a most unsettling manner.

The coaches had been high and wide, with generous windows that she let down for fresh air. Once she dozed, only to wake with her head lolling on the shoulder of a smirking gentleman dressed in a ghastly plaid suit who said a very intimate, breathy hello and tried to hold her hand.

Chicago proved a surging, noisy, sooty city with twangy-voiced people who paid her no attention. She nearly missed her train to Denver and ran the length of the depot shouting for it to wait.

Now she would soon depart for the mining camp called Cripple Creek nestled high in those mocking mountains. Without her trunks, she felt at a loose end and worried that Hilary's dresses might be lost forever.

Feeling nervous in the strange room, she turned up the gas jets in the wall-mounted brass lamps to brighten the scene. Then she dropped across the bed, slept fitfully for two hours and awoke feeling uneasy and wondering for a moment where she was.

Her stomach growled in a most unladylike fashion. She resolved she must eat, but without a change of clothes she felt ashamed to enter the glittering, hushed splendor of the hotel dining room. Doomed to venture forth in the pink wool traveling suit, which now bore the wrinkles and spots of five days' hard, dusty wear, she could only wash her face and tidy her hair, hoping the people of Denver would forgive her appearance. She pinned her hat back onto the high pompadour of her hair and frowned at the stuffed black birds nestling beneath the plumes. They looked as if they had flown the entire two thousand miles from New York.

Pushing her way outside, Daisie stood for a long moment marveling at the heavy carriage traffic. It was full dark now, the black sky dusted with pin-prick stars. Though every window seemed ablaze, between the buildings were murky shadows. From the distance came unfamiliar tunes on rattling pianos.

After walking several blocks, she felt the small red purse hidden in her right high-buttoned shoe rubbing against her already blistered ankle. It reminded her again of the strained departure from Bethinghamshire, and her mother's tearful goodbye. She slowed, wishing her mother could see this fine, modern city.

Loneliness ached in Daisie's chest and she sighed, hearing again her mother's last whispered plea.

"You won't reconsider?" her mother had begged, her face swollen and pale from their week of arguing. "Very well, then. I have something for you." She had handed her a purse no bigger than her palm. "In this is enough money to bring you and your papa back to me."

Daisie hadn't wanted to take it. "You gave me a bank draft yesterday." She frowned at the tightly folded contents—United States bank notes — and felt a prickling of foreboding.

Her mother's voice remained calm, her manner that of a proud but defeated general. "You'll need money for hotels, meals, transportation. I can only hope those people Mr. Bedlow has entrusted you to are — " She stopped, too overcome with frustration even to mention the high-handed way Daisie had arranged her ocean crossing. "If you should spend all I gave you yesterday, I want to be certain you can get home. In this purse is my heart, Daisie. If you can't find your papa, you must come back to me."

Daisie's throat tightened over unshed tears.

"Come back to me," her mother whispered again, gathering Daisie into her arms. She couldn't let go. "Come back to me."

Daisie had set out on her impetuous journey with forced confidence, ignoring her rising doubts and second thoughts. At odd moments she feared that her father might be dead, that her journey would prove futile, that it was already placing too much strain on her mother.

She had hesitated at the Bethinghamshire station, regretting her rash decision, regretting going behind her mother's back to Mr. Bedlow.

Forcing those disturbing thoughts from her mind, she had boarded first the train to London, then the steamer for America. Stubbornly, she had tucked her mother's little purse in her shoe as a precaution against robbery, and now it rubbed, like her conscience, reminding her that finding her father was taking far longer than she'd expected. Still, she had traced him this far. She tossed her head to drive away lingering uneasiness.

Propelled by her hunger, she marched along, constantly aware of the watching darkness and of the myriad smells pouring from promising-looking restaurants. Each time she paused at a door, she became too self-conscious to enter. She was unescorted, and in the last five days she had learned that being alone made her suspect. Men felt at liberty to speak to her. Suddenly even hunger couldn't overcome her dread of what she might encounter alone in a restaurant. Perhaps she would have to brave the dining room.

"What a fool I am," she thought, retracing her steps, thinking she would soon see a familiar building around the next corner. She couldn't get over how new, how up-and-coming the city looked, with its telephone poles and sweeps of wires overhead.

She was so engrossed in writing a mental letter to her sister describing this amazing city at the foot of the Rockies that it was some time before she realized her steps had carried her into shabby and sinister streets. Here, the buildings were crudely constructed, their windows dimly lit and the walkways less crowded.

Now the odors from the yawning doorways of the eating places were unappetizing. Men lurched into her path, eyeing her and murmuring half-heard invitations that set her blood singing with indignant alarm.

Heels clattering, she rushed on, realizing she had lost her way. Many stores were dark; the raucous music was louder. The shadows between buildings revealed shapes of stooped men, lurking, watching, moving toward her with intent.

She was almost running now, her ribs crushed beneath her stays, her stomach a knot of fear. Which way to turn? How far to go? *Where* to go?

Daisie, you idiot, she thought, wanting only the safety of her room.

Ahead, she saw the hulking figure of a man step from the shadows. He stood weaving in the middle of the walkway, his boots, which were caked with dried mud, planted far apart, his hands in his pockets.

Charged with alarm, Daisie slowed, loath to pass him.

He started toward her, tentatively at first, watching her from beneath the thicket of his eyebrows. ''Goo' evening,'' he mumbled, falling into step beside her. ''Wanna drink with me?''

''No!'' she panted, hurrying on, clutching her reticule against her stomach.

He lumbered along with her, reeking of smoke and liquor, his words hushed, insinuating, his clothes smelling ripely of sweat. His belly bulged from the flaps of his rumpled brown coat, and his bagging gray trousers were darkly greasy where he was now wiping his thick-fingered hands.

''Come on, lil' lady. Jus' a lil' drink.'' He edged in front of her, forcing her to slow, his odor surrounding him like an aura.

''Leave me alone,'' she hissed.

"Wannna get to know me? I can be real nice, lil' lady."

Speechless, Daisie gave him a withering look and then rushed ahead blindly, too terrified to think.

"Hey! Lil' lady, hold up there! No' so fast. Don't turn up your lil' nose at me. I'm as good as the next feller. Have a drink with me. Be sociable. You know how to be real nice to a man, I'll bet." He caught up to her and seized her arm. "You're real pretty, honey. Gimme a smile."

His touch was loathsome. Shuddering, Daisie jerked free. She wanted to slap him, curse him, but her strongest impulse was to run. In his eyes was a smiling anger she instinctively understood. She stumbled to the curb to avoid him, quelling her urge to scream.

"Come on, honey," he said, swinging in front of her again, blocking the way. "My money's good. Smile for me real pretty. I know your kind. Don't go looking like I'm dirt. You're no better." As his hands came toward her, she backed against a lamppost.

"Get out of my way!" she demanded, reeling with terrified fury. "If ... if you tell me how to get back to the Brown Palace, I'll ... I'll not report you to the police."

The man threw back his head and guffawed so loudly that several people, exiting from what could only be a smoke-filled saloon ahead, turned and stared. "Brown Palace!" he bellowed, holding his belly. "Listen to her! Police, she says!"

As Daisie marched past him, her cheeks burning and her heart hammering, his laughter stopped. His heavy footsteps closed behind her. She spun, saw him glowering at her, lowering his head as if to do battle.

Wildly, Daisie plunged away. When he grabbed her arm, she swung blindly, choking back a scream.

"Wait a minute, you damned hussy—" His lips curled back, exposing dark teeth. He jerked her around, yanking her against his chest.

For a blinding, terrifying moment she felt her breasts crushed against his filthy coat, felt his hand grabbing beneath the bulk of her bustle, sensed his knee pressing between her own.

"I'll show you, you lil' bitch," he growled. She inhaled the sour odor of alcohol on his breath and gagged.

Throwing her hands up to shield her face, she curled her fingers into claws ready to threaten his eyes. When her nails raked across his cheeks, he howled.

"Damned female—" he croaked, flinging her away. Gingerly, he fingered his cheek. His eyes narrowed at the sight of his bloodied fingertips. Then he lunged.

Daisie bolted, arms outstretched, a cry frozen in her throat. Ahead she saw two men and three women watching her, smirking. Another man had detached himself from the group and was striding toward her.

"Oh, lord!" Daisie moaned, threatened fore and aft. She turned, beseeching the second man to stay away, but he swept off his white Stetson, his stride quickening, and gave her an inquiring look with a cocked eyebrow. Daisie turned on her heel and stumbled off the walkway into an alley. Oh, no, she thought, facing the pressing, enveloping darkness! Oh, help!

She backed into the darkness, felt it smothering her like a heavy, dirty cloak. A sinking numbness darkened her thoughts.

The gentleman with the hat stepped between Daisie and the drunk. "What's the trouble here, friend?" he asked softly, his deep voice even, calm, menacingly assured.

Daisie pressed herself against the building, willing herself not to faint.

Standing several inches taller than the weaving drunk, the man with the hat edged nearer, shielding her. She guessed him to be between twenty-five and thirty, with gleaming nut-brown hair dented by the hat. He wore a curiously crude, soft-looking tan coat that appeared to be made of brushed leather. Long dancing strips of the same material fringed the sleeves and hem.

He stepped forward, his muscular thighs outlined by the snug worsted of his trousers. His alert eyes were a clear, cornflower blue. "Can I help?"

She felt like a floundering ship in an inky sea, and he was her refuge, steady, solid and unyielding. Panting, Daisie nodded. "Please! I need directions to the Brown Palace Hotel."

"You're a long way from there," he said smiling. "English, aren't you?" He turned, giving the drunk a look that made him tighten his mouth and glance away.

"Yes," she said tersely, putting a trembling hand to her forehead.

Muttering, the drunk turned. "Just trying to be frien'ly. Didn't mean no harm."

Close to tears, Daisie said, to no one in particular, "I am English, and I am lost. I need a simple direction. I've been on a train for the past five days. I'm exhausted and hungry. And my feet hurt. Please, if you have a kind bone in your body, tell me how to get back to my hotel!"

A sharp, shrill whistle made her jump. The man with the Stetson and leather coat had signaled for a passing carriage. Realizing she could have done that herself, Daisie felt like an utter fool. When a one-horse carriage halted in the street, she mumbled a curt thank you and launched herself toward it.

"Allow me," the man said, grinning, as he handed her up into the vehicle.

She caught the confident grin out of the corner of her eye and felt a surge of resentment that he had seen her in such a befuddled state. He was quite obviously a crude character who had just stepped out of a saloon. He had a faint smell of liquor on him. She shouldn't feel the least bit embarrassed in front of him, but she did feel embarrassed. She couldn't meet his eyes.

She was about to murmur the name of her hotel to the driver when the stranger threw himself into the seat across from her. "Elitch Gardens," he barked to the driver. The carriage jerked away.

"I would be so grateful," Daisie said, sighing raggedly, "if you would allow me to return to my hotel alone. I do thank you very much indeed for saving me. I think that creature meant to rob me. What a dreadful man!"

"I don't think he had money on his mind," her rescuer chuckled, his expression wry.

She glanced into the blue eyes. "I beg your pardon!"

"I said, he wasn't after your money."

Daisie's cheeks flooded with painful heat. A gentleman would not have said so. "What are you grinning at?" she snapped, squirming with embarrassment.

"Keep talking," he said, his teeth starkly white in his smiling, sun-darkened face. "I've never heard anyone speak so beautifully."

He gave her a look that made her heart flutter. Leaning forward, he braced himself with a broad palm on the back of her seat near her head. She realized that his face was coming toward her — a remarkably handsome face — and that his lips were soft and moist and parted as if he intended to kiss her . . . .

"Oh, please," she cried, pushing him back with both hands. "Please, just leave me alone!" That fleeting touch against his hard, broad chest made her tingle with awareness. "I'm not in the habit of speaking to strangers, much less allowing them to . . . to . . . kiss me!"

"Oh, was I going to kiss you?" he asked, settling back, watching her, letting his eyes travel over her face and then wander downward to take in the provocative swell of her bosom, the tiny waist and the trim outline beneath the fashionably draped skirt.

What insolence! she thought, acutely aware of his appraising look. She had never felt more vulnerable. Perhaps this man was even more dangerous than the other!

He chuckled. It was as though he could read her mind.

Pinching her mouth into a narrow line, Daisie did a good imitation of an insulted old maid. Within moments they had arrived just west of town at a place lit with a thousand lights, a vast garden adrift with orchestra music and laughter. Daisie's body stiffened with alarm. "This isn't my hotel!"

"I'm treating you to dinner. Allow me to introduce myself—"

Daisie erupted from the carriage. "I do not dine with strangers," she said crisply, marching away toward three carriages standing near the high ornate gates of the place. "This may be America, but I am still an English lady and do not have to associate with impertinent gentlemen."

His warm laughter followed her, drifting around her like a cloud. Of all the men she'd seen in America so far, this rude one was certainly the handsomest. She clenched her fists. The conceit, thinking she would dine with him!

Hailing another carriage, she threw herself in. "Brown Palace!" she snapped. Turning back, she saw the stranger disappearing between the gates. He went in as if he owned the whole state, and she felt grudging admiration for him and then sadness that it had not been proper for her to accept his invitation.

"What is this . . . garden?" she asked, leaning back as the carriage surged forward.

"The amusement park, miss." The driver chuckled under his breath.

She sagged into the hard seat, wondering if ever again she'd have a meal. Her stomach ached now, and suddenly she was overcome with a fit of shaking that would not stop.

The image of the Stetsoned stranger danced before her mind's eye all the way back to the hotel. The straight white teeth, the soft, sensuous-looking full lips, the shining brown hair. Wide shoulders, a full strong chest, powerful, commanding arms. Thighs bulging with muscles, a confident stride, tooled leather boots tipped in silver . . . .

As she dragged herself into the hotel and learned that indeed they did have room service, it was the stranger's laugh that haunted her. When the waiter brought her meal half an hour later, she overtipped him. "Wake me as *soon* as my trunks arrive," she said, tipping him again and then trying to remember if she'd already done so.

When the door closed, she fell on the tray, breathing in the tantalizing aroma of soup and fresh bread. Tears stung her eyes as she dropped onto the bed and ate with abandon, vowing that when she finally found her papa—if she found him—she would get to the bottom of this gold-fever business. She would find out if gold was worth all the trauma she and her family had gone through.

Chapter Three

Daisie pressed herself against the side of the lurching, rocking, narrow-gauge coach car. Two feet outside the sooty window reared a sheer rock wall so high she could see no sky. The jagged gray and black granite was a huge jumble of slanting, angular slabs so massive, so overpowering that Daisie was glad no one on the train had heard her call these beastly granite monsters "hills."

On the other side of the coach car was nothing — or so it seemed to Daisie, who gasped softly whenever she chanced to glance beyond those windows. The narrow-gauge tracks clung by some serpentine magic to the pitifully narrow shelf hacked in the side of the mountain that twisted ever upward, one side walled by that surly rock face, the other side dropping off fifty feet or more to a cheerfully gurgling white-water creek. The sight of the sheer drop made her stomach lurch. Forcing herself to relax, she tried to open her fists, but it was hopeless. Her entire body was a fist, every muscle tensed for that one horrendous moment when they would all crash into the gorge.

The man in the seat beside her leaned back, watching her with amusement. "Scared?" he asked, rubbing his hands on his denim overalls.

"Oh . . . no," Daisie said, smiling hastily, craning her neck as if she looked forward to the next vista yawning beyond the far windows. Forcing herself to look did seem to ease her vertigo. She gave the man a dismissing nod and returned her attention to the more secure view outside her own window.

Since leaving Denver she'd been acutely aware of strangers around her. She couldn't forget the frightening incident of her first night in Denver and now scanned the nodding heads of the travelers crammed into the coach car. None of the men leered at her, and no one had approached her. Convinced she could now anticipate and avoid any danger, she lifted her eyes to the windows and settled back.

Ahead, the canyon broadened somewhat, revealing a blur of distant mountains, bald and naked in the brilliant sunlight. They were treeless, faintly pink tinged with gray, and always sporting those chilly, blue-white pockets of snow in the crevices.

The turquoise sky was a welcome sight, although it reminded Daisie that the train seemed to be climbing toward it with ridiculous eagerness, a relentless upward chug punctuated by occasional shrill bursts from the steam whistle. At one point the curve ahead turned back so sharply she saw the black engine with its massive smoke-stack dragging them on. Plumes of black smoke rushed backward, enveloping the cars filled with eager, gold-hungry travelers.

Abruptly, the canyon opened out and it was as if the sheer rock faces and dizzying drops had been nothing but a bad dream. The train rattled and lurched across a high-altitude, tundra-like prairie broken by lumps of scrubby oak bushes and sporting an occasional dead pine, its limbs twisted by a devilish wind.

In the distance, stands of lodgepole pines, tall, straight and nearly free of limbs except for clumps at the top, reached for the cloudless sky. Among the pines were spruces, their needles tinged blue, the shapes tall, conical and stately.

The hills rolled gently, dotted with orange-red Indian paintbrush, scatterings of frail, fluted pink flowers ranging from pale to near-red, little blue cornflowers, yellow-petaled daisies, tiny mounds of pincushion cactus, jabbing yucca cactus, and the dusty-looking, faintly green sagebrush.

As the way curved again, she glimpsed distant mountains, jagged and bleak, harboring large masses of leftover snow above the haunting line where nothing could grow — the timberline. Surely this Cripple Creek town where her father had gone was not that high? Already the thin air made it difficult to breathe.

With amazing swiftness, a sheer rock wall blotted the view. Turning, Daisie watched massive boulders the size of Denver's largest buildings forming a stair-step terrace sweeping downward to a narrow silver ribbon of a creek lost so far below she couldn't imagine how far down it was.

"Pardon me!" she said, realizing she had backed away from the window and was nearly sitting in the gentleman's lap. "These heights are a bit unsettling."

"Some of these mountains are more than fourteen-thousand feet high," he said, smiling at her, leaning closer as if they were now friends. "Imagine that. Two miles straight up into God's heaven." He scratched his bewhiskered face. "You ain't never been in these mountains before, I can see that plain enough. Come far?"

Not caring to encourage him, she let her cordial expression fade. He backed off, his eyes dimming, and tipped his hat down over his eyes. Daisie sighed, grateful for his sensitivity, and let the rocking car lull her back to relaxation.

Her arms and neck had just begun to unknot when she noticed a man ahead in a fringed leather coat stand to flip the reversible cane seat so he could ride facing backwards.

He held a deck of playing cards, and his white teeth gleamed as he smiled at his companions.

Daisie's heart leaped. She edged lower in her seat, wishing she could pull her hat down to cover her face, too. Her cheeks grew hot. It was the man who had helped her in Denver!

Their eyes met. Daisie looked quickly down, hating her response to seeing him again. Keep calm, she told herself, looking back out the window. At the scene outside she felt a nearly physical lurch of vertigo that was unpleasant and unsettling. Oh Papa, she thought, clamping her eyes closed and balling her hands into fists. Why couldn't you have stayed home?

She opened her eyes. He was watching her, grinning. He was jamming the cards into his coat pocket and walking toward her.

"You're the English lady from Denver," he said, extending his hand as if she should shake it like a man. Seeing that she had no intention of acknowledging him, he tapped the gentleman seated next to Daisie on the shoulder and muttered, "Do you mind, friend? If I could just have a moment . . . ."

Uncertainly, Daisie's seatmate rose, looking at Daisie as if he expected her to ask him to remain and protect her. Daisie ignored him and, instead, tried to push her hatboxes, which were wedged at her feet, into the stranger's way.

Watching her struggles, the corners of his mouth turned up. "Did you manage to get back to your hotel safely?" he asked, so loudly that all the car's occupants paused in their various conversations to eavesdrop.

"It would seem so, wouldn't it?" How could she rid herself of this menace?

"And you got some dinner?"

"Yes, thank you." Would she be forced to look at him and let him see her reaction to him? Couldn't he see she was a lady and not accustomed to speak to strangers?

Finally he broke the growing silence. "I just wondered," he said. His voice registered no chagrin that she had refused to look at him. "I was concerned, after that attack . . . ." Aware suddenly that ears were straining toward him, hanging on every word, his voice trailed off.

Her insides in turmoil, Daisie stared steadily out of the window. The train whisked by a place that had been blasted through a solid outcropping of rock. The rock wall swooped past the window so suddenly Daisie reared back.

"Pretty sight, these mountains," the man went on, leaning one hand on the back of her seat only a few inches from her shoulder. His voice was pleasantly deep and warm, not particularly cultivated, but not slovenly or ignorant-sounding, either.

She said nothing, but she was more aware of him than she ever had been of a man. She felt the gentle brush of his breath against her cheek. He smelled of fresh mountain air, of clean, sun-dried linen, warm and refreshing. His presence seemed to electrify the air between them. He had a curious power over her, the power to draw blood to her cheeks, cause her breathing to become constricted and render her palms damp.

After a pause, he straightened, withdrew a long narrow cigar from his breast pocket and lighted it with a lucifer match scraped against his boot sole. When he leaned back down, the aroma of a fine, sweet tobacco swirled around him. His voice registering a warmer, deeper, more intimately friendly tone, he said, "I know it's not polite for me to speak to you, Miss . . . ?" His words trailed off on an expectant note.

She refused to provide her name. A deliciously exciting shiver went through her, but she did her best to ignore it. He was attracted to her, she thought, her heart lifting. It was quite impossible. And so wonderful. . . .

Softly, he cleared his throat. "In these mountains politeness doesn't count for much. A man doesn't get anywhere with it — politeness, I mean. It doesn't fill his pockets with gold, or get him acquainted with likely young women."

Likely, was she? Her eyes narrowed, blurring the astonishing views that changed with every chug and kept her heart leaping with alarm. At least, she hoped it was the view that was causing her heart to leap.

"I'm a man who goes after things. I don't hang back just because the etiquette books say I should. That's why I've been so forward with you, Miss . . . ?" He sighed when she still refused to speak.

"Folks say Tyler Reede is a forward man. Honest, trustworthy, not too bad off in his financial dealings, a man of land, a respected man, handy with a deck of cards on a long, dull train ride, but not corrupted by Lady Luck. He's friendly, charming, not a bad sight on his better days, but possibly the worse for wear after a trip to the Queen of the Plains. That's Denver, in case you didn't know, ma'am. He'll help anybody out, no good reason needed. He's got an eye for pretty ladies, and likes to step right in and make things happen."

Quivering, she said nothing. Who did he think she was that he would address her in this way? Did he think she was a common tart, as that odious fellow who had grabbed her in Denver thought?

Her cheeks felt on fire. Several men ahead had turned and were smirking at her, their eyes hungrily taking in her features below the wheat-gold swell of her pompadour and the wilted plumes of her traveling hat. The coach car had become suddenly still.

The wide, manicured hand of the charming stranger appeared extended before her again. His wasn't the hand of a dandy, but appeared to be acquainted with a little hard work. Still, it was clean and strong-looking, an honest hand.

"I'm Tyler Reede, that forward fellow you've already heard so much about," he said, his voice light, confident, charming.

Involuntarily, the corners of Daisie's mouth turned up. He was irresistible. Oh, dear. What would her mama advise? She would not approve if Daisie let down her reserve for this man, compelling though he was. Bashfully, blushing a little, she kept her eyes fixed on the window. The uncomfortable silence between them grew almost painful. Why couldn't he leave her alone?

Finally he straightened. Staring down at her, his smile gone, he puffed twice more on the narrow cigar, then turned away. "Maybe you'll feel more like talking later," he muttered, moving back up the aisle to his seat.

Daisie felt suddenly bereft. She might have been a little more cordial. After all, what would she have done if he hadn't come along and rescued her from that drunk? She watched him settle himself in his seat and take up his conversation. A woman in a red plumed hat was seated across from him.

Jealous in spite of herself, Daisie stuck out her chin but felt confused and lonely. Tyler Reede shuffled the cards but didn't glance up. Around Daisie, conversations started up again. Her seatmate returned, clearing his throat as if he'd like to speak to her. She ignored him, wishing she knew a decent, effective way to deal with these men.

The train made several brief stops as it continued to Cripple Creek. Each mining camp seemed slightly more habitable than the last, but the dismal collections of hastily built raw-pine shacks and streaked canvas tents made Daisie's imagination race with the horrid possibilities awaiting her.

Where would she look if her father had moved on? Again she planned how she would pursue her father, from questioning the desk clerks of every hotel—if there were such luxuries as hotels —to alerting the sheriff—if there was a sheriff—that her father was missing.

After her trunks had been located (in Nebraska) and forwarded to her, she had checked with the Brown Palace Hotel's manager and looked at the register signed by her father, ''Lord'' Browning, when he had checked out in March. Learning she was the ''lord's'' daughter, the hotel staff had treated her with the greatest respect, which was pleasant and gratifying, although she felt embarrassed that her papa was passing himself off as something he was not. He had worked hard to buy the cabinet-making business he so loved, but it hadn't been enough to survive hard times and the tight money of the past three years.

Suddenly it was all gone, and he had come to this godforsaken place to seek a fortune with which he intended to buy everything back. Why was he calling himself a lord? Had he lost his mind?

Her seatmate got off the train at Victor, leaving her the first privacy she had had for what seemed like an eternity. Relieved to be alone, she burrowed into her reticule and counted out the dwindling coins and bills like a miser. Fretting, she realized she had spent more than she should have since arriving in Denver. She hadn't even thought to take a room in a less expensive hotel. Was she so used to the finer things that she couldn't resist overspending? A weight of dread settled in the pit of her stomach.

Wondering if that same habit of comfort had plagued her father, she strained to distract herself by watching the by now not-so-frightening mountainscape as the train twisted its way to its final destination — the boom town where gold was making headlines around the world.

The terrain was disappointingly tame. The highest mountains loomed in the distance, hidden for the most part by gently rolling closer mountains. There were no wonderful pine forests. The land was barren except for scrubby bushes and occasional boulders lying about.

Everywhere, diggings and mine tailings exposed the red, raw-looking Colorado soil to the sun. Daisie saw men leading burros across expanses of uneven land toward nothing in particular. There was a peacefulness about the high valley, and yet a haunting sense of isolation that made her suddenly afraid.

Unexpectedly, Tyler Reede slipped into the now empty seat beside her. "Getting off in Cripple Creek?"

She found it difficult to remain silent in spite of the warnings drummed into her by a careful upbringing. "Yes," she answered briefly.

"I thought so. There's nowhere else to get off." After a lengthy silence, he said softly, "Have I done something terrible to make you ignore me like this?"

She sighed. "I don't wish to offend you, Mr. Reede, but I am not in the habit of striking up conversations with men I don't know. In England a proper young woman would not think of doing so."

His mouth worked into a smile. "But we *have* been introduced. I'm Tyler Reede. Tell me who you're meeting in Cripple Creek. I probably know him. That will make us acquaintances, won't it?"

"Second-hand," she said before she could stop herself. He seemed able to draw words right out of her. Quickly she busied herself with the crushed and battered hatboxes chafing at her legs.

"Can I help with those?"

She glanced at him, at the smiling, dancing eyes penetrating her own, straying to her lips, sinking lower to admire her bosom as if she was a delicious treasure. Panic reared in her mind. Under her breath she whispered, "If you don't stop annoying me, Mr. Reede, I most certainly will tell the man I'm meeting all about you."

Stiffening, he straightened, his smile falling away. She found his suddenly sober look intimidating. "Pardon me," he said.

The change in his expression unsettled her, and for an instant she was afraid he might prove far less gentlemanly than she had assumed. Her words had effectively driven him away, but now he thought less of her. She was traveling alone, to meet a man. Why hadn't she said the man was her father? Her heart sank. Further explanations died on her lips.

Mr. Tyler Reede rose from the seat next to her, tipped his white Stetson and strode to the end of the car, where he let himself through the door onto the open platform. The train shrieked into Cripple Creek's rail depot, disgorging steam, screeching and grinding to a stop. Not only had she missed her first glimpse of the camp, but Mr. Reede had managed to spoil her day.

Moments later she was off the train, dropping her hatboxes and carpetbag to the dusty wooden platform. She clutched at her hat for fear the steady, cool, mountain breeze would tear it free of the pins. She stood gaping at the town, her melancholy dissolving into wonder.

The town bustled with excitement. Indeed, it looked as if it had been built just in time for her arrival, and everyone was hurrying to finish. The street was narrower than those in Denver — hardly a street really, just a barren, wheel-rutted dirt space between the store fronts.

Some of the older buildings — a few years old at the most — sported wooden walkways in front, but most opened to the bare, pink soil. The street stretched several blocks away down a steepish hill and ended as it began, with the scrubby land stretching up the other side of the basin-shaped valley.

She could see rooftops stretching for several streets to either side. Off to the left, the land rose, making some of the streets quite steep.

Clustered thickly in front of every building were men, clad

mostly in dark worsted coats and denim trousers. In the distance a few bright parasols bobbed above the dense thicket of bowler and Stetson hats. Women seemed to be few in these mountains. Several wagons rolled along in front of Daisie, bringing up the dust and making her cough. She moved to the side and wondered at last if she could hire a carriage.

To her utter self-disgust, she found herself looking around in hopes that the impudent Mr. Reede would hail one for her, but he had disappeared.

Behind her the locomotive stood hissing impatiently, huffing as if eager to return to the wilds of the rocky canyons. The elk antlers anchored just below the headlamp gave the engine the appearance of being alive and dangerous.

Around her the clamor of dispersing passengers lessened. In the distance the faint call of an out-of-tune piano, the high, frantic cacophony of a nickelodeon and the low hum of eager voices all talking one thing — gold — blended into the untamed spirit of this wild, half-built camp.

Clutching her reticule and shivering as the cool breeze penetrated the fine wool of her pink traveling jacket, Daisie hesitated, unable to decide where to go first.

"Need a lift, ma'am?" someone said from behind her.

Whirling, she nodded like a lost child to the man in a leather apron. "Please, yes. To the nearest hotel . . . a nice one."

"That'll be the Colorado Hotel, ma'am," the man said. He was pulling a wooden trolley by a long handle. On the trolley were her trunks.

Looking at the two large trunks and the one small one, Daisie suddenly thought how foolish she must appear. Surely here all she needed were sturdy walking shoes. She rubbed her tender ankle where the purse was hidden. She would look far less conspicuous wearing a badly tailored jacket and denim trousers. Certainly she would be able to breathe more easily.

The tall, angular porter shifted a large tobacco chaw to his other cheek and grinned, tipping his rain-ruined hat. "Nice to see a lady in town. Staying long?" His light blue eyes took in her face and figure with a single impudent sweep.

"I don't know," she said, looking away uneasily, fixing her eyes on the constant, surging motion in the street. She saw telephone poles with one wire attached jutting up along one side of the street — a sign of civilization, despite the town's rough appearance.

"I can't seem to get my breath," Daisie said, pressing her hand to her throat.

"It's the altitude," the porter said, as if pleased to be able to explain why she was suffocating. "Nine thousand and some feet up, Cripple Creek is. It gets to all the greenhorns at first. You'll get used to it. Soon the clean air'll have you kicking up your heels half the night." He winked.

Taken aback, Daisie narrowed her eyes. Was the state populated only with such unmannerly creatures? Her mother and Hilary Arnold had been right to worry about her traveling alone.

The man made a face and turned away to signal to someone. Within moments a buckboard wagon stopped in the dusty street before Daisie. The driver seated on the single spring bench at the head of the buckboard glanced in her direction, raised one curious black eyebrow and spat on the far side. After several moments he looped the reins over the longest, thickest brake lever she'd ever seen. She thought of the steep mountain roads and was grateful she had been able to take a train all this way.

He leaped down and held out his hand.

Blinking, Daisie stared at him. The porter hoisted one trunk onto the bed of the wagon. "Ye gods, this un's heavy. Got gold in these things? Must be a ton of it."

The two mules in harness stood dumbly staring at the ground. Daisie felt a surge of sympathy for them. The driver began to look annoyed.

"Oh, you want me to *sit* up *there*?" she said over her embarrassment. Taking the man's work-dirty hand, glad for her gloves, she felt him throw her up onto the seat. The second trunk dropped like a boulder into the wagon, and the porter tossed the third smaller trunk in after it.

"Careful of my hatboxes!" Daisie exclaimed, thinking of all

the trouble she'd gone to on their account.

Tipping his hat, he deposited them into her weary hands.

"Colorado Hotel," the porter barked to the driver who lurched against Daisie without so much as a hello. She wondered if he was deliberately rubbing her arm with his own and edged as far away as possible.

The trip down the main street was an embarrassment. Every man turned to stare at her. Each tipped his hat. The women, the few Daisie saw, looked frankly curious. No reserved behaviour here, Daisie thought, wondering if she'd ever grow used to being treated with such familiarity.

Snapping his whip, the driver yelled, "Hey, you! Clear outta my way!"

Several men, all dressed in dusty brown suits, turned sullenly, regarded Daisie and her conveyance and with a remarkable lethargy edged away just enough so the driver could maneuver close to the Colorado Hotel's boardwalk. "Colorado Ho-tel!" the driver barked as if he had ambitions of becoming a train conductor.

Daisie felt eyes on her from everywhere as she climbed down, less worried about showing too much petticoat than that someone might notice the peculiar bulge in her right high-buttoned shoe.

She paid the driver and tipped him when he unloaded her trunks and dropped them near the door. She thanked him as he ambled off toward what she supposed was the nearest drinking establishment. Saloons seemed to alternate with more respectable buildings all along the street.

Lifting her head and trying to disregard all the speculative stares, Daisie took herself inside what could only loosely be described as a hotel.

Fashioned of raw, sun-bleached pine, the building stood two stories high. It was wide enough for rooms on either side of a narrow upper hall and deep enough to sport a large barren lobby. She registered, paid in advance and waited for a bellman to appear.

The interior of the "hotel" was unvarnished yellow pine liberally decorated with knot holes. Several benches built of unstripped pine limbs stood along either wall, and the desk was two thick planks balanced on two barrels. Her shoes gritted on the bare floor, which was heavily dusted with the now-familiar reddish soil. A single tin hurricane lantern dangled from a chain and hook anchored in a crossbeam.

"I wonder if you could help me?" she said to the clerk as she watched the first of her trunks disappear up the roughly hewn pine stairs into the hotel's upper recesses.

Annoyed, the clerk glanced up. Several men from outside surged in, talking loudly. Giving Daisie a cursory glance, they thundered up the stairs, making her wonder how she might defend herself if one of those creatures, drunk and disoriented, happened to enter her room that night by mistake.

"Do your rooms have locks?" she asked, with what she hoped was a confident smile to the clerk.

The clerk's face was expressionless. "They have doors," he said. Then he grinned as if joking. "We've had ladies here before. Just holler if you get into hot water."

Daisie felt her face blanch. Recovering, she attempted a more businesslike approach. "I require your help on another matter. I'm here to locate my father, Gregory Browning."

His face became expressionless once more.

"*Lord* Browning." She got a secret thrill at attaching the title to her papa's name. "He may be staying in this hotel. Or he may have stayed here some months ago. Would it be too much to ask to look at your register?"

The clerk pondered her request for what seemed like several minutes. "Look at my register? You mean this register? This here book?" He scratched his head.

"Lord Browning is my father. I'm looking for him." Boldly she reached for the register, turned it and began thumbing back through the pages. It was a surprisingly thick ledger. Page after page of entries — some written with a flourish, some printed laboriously, some consisting only of painfully executed X's.

"Where might I find the entries for March?"

He watched her turn the pages. At last he said, "That's another book. I'd have to get it."

She smiled and resisted batting her eyelashes at him. "Would you? I've come all the way from England — " She broke off, pausing for effect.

"England?" he said as if he had never heard of the place.

"Might I speak with the manager?"

"I'm the manager." He watched her find the most recently used page and return the register to his care.

"The owner, then?" she asked.

"He's in Denver, I think. I'll find the book, later." He looked up to indicate he was suddenly busy. "Facilities out back," he mumbled, his face turning scarlet.

Horrified, Daisie looked in the direction of his hasty gesture, toward a narrow back hall. Beyond it, she saw a rear door yawning into a barren yard where a privy stood. Behind that was the rear of another building. Laundry flapped from a rope slung between two shacks. Her heart dropped into her shoes.

Giving the clerk a curt nod, she fled toward the stairs, lifted her skirts and noticed several gentleman watching her with a kind of yearning. On the upper floor, she found the door of number six standing open and her trunks lying on their ends at the foot of a narrow, rusted iron bed.

Her room was the last at the back, on the right. The window stood open. It had no curtains. The bedsprings were without a mattress. For a moment Daisie wondered if someone had stolen the mattress. Perhaps it was being aired.

She crossed to the window and looked down into the backyard, out across a clutter of rooftops and a scattering of tents on the outskirts, to the scrubby land stretching toward the breastworks of the mountains.

Turning back, she regarded the room and the bare bedsprings with a sigh. At least she would not have to worry about bedbugs, she thought. Suddenly she was ready to collapse with fatigue, and at the same time afraid to be alone in this place of rough strangers.

She pushed the door closed by hooking her fingers into an open knothole. The door had no knob, no lock, no protection of any kind against molesters. Grinning suddenly, Daisie pushed and nudged the heaviest trunk in front of it. ''Let them try to get past that,'' she said to herself, dusting her hands.

The four empty corners echoed with her words. Bark still clung to the windowsill. The walls bore visible marks from a roughcut saw. There wasn't another stick of furniture in the room. She thought of her bedroom at home and the ivy that grew outside its window. She thought of her soft feather mattress now relegated to a loft in a little cottage in Bethinghamshire. She glared at the iron bedstead and springs.

Daisie licked her lips. Was she doomed to miss supper again? Her throat was parched, her hands dirty. Where would she get water? What would she put it in? She jerked off her hat and threw it down, hearing the long pins fall to the floor. She needed to go out back. She stared sullenly at the trunk guarding her door like a surly, witless mastiff.

She couldn't even sit down. The rusted springs would soil and tear her skirt. No lantern hung from the ceiling, and it was growing dark. She had arrived in the wilderness.

Later, she braved the night to slip out back. As she was returning to her room, she heard the men in the next room discussing something, and moments later they trooped out heedless of the noise they were making. Daisie pressed her door closed just in time to escape their scrutiny, and stood, heart hammering, remembering the drunk's touch.

With the trunk in place before the door, she arranged her oldest clothes on the springs, loosened her stays and crawled into the squeaking excuse for a bed. For hours she fought the jabbing, pinching springs, tossing and turning to find comfort. She had just fallen asleep when a horrendous, grinding scrape brought her to her feet before her eyes were even open,

She saw that the trunk had been moved. A wedge of light came through the partly opened door.

"Who's there?" she hissed, deciding she would have good use for a pistol in this horrid land.

A reeking, hulking man stood in the half-opened doorway. She rushed forward, determined to keep him out. She shoved the door against him. "Get out! This is my room!"

"Eh? Oh,'scuse me." The man staggered back, belched and then reeled toward her again. A half-empty whiskey bottle was clutched in the hand he flung out for balance.

When it looked as though he might drop it at her feet, Daisie snatched the bottle away, pushed the man sharply back into the hall and shoved the door closed with a shudder of relief.

She stared at the bottle, expecting the man to demand it back, but he stumbled away, to fall through some other door with a yelp and a muttered curse. When all was silent again, Daisie nudged the trunk back into place and sank down onto it.

Sniffing the bottle and wrinkling her nose, she felt her mouth water at the thought of a drink — any drink. Surely a sip wouldn't hurt? She wiped the bottle's neck and trickled a little of the burning liquid into her mouth.

Coughing, she felt it scorch all the way to her stomach. Seconds later the relaxing warmth of the liquor spread down her arms, sending a comforting glow through her stomach all the way to her knees. Padding to the window, she looked out at the scattered lights glowing softly yellow all along the now thinly populated street.

Her eyes felt suddenly heavy. She sipped at the bottle again, thinking perhaps the whiskey might help her sleep. As she settled again on the punishing springs, she took a hearty swallow and lay back to let the warmth claim her. In no time the bottle was drained and her head felt as heavy as lead.

Suddenly the bed no longer felt like a pile of rocks. She didn't fear a man forcing his way into her room, didn't feel the gnawing hunger in her stomach or the sting of homesickness in her heart. She slipped into a heavy sleep and dreamed of Tyler Reede — and he did not behave like a gentleman at all!

Chapter Four

Moaning, Daisie clamped her hand over her dry, aching eyes and struggled to a sitting position. As she breathed in the sharp, invigorating cold air in her room, she realized she'd left the window open all night. Then she remembered the man who had stumbled in and, her heart leaping, looked to see if the trunk was still across the door.

Everything spun, and her stomach lurched. She clenched her eyes closed until the spinning stopped. After a moment she lay back convinced that her head was going to split open. That whiskey! Whatever had possessed her to drink it?

Feeling ashamed, weak and ill, she struggled to her feet and padded across the icy floor to the window. An eerie white mist hung in the distant hollows. The mountains beyond were a pale lavender, faint, like a dream. The town was quiet and still.

She breathed in the fragrance of damp earth and pine, but the pain in her head remained. Turning away, she squeezed her temples, resolving that she'd die before taking another drop of whiskey. Head throbbing, she dressed in a sober brown skirt and fitted navy jacket and repacked her trunks. Bending over to button her shoes was agony.

Edging the trunk aside, she peeked out the door. Snores resonated through the hall. Tiptoeing down the stairs, she found the night clerk stretched out asleep on the desk, his muddy boots crossed negligently on the register book, his head pillowed on his wadded-up hat. Men lay propped along the walls or slumped on benches, faces covered by dusty hats, feet encased in muddy boots, battered hands gripping pistols.

Daisie slipped out back, barricaded herself in the dusty privy and emerged moments later, her cheeks burning, to find half a dozen drowsy men staggering toward her from the back door. They were standing in line as she hurried back inside. The desk clerk had rolled onto his side, making the desk lean dangerously.

"Excuse me," Daisie said, nudging his shoulder. "The manager said I could look at the register for March." She nudged him again, harder. "May I look now?"

He sat up, rubbed his face and frowned at her. "March?" He hoisted himself to the floor, scratched himself all over and dug behind the desk. At last, he yanked out a gritty ledger from a stack in the corner. "After some faithless husband, are you? Run out on you, did he?"

"Not at all," Daisie said crisply, concentrating on the pages, scanning the names. "Later today I may send a messenger for my trunks." She glanced up with an impersonal smile. "I may decide to leave town in search of—" Her eye caught her father's name and, with a suddenly trembling finger, she traced the date. Her heart leaped and lunged so hard she couldn't breathe. "What does this mean, this one signature? How many nights did my father stay here?"

The man squinted where she was pointing. "One signature, one night." He yawned, scratched and glanced toward the back hall.

Giving the signature one last look, Daisie thanked the clerk and rushed out the door as if she expected to find her father waiting outside.

It wasn't difficult to understand why her father had stayed in this miserable excuse for a hotel only one night, she thought, pressing out into the bright sunshine and brisk air. Shielding her eyes against the glare, she gritted her teeth, ignored her piercing headache and strode purposefully up the street.

An hour later she was puffing, tottering along a wooden walkway with her heart hammering and her head whirling from lack of air. She had been to every crude hotel and ramshackle boarding house in the town. Not one had another of her father's signatures on record.

She stopped to buy some bread fresh from the oven and nibbled at it. She was fairly starving. At last she spied a prosperous-looking store and decided that if she was going to spend another night in this primitive place, she would at least have her own chamberpot.

Inside, the air still held the faint dusty smell of a recent sweeping and particles of dust hung in the shafts of sunlight that poured in through the high, narrow east-facing windows. Orderly shelves bowed under a wealth of goods, from canned food to stacks of denim trousers.

A petite woman in her mid-twenties, dressed in a dark-brown, high-necked dress, stood behind the back counter. Hearing Daisie's tread on the bare floorboards, she whirled, looking perfectly capable of drawing and firing a pistol.

Her wary expression changed immediately to a wide smile. "Good day! How can I help you, miss?" She had blonde, dry-looking curls done up clumsily. They bobbed stiffly as she rushed around the counter toward Daisie. Though she was not unattractive, the harried, pinched look about her eyes made Daisie suspect she worked long hours. "Welcome to Salter's Emporium," she said heartily. She took in every detail of Daisie's apparel, from her hat to her snug jacket and fringed reticule. "I'm Amelia Salter. So pleased to meet you, Miss . . . ?"

Daisie allowed the energetic girl with quick brown eyes to clasp her hands eagerly. Poor lonely thing, Daisie thought, smiling down at her. "I'm Daisie Browning. I wonder if you might have a . . . ," — hearing someone else enter the store, she lowered her voice —" a chamberpot. I'm staying at such a primitive hotel . . . ."

The young woman nodded understandingly. Turning, she shouted, "Hank? Do we have another chamberpot?" She glanced back toward Daisie, unaware that she had embarrassed her customer to the soles of her dusty shoes. "There's gold enough in these hills to make a person sinfully rich overnight, but hardly a convenience of any sort. We put aside a few necessities, but we're forced to price them rather high. Chamberpots, basins and pitchers break on the way up here. You *do* understand? Let me look. Hank? Hank?'' Her voice grew shrill.

Taking a deep breath, Daisie resolved to get used to American ways.

Amelia clattered efficiently toward a rear door, threw it open and hollered toward the stairs just visible beyond. ''Hank? Get down here right now. We have a customer!''

From above came a creak, then the sound of heavy footsteps, and a tall, boyishly handsome man wearing a starched white shirt and a black string tie came through the doorway. He wore black broadcloth trousers held up by red suspenders. Red armbands kept his sleeve cuffs from sagging below his large-boned wrists. ''Good morning,'' he panted, his dark eyes fastening on Daisie. Gaping, he surged toward her just as Amelia had, and smoothed his palms over his fair, center-parted hair. ''Good morning, indeed!'' he said, rocking to a stop before her. He clasped her hands before she could draw them away and shook them fervently. ''Forgive me for keeping you waiting, miss! Allow me to introduce myself. I'm Henry Salter. Folks call me Hank, and I'd be pleased if you would, too. This is my sister, Amelia. Oh, you've met.'' He gave his sister a hasty look and then returned his complete attention to Daisie. With a smile of wonder, his eyes traveled from her face, to her throat, to the swell of her snugly tailored jacket, to her tiny, cinched waist and her wide worsted skirt, returning at last to her face. Licking his lips, he steered her to the side, away from Amelia's interfering movements. ''Welcome to Cripple Creek.''

Daisie introduced herself, relishing in the formal exchange an echo of her fond and distant past. ''Your sister's been kind enough to help me look for a certain . . . item I need,'' Daisie said, coloring slightly. ''There's so much more I need as well. My hotel is simply . . . .'' She shook her head and cringed as it throbbed.

Hank drank her in, nodding, but not listening. Daisie sensed that his interest went beyond that of an eager, solicitous merchant.

"You'd like a cup of coffee, I'll bet, Miss Browning. Amelia makes pretty good coffee," he said, patting Daisie's shoulder. Again his eyes went over her face and then swept up and down her body, finally coming to rest on her well-covered bosom. "How long will you be staying in Cripple Creek? I'll bet it's rustic compared to what a fine, upstanding lady like yourself is used to."

"A bit," Daisie admitted, feeling uncomfortable beneath his frank scrutiny. "I'm here looking for my father, Lord Browning. I don't suppose you recall such a gentleman coming into your store last spring?"

Amelia moved closer. Her lips still curved up, but her eyes flickered toward Hank. She edged between them so that he was forced to move away from Daisie. "Do we remember an English gentleman named Browning — *Lord* Browning —" she added with emphasis, "coming in here last spring, Hank?"

Hank went to the black potbellied stove in the center of the store and poured coffee from a tin pot as he thought. "I don't recall too many English around here, but last winter — " He rubbed his chin, his eyes turned away. "Your father, you said? Kind of stooped over?"

Daisie briefly explained why her father had left Bethinghamshire. She recounted finding his signature, first at the Brown Palace Hotel, and then just a few hours ago in the Colorado Hotel's register.

"Brown Palace," Amelia echoed, smiling and nodding at Daisie as she smoothed her skirt and plumped her curls. "That's such a nice place to stay."

"Bethinghamshire," Hank said, winking. "I couldn't forget a name like that. I remember an old gentleman with an accent in here last spring. Talkative, too. I didn't recall right off because he came in with a woman—not your mother, surely? She didn't look at all like you. He mentioned going into the mountains to prospect for gold."

Daisie's heart jolted with shock. "A woman?" Her mouth went dry. "What sort of woman?"

"Thought she knew everything, didn't she, Hank?" Amelia

sniffed. "I didn't like her. Not at all. Miss Browning, can I get you something else?" Amelia seemed suddenly to be trying to hurry her on her way.

"Where exactly did my father say he was going?" Daisie asked, restraining herself from clutching at the storekeeper's sleeve.

A woman? A woman!

"Is everything all right?" Amelia cut in. "Your father's not in any trouble, is he?"

Trying to conceive of her father in the company of any woman but her mother, Daisie shook her head. Completely bewildered, she muttered, "I don't know. He hasn't written . . . ." Her words trailed off. Never had she thought another woman might be the reason her father had stopped writing. Suddenly she burned to be on her way. "What did you sell my father? Perhaps he bought a map."

"No problem remembering," Hank said, handing Daisie a tin mug of inky coffee. He allowed himself to pat her shoulder again, her anxiety his convenient excuse for the liberty. "He bought a complete prospecting outfit, a pick, shovel, tin pans for panning gold out of streams, a cooking kettle, a lantern, a hunting knife . . . ." He paused, ticking off the items on his thick fingers.

"Rain slicker," Amelia prompted, smiling. "Bedroll, canned goods, rifle . . . ."

"Not my father!" Daisie exclaimed, shocked. "He detested hunting. He often said he couldn't be all English because he didn't ride to the hunt."

"And a mule," Amelia added.

Daisie turned away, trying to picture her father as one of those forlorn men crossing a barren meadow leading a pack mule. Her father was surely half mad with gold fever to be living in a tent, cooking over an open fire, associating with other women . . . . "Where could he have gone?" she wondered as she sipped the coffee. It tasted like tar.

Hank blocked Daisie's path as she made to leave. "I don't

want to alarm you, Miss Browning, but your father is probably wandering hundreds of miles from here by now. A man and a mule can cover a lot of ground in a few months.''

Shaking her head, Daisie found she couldn't meet Hank's eyes. ''I won't believe that. I can't.''

Hank took her hands again and squeezed them. ''If he'd found gold, we would have heard about it. There's no secrets in this town.''

Amelia nudged Hank out of the way and handed Daisie the paper-wrapped parcel, quoting a price on the chamberpot that made Daisie's heart contract. Withdrawing a gold coin from her reticule, Daisie kept shaking her head. ''I'm sure he's not far from here.''

''Of course,'' Amelia said, drawing Daisie away. ''And you may be right. He may be right here in town, sleeping it off in some dark saloon corner or resting his weary head with his lady friend.''

Hank cleared his throat. ''She wasn't that kind, sister dear.''

At last Amelia saw the effect her words were having on Daisie. ''Dear me, I've said something to upset you. Do sit down.''

''My father would not resort to drinking—or anything else,'' Daisie said, though her voice betrayed her fear that it just might be true.

Hank smiled hastily and cocked his head. ''What my sister meant was, if he hasn't written and he's not at a local hotel and we haven't heard of him striking gold, he might have sold his outfit. If he's feeling down in the mouth, taking comfort where he can find it, he might — '' Hank searched her face. ''All of us are only human, after all.''

''Maybe he bought some land,'' Amelia suggested brightly.

Daisie's hope revived. ''How can I find out if he did?'' She moved toward the door, anxious to avoid Hank's eager touch.

''Go straight to the horse's mouth. There's men in town whose business is to buy and sell claims. One might've staked your father—if your father needed money—for more supplies.''

"I hope your hotel isn't too uncomfortable?" Amelia said, examining Daisie's outfit again with interest. "Is it clean?"

In spite of herself, Daisie's shoulders slumped, and she said ruefully, "I had thought to look for a better place, but the sorry truth is, I'm staying at the best in town this very minute."

Glancing over her shoulder toward her brother, Amelia smiled sweetly, her brown eyes shining. "If you'd be at all interested, we have space upstairs. It's nothing fancy, you understand, but it's clean. We have real beds, not those things thrown together out of a few pine boards."

Daisie smiled, longing to make friends and feel less alone. Amelia's offer sounded wonderful. Feeling cautious, however, she looked back at Hank from the corner of her eye, wondering if he'd prove a nuisance. "Where do you and your brother have your own rooms?"

"Upstairs, by the stairs," Amelia said. "Would you like to have a look around?"

Hank thundered toward the door, holding it open. "Now, don't go pushing Miss Browning." He looked worried. "Let her make up her own mind."

Amelia linked arms with Daisie. "Daisie and I understand one another," Amelia said, with a glance at the rounded, paper-covered parcel Daisie carried. "You'll have more privacy here. It's quiet, and I'd just love having someone cultured to talk to. This town is full of roughneck miners and horsey women, not at all the type I'm used to associating with. Say you'll stay with us. You'll be right to home. Won't she, Hank?" she added meaningfully, turning away from Daisie toward her brother.

Daisie relished the way they were treating her. The company of a friendly woman and clean-cut, handsome man of business might prove just what she needed to help her endure her stay in this place. "All right," she said, breaking into a smile. "I'll have someone deliver my trunks. Would you mind looking after them for me?"

"No trouble," Amelia assured her briskly. "Let me keep your package here, too. You don't want to cart it about, do you? Will you be out long?"

Daisie shrugged, unable to guess.

"Well, take care of yourself wandering about alone," Amelia said. "Don't stay out after dark. We Salters intend to take good care of you. We'll have our evening meal at Ranger's, and I'll see that your trunks are taken upstairs and kept safe and sound in the meantime. Is there anything breakable or of particular value in them?"

They paused outside on the boardwalk. Daisie's attention was immediately drawn to a man loping across the street. She shook her head. "Pardon me, Amelia. Do you know that man?" She pointed.

"Oh!" For an instant Amelia looked startled. "Him?" She sniffed, her eyes following Tyler Reede as his broad-shouldered silhouette disappeared into a saloon. "He's just one of those speculators who buy and sell claims."

"What do you think of him?" Daisie asked, trying to make the question sound casual.

Amelia laughed nervously. "Heavens! I don't associate with men—except those my brother approves, of course. I certainly wouldn't know any man who spends the early morning hours in *that* part of town . . . though he's been in the store a few times. Do *you* know him?" she asked, her tone curious.

"I saw him playing cards on the train yesterday."

"I'm not surprised," Amelia said disdainfully. "I sometimes wonder if this town is a fit place for decent people when his kind are around. You stay away from him, Daisie. You're not used to such rascals, the way we are. You just let Hank and me look after you and you'll do all right."

Oddly, after seeing Tyler Reede in his fringed leather coat, Daisie's thoughts kept returning to the possibility of seeing him again—even though she wasn't sure she cared to. She couldn't get him out of her mind as she had a late brunch at the restaurant Amelia had recommended. The place was crude, but the food was palatable. When the waiter suggested someone to deliver her trunks to the Salters' store, Daisie tipped him generously, then went outside unwilling to admit she was shamefully curious about the forward Mr. Reede.

Relieved that she'd soon be more comfortably established and that the Salters seemed like possible friends, Daisie ventured closer to the streets lined with saloons. She was determined to locate her father. If even only one miner would help her. . . .

Moments later, walking gingerly past the first saloon, Daisie steeled herself for the ordeal. The false front looked respectable enough, but the building was nothing more than a log shack. Two large windows flanked the narrow doorway, from which smoke drifted. The proprieter leaned against a rain barrel, arms folded, watching her.

"I'm looking for an English gentleman calling himself Lord Browning," Daisie said. "I believe my father may be mining in this area."

The fellow twisted his drooping mustaches and shook his head. "Ain't seen him."

"Might I speak with some of your patrons?" Daisie asked, knowing her cheeks were scarlet. She refused to look away.

Shrugging, he spread his palm to show her inside. "Ask away, ma'am."

Moments later she burst from the dismal, whitewashed, smoky interior into the glaring sunshine, wondering what her mother would say about the treatment her delicately nurtured daughter had just endured. Such vulgar insinuations! Such impudent questions! She stalked away in disgust. But she would not give up. Doggedly, she repeated her request in every saloon along the street. When she entered a larger saloon with blood-red-velvet-draped windows, she felt it was the first civilized-looking establishment she'd seen since arriving in Cripple Creek.

Across a large, broad hall crowded with round, clawfooted pedestal tables and sturdy oak chairs stood a long, polished mahogany bar gleaming in the lantern-light. The air was thick with smoke. In the corner was a huge mechanical music machine with cymbals, drums and other instruments encased behind glass, clamoring out the song, "Hot Time in the Old Town Tonight."

Making her way to the gentleman in the purple silk vest who was tending bar, she summoned her courage and resolve once more, and asked her question. "Perhaps a . . . woman here knew him," she added, cringing at the thought. "Or perhaps someone here sold him land. Any help you can give me would be greatly appreciated." Her voice took on a plaintive note she hadn't intended.

Kneading his rosy, rounded cheeks, the bartender regarded her with a twinkle. "I can't say I recollect seeing this father of yours, ma'am, but if you'd like to speak to someone who knows all there is to know about claims in this town, the fella to see is sitting right over there a-smiling at you this very minute."

Whirling, Daisie's eyes met the penetrating blue gaze of Tyler Reede. She looked down, blushing. She had not expected to see him again quite so soon, and especially not in this sort of place. The center of the large room was open to the rafters and Tyler sat at a table in a murky corner beneath the upper floor landing. She glanced up at the landing, which was surrounded by a railing. The tops of several doors were visible from where she stood. A brightly painted woman in a flaming red dress came out of one door, leaned over the railing and waved to Tyler before passing the stairway to enter another room.

"Isn't there someone else in town I can talk to about claims?" she whispered.

"Not a better man than Tyler," the bartender said.

"Could you possibly introduce us?"

The bartender's cheeks rounded. "Just go on over, ma'am. Don't be shy. He'll be glad to help you, whatever your problem."

His raised eyebrow irritated Daisie. "You don't understand —"

She wanted Tyler Reede to approach her. She paused, hoping he might. When he didn't move, and she saw that the bartender had no intention of leaving the vantage point from which he could see all that went on in the broad, nearly empty saloon, she knew she would have to make the first move.

Unfortunately, Tyler Reede was now studiously ignoring her. Summoning her courage, Daisie took several hesitant steps toward him, wishing that she had been more polite to him on the train. What must he think now, seeing her in a saloon?

Stopping three feet from him, she felt oddly that he was much larger than she remembered, and far more intimidating. He finished a half-empty mug of beer and then leaned back, oblivious to her.

"Mr. Reede, might I have a moment of your time?" She sounded stuffy and reserved and longed to be able to sound relaxed and confident of her charm.

He said nothing.

"Mr. Reede, excuse me. I believe we met on the train yesterday. And in Denver . . . ." she continued, her voice now barely more than a whisper. "I need some information about the man I came to Cripple Creek to meet — my . . . my father." She expected him to turn now and smile.

Not moving, he stared straight ahead, saying nothing.

Her voice came out in a weak, embarrassed quaver. "My father — Lord Browning — may have bought some land from you. He came here to do some mining. I would be most grateful if you'd try to remember. He's fiftyish, with thinning gray hair . . . ."

For a moment Tyler Reede looked as if he was going to turn, smile and answer her questions. Her heart lifted and she stepped closer. Then his smooth, handsome face tightened. He turned slightly more toward the wall, away from her.

Oh, such rudeness, she thought, beginning to seethe. How dare he treat her this way? She searched her mind for a way to handle this obstinate man. What English code of behavior could she rely on to get her through this excruciating conversation? "I am truly grateful for your help in Denver, Mr. Reede. I hope you understand that while traveling on the train yesterday I didn't feel it was . . . proper for me to . . . to . . . ." Bewildered, she stopped. She was growing angry now. He was being more than rude. He was deliberately insulting her. "My father stopped writing to my mother last winter. No one has seen him since spring. I've traced him here and I know now he bought prospecting equipment. If you sold him land I'd know where to look . . . ." She shivered at his silent rebuff and stepped back, her spine rigid. "I can see you're no gentleman! My father may need help, but you don't seem to care. I don't think I share your exalted opinion of yourself, *Mister* Reede."

Turning with exquisite slowness, Tyler looked up at her, his blue eyes sharp as he examined her face and then raked her body with critical appraisal. "I'm afraid we haven't been properly introduced," he said, mimicking her accent rather well. "I say, if you don't stop annoying me, I shall have the bartender escort you outside."

Torn between indignation and laughter, Daisie gazed helplessly into the now frankly amused blue eyes. Abruptly, her indignation evaporated. "I did behave rather unbearably yesterday, didn't I?" she said, trying not to smile at her own silliness.

Like the sun beaming from behind a thundercloud, Tyler Reede's face broke into a smile. He extended his wide, attractive hand. "I do want to help, ma'am."

Daintily, Daisie clasped the tips of his fingers and shook them three times. "I'm Daisie Browning of Bethinghamshire, England. I've come to Cripple —"

"The man you came to meet is your *father*?" Tyler asked, rising. He looked down on her, his expression saying with eloquence that he didn't for a moment believe her.

Relieved that he was at least now talking to her, Daisie nodded. Knees weak, she dropped into the nearest chair. Tyler seated himself once again and Daisie leaned forward, hands tightly clenched in her lap, and asked earnestly, "*Have* you seen him?"

"Care for a drink, Miss Browning? I like your name. It suits you."

"Please . . . ." She covered her burning eyes with a trembling hand. Right now the thought of a drink made her feel quite ill again. "This is urgent . . . and I *don't* drink!" Her face flooded with crimson guilt from hairline to throat.

Tyler resumed his mocking expression. "Oh, I see. Not a drop before noon. What about after sundown?"

Head spinning, Daisie stood, toppling the chair behind her, turned on her heel and marched toward the door, into the painfully glaring sunlight. To the devil with Tyler Reede! She'd find her father without his help.

Chapter Five

"Forgive me, Miss Browning!" Tyler Reede called, loping out
of the saloon after her, laughing deep in his throat. "Please,"
he chuckled, touching her elbow and then drawing his hand
away to show he meant no insult. "You can hardly blame me
for teasing you. You have the most wonderful way of speaking.
I'm sorry, Miss Browning. I promise to try to behave like the
gentleman I assure you I am."

Sniffing haughtily, Daisie wished she could storm away, but
the street had since filled with carriages and wagons, choking
the air with dust and making the correct way to go a complete
blur.

Slowly, she turned to look back at Tyler. His face wore a
wide grin. Despite his apology, he looked as though he would
survive perfectly well without her forgiveness. "I don't much
like being teased, Mr. Reede."

"Please, call me Tyler. And watch your step," he added,
steering her adroitly out of the path of a lumbering wagon filled
with barrels of beer.

Ignoring the invitation to call him by his first name, Daisie
said, "If you could simply tell me if you've met or seen my
father . . . ?"

"That's just the point, Miss Browning. I meet a lot of people
in my day-to-day dealings. True, I buy and sell claims, and
stake old geezers who need help, but I'm afraid they all run

together in my mind. Besides, I'm a trusted man among the prospectors hereabouts. I don't betray secrets. Many men ask me to lend them money in confidence. I even loan the use of land to a few, in the hopes that a claim will yield enough gold to cover the purchase price. Let me think about this while you and I go somewhere for a cool drink.''

''I do not drink, Mr. Reede!'' she snapped, marching ahead in hopes of finding a cross street that would take her back to the respectable part of town.

''Coffee?'' he said, still at her elbow.

''If what I had this morning is called coffee, no thank you.'' Then, gathering her wits, she turned back to Tyler. In spite of his smile, she was done with this business of cat and mouse, with herself in the role of the mouse. ''If you manage to recall any useful information, Mr. Reede, you'll find me staying with the Salters.''

He looked puzzled.

''They have rooms to rent,'' she added.

His face registered hastily concealed amusement. That quick, provocative smile undermined her composure still further. ''Oh, *rooms*, of course. I'll be happy to call on you in a day or so, Miss Browning. Let me say that you are the loveliest young woman this town has seen in a long time. If I can do anything to get on better terms with you, please say so. I'm staying at the Gaslight Saloon—you were just in there. I wouldn't come there in person, if I were you,'' he added, winking and reverting to a slight imitation of her accent. ''Oh—don't snarl and spit at me, Miss Browning. Teasing is in my nature. Send a message to me any time. It really isn't safe for you to be on these streets unescorted. If you will permit me to direct you . . . .''

Tyler grasped her elbow firmly, sending shivers of excitement straight to her heart, and steered her toward a street corner where he pointed, grinning as if he was enjoying her discomfiture. She longed to be able to manage by herself, but it seemed for the moment that she was doomed to be rescued by this tall, self-assured man in dancing fringes.

Tipping his hat and making her an exaggeratedly low bow,

Tyler bid her good day. Resisting the strong impulse to storm off in a temper, Daisie moved away with queenly grace.

At the next corner, she turned, as if casually looking around, to see if Reede had watched her grand exit. Beyond the confusion of surging street traffic she saw he had turned from her the moment she began walking. He was just disappearing into the great dark mouth of a livery stable.

Pondering this, after a moment she turned and retraced her steps. He hadn't seemed to have any travel plans when she'd found him in the saloon. Could his sudden need for transportation have anything to do with the questions she'd been asking?

Back on the corner where she had left Tyler Reede, she waited impatiently for several minutes, then dashed across the street, leaving in her wake a cursing mule-team driver and several rearing carriage horses.

Out of breath and fervently wishing her corset was not so tight she reached the sagging livery and edged toward the door.

"I'll be back late," Tyler was saying as he and a tall stable boy backed a black mare between the shafts of a gleaming, blue-trimmed top-buggy. "Send someone to give my regrets to Colonel Darnel and his wife. Tell them I was called away unexpectedly and won't be able to join them for dinner."

"That's the big house up on Gold Street, right, sir?" the gangling stable boy asked, patting the mare and checking the harness.

Tyler nodded as he swung into the seat, took up the whip and tapped at the mare's rump. "It's a downright embarrassment what a man'll do to attract the attention of a pretty young woman. I should've been a buffalo hunter!"

Thunderstruck, Daisie ducked inside to stop him. He was going somewhere because of her questions! He knew something about her father and had refused to tell her! Before she could call to him, Tyler snapped, "Git up!" and the horse and buggy bolted out, leaving Daisie choking on dust and bits of hay.

She slipped back into the alley and reached the corner of the livery at the very moment another buggy with a surrey top pulled up sharply to avoid a collision as Tyler's equipage plunged into the road.

A mule train dragging logs chose that moment to cut in front of Daisie. She backed almost to the wall to avoid the roils of red dust. The slow-motion confusion left all traffic stalled until the twenty or so animals had passed. By then Tyler was well out of earshot.

When she crossed the street, she could see Tyler turning several blocks away to the west, headed out of town. Seething, she gathered up her skirts and started after him, determined to walk to the very ends of the earth to learn where he was going.

A mile or so outside town, she stopped, panting. Her chest was aching, her heart pounding, her mind a turmoil of unlady-like thoughts. Helplessly, she watched the top-buggy, now no bigger than a speck, disappear around a wall of humped boulders more than a mile away.

It might as well have been a hundred miles. She sank to the slanting flat surface of a grayish boulder, contemplated the tiny flecks of glitter in it, and cursed gold with the vehemence of a disappointed child.

She paused long enough to empty her shoes of pebbles. The red purse had rubbed her ankle raw. She covered the sore with her hankie and put the purse in her other shoe, leaving both unbuttoned.

Making her way back along one of the twin wheel tracks that comprised this road through the scrubby brush, she gathered wildflowers to press and send to her mother and Pammie. That evening she'd write suggesting that good news was so close she could almost touch it.

Thoughts of her father made the return walk less difficult than it might have been. The sun was sinking behind the western range when she limped into town yearning for someone to offer her a ride, and yet praying no one would notice the foolish English greenhorn hobbling along in shoes obviously more suited to a parlor than a rugged, stone-strewn road through the wilds.

Those last steps into Salter's Emporium nearly brought tears to Daisie's eyes. Lit from opposite windows now, the store appeared more ramshackle than it had by morning light. "Amelia?" she called out, sounding tired and forlorn. "Anyone here?"

Wincing with every step, Daisie limped to the counter and dropped onto a step-stool. She had almost given in to tears when Amelia and Hank entered by the front door, bickering under their breath.

" . . . not a good idea, I tell you!" Hank hissed.

"The way you were acting, I thought you'd — "

Then Hank saw Daisie drooping dejectedly in the dim corner, and his scowl twisted into an ingratiating grin. "My sweet Miss Browning!" he exclaimed, silencing his sister. "Whatever has happened to you?"

Daisie lifted her head with a weary smile. "I have walked my feet off," she said, laughing at herself.

"Look at your skirt and jacket," Amelia scolded. "You'll never get all the dust off."

Hank and Amelia lifted Daisie to her feet. Amelia's eyes were on Daisie's face, quick to see the pinch of pain in Daisie's eyes as she put weight on her feet again.

"Have you had an accident, Miss Browning? Should I carry you?" Hank asked, his eyes sparkling at the thought.

Amelia pushed him away. "She's not an invalid. Here, Daisie, let me help you up to bed." Amelia drew Daisie away from her brother's eager, fumbling grasp. "We waited such a long time for you, and then decided you must've taken dinner with someone else. Wherever did you go today? We didn't see you."

Daisie was too exhausted to explain. "I haven't yet eaten," she said, letting Amelia help her back into the tiny storage room lined to the ceiling with crates and boxes. The stairs felt scarcely safer than those in the Colorado Hotel. Thinking only of a soft bed with cool, clean sheets and a soothing sponge bath in the privacy of her own little room, Daisie took each step with the courage of a true Englishwoman.

At the top of the stairs, her eyes fell on a wall of faded blue canvas. Someone on the far side of the canvas barrier coughed.

Her eyes shot to the front of the building where the hallway formed of canvas drapes on either side ended at a single window. A heavy-set man, his face and clothes covered with dark, russet-colored dirt, emerged from a flap in the wall, scowled at Daisie, edged past and went down the stairs.

"This way," Amelia said, showing not the slightest sign that she thought this assemblage of "rooms" anything less than adequate. "Your trunks arrived this afternoon. Hank carried them up himself. They are quite heavy, aren't they? I've left your parcel on the bed. You'll have to empty it out back yourself. We charge three dollars a night, but of course you can pay us at the end of the week, or whenever you like, really."

Daisie inched down the hallway in a daze of remorse. A canvas-walled room? Suddenly the Colorado Hotel seemed luxurious compared to this, but to move back would offend her new friends. Was that why Tyler Reede had said, "Oh, *rooms*, of course," in that amused way?

"Here we are!" Amelia announced, lifting a flap near the front. "The best room in the house." She smiled, looking as proud of the dim, musty-smelling cubicle as if it were a palace suite.

One look at the bed and Daisie's heart fell. The "real" bed was a folding cot with a suspiciously uncomfortable look that made Daisie want to weep in despair.

The area that was hers for only three dollars a night (and that was, indeed, considerably less than what she had paid at the Colorado), was five feet wide and six feet long. The cot had been pressed into the corner. The hallway canvas wall lay against the foot of it. An up-ended crate sporting a candle stuck down on a jar lid served as a nightstand.

"I've given you a brand-new candle," Amelia announced proudly, as Daisie squeezed past her trunks, which had been placed alongside the cot, the smaller one tottering on top of the two humpbacks. Scarcely a square inch of space remained in which to stand.

Daisie tried to keep her expression hidden as she dropped onto the cot. She was relieved to find it had a mattress, though it felt about two inches thick and as hard as a tax collector's heart. She bit her lower lip to keep from bursting into tears.

"Anything wrong, Daisie?" Amelia asked, a note of touchiness creeping into her voice.

"My feet," Daisie gasped, jerking up her skirts to reveal the half-hooked shoes. "After today's walk I'm going to need new shoes."

"Heavens, we don't have any white kid shoes like this in all of Cripple Creek!" Amelia said, crouching to help draw them off. "Dear me, Daisie, what's this?" She withdrew a blood-tinged hankie. "You poor thing! Your ankle's raw!" While Daisie leaned back, her lower lip caught between her teeth, Amelia clucked disapprovingly. "Your other ankle's nearly as bad. I'll put your shoes by the nightstand. You must be in agony."

Hearing her shoes drop to the floor, Daisie closed her eyes to keep back tears.

"I'll get some water and salve," Amelia said, rushing away.

The canvas flap fell into place, closing Daisie into the dismal cubicle. She pulled up her skirts and stripped off her stockings to examine each ankle. With her lacy drawers and flounced petticoats exposed, she looked up to see Hank peering through an opening in the flap at her.

"Excuse me," he said huskily, but he didn't turn away.

Daisie pushed her dusty skirts down. "Oh, the salve. Thank you," she said.

Hank remained, eyes fastened on her exposed bare feet.

"Get out of my way," Amelia scolded, shoving Hank aside as she edged in with a slopping tin basin of icy water. "Let me do that for you," she insisted, dampening the covers when she set down the basin, determined to minister to Daisie's blisters.

"You're good to help me, Amelia," Daisie said, giving herself up to some much-needed pampering.

"There," Amelia said, straightening, closing the tin of salve. "Just rest now. We're going to have such fun while you're here." She took up the basin. "I'll fetch you something to eat. When you're rested I want to hear all about England."

Daisie's eyes drooped shut. Though she was still listening to Amelia's patter, Amelia apparently thought she had dropped off, for she tiptoed away. Daisie lay still, willing her weary bones to stop aching.

Later, Amelia brought a meal on a tray from the restaurant across the way. Daisie was so famished she devoured every bite without hesitation. She didn't need to answer Amelia's barrage of questions because the eager young woman answered half of them herself and rushed on.

As Amelia lit the candle, several boarders thumped up the stairs and dropped with groans onto their respective cots. She finally stood. "You must be tired," she said, looking reluctant to leave. "If you need anything, I'll be right across the way. Hank is next to me. Don't be concerned if you hear people moving about in the night. Some of the boarders come and go at odd hours, particularly just before dawn."

"Thank you," Daisie sighed, wishing she was in the Colorado Hotel with that bottle of whiskey to help her sleep.

Smiling, looking pleased with herself, Amelia slipped out.

Daisie supposed she'd manage in this "room" somehow. Perhaps they would let her store a trunk in the hallway. Better still, she might rent the cubicle next to hers. She'd have more room until she found her father and a place for him to come to once they were together again. Pleased with this idea, she undressed beneath the protection of her nightgown, slipped gingerly beneath the sheet and blanket Amelia had tucked around the unforgiving mattress and dropped instantly into a heavy sleep.

She woke at what she thought was dawn. The upper floor of Salter's Emporium rumbled with snoring. She was aware of all the strange, unseen men around her, separated from her only by thin canvas.

Peeking into the hall, she saw no one about. Outside the window the sky glittered with stars so bright she wondered if she had ever really seen stars before. The town's lights glowed softly. Faint sprightly piano music and the clamor of a nickelodeon made her realize she'd slept less than two hours.

Lying back down, shivering beneath the thin covers, she drifted in and out of sleep. The other cots groaned and squeaked as the boarders shifted positions. Occasionally a floorboard creaked.

From the distant mountains came the eerie howl of a lone coyote crying at the moon. A volley of gunfire made Daisie jump and sit listening, heart pounding, for several minutes. Then, burrowing more deeply, she slept again.

Dreaming of Denver, she wandered the dark streets unable to find safety. The drunk appeared ahead, hands stretching out, trying to touch her breasts. Frozen with terror, she couldn't keep his groping fingers from fumbling at her clothes.

Then she realized she wore nothing! More aware of herself as a woman then ever before, she felt every nerve tingle. She ached in a strange, langorous way. Moaning in her throat, she squirmed and stretched, thinking that if Tyler were gently stroking her breasts like that she would die of ecstasy.

The air felt cool on her exposed skin. The reaching, titillating fingers closed over one breast, pressing softly, urgently . . . .

Wrenching away with a strangled cry, Daisie came awake, thrashing at what she thought was a tangle of covers. Her hand struck a stubbled cheek. She smelled the heavy reek of whiskey close to her face and the odor of a man's unwashed body.

Aghast, she fought to get away. In the darkness she couldn't make out the man's features. Was this a nightmare or was someone actually sprawled across her on the cot?

Choking back screams, she dug and raked her nails into anything she touched, hearing the man curse as he fumbled to avoid her. Catching his shins on the side of her heaviest trunk, he got to his feet, groaning and reeled toward the canvas flap. Then he found his way out and staggered along the hallway, mumbling, poking into cubicles and disturbing boarders.

As her heart slowed, Daisie heard him drop onto the cot in another cubicle. Seconds later, all was quiet again except for the man's rising snores. Looking down, she snatched her nightdress closed and shuddered. He *had* fondled her! It had happened so quickly . . . . Should she forget it? He was probably so drunk he wouldn't remember.

Scrambling to her feet, she stood trembling and indecisive. Amelia and Hank should know about the sort of men they were renting to. As she pushed back the flap, she bumped into Hank, who was clad in a calf-length night shirt.

"I heard something," he whispered so softly she still felt she was dreaming. He pressed into her cubicle and backed her against the trunk.

Losing her balance, she grabbed at his shoulders. As if in a waking nightmare, her thighs pressed against Hank's.

To steady her, Hank slipped his hand behind her waist. "I'm here," he whispered. "I know you need me."

"Please! I had . . . a bad dream. Hank! Don't — " Ready to faint with confusion and fright, Daisie could barely choke out her protest.

He pressed one finger against her lips. "Amelia heard you cry out a moment ago. She wanted me to check on you. Oh, Daisie . . . ." He squeezed her tightly against his body. She couldn't mistake his true intentions. His breath brushed hotly against her cheek. "I want to take care of you," he hissed. "I want to — "

As his lips mashed against her cheek, she twisted away. "Let me go!" She hissed. She hit his shoulder with her fist and then flattened her other hand against his face to keep his mouth from touching her again. "Let me go!"

Amelia's whisper made Hank flinch and release her. "Is that you, Hank? What's the matter?"

Hank jerked back through the flap, disappearing from Daisie's sight. He cleared his throat. "Nothing. Go back to sleep."

Weak with shock and disgust, Daisie listened to the floorboards creak as Hank moved away. She grabbed up her clothes but was so befuddled and shaken she finally tore her blanket from the bed and yanked it around her trembling shoulders. Her cheeks felt dry and hot. No man had ever touched her that way.

At last she lay back, waiting and listening for what seemed

like hours, trying to imagine telling Amelia what Hank had said and done. The boarder's drunken fumblings were insignificant by comparison.

To spare Amelia the humiliation, Daisie would simply have to leave and find another hotel, once again risking her safety among strangers. After a time, her eyes grew heavy. Exhaustion temporarily drove out fear and anger, and she sank into restless sleep, only to be awakened near dawn as someone finished dressing and tramped down the stairs.

"Draw the water," Daisie heard Amelia whisper in the gray half-light. "Then I'll put on the coffee. Hungry?"

Hank grumbled something. Immediately, Daisie was alert, tense, wondering if again Hank would seize the opportunity to come to her. More men rose and went down. One remained, snoring with the volume of ten.

She grabbed up her skirt and dragged it on beneath her nightgown. She struggled to tighten her corset laces, seething to think she should be constantly endangered. Moments later Hank thundered down the stairs and said something to his sister. Daisie sagged to the cot, shaking, and then tied the corset laces with a furious jerk.

She was still sitting there when Amelia, all smiles, came in with a breakfast tray.

"You're up and dressed early. Sleep well? Oh, if I looked as beautiful as you this early in the morning, I'd have married a king instead of—" She broke off and flushed red as she set the tray on Daisie's lap. "Instead of turning into an old maid."

"You're being too kind," Daisie said, her voice low and rather cool. "And not kind enough to yourself."

After eating, Daisie wrote to her mother and packed her trunks. She was nearly ready to go out to find another hotel when Amelia announced a picnic-style lunch on a grassy knoll behind the store. Daisie felt obliged to accept the invitation as a parting gesture, but she was scarcely able to eat.

"We're lucky to have this place," Hank said as they finished.

The conversation had been stilted and forced from the moment she joined them. Hank persisted, though, acting his usual solicitous self. "Amelia and I came here last summer, had the place built and opened for business even before the roof was on. It's been a long, hard road for us since leaving home. This time, I think, we're in the right place at the right time."

Daisie refrained from commenting, thinking only of where Hank had been the night before.

In fact, Hank was behaving in such a relaxed, ordinary manner that Daisie began to wonder if she might have dreamed the entire episode. Hank met her gaze openly, leaving her feeling a vague and uneasy guilt that perhaps she had misinterpreted something that had had no sexual overtones at all. The thought made her face flood with shame.

"I think I'll go for a walk now," she said at length, rising, eager to escape from Hank's discomfiting presence.

"But it's so late," Amelia said. "Aren't you going to pick out a new pair of shoes? I've found just the ones for you. Let me show you."

Sighing, Daisie went inside with Amelia.

"Are your ankles better?"

"Much," Daisie said.

"I thought perhaps they were bothering you. You've been quiet today."

Unwilling to express her true thoughts, Daisie forced a smile. "I'm just thinking of Papa. You needn't concern yourself."

Amelia took a wrinkled pair of black high-buttoned shoes from a shelf beneath the counter. "Try these."

They looked secondhand, but Daisie said nothing as she perched on the step-stool and pulled one on. The nails felt ready to come through the inner sole, but, except for a pair of satin dancing slippers, she had nothing else to wear. "These will be fine," Daisie said.

Ringing up the sale, Amelia's expression grew grave and troubled. "I've been thinking of your father myself. Wouldn't it be horrid to come all this way and — "

Knowing what Amelia was about to say, Daisie shut out her

words. She tested the stiff leather with her fingers, wondering if she could continue wearing the red purse —

Her head came up sharply.

"I don't mean to alarm you," Amelia went on, seeing Daisie's ghastly expression. "But surely you've realized he might —"

Daisie clapped both hands over her mouth.

"I'm sorry I've upset you, but . . . . Daisie, what is it?"

Going cold, Daisie said, "Nothing. I just thought of something." She jerked off the shoes and started for the stairs.

"Daisie?"

Daisie slipped upstairs and darted into her cubicle, her only thought for the red purse that had been in her shoe all night. Leaning flat over the two trunks, she caught up the shoes and scrambled back to her feet. She up-ended both, and twin piles of dust and pebbles sifted on to the thin wool blanket. "Oh, no," she breathed, feeling her blood turn to ice. Thrusting her hand into the toe of each shoe, Daisie knew with a sinking heart that the purse was gone.

Dropping to her knees, she scanned the gritty floor beneath her cot. There was nothing on the floor but the chamberpot. She peeked between and around the trunks, jerked aside the up-ended crate, looked behind it, ripped the blanket and coarse linen sheet from the cot.

She heard Hank mounting the stairs and whirled, throwing back the flap.

Seeing her wild expression, his face went strangely soft. He came to her and caught her shoulders. "What's wrong?" he whispered. "Amelia said you looked ill."

For a maddening instant she suspected him — suspected even Amelia — but then saw that no knowledge of the missing purse lurked in his eyes, only a smoldering desire to draw her nearer.

Twisting away, she forced her thoughts back to the purse. "Ask Amelia to come up right away," she pleaded. The purse. Her return passage. How could she get her father home? She'd been spending so freely because . . . .

She yanked the pillow-slip off the pillow, turned the mattress, gave out with a mew of anguish and backed again into Hank's ready embrace. For a moment she sagged against him, needing comfort desperately. Hank caressed her shoulders, trying to turn her to face him.

Amelia trotted up the stairs.

Hank released Daisie as if she'd burned his hands.

"Daisie, I —"

Daisie seized Amelia's sleeve, drew her inside the cubicle and whispered urgently, "Yesterday, did you see something in my shoe?"

"The hankie?" Amelia asked, frowning. "I washed it this morning. Do you need it?"

"In the other shoe. A small — Oh, mercy, if I dropped it out on the road I'll never find it." Daisie paused to think, clenching her fists alongside her temples. Her mind whirled. Finally, she dropped onto the bed. "It was *in* my shoe. I have the blisters to prove it!"

"What are you talking about, Daisie?" Amelia snapped, her tone impatient as she looked back at Hank. She crouched, taking Daisie's hands and patting them. "Tell me what's happened."

Daisie spoke as if to herself. "You helped me pull off my shoes. It might've fallen to the floor. But we heard nothing. It dropped into the shoe, but . . . . Amelia! Do you remember seeing anything in my shoe?" Daisie made a circle with her thumb and index finger. "A little red-leather coin purse about this size?"

Bewildered, her eyes round and clear, Amelia shook her head. "I was thinking only of your poor ankles. I suppose something might've been in there, but —" She reached over the trunk, saw that Daisie already had the shoes and straightened slowly. "Is something important missing?" She glanced at Hank. "Surely you won't miss a few coins."

Daisie rolled her eyes. She looked away to avoid exclaiming she would not behave like such a fool over a few coins.

Now the snorer from the cubicle down the hall stuck his head out. Unshaven and disheveled, bleary-eyed and scowling, he snarled, "What the devil are you people doing? I paid for my night's sleep and I mean to get it."

Daisie scrambled off her cot and confronted him. "Did you stumble into my . . . space last night?"

His face clouded. He *did* remember! "I didn't do nothing!" he yelled, ducking away and grabbing up his belongings. "This ain't no proper hotel, nohow. I don't have to stay here. I want my money back!"

Hank lunged. "You're staying right here till we settle this."

Hank nearly brought down the canvas walls and their rickety wooden framework helping the hungover little miner empty his pockets. Except for a change of socks and a few coins, he had nothing of value.

"How much was in the purse?" Hank asked when he had contemptuously dispatched the man.

Daisie buried her face in her hands. "Enough American banknotes to get my father and me back to England."

Amelia gasped and grabbed Hank's arm.

"I don't suppose anyone could use such large denominations in this town without drawing attention," Daisie said, feeling a glimmer of hope.

Hank rubbed his face, bringing color back to his cheeks. "We have some mighty rich fellas around, and some look like they just crawled out of a cave. Daisie, I am so very sorry."

Daisie was too dejected to object to the extremely unwelcome use of her first name. What did it matter? Her knees buckled. She scarcely had enough money left for a single night at another hotel. She'd assumed that in a few days she'd be on her way back to Denver with her father.

"The sheriff will never believe I was so careless," she moaned. "I feel like such a fool."

"Just sit tight," Hank said, taking her hand and patting it. Then he stormed down the hall, and began going through the cubicles.

"We don't need the sheriff," Amelia said hastily.

"We certainly do," Hank cut in. "You go get him right now."

"But our reputation — " Amelia said with an apologetic smile.

Daisie looked away, too stunned to cry.

A half an hour later the sheriff, a middle-aged man with white side whiskers and a sharp eye, arrived. "Tore up the place but good, I see," he grumbled, giving Hank a knowing look. In the adjacent cubicle he snaked his arm beneath the canvas wall and Daisie saw his hand grope where her shoes had stood.

"A clumsy child could've got them shoes," the sheriff said disgustedly. "Did you hear anything unusual last night, Miss Browning?"

She shuddered, too humiliated to admit *all* that had happened to her the night before. "Everything seemed unusual," she said.

"I blame myself," Amelia wailed.

"Ain't the first time money's been stolen — or'lost' — in this town," the sheriff muttered.

"Well, what's done is done," Daisie sighed, resigned to another night under the same roof. "I'll just have to get more money." Dusting her hands, she stood up. Now that the money was gone, she needn't fear another robbery. "I'll just have to work a little harder to get Papa home, that's all. Do let me tidy my bed now, Hank. I'm worn through."

"When you're ready to leave for home, Daisie, let me lend you — "

"That's very kind of you," Daisie said stiffly. "But I'm sure it won't be necessary."

Rebuffed, Hank backed away. "In my own store," he muttered, going down the hall with the weight of the world on his back. "A thief."

Alone at last, Daisie slumped wearily on her cot. She wondered if she would ever see England again.

Chapter Six

"Pardon me for sneaking up on you like this, but good morning!" Tyler rounded the woodpile and stepped into the backyard of Salter's Emporium.

Seated in the sun just beyond a selection of wagon beds, Daisie whirled. "You startled me!" She put down her hair brush and gathered up her still damp hair, holding it at the nape of her neck. She met his intent, admiring gaze and then glanced away, remembering that her unhappy thoughts were probably reflected on her face.

"Your hair is beautiful, Miss Browning, Don't pull it back that way." He stopped several feet from her and gazed up at her as if memorizing every feature.

Nervously, she adjusted her skirts over her slippered feet and started braiding her hair. The morning breeze lifted stray wheat-gold tendrils along her cheeks and played them into the sunlight.

Looking back, she was disturbed by the warmth of Tyler's gaze. The warmth passed into her, erasing her tension. The worries that had blinded her to the morning's beauty receded. This handsome, irrepressible man made her feel wonderful, made her problems seem suddenly less pressing. No amount of mental scolding could make her turn from him in anger.

He stooped, plucked something from the dust and examined it. "An arrowhead, Miss Browning." He held it out to her. The small, pointed piece of gray flint looked smooth and carefully worked. It felt cool yet sharp in her palm.

"Thank you," she said, recalling why she was supposed to be angry. She attempted a scowl.

Anticipating her first words, Tyler raised his palm. "Now, now, let's not get started off wrong. I heard some terrible news this morning." He placed his boot on a large stone and looked back at the store. His smile turned serious. "You were robbed yesterday."

Daisie's memory of following Tyler out of town was forgotten. She thought of the money she had lost. It was important, certainly, but she was even more concerned and furious about Hank's behavior. Quickly she searched Tyler's face, wondering if he would force his attentions on her if given the opportunity. She couldn't guess, but she sensed that she wouldn't find advances from Tyler nearly so repugnant.

"Even if I find my father now," she said, lowering her eyes. "I'll have no way to get him home."

"You're assuming he has no money," Tyler said, noting every shade and shadow of her expression.

"He would have gone home by now, if he had. My mother gave me that money to make sure that *I* returned safely." Daisie felt a catch in her throat. She paused, struggling to gain control of her voice. "I hurt Mama by leaving, but I was sure I was right to come. Now I've failed her."

Tyler's expression was unsettling. "Anything I can do?"

"Please, I feel humiliated enough as it is. Don't make it worse by offering me money." She sounded ungrateful and didn't mean to. Brightening, she said, "But thank you. I'll manage. Really I will. I've come this far. I'll get home again. This just calls for . . . ingenuity."

Grinning, Tyler shook his head as if to say he admired her pluck. "My offer will remain open, Miss Browning." He straightened. "Where are Hank and Amelia?"

"I didn't realize you were acquainted with the Salters," Daisie said, grateful for the change of subject.

"Everyone knows everyone here. I'm surprised you stayed after being robbed."

Daisie tucked the arrowhead into her palm and stepped down from her spot in the sun. "I can't afford to go anywhere else. Besides, I wouldn't dream of embarrassing them further. All their boarders left without notice last night. Amelia's beside herself about the loss of income."

Tyler sniffed. "They'll survive, Daisie. Excuse me, may I use your first name?"

She found it difficult to meet his eyes. "I really don't know, Mr. Reede. I was terribly angry with you the other day. I still am, as a matter of fact." She forced herself to look at him. Once again his steady blue gaze disconcerted her. She looked quickly away to hide her involuntary smile. Now her heart was racing, and she didn't mind that he was standing so near.

"Would you care to go walking with me?" he asked, the corners of his attractive, expressive mouth turning up.

"Walking is the last thing I want to do now," Daisie said, not realizing how sharp her tone had become.

Tyler slapped his Stetson against his thigh. "Daisie — er, Miss Browning — will you give me just the smallest amount of credit if I confess something to you?"

She had started toward the back door. He touched her arm, restraining her with the warmth of his fingertips. An electric current crackled between them, holding her still, quickening her breathing. "What could you possibly confess to me?"

"That I didn't believe you were searching for your father, that I thought you were an adventuress tracking down a benefactor who had dropped you." He raised a hand to silence her shocked exclamation. "Not that you looked anything less than perfect lady. It's just that a man grows skeptical. Few ladies of good family come to the mining camps. I most humbly beg your forgiveness."

Daisie sighed. "You met me on a disreputable Denver street, travel-worn and short-tempered. I behaved like a ninny on the train. I should be offering my apologies to you. I've never traveled alone, Mr. Reede. I don't seem to be handling myself well. And I reacted very badly to you. You . . . disturbed me."

He leaned close, his voice soft, intimate, penetrating to the depths of her being. "Do I still?"

She tried to breathe and found herself dizzy. "A little," she admitted.

"If you won't go walking with me, Daisie . . .?" His voice trailed away on a note of enquiry.

She blushed and nodded slightly, assenting to the familiar form of address.

He lifted his head and drew a deep breath. His parted lips exposed even, white teeth. "It's partly my fault you were here in this place, in a position to be robbed yesterday."

"Yours? I hardly think so."

"If you won't go walking with me, do me the honor of riding in my top-buggy this afternoon. I'd like to show you the area and let you get to know me better."

"It's not that I won't walk with you. Mr. Reede — "

"Tyler . . . please." His teeth flashed. His clear eyes smiled when he saw victory within reach.

". . . Tyler — it's that I can't." She explained about the little red purse hidden in her shoe and the blisters. "I got those blisters following you yesterday." Pinning him with her sharp gaze, she noted that he seemed alarmed. "I saw you suddenly leave town after I questioned you about my father's whereabouts. It seemed a curious coincidence."

He was about to circle her shoulder with his arm. "Come riding with me then." Glancing back, his face reflected annoyance that they were being interrupted.

Amelia appeared in the rear doorway, her expression unreadable. Her brown and blue calico dress fit poorly, and appeared, even at a distance, to be ill-sewn. As Daisie edged away from Tyler, Amelia's mouth tightened into a disapproving line. Her eyes remained masked in shadow.

Perversely, Daisie found herself turning to Tyler and shaking out her long, damp, wheat-gold hair. "I should like to go riding with you today, Mr. Reede. Until you came along a moment ago I was feeling terribly dreary. Let me get a bonnet and some gloves. Will you mind being seen with me with my hair still damp and uncurled?''

Amelia sauntered toward them, her eyes fixed on Tyler. Her gaze lingered on his coat and snug trousers, the flashing silver tips of his boots, and finally the sun lying warmly on the handsome planes of his face. ''Hello, Tyler.'' The hint of a smile glimmered in her eyes, but she kept her lips in a pout, as if silently reprimanding him for some secret offense. She moved so close to him it struck Daisie as indecent. Daisie abandoned her unbidden desire to show up Amelia and stepped back as Tyler greeted Amelia coolly.

''Morning.''

Daisie felt disgusted with herself for feeling even slightly jealous. ''I might have saved myself all that walking,'' Daisie said to Amelia, ''if you'd introduced me to Tyler earlier. You said you didn't associate with men, however.'' Her tone implied that Amelia was ''associating'' quite freely at the moment.

Briefly Amelia's eyes snapped with anger, but she recovered and darted a smile up at Tyler. ''It's true, I don't associate with men my brother doesn't approve of. And no one approves of a land speculator.'' She moved coquettishly between Tyler and Daisie, her words teasing as she looked longingly into Tyler's eyes.

''That's right,'' Tyler said, his expression darker. ''When you mean the word as you do, Miss Salter.''

Amelia stopped moving, her expression again reproachful. ''You don't come into the store very often any more, Tyler. I remember when you used to come in every morning just to say hello.'' She threw Daisie a triumphant smile. ''Hank warned me not to trust you, but it's wonderful to see you today, Tyler. How did you know Hank was out?''

Tyler settled his hat squarely on his head. He looked more annoyed than pleased by Amelia's flattery.

''I'll be right down, Tyler,'' Daisie said, ducking inside. Halfway up the stairs, Amelia caught her arm. ''You're not going riding with him? Oh, you mustn't, Daisie! He's not the right sort for you. *Trust me*. It'll get all over town and people will whisper about you.''

"*You* seem to think Tyler is all right to flirt with,'' Daisie snapped, puzzled and angry.

"Well, of course he is!'' Amelia laughed, following close on Daisie's heels. "It's what a man like that expects of a woman. You were doing it, too.''

Daisie caught her hair and began twisting it into a scalp-tingling knot.

"Men like that are such cads!'' continued Amelia. "It's fun to taunt them. They don't even realize we're doing it. They have such low tastes in women. Such low standards. And such low . . . desires, if you know what I mean. I would never be sincerely interested in his sort. But I can amuse myself, can't I? He was completely taken in, too.''

"It'll be all right,'' Daisie said, opening her trunk and selecting enough pins to keep her hair knotted and in place. She picked up a shawl that lay in a heap on the tray, part of the fringe caught in the back. She was sure she remembered folding it neatly just that morning. Someone had gone through her belongings! Her heart skipped as she glanced over her shoulder down the canvas hall. "Any new boarders?''

Amelia smiled. "Yes, thank goodness! Two miners who came in on the train just this morning. You were still out back. They haven't heard about the . robbery. I hope our accounts can stand this.'' Her smile wilted briefly, but she brightened again. "We'll manage, just as you will. Let me help you with those bonnet ribbons. Remember, now. You mustn't be taken in by that Tyler Reede's charm. He's a gambler and a ladies' man. You should see some of the painted cows he's been seen with around town. Strumpets, every one. He throws all his ill-gotten money away on worthless drifters and stupid old prospectors. A man like that is not to be trusted. I certainly wouldn't be seen riding with him alone. What would people think? Oh, but I could go with you, Daisie, as a chaperone. Is he taking you to your father? I hope your father hasn't been cheated by that swindler! What would you say to Tyler Reede then, I wonder.''

Daisie's mind reeled. Her father cheated by Tyler . . . . ''I know you have to mind the store while Hank's at the freight office,'' Daisie said, only too glad of an excuse not to accept Amelia's offer. ''I have nothing to fear from Tyler. All my money is gone — ''

Amelia looked pained. ''Nothing to fear! What about your reputation? And Hank's and my reputation, too, for that matter. If something scandalous happens to you, out there, alone with Tyler Reede . . . .'' Amelia's voice registered anguish. ''Why, Hank and I might lose so much business we'd be ruined and have to move away.''

Stung by the ease with which self-interest had replaced Amelia's professed concern for her friend, Daisie drew back. ''Honestly, you have nothing to worry about!''

''I didn't mean to offend you!'' Amelia said, her eyes filling with tears. ''Oh, this is all so distressing! If you must go riding, don't let him take you far. There's no telling what a man like that expects of a girl.''

Possibly, Daisie thought, but she already knew what Hank Salter expected and Tyler couldn't be any worse! She took a key from her reticule and locked the trunk. ''That'll keep curious noses away,'' she said, loudly enough for the new boarders to hear. ''As for Mr. Tyler Reede, he knows better than to be impudent with me. I'm not easily won over. You can tell Hank that, too.''

Amelia's eyes clouded. ''Why Hank?''

Daisie tensed. ''If he should ask where I've gone and why, you might simply explain'' — she felt herself on thin ice — ''that I have no time for romance. I'll soon be on my way, perhaps even in a day or so.''

''I had no idea you'd be able to lay your hands on enough cash to go home so soon.''

''I know some people in New York I can beg a loan from, if it comes to that. Of course, I'll hate doing it. Never a borrower be, Mama always says.''

"Of course." Amelia stood aside as Daisie hurried down the stairs.

"I'll be back long before dark."

Tyler was waiting in the blue-trimmed top-buggy as Daisie hurried out onto the dusty walkway. The southwestern sky had filled with clouds and now looked surprisingly dark. "Where did all this threatening weather come from?" she asked, tightening the shawl about her shoulders.

"You've been lucky with our climate so far," Tyler said, reaching to help her into the buggy. "See you later, Amelia. Regards to Hank," he called back.

"It'll be pouring on you in less than an hour," Amelia scolded. "Shouldn't you wait?"

Tyler tapped the black mare's rump and they were off almost before Daisie could wave.

"Will it rain that quickly?" she asked.

He squinted at the sky. "It's a good estimate, but we'll be near shelter by then. I would wait, Daisie, but I've got it in my mind to take you quite a ways. We need an early start to get back before dark. I don't have a lantern." He turned to her and winked. "Did she warn you about staying out after dark with me?"

Trying not to smile, Daisie concentrated on sightseeing as the buggy moved through town. "I should not dignify that question with an answer."

Laughing, Tyler skillfully steered them between the milling miners crowding the streets. In no time, they were headed out of town on the same road Daisie had walked two days before. After a while, Tyler cleared his throat. "How far along here did you get?"

Daisie strained to see the rock where she'd finally stopped. It seemed hardly possible that she'd gone so far. "There," she said, pointing to a spot some distance ahead. "I was quite determined to know where you were going. I suspect we're going there now."

He settled back, pushed his hat back on his head and looked

somewhat less pleased with himself. "How did you guess?"

"I am not stupid, Tyler, just painfully ignorant of American ways. You know where my father is, don't you? You've seen him and talked to him."

Nodding, he eyed the black clouds ahead and clicked his tongue in his teeth to quicken the mare's pace. "Yes, and I'm puzzled by his response. I met Lord Browning a few days after he arrived last spring. He came to me to buy land, just as you assumed he might."

"Why didn't you tell me? Tyler, I don't really look like a . . . what did you call me? An adventuress?" Her heart skipped.

"No, but let me finish." He thought a moment, his eyes troubled.

She watched the thick lashes veil the penetrating eyes and wondered what he saw when he looked at her.

"Lord Browning told me in confidence that he had no money. He'd sank his last dollar in prospecting equipment. He said he'd pay me double the land's value if he found gold. I told you I loan land, but your father was the first time I tried it, and it was by his suggestion. I felt he was desperate" — here Tyler smiled reassuringly at Daisie — "and I liked him. I loaned him the land with the full knowledge that I might never receive a cent for it."

Daisie hung her head.

"I felt he needed the land more than I, more than I needed the price I might get selling it to someone else. I made the mistake of mentioning the transaction to a less than intelligent acquaintance, who accused me of speculating. Remember, Daisie, you heard it from me first. Supposedly, I'm allowing old men in failing health to work my claims at no pay. They'll keel over and I'll claim their gold."

Coming from Tyler, this explanation sounded perfectly straightforward. "Why are you telling me this now?" she asked.

"Because when you get back, Hank Salter is likely to twist everything around, making you believe I've been working your father like some sort of slave. As far as I'm concerned, the land belongs to your father whether he ever pays me for it or not."

Daisie shivered. When she looked into Tyler's eyes she could not doubt his sincerity. "*Is* my father in failing health?"

Tyler shook his head. "He wasn't then, but over the past few months I've watched him grow weaker. Mining, even panning for gold, is no pastime for a man his age."

"Have you tried to stop him?" Daisie asked, her heart filling with dread.

Tyler sighed, glancing at the clouds again. "No, I haven't. He told me why he left England—about the bankruptcy. A man needs his dignity, Daisie. Since coming to Cripple Creek, he's had that. I didn't tell you at first that I knew the man you were looking for because I wasn't sure you were really his daughter, and then I didn't know what you intended to say to him once you found him. You seem sensitive and caring. By taking you to him now I'm assuming you'll spare his feelings and leave his dignity intact."

"You could wonder that?" she cried. "When I've come all this way?"

He raised an eyebrow.

She drew a deep breath. "True, your first impressions of me were not . . . good. I will be very gentle with Papa. How could I be otherwise? But he is coming home with me." She went on to describe her mother's plight.

Shaking his head, Tyler slowed the buggy. "Be careful how you tell him these things, Daisie. Men are fragile creatures."

"Are they?" she said, smiling a little as she peered from the corners of her eyes.

"Not me, of course," he grinned teasingly.

"Of course not," she chuckled. "You have a heart of stone."

"How did you guess?" he laughed.

"Because your head is full of wood. Of course I will treat my father with the greatest respect—as always. Do we have far to go?"

"A few more miles. It's a good claim, one I felt had promise. Some men I met worked it briefly last year — dynamited a shallow shaft. They found nothing, but they weren't that serious to begin with. They were after adventure, but hard-rock mining is mostly just back-breaking work.''

"You prefer to turn a card or two?'' Daisie ventured lightly, determined to put all her doubts to rest.

Tyler was slow to answer. "Amelia did a thorough job on my character, I see.''

Daisie nodded, unwilling to ask about the "painted cows." She smiled a little, but in spite of his easy manner and convincing explanation she still didn't feel sure he was the sort of man she ought to find herself attracted to. She waited for Tyler to make a remark about the Salters' characters, but he remained silent, probing her eyes with his own and succeeding only in making her forget the questions that remained.

"Your father's a stubborn man."

Daisie certainly agreed there.

"He sprained his ankle badly about three weeks ago. I dragged him into town to have it looked after. He told me then that he was alone in the world, that there was no one for me to contact should he become seriously injured or — ''

"Why should he say such a thing?'' Daisie cried. "We don't blame him for coming here! Surely he knows that!''

"I'm glad to hear you feel that way,'' Tyler said.

"Is there anything more I should know?''

Tyler had reached the rock where she had stopped when following him. The road descended toward the huge group of boulders where he had disappeared from sight. Heavy raindrops began pelting into the dust. Amazed, Daisie watched them sail down from the clouds like clear stones. "Git up!'' Tyler said, snapping the whip.

In moments they had rounded the boulders and stopped beneath a protective overhang of large, angular rocks slanting toward the angry sky. The mare whinnied as a gray sheet of rain advanced across the nearby hills. The night-dark clouds sank to the distant mountains, obliterating them, enclosing Tyler and Daisie in soft, murky, moist shadows.

Suddenly the air rushed cool, ripe and rich across Daisie's face, plucking gold strands from her knotted hair and snapping them across her cheeks. Tyler slipped his arm around her, drawing her close, shielding her from the chill.

"I don't think we'll get too wet here," he said softly, turning to gaze at her.

Electrified by his touch, Daisie nearly forgot what she had been waiting for him to say. His arm felt solid and warm across her back. He pulled her closer as a bolt of blazing white lightning split the sky. Distant thunder muttered moments later, shaking the buggy.

"Is there anything more, Tyler?" she asked, her voice small and careful.

"I asked your father again the other day if he had any family. He said he didn't, but I could see he was lying. And he knew I knew. Why would I ask if someone hadn't come here for him? I'm not certain he'll be glad to see you. I'm sorry I didn't believe you before. I'm sorry you had to go on worrying and wondering, and that you lost your money."

Daisie's body began tingling all over. His voice had grown husky and gentle. If she looked up into Tyler's eyes she'd be lost.

Her eyes went up. She saw that wonderful cornflower-blue gaze, the sun-darkened crinkles in the corners of his eyes when he smiled, the little turning up of his lips, the rounding of his cheeks, that wonderful, easy, masculine face drawing closer.

Rain drenched everything around them, beating down the tall grasses, pummeling the pink dust into sienna-red mud. The air filled with a fine cooling spray that settled on them like a silver mist. Tyler's hand looked wide and capable with the thick brown leather reins laced between his fingers.

He moved closer, watching her eyes for every flicker of emotion revealed in them. She knew her expression was too soft, too willing, but the desire to have Tyler suddenly more than a friend persisted. She had thought of him and dreamed of him, and those thoughts and dreams had gone well beyond friendship. Hank's unwelcome advances had kindled something in her, awakened the yearnings she had abandoned as beyond hope while engaged to Norwood. Tyler was the lion she had dreamed of and now, as if he might actually do her harm, she sat small and still in the circle of his arms, waiting, wanting to be devoured.

His arm tightened around her shoulders again, setting her blood racing. His fingertips touched her cheek, turning her to face him. She breathed in the costly aroma of his leather coat, the sweet masculine warmth of his sun-browned cheek. She saw her own image reflected in his eyes, and that was how she wanted it always to be.

Tyler closed his eyes and moved still closer. She drew back, reluctant to commit herself to a kiss so suddenly, yet wanting him to kiss her more than she had ever wanted anything. His palm curved along her cheek, guiding her, tilting her face up. Then his lips were on hers, flooding her with warm, delicious desire in an uncontrollable torrent. His lips were soft and giving, moving against hers as if tasting them, memorizing them, owning them.

Suddenly he released her and pulled away, looking aside, frowning in puzzlement at the wall of water just beyond the rocky overhang. Water poured from the upper boulders in thick silver cascades, dashing the red soil to a muddy froth, washing in twisting rivulets toward the nearly invisible road. ''I didn't mean to do that,'' he whispered.

Daisie sat transfixed. She had let him kiss her and now wanted him never to stop. She turned to him, eyes wide and yearning. He blinked, drawing her into an embrace instantly. Their lips met, tentatively, exploringly. She returned his kiss, giving him the intensity she had dreamed of giving all her life. No longer could she hear the rain or thunder. Her heart was the thunder, pounding in her chest. Her mind was the storm, whirling and crashing with wonder that a kiss could be so much.

She strained against him, wanting him to crush her into himself, and when his hand closed over her breast it was as if no blouse and chemise and corset cover protected her from his caress. No man had ever touched her that way.

She thought momentarily of the miner and Hank and with a gasp, turned her lips aside to lay her cheek against Tyler's and remember how to breathe.

Then she drew away, covering her moist lips with trembling fingertips. The rain lessened suddenly. She watched the darkness lift. A shaft of sunlight broke through the clouds, falling on the glistening branches of a lush green pine twisting up between the slanting layers of rock. In moments the rain had passed, leaving them beneath the dripping overhang in the midst of a shallow red wash. The rainwater poured down the slope, carving runnels in the soaked soil, sparkling on all surfaces, dazzling them with its suddenness.

Daisie adjusted the ruffles down the front of her blouse. She smoothed and dusted her skirt, noticed that the shawl had fallen from her shoulders and drew it up for reassurance. How could she face her father with her mind in such turmoil?

Without a word, Tyler clicked his tongue and moved the buggy out into the blazing sunlight that now poured through a rent in the clouds. Except for the thick red mud clinging to the buggy wheels and the rain-washed rocks, there might never have been a storm.

Daisie concentrated on gaining control of her wanton thoughts that called for more than kisses. And, as they rode, Amelia's words came back to darken the glow, to trouble the memory and to make Daisie wonder if Tyler kissed his "painted cows" that way.

Nervous, she almost giggled. She wanted to believe he had never kissed anyone with that intensity.

After another mile, Tyler slowed almost to a stop. The creek ahead, murky with mud, gushed across the road. "Your father's claim is just up this hill. I hope I haven't done something to make you hate me."

She had no idea what to say. A hundred replies raced through her head, but none of them was appropriate.

"Daisie?" He looked at her inquiringly as the buggy bumped through the creek and rocked to a stop on the far side.

"Please," she whispered. "My feelings are all confused." She smiled a little and blushed what she knew was the blush of a lifetime.

Suddenly he was grinning, his teeth like the sun through the clouds. "Damned if you aren't the most beautiful girl I've ever met! Don't tell your father about the robbery. Just try to convince him to come back to town. I'll see to it you have a place to stay and tickets home, though I hate the idea of you leaving—"

"Oh, Tyler," Daisie sighed. "You've gone and spoiled everything. I can't accept money from you." Not now, she thought. Not when she was so afraid she had just fallen in love with him. "I mean no offense. I'll write those people I stayed with in New York. I think they'll help."

His eyes registered instant regret that he had mentioned money. "But I want to help."

"I'll leave Papa his dignity if you leave us our pride. If I can't get a loan from the Arnolds, I'll consider your offer. Truly I will." She was tempted to put her hand on his cheek.

He guided the buggy up a steep incline and approached a pleasant forest of lodgepole pines and aspens. Rocky clearings covered with wild flowers surrounded huge gray boulders jutting up among the pines. The aroma of beds of drying pine needles enriched the exhilarating air. They came to a stretch of large flat stones the mare had trouble crossing. Then they were in a lush grassy meadow, the buggy wheels rim deep in red mud. A wide creek cut across the meadow. Tyler stopped the buggy and leaped down. "I should have told you to wear old shoes."

Ahead, across the creek, were a group of pine stumps and a half-built dugout cabin on the side of a low bluff. Beyond that, up a hill, was a sagging gray-white camp tent. Nearby, the sodden remains of a fire smoldered in a circle of blackened stones. A cooking pot, suspended from an arrangement of sticks, hung over it. A blue plaid shirt and a red union suit lay drying on a scrub oak. Twigs, branches and deadwood lay alongside the tent with a pick, shovel and lantern.

"I don't see him," Tyler whispered. "The fire obviously just went out in the rain, so he can't be far."

"Papa?" she cried out as Tyler helped her down. Her ugly

K.O.G.—6

new shoes sank heel-deep in mud. "Papa? I know you're here!" She gathered up her skirts and slogged across the meadow toward the creek.

A man stood up in the middle of the half-built cabin. Shielding his eyes against the sinking sun, he stepped up and out through the cabin's "doorway". From there the barren muddy ground sloped down to the creek.

"Tyler, my boy, you didn't tell me the dugout would hold rainwater better than a teapot," he said, his cultivated English accent setting Daisie's heart racing for joy. He straightened red suspenders over his rounded shoulders. His ragged worsted trousers dripped red mud to the knees. "Come show me how to drain it."

Daisie picked her way across the sodden meadow, tried to leap the creek and soaked her left shoe. Filled with confusion and questions, she approached the mud-covered man. He was almost bald now, and looked ten years older. Though tired-looking, his eyes were bright.

"Papa! Don't you know me?" Daisie cried, almost in tears. "I've come all this way for you."

He gave Tyler a reproachful look. "Did you have to bring her?" He limped down into the dugout, but by then Daisie had reached him and caught his tattered sleeve.

"Papa, don't turn away from me. I've been so afraid something terrible had happened to you. Mama's been so worried — " with difficulty she fought for a calmer tone. "Papa, are you all right? Don't be angry with me for finding you. Please, look at me."

Sighing, he paused, pressing his lips together as if trying not to smile. It was as if to say hello to her would be to admit defeat. "I was going to write as soon as I found one small speck of gold, one grain, one tiny flake . . . ." His eyes filled with anguish as he wrapped his arms around Daisie and held her against his trembling, frail frame. "Good lord, Daisie, it is wonderful to see you."

Daisie couldn't hold him tightly enough. "Tell me you're well. Tyler says you sprained your ankle. What are you doing walking on it? You know that I'm here to take you home, with gold or without." She wanted to shake him.

He pulled away, stubbornly frowning.

"Oh yes, Papa. We're going back into town right now and have a doctor look at that ankle. You've got to forget this foolishness and come home with me to Mama and Pammie. We need you. Oh yes, Papa . . . ."

The anguished look in his eyes evaporated, replaced by fierce determination. That must have been how she had looked to her mother the day she decided to come and find her father. Her heart began thudding with alarm.

"Young woman, I am still your papa. You will not speak to me in that manner. I'm not leaving, not till I've struck gold and made the fortune I promised your mother." His voice took on a strength she knew would be difficult to overcome. "The gold's here. Tyler says the lay of the land is just right for it. See the quartz formations all around? That's a sure sign. This young fellow's been good enough to show me how and where to look, so I'm staying, Daisie, just as surely as I've been here all this time. I'll write to your mother and explain as best I can. She'll understand. She knows me." He turned toward the tent. His hesitant steps betrayed the pain he felt when walking.

"I'm not going back without you," Daisie said, her voice equally strong and determined.

Her father faltered.

"All right now," Tyler said, stepping between them. He took Daisie's elbow and then her father's. "Let's start again. Daisie, you say, 'Hello, Papa,' like a good girl. Sir, you say, 'Hello, Daisie. How was the trip?' I'll build up the fire and warm up the coffee. We'll talk this out like civilized adults."

Gregory Browning's stubbled chin came up as his lips pursed. "My boy, you're out of your jurisdiction here."

"No, sir, I don't think so. Daisie's come a long way. You have a lot to talk about. Let's start off right. I see you're still limping. Another visit to the doctor wouldn't hurt. I'll take you both to dinner."

Gregory Browning's eyes began to twinkle. He winked at

Daisie. "He's got a way about him, doesn't he? I may as well ask how you found me, Daisie."

"It wasn't easy!"

Tyler joggled her elbow enough to remind her not to explode.

"Quite the spot your papa's got here, don't you think, Daisie?" Tyler said, offering her a choice seat on a rounded boulder near the fire.

"Just charming," she muttered, glancing around, suddenly struck by the view of the basin, the closeness of the mountains behind and the immense sweep of the cloudy sky overhead.

"It's the finest claim in the whole state," Gregory Browning said, taking his place on a wobbly pine bench opposite Daisie. He put his finger beside his nose. "I've got a nose for gold, my girl. It's here, right under my feet, probably, although I've mostly been panning in the creek. I'd get more done if I wasn't chopping down trees all the day long. Tyler," he said, looking up, his bright blue eyes narrowed, "I took your advice and dug that spot for the cabin."

Tyler nodded.

"And now the bloody thing has a foot of water in it . . . excuse me, my dear. How am I going to live in that?"

Tyler swept off his hat and wiped his brow. He cast his eyes about, studied the sky and then sighed. "I'll take care of it while you two talk. Mind you, now, no arguing or I'll throw you both over my shoulder and take you back to town."

He peeled off his fringed jacket, revealing a finely made white linen shirt. Rolling back the sleeves to the elbow, he took the shovel and marched back down to the roughly rectangular arrangement of logs piled and notched six high. He disappeared into the door opening and began whistling as he dug a trench.

Shovelfuls of red mud sailed over the upper edge of the log walls, falling wetly in the yard. Turning to her father, Daisie saw that he had been watching her. He smiled weakly.

"I've behaved unforgivably, I know, Daisie. Tell your mother I'm sorry to have worried her." His eyes filled with sadness and regret.

"Tell her yourself, Papa. I'm not going back without you. In fact — " She broke off and sighed. She had to tell some of what had happened since he'd left them. "You and I aren't going back right away, not until I get some more money." Her cheeks burned as she explained about her engagement to Norwood, adding quickly that it was already broken. She described her breathtaking ride up the narrow-gauge line to Cripple Creek and finished with the robbery. "So, you see, I've made rather a mess of things. I think the Arnolds will send a bank draft, so we won't be keeping Mama waiting too much longer."

He rubbed his eyes. "Daughter, you're enough like me to understand, so I'll put it to you plainly. I let down your mother when the business failed — no, don't contradict me. A man knows when he's lowered himself in the eyes of his loved ones. I came here believing I could pick up gold like you would pick wildflowers. I was foolish then and perhaps still am."

"I can see prospecting isn't as easy as that, Papa. We don't blame you for coming here, or for not writing, but we do need you at home now."

"What would I do with myself, Daisie? I have no more business. I have nothing." He shook his head. "I can't go back. Not like this. You left when Norwood rejected you. You said so only a moment ago."

"That was another matter entirely," Daisie cried in exasperation.

"We share the same sense of pride, daughter. I'm here to stay until I'm a rich man again and can support your mother as I feel she deserves."

His eyes were darker now and steady. His face looked more wrinkled than she remembered, and leaner, but wonderfully ruddy from the sun. Though his shoulders were stooped and rounded and his hands battered from manual labor, his forearms looked wiry and strong. "At the moment I haven't a shilling to offer her. The bloody truth is, I'm stuck here. And now, it seems, so are you. I do wish with all my heart you had stayed there to look after her."

Daisie took a deep breath and smiled. "I'm not leaving you, Papa." She plucked off her gloves and untied her bonnet ribbons. "I don't think Tyler will mind fetching my trunks. I'll cook for you, and we'll finish this quaint little cabin. You'll look for gold and . . . . What does gold look like, Papa? Is it all yellow and shining, like rings and bracelets among the rocks?"

Her papa looked suddenly haunted, as if to say he wished it was that easy. She stood and looked around the camp. "I'd say you need an extra pair of hands here. Is there room for us both in the tent, or should I — ?"

"Daisie," her father laughed, struggling to his feet and taking her in his arms again. "You can't stay here. It's dirty. It's cold and wet and dangerous. One of my regular night visitors is a bear, I think."

"Stuff and nonsense. Papa, you can't drive me away with fairytales. I am indeed very much like you. And I'm here to stay until you're ready to go home."

His voice rose in alarm. "I forbid it."

Daisie sauntered to the tent and peeked in, standing back as the musty smell of damp blankets filled her nose. "Whew! Papa, this is simply awful." She dragged everything out and began shaking things, looking for bushes to drape everything over. "Mama forbade me to come to America. Look how I obeyed her."

Gregory Browning's expression grew stern, but Daisie only laughed.

Chapter Seven

"Your boots, Tyler. They're ruined," Daisie said, watching Tyler trudge up to the tent and drop onto the wobbly bench.

Puffing and red-faced, Tyler grinned down at his mud-caked boots and soaked trousers. "Cabin's drained, Lord Browning. Anything more you want me to do before I take you both back to town?"

Daisie began to protest, but her father interrupted.

"You know I won't go back, Tyler, my boy. I can't return to my family in disgrace. It's only a matter of time before I find gold." Gregory Browning smiled, but she could see the worry clouding his eyes. "There is something you *can* do for me, however."

Wiping his brow on his sleeve, Tyler waited.

"You can throw this daughter of mine over your shoulder as you threatened and take her with you." His eyes twinkled.

"I won't go!" Daisie said stubbornly. She folded her arms. "Wild horses couldn't drag me."

Stretching out his muddy legs, Tyler sighed. "I've had my fill of you both. If you're coming, Daisie, let's get going before the sun sets. Lord Browning, I'll bring you more supplies in a few — "

"You can bring my trunks, if you will," Daisie went on, ignoring Tyler and her father. "Everything is packed and locked."

Tyler's face reflected a mixture of amusement and concern. "I hope you know what you're doing," he said with a warning note that made Daisie uneasy.

"We'll be perfectly safe here, won't we, Papa? You have been all these months." She nodded firmly, delighted with the prospect of camping out for a night or two.

"Dash it all, Daisie, you'll get cold in the night. The fire goes out, and I'm no grand cook, I assure you. If the coyotes didn't keep one awake all night with their howling or the deer with there tramping through the meadow at all hours, and if that gigantic brown bear weren't around, it would be safe and comfortable enough, I suppose, but it's no place for a woman."

"It won't be any colder than my cubicle at Salter's store and the ground won't be any harder than my mattress, and it doesn't concern me in the least that there are bears in these mountains. I shall be safer here, away from so-called civilized men, than I have been in a good many days. Goodbye Tyler, and thank you for bringing me. Will you come with my trunks tomorrow?"

Looking as if he was masking rising anger, Tyler stood and pulled on his coat. "No. Actually, I had plans. In a few days, maybe . . . ."

Though she was disappointed, Daisie nodded. She'd make do with what she was wearing. "Then it's settled. I'm staying until we find gold or Papa listens to reason, whichever comes first." She was quite certain she'd convince him to go home in a matter of hours.

Tyler crossed the creek, slapped his hat against his leg several times and then looked back at Daisie before clapping the Stetson on his head. He climbed into the buggy and worked at turning it while Daisie, casting her papa surreptitious glances, followed him.

"Changed your mind already?" Tyler said, surprised to see her when she came alongside the buggy.

"Of course not. I just wanted to . . . to say a more proper goodbye and . . . and to thank you for bringing me here today. And for helping Papa."

Tyler tipped back his hat. He looked as if there was a lot he would like to say, but he restrained himself. He straightened and waved to her father. "Fired the rifle lately, Lord Browning?"

"Only yesterday, my boy. I'm not a complete nincompoop. I've plenty of shells, and it didn't get wet."

"See you in a few days then," Tyler called. He turned to Daisie. "Are you sure you want to stay?"

"Completely."

"You'll be very careful?"

She smiled to think he was worried. "Very."

"You won't wander off and get lost?"

"I'll stay right here. I promise."

Tyler caught her hand. He looked intently into her eyes, and if her father hadn't been watching, he might have kissed her. "Keep the rifle loaded, but don't shoot yourself with it. If I could stay, I would."

"That wouldn't do at all," Daisie said, her heart leaping at the thought.

Tyler's eyes grew heavy, his expression gentle. "I want to kiss you again."

"Perhaps you will," she said, a teasing smile on her lips.

He laughed. Releasing her hand, he clucked to the black mare. "Don't talk to any strangers."

She turned away so she wouldn't see Tyler disappear beyond the aspens. The last of the sun went under a bank of dark clouds that lurked against the western range. A chill wind penetrated her thin blouse. She grabbed up her skirts and turned toward camp.

She found her father feeding deadwood to the campfire. Putting her hands on her hips, she pinned him with a stern eye.

He looked up, wonderfully innocent. "What is it now?"

"When were you admitted to the peerage?"

Her father coughed, then rose and busied himself with the pile of firewood next to the tent.

"Papa — or rather, *Lord* Browning." Her voice dropped to a scold. "Impersonating a lord, Papa. Really! What can you be thinking of?"

"I'll have you know, I was not the one who started that nonsense. Once the rumor got around, however, I was given a fine room and excellent treatment everywhere I went. I'm thousands of miles from anyone who could contradict my claim. I didn't see what harm it could do. Americans have such a delightful regard for titles. The impersonation has hurt no one but me. You must have a little more forgiveness in your heart for your old papa."

She went to him and hugged him. "You know I do. I've been just as foolish in my own way." She paused and said briskly, "Well! Now we must forget it all and set about making ourselves more comfortable here in the mountains."

Her father stared across the creek toward the place where Tyler's buggy had disappeared. The sunset cast a warm glow on his creased face as he scanned the shadows among the trees.

Listening, Daisie was struck by the silence, a silence that was not at all quiet but somehow eerie and distant, ageless. The wind whispered in the pines. The creek gurgled. Faint noises in the brush made Daisie edge closer to the fire. "It's like listening to eternity, isn't it, Papa?" she said in a low voice, her arms breaking out in goosebumps.

He smiled quickly for her. "I've spent many an hour searching my soul in this place," he said. "Would you make me some coffee? In all this time I haven't gotten it right."

Feeling as much a pioneer as her ancestors when they emigrated from England to the colonies, Daisie dipped coffee from a nearly empty tin can and poured water from a leaking bucket into the pot. "I've had plenty of practice cooking lately, Papa. Edna doesn't always have time to prepare everything herself."

Her father huddled near the fire. He'd pulled on his suit coat. It was as tattered and dirty as his trousers.

Daisie's breath caught. She looked away, her heart twisting. "How is your mother?"

As the coffee warmed over the fire, Daisie sat and spread her hands to the licking flames. Then she tightened her shawl around her shoulders. She told him about the difficult times she, her mother and Pammie had had since he left. "It wouldn't have been so bad, Papa, but when we didn't hear from you month after month . . . ."

He looked sad. "I have made a terrible mess of my venture, my dear. I lived too high in Denver while waiting for the snow in the mountain passes to melt. By the time I was able to take a coach here I had almost no money left. I suppose you've learned the hard way how expensive these mining camps are."

Daisie nodded. "Outrageous."

He frowned suddenly. "If your mother had to let the gardener and parlor maid go, where did you get the money for this trip?"

"All in good time, Papa. Did you get any of her letters?"

"One or two. I felt so dreary writing that nothing was happening yet, I decided to wait and write to her after I was settled here. I didn't do well at all, as you can see. Tyler has been a tremendous help, but I spent every last coin in my pocket for supplies. That lad at the store seemed to know exactly how much I had. Tyler loaned me the use of this claim, you know. Awfully decent of him. The days went by, and I had no desire to return to civilization. I became like a hermit, panning, fishing, even hunting. It's like a new life compared to my years at the factory, worrying about orders and supplies and whether the craftsmen were about to demand higher wages. I don't feel reduced here, Daisie. I feel as if I've got a part of myself back. I intend to go home rich, of course, and take up the yoke again. But right now I'm thoroughly enjoying myself. When I'm home again I'll buy back the factory and make the changes I couldn't afford before. I've made many grand plans."

"I'd hate to think I was taking you back to a yoke, Papa. Although this looks like hard enough labor to me."

"Of a different sort." He contemplated his hands. "If a man's ingenuity and business sense fail him, he always has his hands. Mine had grown soft. I should like to think I can succeed at something, even hard labor."

"Oh, Papa." Her heart ached over his words.

He shook his head. "I haven't proved to be the best of prospectors yet. My mule ran off the first night. I fretted about that for days until I realized I didn't even need the beast. I began scouring my claim for ore and enjoyed panning in the creek for nuggets and dust.''

''Surely you've found a little, Papa. The town's bursting with miners. I've seen mining companies everywhere.''

''I'm no company, Daisie. I am one man in a hard-rock mining district living on borrowed land . . . and time. It can be done — finding gold on the surface, I mean — and I must do it. But I won't go down into the shafts with the young men. I won't do that. So we must be patient.''

The coffee was ready. Daisie poured two cups and then looked through her father's pitifully small selection of canned goods for something to make for supper. He had no fresh bread except what Tyler brought occasionally from town. He chuckled when she mentioned fresh vegetables.

Wanting to avoid further depressing discussions of home, and unwilling to broach the subject of the woman he had been seen with, Daisie turned to her newest concern. ''What do you think of Tyler Reede, Papa? Do you think he's a good and honest man?''

''I like Tyler. It's difficult not to. He has treated me with kindness and respect. Ordinarily I wouldn't question beyond that.''

Daisie had hoped her father would have no reservations. ''But . . . ?'' she added for him.

''But since coming here I've met cheats of every description. Some have been just as charming and likeable as young Tyler. I've been taken in without the slightest notion of how it happened. And my new so-called friends have shrugged their shoulders and said that that's how it's done out here. Without Tyler's generous loan of this land I'd have to camp somewhere far from the promise of gold, but I can't help but wonder when I'll wake and learn that he's cheated me like all the others.''

''How are we to deal with him, then? How are we to protect ourselves?''

''Let me worry about Tyler, my dear. I'll count him as a

friend until I know differently. That's the only way I can live. And that's one of the reasons I lost my factory,'' he added with a wry smile.

Daisie shivered. By what standards was she to judge Tyler? Could she trust her heart to someone who might be planning to ruin her father? What more could her father lose? Tyler could see they had nothing — she'd been depressingly frank about that.

She noticed the weary tremor of her father's hand as he rubbed his eyes and smoothed his sparse hair. "Don't you have some dry clothes to put on, Papa? It's not good to sit about in those damp, muddy things. I'll wash them for you."

Nodding absently as if suddenly he didn't mind being mothered by a slim young woman in a mud-stained skirt, Daisie's father struggled to stand and limped into the tent as if every bone in his body was going to crack. After a moment he tossed out the muddied trousers.

"I'll tidy up," Daisie said, watching her father curl onto his side. Almost at once he was snoring. How she wished her mother could hear that comforting sound.

As soon as possible she'd tell Tyler her father was not a lord. If he had notions they owned anything of value in England, she'd certainly dispel them. If his true purpose was to dupe an innocent man, he'd get nothing for his trouble. Nothing, that is, but her everlasting hatred.

By the light of the fire, she sat and wondered what her mother and Pammie were doing now. She still thought of them in the old ivy-covered house and had to remind herself of the letter she'd received in New York describing their move to the village.

Frustrated that she couldn't write to her mother now to say that Papa was safe, Daisie snatched up her father's trousers and tramped to the creek's edge. "Now I'm a washerwoman," she muttered. She felt completely alone. Until lately, she'd been surrounded by people whose first concern was to look after her every need. When she was a child the house had been filled with servants all busy with tasks clearly outlined by her mother, a woman used to receiving callers in the parlor, to wearing elegantly cut and embroidered gowns and to living a life of leisurely comfort.

If Daisie had been told she would someday squat alongside an icy mountain creek, beat her papa's ragged trousers against a rock, or contemplate sleeping on the ground, she would never have believed it.

Faint, unidentifiable sounds among the pines and aspens made Daisie freeze. Perhaps night wasn't the time to be far from the campfire. Wringing out the trousers, she looked up and around, feeling small and afraid. What could she say to pry her father free of this place?

Creeping back to the safety of the fire and its warmth, she imagined Tyler asking Amelia for her trunks. Wishing she could watch that interesting scene, she laid out the trousers to dry and put two more thick branches on the fire. Then she crawled into the tent alongside her rumbling father's back and arranged herself beneath the thin, scratchy blanket she'd claimed for herself.

Some day, she thought, she would look back from her sedate parlor and recall this adventure with a fond and wistful smile.

Her father slept with no trouble that first night, but Daisie's eyes remained wide until dawn. She strained her ears at every night sound. Several times her heart hammered in alarm as some creature crept stealthily toward the creek. Most frightening of all was a bold prowler that splashed through the creek, moving away from the tent just when Daisie thought she must jump up and run screaming into the night.

By morning she was groggy and convinced she'd imagined everything. She cooked porridge for her papa, which he ate without sugar or cream. She found the hot, gluey mess impossible to swallow and decided hunger was preferable. By noon she had reconsidered, mixing the porridge with beans. The combination was perfectly horrid. She tried to raise her spirits by telling herself that the early settlers of this vast land had survived on far less, but her stomach found that little comfort.

Her father gave her the grand tour of his new "estate," a

claim twenty rods square. The half-built cabin was his future manor house. Building the cabin over a dugout was supposed to be less work, requiring half as many logs and providing better insulation from wind and cold. He seemed inordinately proud of the ugly, sagging structure.

Tyler had dug a five-inch-wide trench to drain the rainwater down the slope, and the floor had finally begun to dry. "What will you use for a roof, Papa?" Daisie asked, when the day waned and the temperature dropped with the setting sun. She wished the cabin was finished.

"I expect I'll split shingles, my dear," he said. He was writing a letter to her mother on brown wrapping paper.

Daisie slept more easily the second night, partly from exhaustion, but mainly because she expected Tyler the next day and counted this as her last miserable night on ground that chilled her bones with its hard cold.

When Tyler didn't come, Daisie and her father took two more unappetizing meals of warmed beans and coffee. Daisie began to think Tyler had abandoned them.

Tyler didn't come on the third day, either. Daisie desperately wanted a bath and decent food. She felt like a peasant girl on a pig farm. Each afternoon about two, clouds moved up from the southwest, drenched them with a chilling rain and left them to pick their way about in the red mud and dazzling sunshine. Daisie gathered deadwood, although the rough bark wore away the fine ladylike smoothness of her palms. She buoyed her energy dreaming up names to call the charming but tardy Mr. Reede.

She was thoroughly tired and done with her adventure by the third night, aching from head to toe and longing for a decent bed. Her father seemed to think Tyler's non-appearance nothing to worry about and contented himself with squatting by the streams, circling creek gravel in his tin pan and sloshing the icy water out in a rhythmic, hypnotic routine that made Daisie wonder at odd moments if he had regressed to childhood and the mudpie-stage.

She longed to wash her clothes, but she dared not for fear

Tyler would finally appear while she was wearing only petticoats. For that she cursed him, too.

Again that night she crawled beneath the clammy covers inside the musty tent and listened herself into a tense, weary sleep. Some time during that night she woke, heart hammering, hearing again the sound of a large creature splashing ponderously through the creek. Lying petrified next to her snoring father, she listened as the movements outside drew closer. Through the side of the tent she could make out the faint glow of the fire four feet away. Something large passed in front of it, moving nearer, sniffing, breathing in deep, short grunts.

Sitting up, Daisie shook her father's shoulder. "Papa, something's outside!"

Moaning, he woke, listened for a moment and then fumbled alongside the blanket for the rifle. "Quiet!"

She heard the comforting sound of the rifle hammer cocking. The stacked firewood beside the tent scattered when the pick and shovel fell over against the pile. The coffee pot toppled into the fire with a clank and a hiss. The cooking pot followed, clattering against the stones. The canned goods stacked in a crate nearby knocked together and began rolling down the hill.

"What's out there?" she whispered.

"I warned you, Daisie. It's my friend the brown bear. Be quiet. He'll probably go away."

"Can you shoot that thing, Papa?"

"If I must." He edged the tent flap aside. "Sh-h-h."

The sound of snuffling came closer. "How close is he?"

"Close! Shush!"

She clamped her hands over her mouth to keep from screaming. "Are you going to shoot him?"

"Not unless he gives me good cause. Hold still. You're shaking the whole tent."

"I'm not touching the tent!"

The tent shuddered and sagged against Daisie. "Shoot now, Papa! He's on top of us!"

"We're in serious trouble if I only wound him."

Daisie saw the shadow block the firelight again. She heard a growl, felt the threatening presence of the animal close by. Her father raised the rifle, took aim through the tent flap, tensed . . .

There was a brilliant flash, a deafening explosion and the tent was filled with acrid smoke. Daisie's father was thrown against her. She was knocked back against the ridge behind the tent. "Did you hit him?"

"I . . . don't know." Gregory Browning scrambled through the tangle of blankets toward the flap. They could see the campfire through a large hole blasted in the canvas tent wall.

Hands shaking, her father tried to reload the rifle. Daisie peeked out. Thin gray smoke hung over the half-doused fire. The bench and crate lay overturned. She saw no sign of the bear and swallowed in relief over a dry tongue. "I think you scared it away." She closed her eyes, sighing.

Then she heard a snort. The bear had retreated down the hill and was prowling near the cabin doorway, its hulking shape far larger than she had imagined. "Oh, God, Papa . . . ."

Raising its head, the bear started to lumber toward the tent again. Daisie's heart lodged in her throat. She jerked back, scrambled as far away as she could inside the tent and flattened herself against the rear corner. Jagged rocks cut into her back. She hadn't known she could feel such terror.

Her father was still trying to reload. For a moment he paused, drew a deep, shuddering breath and concentrated. Daisie pressed herself back so hard the tent poles gave way, bringing the musty, damp canvas down on their heads. She screamed.

Her father struck at her, his voice dark with fear. "Get hold of yourself!"

She held herself steady, willing her self-control to return. Breathing deeply, she forced herself to think what she must do to save them. A glimmer of light and a breath of smoky night air seeped in. "Don't go out — " Too late, she clutched at her father's arm, but already he had disappeared through the tent flap.

Fighting her way out from under the dirty canvas, Daisie watched sparks settle where her father had stumbled through the logs of the campfire. On the far side, he stood, feet spread, fighting to load the rifle. Ten feet away a hulking brown shadow approached, growling. Her father waved her back, tucked the rifle against his shoulder and fired. The shot went wild and the recoil threw him onto the ground.

Daisie was crouched against the ledge. Never taking her eyes from the now standing, roaring shadow, she squatted and seized two good-sized rocks. Dashing forward, she flung them toward the bear, then quickly grabbed up several more. A hail of rocks flew from her hands in the bear's direction.

One of the rocks struck the bear, making him retreat a few steps. Heartened, Daisie filled her skirt and dashed beyond her papa to the edge of the creek. The bear had gone down on all fours again and was moving away steadily into the velvety darkness.

"Go away! You're not welcome here!" she shouted, stopping only when her supply of rocks was exhausted. Letting out a whoop that echoed off the surrounding hills, she threw her hands in the air. "Let them call us greenhorns after this, Papa!"

"Come back here!"

She watched until the bear disappeared among the pines.

"Daisie, get over here. He'll not be back."

"We'll have him for supper if he does!" she said, splashing through the numbing water.

"You're mad, my dear! I thought you were frightened senseless."

"But I was, Papa! I still am! Oh, what I will say to Tyler when he brings my trunks. Leaving us here all this time to fight bears." She spun about in the dark, giddy with victory. "How often does this 'friend' of yours make an appearance?"

"I've only seen him a few times — and never this close. Daisie, I'm ordering you to go away from here as soon as Tyler comes."

She tripped up the hill, gathering scattered cans and shaking her head. Her father had righted the bench and sank onto it. Hands on hips, she bent before him. "If you want me away from here, just put on your boots and come along. If it were not for me, that beast and you would be waltzing right now."

"He's not after me. He's after my food."

"He's welcome to it. Papa, I'm all for leaving this muddy little camp as soon as possible. I suspect you're ready, too." She looked around, nerves taut.

"I'm weary of your nagging, my girl."

The last of Daisie's control snapped. "Oh, I see! You can stay here for months on end with no regard for those who love you and need you. Well, I have come too far and gone through too much to leave you now. If you think you can force me to go, you have a great deal to learn. Not even a wild bear can drive me away! While you've been playing at finding your fortune, Mama has taken affairs into her own hands, as I have. We've had to make do in your absence. It's time you realized just what that involved."

Scowling, he raised eyes shrouded in shadow. "Just what do you mean, taking affairs into her own hands?"

Instantly regretting her rash words, Daisie squirmed. Could she put him off a little longer, or was this last most devastating bit of truth just what she needed to bring him to reason?

"Mama was forced to sell the house. Well, perhaps I shouldn't put it quite like that. She seemed eager enough to sell it. Soon after I left, she and Pammie moved into the village. I came to find you on money from the sale."

Suddenly, she was trembling. Silent tears trickled down her cheeks. "Mama gave me a special secret reserve for my fare home — yours, too. That's what was stolen from me the other night. I don't know how we'll manage, but we have to go home immediately. Mama can't go on alone. She shouldn't have to."

For several minutes her father sat deathly still. He stared into the scattered, dying coals. Finally, with a stick Daisie nudged the stones back into a circle. She put on more wood, and then stole a look at her father. He would not meet her eyes. After a time he rose to see about the tent.

At dawn, Daisie felt dull and exhausted. The sky lightened to a clear, pale blue. The sun washed the mountainside in golden light. But Daisie was disgusted with herself for lashing out at her father and upsetting him. She watched his rounded back as he continued struggling with the stubborn canvas and tent poles. If she could only have told him more gently . . . .

When she heard the rattle of wagon wheels crossing the rocks on the far side of the aspen grove and realized Tyler was coming at last, she turned away. She didn't want to see him.

She dusted her wrinkled, dirty skirt, feeling ashamed to look little better than a beggar. Her hair hung loose and straight about her shoulders. She'd ruined her hands, and her face was probably dirty. She wished she could hide.

"Morning, Daisie! You're up early," Tyler called, murmuring "whoa" to the dun-colored horse that pulled the buckboard. "Having trouble with the tent, Lord Browning?"

Daisie's father straightened with a groan. "Dash it all, my boy, I can't get this bloody thing back up. One of the poles is bent. We've had a devil of a time since you left. I'll thank you to take Daisie away before I turn her over my knee. I've a mind to give you a sound thrashing for leaving her. Where have you been?"

Just as she expected, Tyler laughed, leaped the creek and joined them. "I was under the impression you both were going to be perfectly safe here. I had to go up to my ranch and found half of my herd scattered. It took two days to round them up. When are you going to throw a couple of logs across that creek so I can save my boots?" He rocked on his heels, surveying the mauled campsite.

"As soon as you fell a couple of trees," Gregory Browning retorted sharply. He remembered himself. "Forgive me, my boy. We had a bad scare in the night. I almost shot myself a bear."

Daisie still hadn't turned to greet Tyler. Perhaps he'd forget she was there.

"Daisie almost brained the beast with her rocks. Of course, she was aiming at me."

"Papa!" Daisie said, blushing. "At least it went away and didn't eat us." Instantly she regretted speaking.

Tyler approached her, cocking his head to catch her reluctant eye. She stared sullenly at his silver-toed boots. The tooled leather had dried badly.

"I told you not to talk to strange bears, Daisie," he said softly.

She gritted her teeth. "Your boots look terrible, Mr. Reede." She wanted to be angry, but already he was melting her resolve.

He sighed. "It's back to Mister and Miss, again, huh? You're angry I was delayed. I am sorry. I couldn't let thousands of dollars worth of steak on the hoof run loose."

She waved him off. "Just unload my trunks and go away for a while. I want to change. Don't look at me. I'm a fright."

Tyler began chuckling. "If only you knew how delightful you look with your hair gleaming with sunlight, your skirt muddy and torn. Like a little match girl."

"*Where* is it torn?" she cried, plucking at the folds. Then she couldn't stop herself from smiling. Her heart filled with a strange but welcome warmth. She looked up into Tyler's face and found herself longing to kiss him hello. When he reached out, she took his hands. The warmth penetrated her gloom, erasing all her doubts. "I'm glad you've come," she said, letting him pull her to her feet.

He laid his wide, strong palm against her cheeks. His cornflower-blue eyes were soft. "*Are* you all right?"

She nodded. "We had a terrible fright, though. Simply terrible. Didn't we, Papa? It was the most enormous bear!"

"I'm sure it only seemed large — "

"Come and look at the footprints. I fetched water by first light and went faint when I saw them." She grabbed his hand to guide him toward the prints. "You must've left town early to be here now," she commented.

"I hadn't intended to leave you here so long. I've been worried about you. It looks like I had good reason."

Several clear prints marked the soft silt along the bank of the creek. Tyler crouched, tracing the outlines. "It *was* big."

Daisie shuddered, remembering the bitter taste of her fear. "I'm so hungry I could eat that bear, fur and all! Do you have any idea how perfectly atrocious tinned food is? For three days straight? Tyler, I'm wild to change my clothes. Where are my trunks?''

Ignoring her, Tyler followed the tracks across the creek to where they disappeared into the meadow. "He must have come from that way."

He made his way through the grass searching for signs. He stooped once and moved on, stooped again and then turned. Plucking a snag of brown fur from the branch of a scrub oak, his face turned serious. "He was very big."

Still barefoot, she stepped into the creek to clean her feet. When she stubbed her toe on the far side she yelped and reached down to grab up the offending rock.

"Where are your shoes?'' Tyler asked, taking her hand when she joined him.

"Muddy and wet, thank you. It has rained every afternoon. I don't see how Papa has stood it."

Absently, Tyler took the rock from her. Turning it over, he squinted at it. "Did you miss me, Daisie?''

She tossed her head. "Not at all. I cursed you when I was hungry and cold. I cursed you when I couldn't sleep. I feel that Papa is on the verge of giving up this venture, and I want him to, desperately. But I want him to be happy, too. He called home and his old business a yoke. Isn't that dreadful? What am I to do?''

She paused to watch Tyler examine the rock. His eyes widened.

"You haven't heard a word I've said! I suppose by the way you're gawking at that rock you're going to tell me we've struck gold."

"This side of the creek isn't part of your father's claim, and it isn't often you pick up gold lying about, but with the blasting over there last year it might have been blown here. I'd say yes, there's a little gold in this rock."

Daisie's skin prickled. "You don't mean it!'' She grabbed his arm. "Don't tease about something so important."

"Look around. Are there more rocks like this?''

"Tyler, please stop teasing. Papa won't take this lightly."

"You've found *something*!'' Tyler said slowly. "The trick

will be figuring out where this float came from. That's what this rock all by itself is called — a *float*. It could have rolled down from the ledge — ''

''I might have thrown it here myself, last night,'' she said, still unwilling to believe.

''I thought I examined that area behind your father's tent. There was nothing there. I've thought all along he might find something farther on, around the knoll.''

Taken aback, Daisie edged away. ''I thought you said there was promise of gold on Papa's claim. If you've thought all along there wasn't — '' She backed away still more. ''I believe you *are* a speculator!''

Straightening, Tyler frowned. ''Speculators, as you call them, make a profit, and I am not going to make a profit out of your father.'' He handed the rock back to her.

''So you claim, Mr. Reede,'' she said. ''But we're not green-horns any longer. We've fought a bear, and we are beginning to understand the way things are done in these hills. I would say buying and selling claims must be a lucrative business for you to wear boots tipped in silver.''

He eyed her, his amusement unnerving. ''Yes, indeed, Miss Browning. I make a great deal of money loaning claims such as this one to unwary, uninformed gentlemen I suspect will never pay me.''

His words, though sarcastic in tone, concealed a grain of truth. He would only have agreed to lend her father use of this claim if he'd known it was no loss to him. That was surely enough to suggest the claim was worthless. Hoping to retreat without revealing her conclusion, Daisie scanned the rocky ledge extending from the aspen grove to the creek. A huge crack gaped where the creek gushed through; above this the ledge rose high and jagged behind the tent, ending in a pine-topped, grassy knoll just beyond.

''You think the float came from that knoll? I disagree. It's too far from here,'' she said confidently. ''I think it came from in there where the creek cuts through the ledge. It flooded the day you brought me here. Water gushed along this way. I can see where debris collected." She pointed to various spots in the meadow where dead grass had snagged around the scrub-oak trunks. "I think the ore was washed down—"

Tyler shook his head. "From perhaps miles upstream."

Scrutinizing the rock, she thought to match the color to one of the many layers high along the ledge. Her lips tightened. The rock didn't look like gold in the slightest, but perhaps along the edge of this side of the creek . . . . "I wonder if you'd be willing to lend us this adjacent claim, Mr. Reede. If Papa wants gold so badly, and we can't yet go home, I'm going to do all I can to help him find it."

"Supposing I don't own this adjoining claim, Miss Browning."

She smiled. "But I'm quite sure you do. If you don't, you'll know who does, and I shall borrow it from him."

"No one but me lends claims, Daisie," he said, his eyes slightly narrowed, as if he was rethinking his earlier estimation of her. He appeared not to like what he was thinking. "I did make a loan this once out of the kindness of my heart. You're asking me to do it again, and not very nicely."

"Oh, must I be nice?" She looked up through her lashes. Her voice was sweetly persuasive, but her eyes snapped. "Please, Tyler?"

Chuckling, Tyler swept off his hat and bowed. "Miss Browning, you drive a hard bargain."

He looked charmed, but she thought she detected something calculating in his eyes. Not for the first time, she wondered what the real Tyler Reede was after.

Chapter Eight

"You didn't bring my trunks?" Daisie said, unable to hide her disappointment.

Tyler tried grinning but saw that Daisie was too upset to endure more teasing. "Amelia wouldn't let me take them!"

That Amelia would hold Daisie's trunks was just too hard to believe. Tyler probably hadn't bothered to go by the store. "What did Amelia say?" Daisie asked, turning back toward camp.

He shook his head. "I wouldn't repeat the crazy things she said, but she and Hank refused to turn them over. I hope nothing's happened to your things."

Daisie cast Tyler a scalding look. She hoped not, too. Gregory Browning was waiting for them. "Coffee, Tyler? What have the two of you been looking at over there?"

Tyler took the rock from Daisie and held it out. "Have a look at this, sir."

"I don't see anything special about — " He stopped and frowned. "Is this what I've been looking for?" Leaping to his feet, he seized Daisie's shoulders. "We've done it!" Turning to Tyler, his eyes blazing, he looked almost frightened. "Is this it? Is this gold?"

"Let me take it to the assayer before you begin spending your fortune, sir," Tyler said, grinning. "But yes, I think there's gold mixed with a little silver in that rock. Want to look for more?"

Her father sank to the bench. Heaving a ragged sigh, he whispered, "We've done it." He put his head in his hands.

Daisie shivered to think this might be yet another disappointment. How could Tyler stand there smiling so openly if . . . ? She pushed aside her confusion. He had loaned her father a worthless claim and stood by while her father ruined his health working it. It was just a strange twist of fate that she happened to find gold on the adjoining claim. Tyler must certainly be surprised by that.

Later, Tyler brought the supplies down from the wagon — supplies Daisie hated to accept. He and her father talked excitedly of the find. Then, while Daisie prepared lunch for them all, the two men hunted among the grasses in the meadow for more ore samples.

Not surprisingly, they didn't talk of leaving the claim. The find had to be guarded. Daisie's father would surely wear himself out looking for the source of the float. And she would continue making do with her dirty clothes.

If ever the moment to tell Tyler the truth about her father had come, it was now. She knew she'd see a change in Tyler then and imagined the scene in humiliating detail. Perhaps he'd laugh and call her father a fool.

After lunch Tyler righted the tent and helped bring in several heavy pieces of deadwood for the fire. Though he remained cheerful with her father, Daisie knew he was watching her, puzzled by her aloof behavior.

As the afternoon passed, Daisie cautioned herself to keep Tyler at a distance, but when her suspicions and anger had receded, her emotions confirmed the strange power he still exercised over her heart.

"Let me walk you to the wagon," Daisie said as Tyler prepared to leave.

He looked surprised and pleased. "I thought you weren't speaking to me," he said as they crossed the meadow to the edge of the aspens where he had left the wagon. After he hitched the horse back into the harness, he waved goodbye to her father. "I'm of two minds about this discovery, Daisie. On the one hand, it's bound to keep your father from returning to England for several more weeks. But don't worry." He patted his breast pocket. "I've got his letter to your mother to mail." He looked at her anxiously. "I couldn't very well say nothing about the ore. What would you think of me then?"

"We should never have known," she said softly.

"What is it then, Daisie? Why are you angry with me? Can you really believe this is all an elaborate set-up to cheat your father? He has nothing I want — or need — except possibly you, and I didn't know you existed until a few days ago."

"It's that I can't be *sure*!" Daisie snapped. "And not being sure makes me angry and afraid. I feel foolish . . . and I detest that."

Tyler sighed, his eyes dark and turbulent.

She folded her arms, bracing herself for the revelation of his true character her next words would bring. "I think there's something more you should know."

He didn't respond.

"Papa has no title. He's not "Lord" Browning at all. Just plain Mr. Browning." She watched for a reaction. She saw only that Tyler was looking deep into her eyes, making her self-conscious and jumpy.

"That's it?" he said after a moment.

"I think that's quite enough. He said it was a harmless rumor, a joke that got out of hand. We haven't any land in England, no grand manor house, no peerage. My mother's few pieces of jewelry have been sold, including one or two heirlooms. We're quite ordinary, actually. I didn't want you to go on carrying any . . . lofty notions about us."

His brows worked. A half smile lingered on his lips. He looked bewildered. Suddenly he cupped Daisie's face with both hands and kissed her.

She struggled free, feeling dizzy. "Why did you do that?"

"Did you think I didn't know all this time that the title was fake?"

She hid her shaking fists behind her back. "You *call* him Lord Browning!" she cried.

"Because it pleases him. Do you think I was born yesterday, Daisie? I've been all over. I went to school in the East. Some of my friends in Denver are pretty high up in politics and the like. I know an English peer wouldn't own only one factory, that losing it wouldn't mean ruin, that his fondest story wouldn't be of how he worked himself up from joiner's apprentice to owner. Daisie, what wild notions do you have about me? How could Hank and Amelia be so convincing when they — ?"

"They have nothing to do with this!" Daisie burst out, turning away. What a fool she was. She wished she'd never spoken. "Goodbye, Tyler. Is it too much to hope you might bring my trunks tomorrow?"

"I told you — "

He grabbed her, turned her and kissed her before she could put up her fists and hold them away. His lips were warm and moist on hers and she sank into his embrace, yearning for the thrill she had known kissing him only a few days ago.

The thrill was there still, but it was more frightening now — confusing, arousing — because in spite of everything she couldn't be sure of her own mind. Her world was upside down.

"Let me go!" she gasped. "Papa will see."

"Your papa likes me, Daisie. He trusts me."

"That's because he's a trusting man. If you betray that trust, Tyler," she hissed against his lips, "I shall hate you."

She expected him to go on kissing her urgently as proof of his honor, but he put her from him, roughly. His mouth had gone tight. He seemed separated from her by a chasm of anger.

"I'm sorry for you, Daisie. That you can't trust me. That you won't. I don't feel the need to do anything extraordinary to impress you. Take me as you find me, Daisie, or take whomever you please. I have no hold on you, whatever you might imagine. Don't build me up as some villain. I'm no such thing. To be a villain takes more guile than I've got time for. If you'll excuse me, I've business waiting in town. When I get the results from the assayer, I'll be back. And in the meantime, have fun with your little suspicions. Maybe they'll keep you warm at night."

He swung up onto the wagon seat and, with a vicious snap of the whip in the air, turned in a tight, creaking circle and rattled off through the aspens. Daisie wanted to shout something horrid, something final, something to which there was no comeback, but she could only turn away with the miserable realization that she was worse than a fool.

The camp looked better after Tyler's visit. The tent stood straight and taut. Only the ragged, blackened hole in the side reminded Daisie of the bear. Tyler had strung a line of empty cans along the far side of the creek to serve as an alarm system, and he had advised her father to store the fresh meat he'd brought inside the cabin where the bear couldn't reach it.

With a feeling of desolation, Daisie glared at the cabin. It needed only a few more days' work to be completed. Tyler had said they would arrange slender pines in a cross-hatch pattern over the top and cover that with grassy blocks of sod. "Won't it be muddy during a rain?" she had asked during lunch.

"I grew up with grass over my head—and mud in my hair," Tyler said, going on to explain that his parents had home-steaded in western Kansas.

Where had she got the idea people would be fooled by her father's false title? Everyone probably knew a real peer wouldn't live as a hermit. Everyone who had met her father had probably been laughing behind his back all this time.

Tyler returned two days later with a second lantern, a pistol, a stout pick and some lumber to build a sluice-box. He brought a variety of tinned food that Daisie hoped they wouldn't need, and a calico dress for her to wear. He still claimed that the Salters refused to release her trunks.

Since she was desperately dirty by then, she accepted the dress grudgingly, adding its cost to a lengthy tally she'd started keeping. She'd repay Tyler for every bean, she swore to herself, watching him and her father together as if no suspicions lay beneath the surface of their words.

The talk was mostly of gold. Though they hadn't found a

single other pebble containing gold, Daisie's father greeted each new day with childlike enthusiasm and energy. Tyler avoided Daisie and she ignored him. It was an uneasy arrangement.

Tyler wasn't proving himself a cheat at all. On the contrary, he said they had found real high-grade gold — at least, one fantastic, mysterious piece of it — and now there was no hope of going home. No hope, either, of redeeming herself in Tyler's eyes. Not that she cared to . . . .

The bear rattled the can-alarm once one night and then left them alone. The days merged into a blur of warm, sunny mornings followed by cool, rainy afternoons and damp, chilly nights. Daisie altered the calico dress to fit and changed into it. She washed her blouse, skirt and petticoats, but the result was dismal. Her irritation grew, but fortunately the campsite kept her busy from dawn until dark. She banked her temper and tried to be patient.

After a week she heard the familiar rattle of rigging and the grate of iron-rimmed wheels on distant rocks. She tensed, expecting Tyler to appear again. Her father was picking his way up the crevice where the creek gushed from the higher ridge. She was about to call to him but broke off as she squinted through the fragile quivering aspen leaves at the two people who were approaching. One was a man in a dark suit and hat, the other a woman in a tan dress with an elaborate ugly bonnet. Daisie felt as if she had forgotten the outside world. Now it came marching back toward her, concerned and somewhat put out.

Straightening, she brushed back her wind-whipped hair and smoothed her dusty calico dress. "Amelia," she called, making herself smile as if she was welcoming them into her old parlor. "How good to see you. And . . . er . . . Hank." She hated to use his first name, but formal address seemed silly when she was standing in the middle of a barren campsite, her feet naked and muddy, her nails dirty and her dress homely in the extreme. "What brings you so far?"

She didn't dwell long on Hank's boxy worsted suit or the stiff black shoes. Glancing at his face and seeing that he still devoured her with his eyes, she turned her attention to Amelia. "Can I warm some coffee for you both? It's quite good for being brewed over a campfire. Papa is — "

Amelia's face mirrored a mixture of feelings, from shock to amusement to deep concern. She stopped on the far side of the gushing creek, her hat sweetly perched on her dry, blonde curls, her face pale and gaping, her gloved hands delightfully silly-looking. "I can hardly believe you're really living here," she said, looking about helplessly for a way to cross. "You look like a squatter!"

Daisie's cheeks went cold. She lifted her chin, refusing to let them see the wave of humiliation that washed over her. "I've been working." She said that as if work was an activity Amelia didn't know — although that was not the case, Daisie was sure. Amelia had been tending store long before Daisie had ever lifted a finger in manual labor.

Hank helped his sister across the creek, waited while she fussed over a few splashes along the hem of her skirt and then joined Daisie beside the snapping campfire. As if entering a funeral parlor, Hank removed his hat. "Miss Browning, we've been deeply concerned about you. Now I see we should have come the moment Tyler Reede proposed to remove your trunks from our care. I sensed you were in trouble then, but Amelia said you'd been warned — "

"Why, Hank, that's not so! I said she'd joined her father. Look, there he is now. Daisie, honey, I said no such thing. That Tyler Reede came back and asked me, right to my face, if he could have your trunks. Goodness only knows what he was going to do with them. I thought at first he might have — " She lowered her dark eyes and pursed her lips. "I thought some harm had come to you. I truly did. I thought to myself, why he's attacked that poor little thing and left her in some gulch where not a soul shall ever see her again, not until her bones are white as snow."

Her humiliation evaporating, Daisie laughed. "Amelia! Your imagination! I asked him to get them for me."

Amelia sputtered. "Oh? Well . . . er . . . we just couldn't let him take them on his word alone. It just didn't set right with either of us. Lord only knows what *his* sort would do."

"I'm all right, as you can see," Daisie said, still laughing. "I don't suppose you thought to bring my trunks with you?"

Hank cut in, moving to pat Daisie's shoulder affectionately. "We weren't sure we'd really find you here. Reede finally told us you were here. We didn't believe it. We thought surely a lady like yourself wouldn't stoop to . . . to this."

Insulted, Daisie tossed her head. "It's quite fun, really."

Clearly Hank wasn't a man one could count on to be tactful. His mind wasn't sufficiently developed for it. "I want you to meet my father. Oh, how stupid of me. Of course, you met him in the spring. Papa? Do come out of there now and say hello to the Salters."

Daisie's father picked his way out of the narrow ravine and stood looking at them. "Morning," he said, sounding rather annoyed. Though he looked about as substantial as a scarecrow, his eyes were clear and penetrating.

Daisie supposed there wasn't the kindest of feelings between her papa and Hank. If the prices in Hank's store had been more reasonable . . . .

"Lord Browning," Amelia said, extending her gloved hand and curtseying as if she was meeting the King of England.

Daisie hid her grin. Hank seemed skittish around her father. Then he apparently reminded himself of something and brightened. He turned the full force of what he probably thought of as his charm on Daisie.

"So, how have you been?" he asked, boldly taking her hand before she could draw away. He stroked her callused palms and clucked sadly over her ragged, darkened fingernails. Then he looked earnestly into her eyes. For a moment Daisie felt as if she was looking at Norwood Poole again, only this "lamb" could be frightening in the dark.

She pulled her hand away.

"We've had some adventures since I decided to stay with Papa," she said brightly. She went on to describe the bear's visit, but out of the corner of her eye she watched Amelia and observed the woman's small dark eyes dart about the camp, reflecting her disdain.

She poured coffee and was pleased when Hank sipped with a startled expression that proved it had an identifiable flavor and didn't corrode his throat as he swallowed.

"Um-m-m, very good, Daisie. You could teach Amelia a thing or two about making coffee. We decided we couldn't go on wondering what had become of you. I'm glad you're well and safe. I see the outfit I sold you is serving you well, Lord Browning."

Daisie's father sputtered but refrained from expressing his true opinion of the expensive supplies.

Refusing to comment on the coffee, Amelia seated herself on the wobbly bench. She raised her brows and looked stuffy and officious. "Daisie," she began, "we've heard some disturbing rumors and thought we should inform you right away."

Hank broke in. "There's been some fast selling of property up here in the last day or so. Have you seen anyone about?"

Looking quickly toward her father, whose expression was reserved, Daisie shook her head. "I don't know what you mean."

"I've heard gold was found up this way. Folks have been buying up claims. What do you make of that?"

Daisie hestitated. Why did Hank look so serious when a gold discovery ought to bring smiles of congratulation? Her father said nothing. Daisie thought suddenly that her father was making himself look almost simple-minded. Immediately on guard, she offered a puzzled smile of her own. "Why, whatever do you mean?" She hedged.

Amelia leaped to her feet. Her bonnet fell back and she snatched impatiently at the ribbons. "I think it's disgraceful! If you've found gold, it's just too impossible to believe! Here your unfortunate father has been working his claim for months. Suddenly you come along, and Tyler Reede takes a fancy to you. Before you know it, you've got gold lying about in chunks. Really, Daisie, it's the oldest trick in the mining districts."

Daisie went cold. "Papa? What does she mean?"

With a sharp look, Hank tried to quiet his sister.

Amelia ignored him and stamped her foot. "It's disgraceful the way some men try to pull the wool over the eyes of innocents. Disgraceful!"

Daisie's father's face grew pale, but he didn't move and didn't speak.

Daisie set her steaming cup on the ground. "What's the oldest trick in mining?"

Hank put his arm around Daisie's shoulder. "She's talking about salting claims. She means she thinks — she and *I* think — that Tyler Reede wanted to impress you. He put some ore-bearing rocks on your claim."

Shivering, Daisie jerked away. "That's impossible! He wouldn't do such a thing!"

Her mind reeling, she wished for time to reflect calmly on the accusation. Salting a claim with ore-bearing rocks. . . . Of course! How very stupid of her not to have guessed that that was where the gold came from. It hadn't come from the knoll or the ledge or some place miles upstream. It had come from Tyler's own pocket.

Whirling, she wished she could silence Hank and erase the pity in Amelia's eyes. Tyler wasn't trying to impress her! He was trying . . . to *own* her! She owed him for food, for the dress on her back, for the health and safety of her father. And soon he'd make her pay. He'd make them both pay in his straightforward, maddening way!

"I warned you about Tyler, but you wouldn't listen," Amelia said, her brows arched. "Speculators will do anything to make their claims more attractive, not to mention the surrounding land. Think of the money that reprobate has made already! Who knows to what lengths he'd go to attract the attention of a decent, innocent young woman like you? I'll bet whatever you found didn't have much gold in it. He wouldn't want to plant a valuable piece of float. That wouldn't pay at all. He planted just enough to tease you."

"I refuse to listen to any more," Daisie cried, loath to confess they were right. It was not Daisie and her father Tyler was exploiting at all! He was making money out of rumors, exploiting the madness of gold fever and the gullibility of fortune-seekers! ''The ore we found wasn't even on our—'' She broke off. She had fallen into the Salters' trap. Now they knew the Brownings had found gold. Daisie wondered how much land Hank had bought since the first whisper of gold reached his ears.

Her father lifted his head. ''I believe enough's been said for the moment, Daisie.'' He moved between Daisie and the Salters. ''I think you'd both better return to town. If there's any question of wrongdoing here, we'll discuss the matter with Mr. Reede personally. But your concern for us is most touching.''

''We've sorry to be the ones to reveal this, Lord Browning, but we felt we owed it to you,'' Hank said. Daisie thought his air of concern a trifle exaggerated.

''It was good of you to come,'' Gregory Browning muttered. ''Daisie?'' he said turning to her with remarkable calm. ''Daisie, I want you to go back to town with the Salters. I want you to go now, this very minute, with no arguing. Do you hear me, daughter? I want you to go.''

''But Papa—''

''I'm not going to order you, Daisie. I know you'll do as I ask like a good girl. We've worked hard here and you need a rest. I know you want to write to your mama . . . and to the Arnolds.''

Daisie wasn't sure what her father was getting at. Did he want her to ask the Arnolds for that loan now? Her heart lifted. If he was prepared to go home. . . . She thought how devastated he must feel. She wanted to put her arms around him, but she held herself rigid in front of the Salters. How could she leave him alone to contemplate Tyler's betrayal?

''As soon as you can, Daisie, I want you to find Tyler and request he come out here. I want to discuss this accusation with him directly.''

Hank interrupted, his eyes worried. ''You're not going to come right out and tell him you know he salted this claim, Lord Browning! He'll only deny everything. He's a clever man. He has to be to stay in business the way he does and not get run out of town. Or shot."

"We're so sorry, Daisie," Amelia said, sighing and dabbing at the corners of her eyes. "Of course you must come back to the store. Your trunks are right where you left them. I imagine you're desperate for a bath and a decent dress. Where did you get that rag? It looks like something a servant would wear. When I think of how fine and sweet you looked that first morning we met you. . . . And now, your hair . . . and those sunburned cheeks. You're as brown-skinned as an Indian! It breaks my heart!"

Daisie wanted to scream. How could she go back to that store where Hank's eyes — and hands — would be on her whenever the opportunity arose? And yet to be clean and dry and warm even for a day or two. . . .

"Lord Browning," Hank went on, "you must deal with this speculator as cleverly as possible. It's the only thing he understands. If he salted this claim, his intentions can't be honorable. He can't be trying to sell you land. This claim's already yours. But he must expect to profit in some other way. You have to get him to reveal just what he's up to."

Daisie shook her head and kept shaking it, wanting to deny all their accusations against Tyler. She wanted to believe that the passionate embrace beneath the rocky overhand during the storm had been as sincere on his part as it had been on hers. She wanted to trust the feelings she had for Tyler — intense, tumultuous feelings she hadn't been able to tear from her heart. How could she fall in love with a man who was crooked and deceitful?

What a fool he must think her. She was ashamed she had ever let him close to her. She had actually wanted more than kisses! She had dreamed of giving him all she had to give, and she knew that if she were to see him again that very moment he would blind her with his flashing smile and melt her defenses with his touch. It would have been so much easier to marry Norwood!

Clearly, her father wanted her to return to beg a loan from the Arnolds. At last he was ready to go home. But she felt none of the sense of victory she had expected to feel. This was the final crushing blow to his pride.

"All right, Papa," she said softly, startling them all. "I'll go. You'll come along later?"

"After I've done some thinking." He dismissed them all and turned away, ducking inside the tent.

"I'll get my shoes," Daisie said, following her father, embracing him silently within the privacy of their musty, damp little home. Moments later she presented herself to the Salters feeling as well as looking like a squatter. She didn't look forward to the embarrassing ride into town. She smiled humorlessly as Hank took her elbow and helped her across the creek.

As Daisie seated herself in the Salters' neat buggy, she looked wistfully back at her father, standing alone now in the camp in front of the tent. He seemed to belong there. It was sad to think he'd soon be torn away.

Narrowing her eyes until the scenery blurred, she set her teeth, ignoring Amelia's chatter and Hank's too-familiar nudges and pats. How was she going to wring the truth from that blue-eyed man with the ostentatious fringed jacket and the silver-tipped boots? And how could she get back at him?

Chapter Nine

Drumming her fingers, Daisie leaned against her trunk and gazed out the small dirty upper window of Salter's Emporium at the choked street below. Customers streamed in and came out a while later laden with packages. Amelia refused to let Daisie go to the post office unaccompanied, and yet was so busy she couldn't leave the store. Daisie felt tempted to go without her, but hated braving the crowded streets.

The main street surged with loud, rowdy newcomers. Heavy wagon traffic kept the dust stirred. On the outskirts, shacks and tents mushroomed, while everywhere miners swarmed to and from the mining companies that sprouted tall, raw pine buildings housing elevator shafts and stamp mills. Cripple Creek's staggering boom showed no signs of abating.

At length, Amelia dragged to the top of the stairs, her curls askew and her lips pinched with irritation. She untied her work apron and disappeared into her cubicle for a moment.

"You look worn thin," Daisie said, picking up the thick letter she had written to her mother. "Are you ready to go?" She also had a letter for Mr. Arnold that had taken hours to word. She hated to mail it, but the letter was necessary to explain the telegraph message she intended to send first.

Amelia came out, plumping her hair. "I thought you might be napping. I'm ready if you are." A white lace collar pinned to her otherwise plain black dress made her look less severe.

"What a morning! I am tired, but I like it when a trainload of empty-handed, full-pocketed gold hunters gets in."

"I'm glad to hear business is good," Daisie said, hoping she sounded sincere.

They emerged into the dusty clamor outside the store, two slim young women in bonnets, gloves and high-buttoned shoes, their slightly draped and bustled dark skirts looking curiously formal among the shapeless clothes of the miners. Sheer linen blouses with large puffy sleeves gave the two women a look of frail refinement. Daisie relished being clean and decently dressed again. She walked with her head high, ignoring the dozens of men who turned to watch her pass.

After she'd posted her letters, she and Amelia fought their way through the crowds and traffic to the telegraph office. They waited in line for half an hour before Daisie could send her message: "Father safe. Urgently need two return fares, please. Letter follows. Gratefully, Daisie Browning."

"Your friends must be wealthy to send so much," Amelia said as they pushed their way out of the building. "Where in New York State do they live?"

"In the north," Daisie said. "I stayed with them for almost two weeks before coming west. They were wonderful to me."

"I suppose they had a fine house?"

Daisie raised her eyebrows and nodded. "Lovely. I especially enjoyed the solarium. Mr. Arnold's hobby is raising orchids. He also has quite a collection of animal trophies from his African travels, but I found those disturbing. My father never hunted for sport. I seem to have taken up his opinions."

"Was it as nice there as your home in England? I mean, them being American and all. You English do everything in such a fancy way."

"Much nicer, actually."

Amelia looked disbelieving. "Really?"

"They'll understand I mean to repay them for this loan," Daisie said, smarting to think they'd get the message before the letter. They'd nod and agree they'd warned her about going west alone, but at this point Daisie couldn't dwell on her folly.

That her father was ready to go home was her only concern.

"You must be longing for England," Amelia said, tucking her hand in Daisie's elbow.

Daisie shook her head. "Let's not talk about it. I'm dreadfully homesick."

Amelia sighed. "You're lucky to be able to travel, but you're right. It's such a short time until you leave us. Let's think about how we can raise your spirits. You probably haven't heard about the dance next week. Would you like to go? It'll be crude compared to the grand balls you've attended, but I think it'll be fun."

Before Daisie could assure Amelia she'd never been to a grand ball, only a few formal cotillions after she came out, they had arrived at the store. The dance sounded interesting, but her thoughts returned to her remaining chore: Tyler Reede. Her father wanted to see him — and so did she!

As Amelia went back to work, Daisie resigned herself to a boring afternoon of resting and then watching Amelia cater to her customers while Hank supervised the unloading of goods in the rear. He paid so little attention to Daisie she wondered if she'd finally discouraged him. Since returning, he'd given her no cause for worry.

Late in the afternoon she wrote Tyler a message and took extra care copying the note onto her precious pink and cream stationery — a present on her eighteenth birthday two years before.

She had thrown out a detailed letter explaining her disappointment and disgust at his practice of salting claims and decided against a terse note conveying fury without explanation. At last she had settled on a simple message.

Father is most anxious to talk with you.
Please let me know when you can see him,
Cordially, Daisie Browning.

She wondered whom she might get to deliver the note to the saloon and thought Hank might advise her. She found him talking privately to a customer and waited until he was done. When Hank turned to her, it was the first time they'd been alone together since the night her money was stolen. She found herself tongue-tied and yet curious to know how he'd behave.

"I wonder if you would deliver this for me," Daisie said, watching Hank's eyes fall on Tyler's name written with a flourish across the pink envelope. "Father's waiting to talk to . . Mr. Reede."

"It's a mistake to tell Reede he knows the truth," Hank said. "Or is this personal?"

Daisie flushed. "I have no personal interest in Tyler."

Hank edged closer. She looked up into his face, feeling a repulsion as strong in its way as the attraction she felt toward Tyler. Hank unnerved her. His eyes darkened, and he smiled a little. Clearly his interest in her hadn't diminished.

"I'd take it for you, Daisie, but I'm not in the habit of going to saloons." His voice was husky with reproach.

Seeing that Amelia was busy with two lady customers, Daisie decided she couldn't wait until Amelia was again free. If Daisie delivered the note herself, she might have the chance to talk to Tyler and confront him.

Throwing Hank a too-bright smile she said resignedly, "Never mind, then."

She went upstairs as if to put the note away, but instead took her shawl and slipped quietly down the stairs and out the storeroom door while Hank and Amelia whispered near the cash register.

Hoping they would remain busy long enough for her to get to the saloon and back without being missed, Daisie slipped out to the street. Glad to be alone with her thoughts, she hurried along, carefully avoiding eye contact with strangers.

Street traffic had lessened, and the dust had settled a bit. Warm yellow light filled the windows of eating houses, hotels and saloons. Doors stood open to catch the mild evening air.

Making good time, Daisie reached the Gaslight without incident. As she had feared, it was already crowded, noisy and smoky. She wondered what attraction the place had for Tyler.

At one time she would have thought him a cut above those standing thick at the mahogany bar, but she had been wrong about so much.

She craned her neck to survey the men seated at the round tables. At last she went to the bar, as self-conscious and embarrassed as if she were undressing in public. Ignoring throaty queries and leering invitations from the miners who ogled her, she caught the bartender's eye. "I've got an important message for Tyler Reede. Where can I find him?"

The bartender, whom she recognized from her first visit, leaned on his meaty forearm. "Ain't seen him in a while, ma'am. I'll take the message if you want."

She shook her head. "Can you suggest where I might find him?"

He eyed her and ran his tongue around his teeth. "Maybe Carla knows where he is. Francine?" he called to a woman perched on a miner's knee at a nearby table. "Is Carla upstairs?"

She made a face. "How should I know?" But at the bartender's jerked thumb, she went to the stairs and shouted Carla's name. Moments later a young woman in a scarlet dress with a plunging neckline appeared and leaned over the railing. "You screeched, Frannie?"

"Some . . . *lady* to see you," Francine smirked, looking back at Daisie as if Daisie was the one wearing gaudy paint on her cheeks and eyelids.

Carla rustled down the stairs, holding her skirts high enough to give a generous look at her rich lace petticoats and dark stockings. She bestowed smiles and familiar caresses as she crossed the room, coming at last to look up at Daisie curiously.

Her russet hair was a pile of rolls and ringlets. Daisie tried not to stare at the blue eyes masked with dark liner, the glinting paste diamonds in her ears and the scarlet velvet ribbon that circled her throat.

Carla leaned on the bar, arching forward enough to display the full depth of her cleavage. She winked at a man next to Daisie, making his tongue fairly hang out. "What can I do for *you*, honey?" she crooned at Daisie.

"I . . . er, I have a message for . . . for Tyler Reede. Can you tell me where I can find him?"

"I can, but I won't. What'll you have?"

"I . . what do you mean?"

"What do you want from the bar? To drink. It's on me." Carla gave Daisie a once-over look and raised an eyebrow. She propped her foot on the brass rail and nudged a spittoon with her toe as if toying with the idea of spilling the contents on Daisie's shoes.

Fighting panic, Daisie stiffened her spine. "I'll have a whiskey." She was grateful the room was dim enough to hide her blush.

Looking surprised, Carla nodded to the bartender. "What do you want to see Tyler about? Don't bother telling me who you are. I know just by listening to you. You're that high-minded little — pardon my French — la-dee-da *lady* from ol' London town. I've heard my fill of you. Here, you got a message for him? I'll see he gets it." She grabbed the note before Daisie could protest.

The bartender took extra care polishing Daisie's glass. He filled it to the top with amber liquid Daisie knew would give her courage.

Carla tore open the note and read it, looking disappointed. "I thought it'd be something mean—or mushy. Didn't know which. Drink up, honey. That stuff ain't cheap." She made great show of tucking Daisie's pink note deep into the bosom of her straining gown. Then she patted and arranged herself while sending provocative glances to the watching men.

Daisie lifted the little whiskey glass to her lips and drank. Some of the men cheered, making her choke on the last burning swallow. The warmth spread to her limbs, and she felt strengthened.

"You've been most kind," she croaked.

Carla raised her darkened brows and, a hand on her hip, pranced in a mincing circle. "Oh, quite right, dearie. Let's all knock back a cup of tea, shall we, boys?"

Her audience roared. Daisie gave the leering bartender a

bewildered look of thanks and turned toward the door. Seconds later Carla grabbed her elbow.

"Let me give you a piece of advice, honey." She patted Daisie's cheek as if she longed to slap it. "Either be nice to Tyler or leave him alone. Cut the stiff-upper-lip treatment. I happen to think he's the nicest man to cross my path in a good long while. I wish you'd never set foot in America. I wish to hell you'd go back to wherever it is you came from and stay there."

The whiskey had taken the edge off Daisie's nervousness. She stared levelly at Carla until the woman gave her a disgusted sniff and marched away.

"Anybody for a game of cricket with ol' Carla?" she called, swirling her short skirts and flirting her way around the room.

Daisie escaped to the crisp, clean evening air outside and hurried away down the darkened streets. The deep menacing shadows between the buildings and shacks rang with Carla's mocking words.

Daisie spent the next two torturously slow days worrying about her papa alone at the campsite.

She fretted over how the Arnolds would react to her telegram, and wondered how long she'd be forced to wait for a reply. And she heard nothing from Tyler. She couldn't bring herself to return to the Gaslight to ask Carla if she'd delivered the note.

By the day of the dance, Daisie had been five days in limbo. She welcomed the pleasant diversion of curling her hair up in pink ribbons and fussing with face creams and the nail buffer. Among the gowns Hilary had given her was a pale sprigged satin with a fitted bodice and lace flounces at the elbows. The under portion of the double skirt was cut to form a slight train, and the overskirt drew back and up with gathers at the side trimmed with large blue bows. Finishing touches were a triple row of royal-blue braid trimming and tiny buttons from the lace-trimmed neckline to the waist. She had tried it on only once to have it altered, and had forgotten she was a bit more well-endowed than Hilary. The bodice fit quite tightly, outlining the fullness of her breasts, emphasizing their swell above the low, lace-edged neckline. The waist was agonizingly small, so she'd have to lace more tightly than usual.

She hung the gown up that morning to let the wrinkles fall out. As she selected her underthings and fluffed her nicest petticoats, she kept getting the feeling that her belongings had been searched. Her best drawers and silk corset cover were missing. A hat pin turned up in the wrong trunk and some things lay upside down or squashed in corners, as if hastily repacked. Though she examined the locks of all three trunks, she saw no evidence of tampering.

Her off-white high-heeled dancing slippers were a fair match for the frock and sported stiff bows on the toes. She was glad now she'd decided to bring them along. When Amelia came up after a busy day behind the counter, she ducked in to see how Daisie was doing and eyed the gown enviously.

"It's not too much, is it?" Daisie asked, having alternately worried all day about measuring up to the Cripple Creek ladies or outshining them.

"It's . . . very nice, Daisie. From Paris?"

Daisie hadn't given the sewn-in seamstress's label a thought. "I . . . er . . . don't remember." She hated confessing that the gowns were secondhand.

Amelia fingered the deep flounce along the hem. "You'll attract attention in this, that's for sure."

"Would you help me lace in a few minutes? I'll be happy to help you. I lace my younger sister all the time."

Giving Daisie a peculiar look, one that made Daisie think Amelia suddenly hated her, Amelia agreed to slip in later. She appeared eventually wearing a silk wrapper printed with huge orange, yellow and purple flowers. She eyed Daisie in her long lacy drawers, white silk stockings and whalebone corset. "My, aren't we done up," she said, taking the corset laces. "Too bad Tyler can't see you like this. He'd drag you into the nearest alley."

"What a thing to say!" Daisie said, laughing off her embarrassment. She had been wondering that very thing. What would

Tyler say if he could see her now, half dressed . . . ? Her heart skipped a beat.

"Oh, I've seen the way he looks at you," Amelia said, yanking the laces until Daisie thought the woman was trying to suffocate her.

Panting, Daisie waved for Amelia to stop pulling. "That's . . . fine. Thank you!"

"Tyler will be at the dance, I'll bet. He never misses a chance to be around women. Will you dance with him, knowing he salted your father's claim?"

Daisie hated being put on the spot. "Let me help you lace now. It's getting late."

"That's all right. I don't need a corset like you do. As soon as you're dressed Hank wants to get up here to change into his best suit. We shouldn't keep him waiting with our silly talk. But I'll bet Tyler will think the most indecent things about you tonight with your . . . *charms* all squashed up like that. I wouldn't be surprised if he . . . *manhandles* you."

Made uneasy by Amelia's tone, Daisie forced herself not to reply.

Amelia paused to look longingly at a box sitting in the smaller trunk's tray. "What's in that?"

"Some things my New York friend . . . loaned me," Daisie said, opening the box. "Would you like to wear these earrings?"

Amelia snatched at them, looking almost angry that Daisie had offered. She also helped herself to a gaudy necklace — one that Daisie disliked. "You don't mind, do you? You have more here than you can possibly wear at one time."

"Help yourself," Daisie said, watching Amelia's dark eyes glint as she pawed through the other baubles.

Selecting several rings, Amelia hurried away to finish dressing. Moments later she emerged from her cubicle wearing a pink muslin gown with a crooked scooped neckline, a gathered waist and a single narrow flounce attached about half way down the single skirt. The flounce was lower on the left side than the right. The jewelry made her look like a gypsy.

Hoping her face didn't give away her opinion of the homely

dress, Daisie finished jabbing the tortoise-shell combs into her hair, lifting her nearly perfect curls into a cascade of soft gold from the crown of her head to just past her shoulders.

"You look wonderful, Amelia," Daisie said. She wondered privately why the poor woman's yellow hair always looked so dreadfully dull. The notion that Amelia might be trying a home-made method of lightening it crossed Daisie's mind. "Will I do to meet the wives of mining company presidents?" she asked.

Amelia's dark eyes snapped. "Well, that watered-down color tends to make your skin look even darker, but on you freckles are adorable."

"I'm so glad you think so," Daisie said, wondering if Amelia was genuinely obtuse or simply jealous.

Amelia turned away, her head stiffly erect. "I'll close up while Hank changes. He wanted to take a buggy, but I think we can walk, don't you?"

Daisie supposed she should have dressed in something plain, but after being called a freckled squatter more times than she could bear, she couldn't help enjoying the feel of smooth silk against her legs, the tickle of lace against her arms and the cool kiss of the night air on her throat and shoulders. Even the crushing hug of her corset was exciting and somehow arousing. She thought her full heavy skirts whispered approvingly as she made her way down the narrow stairs. When she emerged into the store's dark and deserted main room, she got a secret thrill when Hank first turned and saw her. Though he was a repugnant buffoon, she couldn't help being gratified by the lusting look of admiration that crossed his face. There were moments when a woman needed to feel desired.

Amelia turned away, absorbed in counting the day's receipts. Hank said nothing, but his eyes spoke volumes. Daisie kept her expression pleasant but aloof. Hank might look, but he had best keep his distance. If he felt moved to ask for a dance tonight she hoped she would be able to reject him without a scene. If he so much as touched her improperly she'd expose him as the masher he was, and Amelia's reputation and sensibilities be damned!

"Daisie," Hank said, releasing his breath in a long sigh. "You look beautiful."

"Thank you," she said. "Doesn't Amelia look pretty in pink?"

Hank glanced at his sister. "Stand up straight. Your hem's crooked or something," he said, appraising her gown with a critical eye.

Amelia's lips pressed together in a furious line. "It's the way I sewed on the ruffle. You said before it didn't show."

He shrugged. "I forgot. It doesn't, really. It must be the light. I'll be right down." Stumbling over his feet as he turned, he hurried into the storeroom and up the stairs.

When he came down his fair hair glistened, slicked back behind his ears like cornsilk. He wore a wide, stiff celluloid collar and a string tie with a large turquoise nugget in its clasp. His blue satin vest shone. Across it was draped an ostentatious watch chain that Daisie suspected was gold plate.

Offering an arm each to Daisie and Amelia, Hank smiled affectedly. Daisie hated to start the promising evening with an insult, and Hank had been behaving since she returned, so she took his arm, and they all went out.

As they approached the town hall, Daisie saw that most of the gentlemen wore fine black broadcloth frockcoats and snug formal trousers over heavy mining boots. The ladies wore nicely done-up dresses with ruffles, bows and lace, although none could compare with Daisie's. Everyone turned to stare at Daisie. She smiled and casually withdrew her hand from Hank's elbow lest anyone mistake him for her escort. She had never before felt quite so on display, not even at her own coming out party. Every eye was on her. The women were clearly assessing her exceptional gown. Smiling graciously at every person bold enough to meet her gaze, Daisie made her way inside.

An assortment of chairs stood along the bare pine walls. Lanterns hung from the high ceiling, flooding the crowded noisy room with garish yellow light.

In the far corner on a rough platform sat the orchestra, a

group of locals tuning up fiddles, a bass drum and a trumpet. A thin man struggled onto the platform with a gleaming tuba. A withered little woman with snow-white hair took her place apologetically and sat primly holding a flute. An elderly gentleman with a magnificent beard began hawing with a concertina. Daisie winced as they played something that sounded all too vaguely like the Blue Danube Waltz. The woman with the flute was the only one on key.

Daisie nodded at all those who were inspecting her from hair to hem, and waited for Amelia to begin introductions. When Amelia remained silent and pouting as though glued to Hank's side, Daisie pitied the woman's lack of social grace. She realized that Amelia knew the townsfolk only as customers, not as friends. Perhaps it was the emporium's prices that made everyone less than eager to welcome the Salters, and Daisie, to the dance.

"Look at the way all these cows are staring at us," Amelia hissed, glaring at the chattering, chuckling clusters of townspeople. "Just see if I give them a good price the next time they're in our store."

Hank shook her arm sharply. "They'll hear you."

"I don't care! I don't like being laughed at. Look how they're snickering at Daisie. It's disgraceful. We shouldn't have come."

Uncomfortable, Daisie separated herself from Hank and Amelia and smiled automatically at a nearby curious couple. The orchestra attempted another waltz and Daisie forced herself not to cringe.

"Aren't they just awful?" Amelia said, taking Daisie's arm. "Let's find some chairs."

"Actually, I'd like to keep moving around," Daisie said. "This is my first chance to see Cripple Creek's residents."

"I would have taken you calling if I'd had the time," Amelia said.

"Of course, I understand," Daisie said. She understood more than Amelia realized. "I'd like to meet some of these people now," she said, knowing she was being cruel to place Amelia in an embarrassing position, but unable to help herself.

Before Amelia could think of an excuse to avoid making introductions, Hank stepped up to Daisie and bowed. "May I have this dance?" he asked, looking frankly at Daisie's low-cut neckline.

She tensed, wanting to refuse, but he had her hand and was turning her toward the dancers moving in the middle of the room. Serious, almost frowning, he rigidly two-stepped her in a circle, leaving Amelia to watch glumly from the sidelines.

"You're the most beautiful woman here," Hank whispered. "And you know it," he added earnestly.

"Hardly," Daisie said, knowing that her expression had soured. "You're hurting my fingers."

He loosened his grip and then hugged her more tightly, bumping her legs with his sharp knees.

"Hank, please," she hissed, eyeing the crowd to see if anyone was watching her struggle. She needed rescuing badly, but not even Tyler could help her now. He was equally undesirable. "You're embarassing me. I don't find dancing this . . . close at all enjoyable or — ouch! — proper!"

"I want to do more than —"

A tall gentleman, reeking of bay rum, tapped Hank's shoulder. "You ol' buzzard, where'd you find this little beauty?" He winked at Hank and gazed down at Daisie's bodice where her creamy skin swelled above the narrow lace ruffles. "Don't keep her all to yourself. Let me have a turn with her."

"I don't think Daisie wants to —"

"I'm cutting in, Salter. Don't make me raise my freight rates for all that heavy equipment I haul up from the Springs for you that you still owe me for."

Releasing her, Hank scowled as the stranger whirled Daisie away. Moments later another gentleman took Daisie in his trembling arms. He had barely time to mumble his name and ask hers before yet another man cut in. And another.

Five songs later Daisie pantingly begged off and slipped through the crowd in search of the door and fresh air. She had seen no sign of Tyler. Despite the excitement of being the object of nearly every man's interest, he was the only one on her mind.

She couldn't reach the doorway for knots of milling men. Dropping into a chair, she watched Hank two-stepping his sister in a far corner. By the jostle of Amelia's curls and Hank's reddened face, she knew they were arguing.

"What brings you to Cripple Creek, ma'am?" a man asked, lurching to a stop in front of her. He bowed, his eyes as slicked as the sides of a week-old herring.

Blinking at the stocky man's audacity, Daisie stared at the watch fob swinging from a heavy gold chain draped across the bulging front of his vest. The large lumpy nugget of soft lustrous yellow metal made her seethe to think such crude, impertinent men could be rich while her father lived in a hovel.

"The name's Belvis Laker. I just come up from Leadville to see how this here boom is coming along. Got me three claims working, and me and my hired boys, we're pulling two hundred dollars a day. Ain't bad, considering. I see you ain't married — no rings on your hand there. Can't see no escort hanging about, neither. A sane man wouldn't let a humdinger like you out of his sight a minute. Care to dance? I got a bottle of whiskey up in my hotel suite, too, if you're dry."

Blood rushed to Daisie's cheeks. Her heart raced with indignation. Oh, what she would say if she did have a drink of whiskey near. She straightened, face composed in a bland, aloof expression. After a moment of pointed silence, she looked about as if suddenly remembering something and rose from her seat.

As if seeing the man for the first time, Daisie gave him a brief, puzzled smile, said, "Oh, excuse me," and moved briskly away around the room to the other side. If only Hank were as easy to ignore.

Standing alone, Daisie sensed that the milling miners skirting the center group of dancers were giving her a wide berth. She felt lonely and wished suddenly that she hadn't come. Several ladies looked at her and her gown with curiosity mixed with speculation and then turned away to exchange rather loud opinions of the Salters' "friend." Annoyed, Daisie forced herself to look amused and interested in everything around her. She'd not let them see she was aware they were snubbing her.

She had about decided to leave when she turned and saw a man in a fringed coat watching her from the doorway. He swept off his Stetson and grinned. All her discomfort vanished. For one breathless instant Daisie felt gloriously beautiful, like the most beautiful woman in the room — or maybe in the world. Her body tingled and she felt a surge of delight at seeing that face, that smile, those cornflower blue eyes that made her want to hold out her arms and say save me!

But then the joy was gone, erased by the fact that the smile and eyes belonged to a speculator who was exploiting the Brownings to further some scheme of his own.

She wanted to run. She wanted to freeze Tyler with her indifferent silence and excuse herself, just as she had that fellow who offered her whiskey in his suite.

She wanted to turn away. But an uncontrollable little smile turned up her lips. She felt the blindness of her desire for Tyler overtaking her better judgment. She felt the sinking, melting, yielding weakness in her legs and stood helpless as Tyler approached, teeth flashing and fringes dancing.

"You really put Laker in his place, Miss Browning. I guess there's a lot to be said for propriety. Good evening. Are we on speaking terms or must I slay a dragon or two to be worthy of you tonight?" He cocked his head and smiled irresistibly.

"How nice to see you, Tyler."

"Oh, yes. Fine weather we're having. What other polite exchanges must we endure? You're looking ravishing, enchanting, delectable and other assorted things I shall not mention for fear you'll slap me. Where, may I ask, are your heel-dogging companions, the Salters?"

Sighing, Daisie shook her head. She couldn't seem to summon enough anger to reject him. "Why didn't you answer my note?'' She realized that many people were eavesdropping and that her question sounded most interesting, offering unlimited room for conjecture.

"Note? I've been out of town for more than a week — in Denver, if you're curious. I didn't get out to the claim until this morning. Your father told me you'd been here nearly as long. At the Salters. Are you a glutton for punishment or do you really enjoy their company?''

"Is Papa doing all right?'' she broke in. "I hate being away. I'm . . . waiting for an important letter.''

"He looked well. If I'd known you were in town I would have come to see you before going out. I could have given you a ride."

Daisie narrowed her eyes. "How is Carla?"

Tyler's brows drew together. "You know her?''

"We met, briefly. I believe she's quite fond of you.'' Daisie's voice was cool.

"We've been friends quite a while. How did you meet her?''

"I gave her a note, which she said she'd pass on to you. When you didn't answer it, I thought — —''

Tyler saw Hank and Amelia closing in on them. "We can't talk here. Will you come out — Oh, Colonel Darnel, excuse me." He signaled to a man nearby. "I'd like this gentleman to meet you, Daisie.''

Amelia caught Tyler's sleeve just as he was about to lead Daisie away. "Tyler, you bad boy, isn't it awful how all the men are swarming around Daisie? It's almost indecent. They don't even see me.'' She pouted, rolling her eyes. "I'm so jealous. Won't you dance with me and make me feel better?''

Hank scowled. "Tyler probably doesn't dance,'' he said. "How are you, Reede?''

Tyler sighed, turned a patient smile on Amelia and patted her hand. "Amelia, you remember Colonel Darnel. Colonel, this is Miss Amelia Salter and her brother Hank. And *this* is Daisie.''

The colonel, a large, tall man who looked as if he missed his cigar, spoke gravely, nodding, his eyes never leaving Daisie's face. Taking her hand, he smiled. "I hear your father made a small strike. My congratulations."

"How very kind, Colonel," Daisie said.

"Isn't it just uncanny how it happened, too?" Amelia said, eyeing Daisie. "And so soon after Daisie met Tyler."

Daisie tried to remain polite. "Do you own many claims, Colonel?"

"A few. Tyler and I do a little business in land now and again. How's the store, Salter? Did you get that loan you were after?"

Hank mumbled something. He seemed more interested in keeping an eye on his sister, who was sidling next to Tyler, than in talking to the colonel.

The colonel made no remark but exchanged pointed looks with Tyler, noted Amelia's hands locked possessively around Tyler's elbow and returned his attention to Daisie.

For ten agonizing minutes they exchanged pleasantries about England, the East and travel in general, while Daisie fumed impatiently to be alone with Tyler and ask about his meeting with her father.

Just when Daisie thought she and Tyler might break away, Hank gave Amelia one last hot look of warning and swept Daisie into his arms. "I never did get a complete dance with you."

Daisie squawked with surprise, "If you don't mind, I'd rather — "

Amelia tipped up a triumphant face to Tyler, whispered something and led him onto the dance floor, too. Daisie was forced to follow Hank's lead while straining to watch Tyler and Amelia together.

"I imagine you've noticed my sister's pretty interested in that scoundrel, Tyler," Hank said, his voice low. "She can't seem to help herself. He uses some kind of animal magnetism on his women. I try to keep Amelia away from him, but — "

Daisie watched Tyler swirl Amelia effortlessly around the floor, holding her far tighter than Daisie thought necessary. Shutting out the vexing sight, she concentrated on avoiding Hank's leaden feet.

"Have you noticed how interested I am in you?" He backed her into a burly miner with a beard. "Watch it," he snapped, jerking Daisie aside.

Daisie tried to slip free. "I'm tired, Hank. I don't want to dance now."

His grip tightened. "I want you to look at me like you do Tyler."

Daisie stumbled. "I couldn't . . I don't . . . . Let me go! I don't want to dance with you any longer. I think you know precisely how I feel about you."

Hank somehow managed to keep her circling, backing and backing until they were in a corner. His eyes were steady, his lips moist as he licked them. "I want permission to court you."

"Don't be silly."

His arm tightened hurtfully around her waist. "I am very serious. I love you."

"Don't say that! I mean it, Hank, don't or I'll — I won't go back to the store, and Amelia will want to know why. I'll . . . I'll tell her what happened the night my money disappeared!"

"What happened?" he whispered.

"Why, you — " She lowered her voice and ducked her head. "You grabbed me!"

"I thought you called out to me!" he said with a look of injured innocence. "There's been something between us from the moment we met."

Revulsion, she thought. "Let me go!"

"I want to court you!"

"In another week I'll have left Cripple Creek forever," Daisie hissed. "I have no intention of entering on a relationship with anyone. And I might add that you're not treating me as a lady wishes to be treated. How can I allow you to court me when you behave like a boor? Release my hand!"

His head came forward as if he meant to persuade her with a kiss. After an instant of startled panic, Daisie stumbled. "Oh! My ankle. Do let's sit down." She limped dramatically to the sidelines. Dancers turned. Confused, Hank released his crush-

ing grip on her. Then understanding dawned. With hands everywhere they didn't belong, he assisted her to a chair, fussing for
the sake of the gathering crowd and asking if he must fetch the
doctor. Tyler had been watching and joined them, Amelia close
at his heels.

In the commotion, Tyler managed to take Daisie's hand.
They disappeared out the door, leaving behind a crowd of people all talking at once.

"I'm surprised you didn't slap him," Tyler said, as they
hurried along the deserted street.

"I wanted to!" she said. She was shaking with fury. "He
has the most peculiar notion that I like him. Nothing could
be further from the truth. I wouldn't stay at their store if I had
a penny left to my name. I spent the last of my money on a
telegram. If the reply doesn't come soon — " She shuddered
to imagine going back to that cubicle now without a pistol to
hold Hank at bay.

"You're the star of the dance tonight, Daisie. I've never seen
anyone more beautiful than you. I thought Amelia would kill
you with her jealous stares."

"You dance quite nicely, Tyler. Did Amelia teach you, or
was it Carla?"

He sighed, assuming a patient expression. "I can see we have
a great deal to talk over."

"We certainly do."

Daisie let him steer her into the comforting privacy of the
surrounding darkness. He seemed to know the way toward
solitude and calm.

"Your father and I finished roofing the cabin today. He moved
in and likes it. At least he's safe from that bear. He said you
came to town to contact your friends for that loan."

She strolled silently with Tyler, wondering how she might
approach him on the subject that had kept her awake for so
many nights — the question of his salting the claim. If she and
her papa left soon, did it matter how Tyler earned his money?

"Will Papa and I find it difficult returning the two claims to you, Tyler?'' She thought perhaps that would draw him out.

"I consider both claims his . . . and yours. You may sell them, if you like.''

For what pittance? she wondered.

"You might get a good price.''

"Oh, yes, I forgot, because of the float you and I . . . found.''

"You don't sound pleased by the prospect. Not that I thought your father would want to sell, but it's an option.''

They reached a freight office where, outside the door, stood a narrow bench. Tyler dusted it. Daisie sank down, her thoughts and emotions in turmoil. Just being near Tyler emptied her head of logic, making even the salting of a claim and the resulting unfair profits from land sales seem unimportant.

"Your father was quite   distant today,'' Tyler said, taking Daisie's hand. "The two of you are sometimes very confusing. I never know where I stand. When I first took you to the camp I felt everything was fine between us — more than fine, if you want to know. When you got the idea I was trying to entrap you with another claim — which you asked to have — I felt in time you'd see for yourself I wanted only to be of help to you and your father. You seemed to enjoy being angry with me.'' He paused and thought. "I decided not to get involved with you, since you were bound to leave. Yet I can't seem to get you out of my blood, Daisie. Now I see you're still cherishing false ideas about me. I don't care for suspicious, difficult women. I'll say this much; Carla and I are friends. I'm aware she cares more for me than I do for her. I've made myself clear on that point. I don't lead her on. You'll have to accept that, because I won't defend myself to you every time you take it into your head to distrust me. I still feel distance between us and want to clear it up.''

She felt nothing but the warm pressure of his fingers wrapped around hers. Not wanting to spoil the moment, she said nothing. Her face suddenly flared hot and prickly as words spilled out of her mouth from nowhere. "Tyler, would you kiss me?''

The excitement of her unexpected question trembled between them. She turned her face to look directly into Tyler's eyes.

She saw warmth and an eagerness as delightful and gratifying as that she had once seen in Norwood's eyes and saw constantly in Hank's. But with Tyler she knew there was more — an exchange of that warmth and eagerness between his eyes and her own and a response from her that made all logical thought impossible. Was Tyler sincere, or was he simply an expert at seduction? Did it matter? He held her spellbound. For this dark, silent, charged moment she wanted to be spellbound, helpless, in his control.

Expecting something explosive, Daisie was surprised when Tyler's lips pressed chastely against her own for only a second. Then he drew away. "Was that some sort of test?"

She pulled away suddenly. It had been and she hadn't known it. "I'm not being straightforward, Tyler. I'm sorry. Something is on my mind . . . and on Papa's. Something quite serious."

He didn't attempt to take her hand again, though he moved more tightly against her, forcing her to remain in contact with his side, confusing her with the hard press of his leg against hers. All she wanted was to fall against him and feel again that possessive passion he had let her taste that first day on the way to camp.

Drawing a clean, cold breath and shivering, Daisie spoke her thoughts as best she could. "Last week when you brought the ore sample from the assayer, you said it was high-grade ore."

He nodded.

"And when I asked for the adjoining claim you let us have it on loan as well as the first."

He continued to nod.

"Since then we've heard that several claims near ours were sold, likely bringing sizable profits to the sellers."

"That happened, yes," Tyler said.

Her head began throbbing. She put her fingertips to her forehead. Her throat became thick and she couldn't speak without revealing her emotions. Softly, she asked, "What is salting a claim?"

She heard his breath drawn in sharply. His leg was no longer pressed against hers. The sudden lowering of his voice reflected his instant, cold understanding. "Someone's accused me of salting your father's claim?"

She hung her head as if she was the culprit.

"Hank or Amelia? Or both?" he asked dryly.

"They rode out . . . and told us what they suspected. Papa told me to return to town and get the loan so we can go home. But I wanted to talk to you — " She lifted her face "I gave Carla the note, and she assured me she would pass it on to you."

"You just figured I didn't bother to answer," Tyler said darkly. He tapped his hat against his knee. "I didn't get it, Daisie."

"Never mind, then. Just tell me you didn't salt the claim, and I'll put the entire matter out of my mind."

"That's all it will take to convince you this time?" he asked.

"Yes, I see that it doesn't matter. Papa and I will be gone soon, regardless. I shall never . see you again." Her heart twisted.

"What is it that makes you distrust me?" Tyler seized her shoulders. "Look at me. Tell me you think that I'd swindle old men and that I'd stoop to attract your favor by dropping gold ore at your feet."

He shook her slightly, and her eyes widened. She wanted him to go on shaking the silly notions out of her head until he — And he did just as she wanted. He drew her close and kissed her deeply, bending her to him with the force of his gentle strength, molding his lips against hers with a fierce determination.

Then suddenly he released her. He stood, clapped his hat on and glanced down as if about to say something. His mouth twisted into a hard line of self-control. "Come on!" He brought her to her feet, not roughly, but not as a lover might.

"You haven't said you didn't do it," she blurted, stumbling after him.

He whirled. "You tell me, Daisie!"

He was not laughing. That surprised her. She had asked him to his face because in her imagination she'd heard him laugh at the accusations.

His anger frightened her. She didn't want to be with him now. Ahead was the comforting darkness, and beyond the glare of the brightly lit town hall and the ear-splitting orchestra music. She didn't want to go back. She didn't want to fight off Hank and spar with Amelia.

"Tyler, please."

"Not this time, Daisie! I'm taking you back to your *friends*. Don't worry, I won't start a fight with Hank. He's not worth the effort. I hope you come to see that, in time. I'd say more, but my mother taught me to keep my ungentlemanly thoughts to myself. She may have plowed her own fields and had the hands of a farmer, but she was a lady, and *her* loyalty was beyond question. She judged men by their eyes, not their words. What do you see in my eyes, Daisie?" He pushed his face close to hers.

She wouldn't look at him. "I've been accosted, ogled and robbed. Every man I meet thinks me fair game. I don't know you, and if you want to know what I see in your eyes, I'm just not sure! You've made money because of our 'strike,' so it shouldn't matter to you what I see when I look at you. And, after all, you can come and go as you please, while Papa and I are prisoners here! If I'm careful and that inconveniences you when you're feeling . . . romantic . . . then I'm terribly sorry! But if you were innocent of profiting by my father's reduced position you wouldn't get so angry when I try to be honest with you. You've taken my questions badly. I expected better."

He laughed bitterly. "My mother also warned me about the upper classes, their public manners and private opinions. You're awfully proper, Miss Browning, but inside I fear you're like all the rest — suspicious and coy."

"That's not fair." Her words came out small and hurt.

He looked startled, as if he realized he had wounded her more than he intended.

"I can get back to the dance alone, thank you," she said, feeling her eyes stinging with tears.

He stood a long moment, arms hanging at his sides, the fringes no longer dancing. Then he struck off, taking long angry strides away toward the saloons, the card tables and the voluptuous, gaudy women who knew how to please him.

It was just as well, she told herself, watching him disappear. She'd be leaving soon. A moan escaped from her tight throat. She paused in a shadow, forcing her thoughts away from Tyler and the soft brush of his warm lips. Soon she'd be home with her mother again. Then she would cry, she thought, remembering his smile and the press of his hand. Then she would cry.

Chapter Ten

"What does she say?" Amelia asked as she and Daisie emerged from the post office.

Daisie paused. "I can't read and walk, too." She read several lines of Hilary Arnold's letter and then sighed. "I knew she'd be upset."

"Let me see the bank draft. I've never seen so much money on one piece of papper. Oh, she did send a lot, didn't she? Isn't that nice." Amelia handed back the bank draft, her eyes shining.

A carriage clattered by, covering them with dust. Coughing, Daisie shook out the letter and continued reading. Oh, dear, Mrs. Arnold really *was* upset! "I felt it my duty to inform your poor mother of this request," Daisie read. "That is why my reply is so long in arriving. I wanted her to know of your difficulties. She was most distressed to learn you had lost the passage money she gave you and regretted ever having you come to America with us. I blame myself entirely . . . ."

Daisie had hated lying to her mother, but even less had she wanted to tell her she had been robbed. Her mother might imagine pistols and bandits and die of fright. Bearing her shame, Daisie read on to the end. "My husband and I agree that you must return to us at once. I've sent ample funds to bring both you and your father back, but regardless, *you* must return. This has gone on long enough. I fear this is all putting your dear mother under a terrible strain."

Wilting with remorse, Daisie lifted her eyes. "She's hiding something. Mother must be ill." Forgetting Amelia, she rushed toward the bank. Even there she could find no peace. Miners stood ten deep at each of the three tellers' windows. Some held chamois bags of gold dust. Others brandished paychecks. While in line, Daisie reread the letter. "I wonder why she didn't send along Mother's letter," she thought out loud as Amelia tried to read over her shoulder.

After cashing the bank draft, Daisie folded the thick stack of bills into her reticule, thrilled to think that tomorrow she'd take her father by the collar — if necessary — and head home. She and Amelia returned to the store, where Daisie busied herself packing. Amelia had little to say, and Hank stayed as far from Daisie as possible. She was glad of that.

Hank closed the store that evening as usual, and they took their supper at a nearby restaurant. "This may be my last night in Cripple Creek," Daisie said over dessert.

"We'll miss you," Amelia said, her eyes warmer than they had been in some time.

Hank gazed at Daisie reproachfully, and at odd moments she found him brushing against her, reaching for something and letting his hand linger over hers. She was afraid he might blurt out his feelings again, so did her best to keep the frequent lulls in the conversation filled with inane talk. She discussed Norwood and his family's estate. As the names Lord and Lady Poole rolled off her tongue, she realized that Hank and Amelia probably thought she was discussing equals. She didn't bother to enlighten them.

"I think I shall rent a small wagon tomorrow for my trunks," she said as they left the restaurant and walked toward the darkened store. Amelia went inside, but Hank detained Daisie at the side door in what amounted to an alleyway.

"May I talk to you, Daisie?" he asked, his voice low and husky as he blocked her way.

Instantly she was on the alert. "Please, Hank. Let's part on friendly terms."

Before she could move out of his reach, he grabbed her and

hugged her. His open mouth sought her lips, but when she kept twisting away he whispered, "I love you! Let me take care of you and your father. I'll build him a real cabin. I'll give him everything he needs. Say you love me, too! Daisie, darling, you're so beautiful — "

She struggled to break his hold and was alarmed by how strong he was. "I warned you before, Hank. Stop it. You're hurting me!"

He seized the back of her head, trying to hold her still long enough so he could kiss her. Roughly he pinned her arms behind her back. The more she struggled the worse it hurt, so finally she stopped resisting.

"Hank — "

His mouth closed hotly over hers. He forced his tongue deep into her mouth, making her moan in protest.

"Stop it!" she gasped, jerking free at last. "How can you treat me this way and call it love? You don't know the meaning of the word!"

She whirled away, making for the door. "I wouldn't spend another night under the same roof with you if my life depended on it."

He caught her arm. "I'm sorry! I don't know what I'm doing. You've got me crazy for you. The way you kept looking at Tyler Reede, I thought you wanted to be treated like a . . . like that. I didn't know what I was doing. Don't tell Amelia!"

"I will! I will tell her!"

"Tyler Reede will take you for all you're worth. Let me help you! You can't leave town without selling your claim and he won't give your father a tenth of its value. Let me handle the deal. I know ways to get around Tyler!"

Daisie bit back a sharp retort.

"Tyler Reede's after whatever he can get," Hank hissed, his teeth bared. "If he hasn't gotten it from you already."

Ice flooding Daisie's veins, she paused and leveled scorn-filled eyes at him. "You're a fine one to talk! Tyler's a thousand times better than you'll ever be! Get out of my way, and don't touch me again. Ever! I'll send someone for my trunks — "

"I didn't mean it! Say you forgive me, Daisie! I'm out of my head. Look what you've done to me. I'm a good, decent man, but you've driven me crazy. I've tried to keep away from you, but when I see how you look at me I think you're yearning for me as much as I am for you. Don't turn away. Let me — "

He swung her around and wrenched her against his chest, holding her painfully hard against him. She felt herself being bent backwards and, as his mouth smothered her again, a scream rose in her throat, and she clawed to be free. A cry of protest broke from her when he drove his knee between her thighs, nudging her in a way that left her in no doubt about his intentions.

"My God, what are you doing?" Amelia came out the side door and stood for a moment dumbfounded before tearing Hank's hands away from Daisie's bodice. "Let her go, you damn fool!" she screamed, pummeling his arm, her teeth gritted and her eyes blazing. "Do you want somebody to see this?" She slugged his ear with a yelp of fury and started slapping at his head and neck. "Don't touch her like that! Damn you! Damn you, you stupid jackass!"

Clutching his head, Hank released Daisie and staggered away.

"What the hell are you doing?" Amelia screeched, swinging at Hank. "Are you crazy? Do you know what you've done — " She clutched at her hair and whirled. "I'm sorry, Daisie! I don't know what's come over him. Let's get inside before someone hears us."

Hank stared open-mouthed at Daisie. His slicked hair stood on end, and he appeared dazed and confused.

Daisie shuddered. "I'm sleeping somewhere else tonight, thank you." She pushed past Amelia and raced into the building and up the stairs. Once inside her cubicle she couldn't think what to do. She was trembling so much she had to sit down. Opening the small trunk, she reached for her nightdress to begin packing, but her heart quailed. Where would she go?

Below, she heard Amelia and Hank arguing amid the sound of scuffling and slaps. Daisie clutched at the cash that she'd laced beneath the front of her corset that afternoon. She had to take out enough to rent a room. Her hands shook so that she could barely count out the bills, but she gritted her teeth. She would *not* cry.

Heavy footsteps came up the stairs. Daisie's head jerked up. Her heart leaped in terror. "Who's there?" she cried, wondering if it was Hank coming to have his way after all.

"Somebody who's going to see about it if you don't stop carrying on," growled a surly voice near the stairs.

Daisie almost wept with relief. Hank wouldn't dare hurt her with someone else near.

White-faced and disheveled, Amelia tore the canvas flap aside. Her burning eyes raked Daisie from head to toe and then took in the open trunk. "You don't have to go. Hank's got his senses back. I'll make him stay outside all night. It's what he deserves."

"It doesn't matter to me where he goes tonight. I've had enough of him! This isn't the first time Hank has forced his brutal advances on me, I assure you! I think he's dangerous."

Amelia steadied herself. "Not the first . . . ?"

"He's been pawing me and making suggestive remarks from the very beginning," Daisie spat. "Your brother is an animal."

Gathering her wits, Amelia let the flap fall shut behind her and edged close. Daisie felt a surge of renewed alarm.

"Let me explain — "

"Shut up out there, or I'm getting my five dollars back and renting somewhere else!" the unseen boarder called.

Amelia threw back her head. "Shut up yourself! See if you can find another room this late."

Daisie closed the small trunk and grabbed up her shawl.

Amelia stepped in her way. "Now listen here, Daisie. My brother didn't do anything he didn't think you already wanted. You've been smiling and sweet-talking him all along. He just naturally assumed you liked him. You've driven him to this, and I saw it coming, but I didn't say anything because I figured you didn't know any better. Maybe Tyler understands what you're up to when you flirt with him, but Hank took you seriously."

"I never — "

Amelia shook her mussed curls. Her eyes were angry. "I

warned you about so many things. About riding alone with Tyler, about wearing that . . . that shocking dress. Only a Jezebel would display her bosoms that way! Don't think we didn't hear about you drinking in that saloon, either. Disgraceful! I can't hold up my head in this town, thanks to your low behavior. You saw how I was shunned at the dance."

Thunderstruck, Daisie dropped to the cot. "Your brother is no gentleman," she hissed. "If you hadn't stopped him, he would have raped me. And I'll bet I'm not the only woman he's assaulted. I am not staying here another night! Get out of my way!" She moved to get up, but Amelia shoved her back.

"You haven't a hope of finding another room tonight. This is a boom town, remember. Men fight to sleep under a table."

"They're not flocking here, I see," Daisie snapped.

"I'm trying to be nice about this, Daisie."

"You're trying — " Daisie laughed and sat seething. Did it matter if she stayed one more night? Did it matter what she did now that she could leave?

Amelia folded her arms across her breast and lifted her chin, eyebrows raised, cheeks hollow and mouth pursed. "I've thrown my own brother out into the cold. What more do you want? You've succeeded in ruining us, and you've destroyed my brother. Led him on, broken his heart and shamed him! You taunt him and then condemn him when he confesses his love. You're no better than that painted *cow* you were seen drinking with in the saloon. Everyone is talking about that little trick of yours. When you were robbed, why didn't you just go out and earn back the money *that way*? It obviously comes to you naturally."

Too stunned to speak, Daisie reared up and tried to slap Amelia. "You — You ugly little — You're little better than a hussy yourself, Amelia Salter!"

Amelia blocked her swing. "That's right. Call me names! I've tried to be your friend. It hasn't been easy the way you've had your nose so far up in the air."

"Just shut up!" Daisie said, hot anger suddenly turning to icy hate. "If I stay tonight will you just *shut up*?"

Amelia stood rigid, fists clenched at her sides. Her eyes moved to every corner of the cubicle as she fought for composure. At last she looked at Daisie with such loathing Daisie suspected she must be mad to say she'd stay. But Amelia was right, rooms were terribly scarce. She dared not remain on the streets alone, not with hundreds of dollars laced beneath her corset, not with Hank Salter wandering loose.

"Will you lock Hank out?" Daisie said.

"Yes," Amelia hissed. "Yes! For the Queen of England I'll do anything. You know," she added, her eyes glinting with hatred, "I liked you better as a dirty, freckle-faced little squatter. At least then you didn't look down on everyone. I hope your bag of money keeps you warm tonight, Daisie Browning, because it's a sure bet you haven't a friend left in this town."

"If I led Hank on I most certainly did not mean to."

"Oh, no, of course not!" Amelia sneered. "I don't see how one person can cause so much pain! My brother deserves better! I never saw Hank behave like that. Never! I doubt he ever kissed a girl before."

Daisie found that exceedingly difficult to believe. "If he lays another hand on me, I'll have him arrested," she said softly, meaning every word.

The boarder's voice boomed out. "Aren't you females done blubbering yet?"

Whirling, Amelia stormed out through the flap and down the hall. "You want quiet, fella?" she screamed. "You've got it. Get out! Here's your damn five dollars back. Get out and don't come back. I'm sick of being forced to take in boarders. Filthy, lazy and ungrateful, every one! A person's got to make a living and tries to be decent . . . . I'm sick to death of trying! Get out before I have my brother throw you out!"

Daisie listened as the man scrambled down the stairs muttering, "Damned, crazy females . . . ."

A few minutes later Amelia went down the stairs and out the side door, slamming it. Her voice carried from outside where apparently Hank had been waiting. A few harsh words were abruptly hushed. After a lengthy silence, Daisie investigated each cubicle to be certain she was alone. With her ear cocked for Amelia's return, she loosened her stays and took out the thick stack of bills. As she changed into her nightdress, she thought again of leaving, but decided that, as long as Hank was locked outside, she'd endure one last night in the cubicle. She hated abandoning the trunks again, but if she remained and hired a wagon in the morning, she'd be able to haul them safely herself, instead of having to rely on Amelia to release them to a messenger.

She tied the money up in her stockings and rolled that into a neat package inside her corset, tying everything with the corset laces. Let someone try to get this money, she thought. She decided to tie the package to the legs of the cot. As she lay down with a heavy heart, she listened for Amelia, remembering all the ugly things that had been said.

A quarter of an hour later, Amelia came up, sniffing loudly. "I've locked both doors. You can check them if you don't believe me. Hank's gone, so you don't have to worry about him trying to get in."

"Thank you," Daisie whispered. Why, why, why did she feel as if she had done something terrible? Why did every man treat her like a tramp? Unhappily, she drifted into sleep, longing for home.

Coughing, Daisie reared up. Throwing off the blanket, she sprang to her feet, stumbling in dazed circles. With eyes stinging, nostrils choked with thick, dark smoke, she fumbled in the darkness trying to get her bearings. Smoke?

Smoke! Without another thought, she flailed at the canvas flap as Amelia screamed, "Fire!"

Daisie was nearly to the stairs when she crashed into Amelia and the two of them slid and bumped their way to the bottom in grunts and wails of terror.

Daisie grabbed at the barred outside door. "How do I open it?" she screamed, jerking at the handle.

Everything was so dark! The smoke was choking her. Behind, a high stack of crates tumbled to the floor, grazing her shoulder.

She grabbed at the door to the main room but saw a raging orange glow coming from the crack beneath it. She clutched Amelia's arm. "Don't go in there!"

"The store! We'll be ruined!" Amelia shrieked, yanking at the locked inner door. Almost at her touch it ignited from top to bottom in a rectangle of licking orange flames that seared their faces and drove them backwards against the stairs.

Amelia's tortured scream filled the darkness. "Help! Hank, help!"

Daisie fumbled to get the outside door open, pinching her fingers badly as she lifted the stout wooden bar that held it closed. She almost knocked Amelia silly flinging it out of the way. They burst into the chilled night air, gasping and sobbing. Above, the inky sky glittered, but was quickly covered by a swell of angry black smoke billowing into the sky.

"Fire! Fire!" Amelia screamed, shoving Daisie out of her way as she dashed for the street.

Daisie staggered, rubbing her burning eyes. Coughing painfully, she stumbled away from the heat and roaring flames to lean against the wall of the barbershop next door. For several seconds she rested there, her lungs aching, knowing nothing but that she was safe.

Men swarmed in from every direction, yelling and coughing. Some called excitedly, "Look't her burn!"

Daisie shielded her eyes against the blinding glare. Hank ran around from the front of the store, his face twisted with agonized disbelief. "Oh, no! Not my store!" he yelled at the top of his lungs. He made one attempt for the rear door but met a roaring wall of reaching, surging flames. He dashed around to the front again, grabbing at his hair, waving his arms. "No! No-o-o!"

Men rushed into the space between the buildings, crashing into Daisie, knocking her off balance. Brilliant yellow-white flames leaped and danced in the side windows. A furious glow poured fourth from the large front windows. Smoke curled thickly from beneath the doors and from cracks around the side windows. Shouting, running men were everywhere. Then the windows began to shatter, raining hot glass onto the roaring men fighting to get out of the way.

Bowled over, Daisie clawed her way to her feet, grabbing whatever arm or shoulder she could find. She fought her way to the street and ran crying away. Her lungs burned, the gravel stung her feet. She could feel the clammy night air swirling against her skin, cutting through her thin cambric nightdress as if she was wearing nothing.

When two strong arms clamped around her, she screamed and fought to be free. Then she saw the cornflower blue eyes, the mouth she knew so well, the curve of a hard, handsome cheek. She let Tyler gather her up as she buried her face against his chest, panting and sobbing with relief.

His hands were strong, almost hot against her shoulder blades. She could feel the lapels of his coat feathery soft against her cheeks, and the hard bite of his silver belt buckle against her waist.

"Tyler! Tyler!" she coughed, feeling his hands slipping to her waist to lift her slightly against him, then moving around just enough to graze the sides of her breasts. "Hold me!" she cried, straining her face upwards, tucking her face into the strong, corded warmth of his neck and shoulder. She kissed the warm skin, coiled her arms around his neck, lacing her fingers into his brown, silky hair. She felt rather than heard him moan in response.

In the distance the fire bell clanged raucously. Spectators roared with excitement. Seconds later came the frantic, muted thunder of galloping horses. Someone shouted orders through a horn. A large group of men tried to salvage parts heaped behind the store by carrying them out into the safety of the street. Somewhere Hank was shouting for help, shouting and shouting, as if all those crowding around were unwilling, or too slow to suit him.

Sniffing, trembling, Daisie drew away from Tyler, aware she had been pawing him. She went limp. "I've had enough. I shall be so glad when — "

Her head came up. Her heart stopped. She screamed and

started running back toward the flames, arms outstretched. "The money!"

Tyler chased her and caught her roughly around the waist. Grunting, she felt herself whipped around and held, her feet dangling off the ground.

"Tyler, the money! Let me go! I must get — "

"Have you gone crazy? You can't go back in there!"

Wailing, she struggled and twisted to look back, to see the triumphant flames curling out of the upper window. Smoke oozed all along the roof line. If only she could faint, she thought. Everything was so hopeless.

Tyler slung her effortlessly into his arms and carried her to the nearest walkway. There it was dark, cool, private. Men rushed by, but she paid them no heed. Tyler sat her on the edge of the walkway, squatted before her and peered into her face. "Are you hurt?" He brushed back some hair blowing across her eyes and then laid his hand against her forehead.

She shook her head.

"Some of your hair's been badly singed," he said softly. "Are you sure you're not hurt? Let me see your hands."

She allowed him to examine her hands. Feeling her mouth turning down at the corners, she turned away so that he would not see her cry. Then he was slipping his warm, heavy fringed coat over her shivering shoulders. She clutched it around herself, huddling inside it like a child.

"What are you doing here? Where did you come from?" she asked, feeling hopelessly weary.

"I was drinking with some friends when we heard somebody yell fire. I went out to see where it was. I thought it looked like it was over this way, so I came to have a closer look. When I saw it *was* the store, you were running and screaming down the street toward me. Do you know how it started?"

"I don't care. I hate this town! This afternoon I got the money I've been waiting for for nearly two weeks, and now — " Her voice caught. She wanted to scream.

"Then you'll be — " Tyler's eyes widened and grew soft with pity. "The money's still inside? I'm so sorry, Daisie."

She shook her head and laughed. "I don't believe it! Twice! How will I ever explain?"

"Let's go back and have a look. Maybe they can salvage something. It'll take a hot fire to destroy the contents of your trunks. Daisie. Daisie, look at me. It's only money. Thank God it wasn't you!"

He kissed her lightly, but she went on weeping. "I shall never get home!" She collapsed against him, feeling weak and drained. Then she thought of all her pretty frocks, all lost. "The money wasn't in a trunk, Tyler." She looked up and laughed at herself as she went on sobbing. "I didn't want to be robbed again, so I tied it to the bed . . . all done up in my corset and laces."

He broke into a grin. Then he was laughing. Pulling her to her feet, he drew her close and held her, patting her gently. "Daisie, Daisie, my precious. You are so wonderfully dear."

She lifted her face and let his mouth cover hers. It was warm, gentle, tantalizingly soft. She strained against him, grateful for his comfort and strength. When his hands tightened around her back, caressing her through the thin nightdress, she didn't feel afraid or draw away. She wanted him to hold her and never let her go. For a wild moment she wanted everything with him, and she let her desire pulse in her response.

Tyler tore himself free and looked down into her eyes, his own only shadows. Dragging in a ragged breath, he turned to look back at the building. The store's walls looked starkly black, the windows blazing orange, the roof a sea of yellow-white flame reaching and reaching upward into a black thunderhead of smoke. "Your cash is gone, then."

He drew her along to the edge of the crowd. Working frantically, the fire brigade was pumping a stout stream of water in the front windows, but it was clearly hopeless.

In a cascade of orange and red, the left front of the store collapsed. A smoldering lump rolled to a stop in the rubble, but as two men attempted to jockey it away with long poles, the trunk caught and blazed. Daisie imagined her engraved stationery turning to ash, her hankies, stockings and sewing kit so much black waste. She leaned against Tyler's solid strength and groaned.

Wind scattered firebrands onto neighboring rooftops. The crowd shifted, interested now in the furniture store next door. A distraught owner appeared in trousers and nightshirt, yelling for help. Everyone began carting goods into the street when a portion of the roof caught in the rear where the pumper couldn't reach.

Smaller fires started up behind the flaming store and men rushed off to beat them out. Daisie didn't see Amelia anywhere, but Hank stood in front, wringing his hands and moaning, "I'm ruined. I'm ruined!"

From nearby came a muttered reply. "I don't know what *he's* going to do, but *I'll* be a sight better off not having to pay his prices. *Bloodsucker*."

Hank whirled, his face baleful in the orange glare and smoky shadows. "Who said that? I demand to know who said that!" His wild, enflamed eyes fell on Tyler standing with his arm around Daisie. Hank's hands curled into huge fists and he started toward them.

"Let's go, Tyler. I had trouble with Hank earlier tonight."

Tyler looked concerned, but he had no time to ask Daisie what she meant. Hank stuck his face nose to nose with Tyler's. His arms hung loose as if ready to grab Tyler's throat. "Say that to my face, Reede. I dare you."

An amused murmur rippled through the crowd.

"Let's go," Daisie whispered to Tyler. "There's nothing left of my belongings." Fearfully, she tugged on his arm.

Tyler grinned. "I didn't hear anybody say anything."

"Say it to my face!"

"At least I didn't hear anything new." Tyler didn't flinch as he stepped away from Daisie, flexing his muscled arms.

Hank lunged, but half a dozen men grabbed him, holding him back. "Dammit, let me at him! He's got it coming, going after Amelia the way he did once! I'll show him! Let me go!"

He struggled to break free, but the men held him fast. "First you go after Amelia. Then you go after Daisie, too. You stole my girl! How many women do you need, Reede? Fight me like a man! I'll take you apart. You've always been trouble for me, and I mean to get even. Let me at him!''

"Be reasonable, Salter," someone said, but Hank jabbed with his elbows, throwing the men holding him off balance.

Tyler gave Hank a look of contempt, scathing words dancing in his snapping eyes, but he said nothing and turned away. With incredible calm he walked down the street as if his face wasn't black with rage.

"Look at him!" Hank yelled. "What's he doing here? Why's he hanging around my store this time of night? He belongs in a saloon, drinking with his whores! He's a goddamned speculator! He's making money off you dumb people. He's faked a gold strike and now everybody's buying up his claims!''

"That's enough, Hank," Tyler said, pausing twenty feet away, his voice deeply menacing.

"Ask her! She's probably in on it with him!"

Daisie went cold.

Tyler turned. "If I'm a speculator, you're a bloodsucker.'' He glanced angrily at Daisie. "Everyone in this town knows Hank Salter charges everybody double, and he bleeds ignorant greenhorns triple for everything they buy. He charged your father four times what the prospecting equipment was worth.''

The gathered men murmured darkly, but another blaze had started on the roof next to the furniture store. It was possible the whole street might go up in flames. Everyone turned away, arguing how best to save the other shacks. The pumper turned away from Hank's store, leaving it to collapse in puffs and plumes of flame. Daisie edged back as the men forgot Hank and Tyler's dispute and ran to man the buckets.

Hank looked at the fountains of sparks, his face etched with anguish. He gave Daisie one searing look, then brushed past her to pound down the street after Tyler. "Did you set fire to my store, Reede? Is that your way of getting Daisie for your string? It won't do you any good. She knows what you are.''

Tyler waited, head back, eyes half closed, lips compressed.

"Tyler, don't listen to him! He's crazy!'' Daisie cried.

The two men became a tornado of fists and shouts. Hank was still reaching for Tyler's throat as Tyler drove his fist into Hank's face with a teeth-gritting smile. Staggering back, grunting, Hank swung awkwardly, obviously stunned and disoriented by the first blow. His fist grazed Tyler's jaw, but Tyler swung again, sinking his fury deep into Hank's belly, again and again.

Doubling, Hank began to sink to his knees. Then he rallied, driving Tyler back with a flurry of blows that ended when Tyler delivered a mighty roundhouse that sent Hank sailing backwards. He landed heavily, with a grunt, and lay stunned.

Tyler dropped onto Hank's chest, pummeling his face, his expression deadly. "You want to lie about me, Salter, I'm going to make you eat your lies!"

"Stop!" Daisie screamed, running to them, trying to pull Tyler to his feet. Hank's face was covered with blood. "Don't, Tyler. Please!"

"He fired my store," Hank mumbled through swelling lips. "I'll have him behind bars by morning."

Daisie jerked at Tyler's collar. "Don't hit him again! Get up! Get hold of yourself! You could kill him. He's not worth it."

Staggering to his feet, Tyler drew his forearm across his bleeding lips. Daisie reached for his arm, but he flung her away.

"Reede did seem to show up pretty quick," an onlooker remarked, watching Tyler stumble away, the back of his bloodied hand against his mouth. But she had been *in* that store, Daisie thought. Tyler might make money from a staged gold strike on her father's claim, but he'd never set fire to a building with her — or anyone else — in it.

She ran after Tyler, but he threw her hands off and lurched away. Daisie stopped and looked back at the store still engulfed in flames. Fire was sweeping across the roof of the furniture store. *Could* Tyler do such a thing? Had Hank charged her father four times as much as he should have? She looked down at Hank lying on his back, moaning. They were alone now, with everyone else two stores away up the crowded street. She wanted to shake the truth from Hank. She didn't see Amelia anywhere. She wondered suddenly if she'd been hurt.

"Daisie," Hank moaned, lifting a limp, bloody hand. "Help me up."

She couldn't move. Help him? She almost laughed.

When someone appeared at her elbow and softly spoke her name, she jumped, ready to scream.

"I don't suppose you remember me, Miss Browning," the tall gentleman said. "We met at the dance. Were you introduced to my wife?"

Daisie clutched demurely at Tyler's coat still hanging around her shoulders. "Oh, Colonel Darnel, you startled me! I can't seem to think. . . . Yes, I believe I did meet your wife. She was most kind."

"You must be cold. Allow me to take you home where my wife can look after you. We have a comfortable guest room. You're welcome to stay as long as you like."

His soft, low voice filled her with gratitude. "You're too kind. I don't know what else to do. It would only be for one night. I . . . must return to my father's camp."

"You're welcome to stay as long as you like, nevertheless. Come along, my dear. And you mustn't call me Colonel. You must call me Stanley. Now, how about a nice, hot toddy to calm your nerves? Martha says I make the finest toddy west of the Mississippi River. I don't believe I caught what part of England you're from . . . ?"

As they moved down the street away from the smoke and commotion, Daisie let him weave his aura of comfort around her. "Might I beg a ride out to my father's camp in the morning?" she asked as they climbed Gold Street's hill and turned in at a tall house resplendent with gingerbread trim.

"I am at your disposal, Miss Browning. Come right in. Martha, dear, look at the poor lost kitten I've brought you. Could you see the fire from the window? Hank Salter's store is gone and Henry Danson's is on fire."

Daisie looked into the sympathetic face of a woman, wearing a gray silk dressing gown and a nightcap, whom she recognized from the dance. The woman was in her late thirties, with a wide, welcoming face and the clucking manner of a mother.

"Just look at you, dear. We're going to have to cut away some of that lovely hair." She put her arm around Daisie. "Now come upstairs and tell me all about it. . . ."

Chapter Eleven

"We were only in New York once, but I found it a lovely place. Now, Daisie, turn your head a little more. There, I think that should do it. Won't your mother be surprised to see you've fringed your forelocks?"

"She'll be heartbroken," Daisie sighed, smiling into the looking glass. "But I think I like it. Thank you." She supposed now she looked a little like a woodland fairy with gold fringes framing her tanned face. Her hair hadn't been singed too badly. She was glad the back had been spared. Coiling the heavy length into a knot, she pinned it in place and stood up from the dressing table. Mrs. Darnel had loaned her an old-fashioned shirtwaist blouse with delicate lace insets and a heavy wool skirt in a wretched shade of forest green. The waist was several inches too large, so they had made bulgy folds and basted them.

"Now, let's go down for a bite of breakfast. Later I'll hunt up some other things for you to wear."

"This is more than generous," Daisie protested.

"Nonsense. A girl as pretty as you needs more than one change of clothes."

"Not on a mountainside."

"Well, I've been hoping you'd decide to stay with us a while. We have so much to talk about. Oh, I am hungry! Isn't it amazing the variety of foods we can get here in the mountains? At a price, of course. Would you care for some bananas? I can't

get enough of them. Oh! I wonder who's at the door this early."
Mrs. Darnel went to the window and craned her neck to see
who had started knocking. "I can't see onto the front porch
from here."

Moments later Sayrah, Mrs. Darnel's maid called from the
foot of the narrow stairs. "Flowers for Miss Browning, ma'am."

Daisie's head came up. Tyler! She followed her hostess into
the narrow upstairs hall and went down to a wonderful bunch of
wildflowers done up with a huge blue satin ribbon. She plucked
the tiny white card from the bouquet and opened it, expecting to
see Tyler's name smiling at her.

"Begging your forgiveness. Henry Salter," she read.

Daisie wilted. "Oh." She forced a smile and gave the flowers back to the maid.

Mrs. Darnel had already disappeared into her parlor, chattering eagerly about the fire and asking her husband what he had
learned on his trip to town early that morning. Back in the
dining room, which commanded a view of the town's jumbled
rooftops, she clucked her tongue when Daisie joined them.

"Did you hear? Six buildings lost in the night. What a terrible shame. We have coffee and fresh rolls, with fruit, dear. And
do try a banana."

As they finished breakfast, Daisie tried to convince her host that
she was too out of practice to play their lovely piano, a massive
black grand, when another knock came at the front door.

Sayrah curtsied in the doorway. "Hank Salter and his sister
to see Miss Browning, ma'am."

"Isn't that nice," Mrs. Darnel said blandly. "They've just
lost an entire business, but they take the time to see you're all
right. I wouldn't have thought they'd . . . . You may receive
them in the parlor, dear. I'll make myself scarce."

Inwardly, Daisie groaned. She never wanted to see either of
those two again. Rising from the dining table, she turned as if
facing a firing squad and moved into the parlor. Hank entered
and stared at her. One side of his face was badly bruised. His
lips were swollen and his eyes rimmed with red. Looking sullen

and defensive, he glanced at Amelia crowding in behind him. The maid drew the sliding doors to the hall closed.

Amelia nudged her brother.

"I've come to beg your forgiveness," Hank said woodenly, turning a glossy new hat in circles. His brown ready-to-wear suit still had wrinkles where it had been folded in the box. The shirt collar looked as if it was strangling him. His bow tie was crooked.

"I'm sorry about the store, Hank, Amelia." Daisie refused to say more. When Hank stepped closer, she backed into the table, rattling the tableware.

"I don't know how I could've treated you as I did yesterday, Miss Browning," he said, looking proper and reserved. "I can't put my life back in order until you've forgiven me . . . for everything."

Terrified that the Darnels might overhear, Daisie broke in. "It's forgotten," she whispered.

Amelia's rumpled gray and tan dress appeared to have been in storage for some time — it reeked of moth balls and the skirt hung in stiff folds about her ankles. On her face was a grave, melodramatic expression that made Daisie want to laugh. "Your trunks were destroyed, Daisie. And you disappeared so quickly last night that neither of us could ask if you had time to grab up all that money you got at the bank yesterday."

Stiffening, Daisie shook her head.

Amelia moaned as if the money had been hers. "A tragedy! If only we could help." She didn't wait for Daisie's polite protest. "We lost everything, too, everything except some equipment our friends saved from behind the store. We had insurance, but — " She reached into her sleeve for a hankie and dabbed at her dry eyes.

So much for their ruination, Daisie thought, the taste in her mouth bitter. "It was thoughtful of you to stop by. Thank you for the bouquet. Goodbye — "

The sound of a buggy arriving out front drew Amelia to the window. Making a face, she turned quickly to Daisie. "No matter what people say, we didn't overcharge your father! And

I beg forgiveness for all the terrible things I said."

Rapping at the front door and the murmur of voices in the hall could be heard over Amelia's apology, but she plunged on. "Hank is willing to make amends for his behavior. If you feel you've been compromised, he'll marry you."

Daisie choked back an incredulous laugh. "Marry!"

Mrs. Darnel tapped at the parlor door and slid it open. "Goodness me, dear, you're a popular young lady! Tyler Reede to see you. Go right in, Tyler."

Tyler swung in, looking startlingly unlike himself in a dark, tailored, worsted frockcoat. He smiled when he saw Daisie in the archway, but his smile faded when he realized she wasn't alone. "Oh — I didn't know you had visitors. Just wanted to make sure you were all right, Daisie." His gaze was somber, his eyes narrow and suspicious. Daisie wished she could make Hank and Amelia vanish.

Tyler looked wonderful, his shining brown hair combed back, his skin glowing with health. Mrs. Darnel came in with his fringed leather coat and he took it without a word, throwing it over his arm. Hidden beneath the heavy folds and fringes he clutched a handful of flowers Daisie longed for him to present. He seemed to forget he had them and turned toward the door.

"You're not going already?" Daisie cried.

Tyler let his gaze wander toward Hank and Amelia. Amelia cast him a longing glance that made it crystal clear why she so disapproved of Daisie's association with Tyler. Daisie stiffened even more.

"I would have been here earlier, Daisie," Tyler said, "but I was tied up most of last night and this morning answering ridiculous charges that I started the fire at Salter's Emporium."

Daisie couldn't help glaring at Hank. "Has anyone determined what *really* started it?" she asked.

Amelia and Hank burst into talk. Despite what people said, it was impossible, they both exclaimed, that the fire had broken out when a lamp had overturned near the counter. Their argument raged, but Daisie tuned it out, looking only at Tyler.

Tyler's eyes were filled with questions, but he voiced only

one. "Are you going back to your father now?"

She nodded. "Won't you wait? Hank and Amelia were just leaving."

Amelia glared at Daisie. "We were concerned about you! If you're going to throw us out — "

Daisie sighed. "Surely after everything that's happened — "

Perhaps fearing that Daisie might mention some of what had happened the night before, Amelia grabbed her brother's arm. "We know when we're not welcome!"

But Tyler didn't wait for Amelia to complete her performance. He joined Mrs. Darnel and the colonel in the hall and spoke to them softly before he went out.

Feeling peevish that he was gone so quickly and that she hadn't had a moment to talk privately with him, Daisie went to Amelia and took her elbow. "Where will you stay until you rebuild the store?" she asked, steering the young woman toward the front hall. Hank was forced to follow.

"We'll live in a tent, I suppose," Amelia muttered.

Hank brushed against Daisie as he went out the front door after Amelia.

Daisie shuddered. "I hope it's a good tent and doesn't cost your last cent."

Amelia stopped on the porch and her eyes widened. "From the day we came to this town we've done an honest business and charged prices we felt were fair."

"No more, Amelia, please! Just go. We have nothing more to discuss. I wish you all the best in starting over."

Hank turned pleading eyes on her. Did he really love her? she wondered, genuinely puzzled.

"Goodbye," Daisie said, closing the door.

"Are they gone?" Mrs. Darnel whispered, entering the rear hall. "What a highly strung pair. Not your sort at all. Did you see that rag Amelia wore to the dance? And the way she pouted and slouched like an ill-mannered child? No one I know in this town cared for that store of theirs. Terrible prices! I'm surprised they went into the shop-keeping business, actually. They weren't at all suited to it. Hank was rude and treated his customers with contempt. Amelia wouldn't help a soul. It's not the proper way for people building a business to behave. I'm glad to see you didn't encourage them. The man had designs on you. That was obvious, but of course, you're a lady and didn't respond. When I heard those rumors about you — about the drinking, dear — I told Stanley it had to be a mistake. And then Tyler explained that you'd been delivering a note to him. I keep telling Tyler he should live in a hotel like a gentleman, but he says hotels are lonely. Of course, he's closer to the miners in his saloon, but I've told him time and again it just doesn't look right. I think you should rest before going out to your father That fire surely strained your nerves to the limit. We could spend a few days sewing you something that fits. I'd enjoy your company."

Tempted, Daisie finally shook her head. "I couldn't. I haven't seen Papa in weeks, and I must explain about the destroyed money." She laughed a little. "I'm afraid he'll be only too glad we're stranded here."

Later in the afternoon, as Daisie prepared to climb into Colonel Darnel's top-buggy, she saw the fistful of flowers Tyler had been holding that morning.

They were limp now, lying in the tall grass alongside the gatepost. She picked them up, climbed into the buggy and held them in her lap. In their wilted state they seemed to symbolize her relationship with Tyler. The colonel chatted amiably as they rode down the steep street into town and past the charred ruins of the six burnt-out stores. Men were raking through the smol dering debris, and a wagon loaded with lumber was pulling up as the colonel started away.

Refusing to think how she might have saved the money — she'd lain awake all night berating herself — Daisie forced herself to take a deep breath and hold up her head. She was glad to be returning to the comforting solitude of the mountains

The colonel amused her with stories as she directed him out of town past the overhanging rocky slabs and through the creek ford to the stretch of broad rocks leading to the aspen grove.

"It's dangerous to go much further," Daisie said, telling him where to turn and stop. Not waiting for the colonel to help her, she leaped down and dashed through the cool green shadows to stand at the edge of the meadow and look down at the camp.

"Papa still has his alarm system strung up." She pointed as the colonel joined her and explained about the bear alarm. "Come and meet my papa. He'll enjoy the company."

Jerking off the oversized high-buttoned shoes Mrs. Darnel had given her, she splashed across the creek, gasping and laughing at the icy shock of the water.

The tent still stood snugly backed against the raw rocky ledge. No fire burned in the circle of stones before it. Instead, a thin curl of smoke lifted from the mud-and-stick chimney at the side of the cabin. Now roofed over with sod, the cabin looked more like a cave than a house. The grass atop it was still green and growing, dotted with little yellow and pink flowers. The gaps between the logs had been packed with mud, giving the whole place a dirty, reddish color, as if the structure had sprouted from the earth like a mushroom.

The cabin had no door yet, and there was no window. Along the low grassy bluff was a pile of firewood. Someone had been splitting logs on nearby stump. She doubted that her father was up to such strenuous labor.

She trotted to the door and peeked in, inhaling the rich aroma of damp, cool earth inside. Going in, she saw that the fire was almost out, and added some wood.

Her father had fashioned a nice low bed from pine boughs. A quick peek under the heap of blankets showed that his mattress was a pile of pine needles. A wobbly bench leaned near the hearth, which was an arrangement of flat, pinkish flagstones. The cooking pot held some stew, and the crate of canned goods looked well stocked. She wondered if Tyler was still keeping her father in supplies. Her heart warmed to think of Tyler's continuing concern.

There was room for little else in the dark, confined cabin.

Another bed would take all the remaining space. "It's a good thing I don't have my trunks to get in the way," she said to herself with a twinge of sorrow

She ducked outside, to see the colonel and her father on the far side of the creek where the aspen grove climbed the ridge The colonel was talking excitedly, and her father was nodding as they headed back toward the cabin.

As he crossed the creek, Gregory Browning paused and looked at Daisie with a sigh. She gathered that he knew now of the fire, and ran to throw her arms around his neck. He embraced her as if unable to let her go. Then he held her back for a stern inspection. "So, my dear, you've survived yet another adventure." He frowned at her trimmed hair in front, and plucked at the wispy tendrils. Then he smiled with his lips pursed. "Dash it all, Daisie, why didn't you go home the moment you had the cash in hand?"

She sputtered in protest, until she realized that he was teasing Seated in front of the cabin, she spilled out the whole weary story, ending sadly with, "I thought today I'd be taking you home." But she could see that her father wasn't sorry to be staying. "I wrote to Mama and left the letter with Mrs. Darnel She'll mail it today."

The colonel broke in. "I should think, Lord Browning, that a letter to your lawyer would bring whatever funds you require from your bank in London. In the meantime, I'd be glad to help in any way I can. You needn't stay here simply because you've exhausted your American currency. My house has plenty of room, and I imagine you'd prefer talking with some of my investor friends than hacking about with a pickax here. If there's gold on this claim, we'll get at it!"

Daisie looked away, afraid she'd blurt out that there was no London bank account, and probably no gold. After coffee and a pleasant visit, the colonel took his leave. Once again Daisie and her papa were alone.

"I missed you, Papa," she said, hugging him again.

When they went into the cabin, Daisie felt she was stepping into a dark and musty warren.

"You take my bed tonight," her father insisted. He plucked several likely branches from the woodpile. "I'll begin making you a bed of your own tomorrow. And you'll need a stool."

"Have you found any more gold?" she asked.

"You forget, you are the one who found the original ore. I think it's been hiding, waiting for you to come back to find the rest.

"When you talked to Tyler about the accusation the Salters made, what did he say?"

"I never mentioned it." His gaze was serene.

"But he's been back since, hasn't he? *I* asked him about it! Why didn't you?"

Her father frowned. "To question him would destroy our friendship."

"Don't be so naive! He behaved as if — " Daisie stopped, ashamed to have spoken so disrespectfully to her father. "I'm not any surer of what he did or didn't do than I was the day Hank and Amelia came here. Papa, am I mad to be so confused?"

A smile tugged at his lips. "We've been hurt, Daisie, but we mustn't go on living with suspicion. Let others, the cheaters and frauds, live like that. We must have open hearts."

"You said yourself that one of the reasons your business failed was that you were too trusting!"

He nodded. "What do I want with business associates who cheat me? I'm glad to be away from the madness of the business world. When the colonel offered to introduce me to some investors, I recoiled at the prospect. I'm happy here, Daisie. I've decided that if. . . *when* we strike gold, we'll not go back to the old way of life. We'll bring Mother and Pammie here and build a solid little house. If Pammie wants to go back for schooling or marriage, that will be her choice. I'm happy here. Don't keep trying to tear me away. Let a tired old man have his wish. What else is life for but to live and enjoy? Must I struggle and strive to feel alive? I leave that to the colonel and the mining companies . . . and the Salters."

"I don't think you mind having found no gold!"

He smiled as if to say that at last she was beginning to understand — that here he had what he'd left England to find — inner peace.

Several days later a wagon stopped in the aspen glen. Daisie had just finished fashioning a broom out of coarse meadow grass and jumped up hoping to see Tyler.

"Did I hear a wagon?" her father asked, coming out of the cabin, looking more rested for having slept late. He squinted across the meadow. "What does *he* want?"

Hank Salter leaped down from a wagon piled with sacks and crates. Daisie had told her father a little of what had been said and done while she was staying in town, but she had left out a lot. She edged back toward the cabin doorway. The rifle stood just inside.

"Ah, Lord Browning, nice to see you again!" Hank loped across the creek carrying a huge crate. "I've brought some provisions!"

"Might as well take them back," Daisie's father said. "I can't pay, and I won't buy on credit . . . from you."

"Don't worry about it!" Hank said, setting the crate down. "Consider it a gift."

"Too bad about your store," her father said.

"Well, we've already got the new framework up. Amelia's arguing with the builder. She asked me to say hello. Afternoon, Daisie." He smiled eagerly.

Did he think she had forgotten? She turned away, saying nothing.

He made three trips back to the wagon, carting goods they did need desperately, but which Daisie didn't want to accept. "We really don't want all this," she said once, but Hank ignored her. When he was done, he patted his breast pocket and drew out a small envelope.

"A letter?" Daisie asked excitedly, reaching for it.

Hank grinned and shook his head. "No, a settlement for the belongings you lost in our fire. I feels it's a fair sum — "

She withdrew her hand as if she'd been stung. She'd never take money from him! "No thank you."

"Very well then. Mind if I sit? Those crates were heavy. Think a hundred pounds of flour'll last you a while?" He put the envelope back in his pocket.

Daisie's father watched the exchange, especially Daisie's reaction to Hank. After a moment he held out his hand. "Thank you for coming, Salter."

"Well, sir, I was hoping to take Daisie riding this afternoon."

Daisie's breath rushed out. "Riding! No, thank you! I'm much too busy. Good day!" She started into the cabin.

"A short walk then," Hank smiled, looking around admiringly at the campsite. "I'd like to see your land . . . and your mine."

So that was it, Daisie thought. Hank wanted to know how much gold they had.

"I don't wish to be inhospitable, Salter, but there's no mine here. The claim was salted, remember?" her father said.

Hank's smile twisted. "Daisie? Won't you reconsider?"

She gave him a look of loathing.

"I never seem to say the right thing around your lovely daughter, Lord Browning," Hank sighed, still seated on a stout log next to the cabin.

"Who set fire to your store, Hank? Any news?" Daisie asked, her tone icy as she gazed unseeing into the dark cabin.

Hank's shoulders rounded. "I said things that night . . . . Can't you forget? And forgive?" He stood up and moved toward Daisie, skirting her father with a quick, dismissing nod. "I'll ask your father for permission to court you. Would that make you see how serious I am?"

Her father looked rather shocked.

"I don't care to go walking with you, Hank! I don't care to ride with you. I have no desire to be courted by you. Is that clear?" Daisie's voice rose. If he mentioned marriage in front of her father, she'd scream!

"Put in a good word for me, sir! I want to help you both, build you a decent home, bring supplies, set up a mining company — "

At the sound of laughter behind them, they turned.

"Salter, am I never going to see Daisie without you around? Take your lies back to town. Next time they have a tall-tale, lying and spitting contest, you'll win all three, hands down."

Tyler stood in the meadow, coat fringes swinging, hat in hand, legs planted apart. Daisie thought he was the grandest sight she'd ever seen. He led a chestnut horse down through the deep grasses, crossed the creek without regard for his boots, and tied his mount to a nearby bush.

To find her here with Hank . . . . She felt ready to explode with fury and frustration. All she wanted was to be alone with Tyler.

Hank's face darkened to scarlet. He backed away and crossed the creek a good ten feet from where Tyler stood. "I'll leave it to you, Lord Browning. Is this the sort of man you want chasing after your daughter? A man who lives at a saloon and carries on with painted women? A man who has dallied with the affections of my sister and salted the claims of honest men like you? I'll be back next week with more supplies," he finished.

"No need," Gregory Browning said quietly. "Tyler brings us everything."

"Perhaps lately," Hank said, a sniff in his words. "But what will become of you when he tires of Daisie and one of those painted ladies of his claims his attention, instead?"

Tyler just laughed and shook his head. He went to her father, shook his hand and clapped him on the back. "You're looking better, sir. Goodbye, Salter. Don't be surprised if you find all these expensive supplies dumped in the creek."

Eyes narrowed, Hank stalked away. When Daisie heard his wagon rattle away she sighed with relief. "I'm so glad you came, Tyler," she said.

Briefly he took her hand and squeezed it, filling her with excitement and warmth. "You look well, too, Daisie. Your hair is pretty that way." He turned to her father. "Found much ore for me to take in?"

"Not looking terribly hard, my boy. Doesn't seem much point."

"That's a shame," Tyler said. "Anything I can get you on

my next trip from town? It looks as if Hank thought of everything today."

"Dumping it in the creek is an excellent idea," Daisie muttered. "I'd choke on that food."

"Look here, Tyler, we didn't ask that worm out here. He's set his sights on Daisie, but I can't imagine he believes he's got a chance with her. He's an oaf. I wouldn't have the likes of him as a son-in-law if I was dying in debtor's prison."

"Papa!" Daisie laughed, squirming with delight and embarrassment. "Ask Tyler to supper. I know it'll mean getting back late, Tyler, but we'd enjoy your company."

"I wouldn't mind staying," Tyler said, winking. "I brought my bedroll. How do you feel about that, sir?"

Her father's forehead creased. "I'd welcome your company. But not a word about gold tonight. I trust you, my boy. Eat with us." He nodded his head. "Yes, I like you, son. Can't help myself."

Tyler gathered firewood while Daisie mixed her best biscuits and finally decided to cook the roasting chicken Hank had brought. Skewering it on a green stick, she set Tyler to turning it over the fire outside the cabin while he amused her father with stories from town. Among the supplies Hank had brought, she discovered wine and fresh vegetables and even imported chocolates in a tin.

They ate and talked. They laughed when Tyler related stories of his boyhood on the prairie homestead. Daisie countered with the mischief she and Pammie had got into in the old house. The wine was delicious and made Daisie warm and giddy. The conversation turned solemn, however, and her father looked lonely when she spoke of her mama and of home.

Tyler told them of his father's crippling accident one spring and death six months later that left his mother to carry on alone. In the end they lost the homestead. Tyler's mother passed away in her sleep and his brothers went East. Tyler roamed westward, moving from mining camp to mining camp, his only steady income from repaid loans to friends and the buying and selling of small bits of land. "I staked people I believed needed a chance, and months, sometimes years later, they'd come back, thanking me in cash." Tyler's eyes grew distant and gentle. "I do it now more for that than for the repayment. And in case the boom doesn't last, I started a small ranch."

"I remember the day I opened the morning newspaper to read that gold had been discovered in Colorado," her father said, forgetting he wanted no talk of gold.

The next day, Daisie remembered, he had appeared in his travelling coat, valise in hand.

" 'I'm going to America,' I said to your mother," her father recalled. "Going to America." He began to chuckle. "I thought it'd be like a vacation. I thought I'd find gold lying about."

"You've found something better," Daisie reminded him.

"So I have. But I still need a little money to care for your mother and Pammie."

"Any trouble with the bear lately?" Tyler asked, stretching and planting his heels in the dirt. He knew they must get off the subject of money and home.

"The beast doesn't fit through the doorway!" Daisie's father laughed, sounding as if he had seen the bear try.

Tyler's expression turned serious. "You intend to stay here then, both of you? For how long?"

"We can't go home until we have passage," Daisie said. "I can't ask the Arnolds for another loan. And anyway I'd be terrified to cash another bank draft. Something would be bound to happen."

Tyler appeared to have difficulty controlling his exasperation. "Any number of people in town can assist you, if you really want to go home. And even if you don't, a house in town would be far safer than here. I get the impression you're not very eager to do either.

Daisie's father chuckled. "That's the thing, my boy. I have no desire to go back and no desire to live in a town. I like these mountains. I like this spot. I have a cabin, a little food, the open sky, running water. What more do I need?"

"You've never been in these mountains during the winter. You're not up to the hardship, sir. I intend no disrespect."

"Now, now, no need to spoil a pleasant evening with tales of danger, my boy."

"Three feet of snow or more will cover this area from November until March. If the winter is bad, the snow will be deeper, begin earlier and stay longer. It will bury the cabin. You won't be able to get to the road, possibly not even to the creek. Firewood will be difficult, if not impossible, to find. The cabin's not big enough to hold supplies to last six months. And the cold . . . twenty degrees below zero is common."

"Tyler, stop," Daisie said softly. "We'll go before then."

"If you're going to be depressing, my boy, I shall go to bed." Daisie's father pulled himself to his feet, groaned and pressed at his back. "I'm getting lazy and spoiled. Daisie's been making me rest while she plays nanny and nursemaid."

He hobbled inside, winking back over his shoulder at Tyler and Daisie. "Don't stay out in the cold long, my girl."

Darkness had fallen as they talked. Now the chill of the night was upon them. Daisie huddled in one of Mrs. Darnel's old shawls while Tyler poured the last of the wine into her tin cup. The glow was beginning to wear off.

For a while after her father had gone in she and Tyler didn't speak. Daisie could think of nothing to say. All the obvious topics led back to money, and she was weary of it. She wanted the talk to be personal and agreeable, but personal talk would lead to the subject of Hank and why he'd been at the Darnels' and here at camp. She didn't want to explain herself. She didn't want to think about dance-hall women, either, or about what Hank had said about Tyler "dallying" with Amelia. She wanted to think of herself and Tyler, together, alone.

Finally she remembered her list. "Could you bring these things when you have the time, Tyler?" she asked, leaning across to hand him the scrap of paper she'd pulled from her skirt pocket.

"My pleasure."

"I can't pay yet."

He looked at her as if to say payment was not a concern.

"We haven't a single coin between us. To take all this charity is demeaning to Papa. I was once a spoiled child. I never gave a thought to where my clothes or food came from. When Papa left us I thought he'd gone mad, but now I know what it means to need money, to be willing to go anywhere, do anything for it."

He sat attentively, offering no loans, pressing for no alternatives.

"But I can sew quite well. I want to stay with Papa as long as necessary. I like this quiet meadow. I think to work would be just the thing for me. Could you possibly find me some business? I can make aprons and bonnets, and I'm even a fair hand at making simple dresses."

His face split into a grin. "I'm glad you've finally asked me for *something*. I can certainly find some piece-work for you. And of course I'll bring the supplies. But what can I bring to please just you?"

"That will please me," she said, feeling relieved. "A girl can gather firewood only so long before she begins to feel like a . . . a pack mule."

Chuckling softly, Tyler stood. He caught her hand and pulled her to her feet. When he drew her close, he smiled, his eyes going over her face as if seeing her for the first time. "I like these little curls," he said, softly blowing on her fringed locks.

There was so much she wanted to ask him, all of it unpleasant. Her doubts about him were still strong, but in spite of Hank's accusations and Amelia's insinuations, she wanted to believe Tyler was a decent man. If she turned out to be wrong, that would be her secret sorrow. But if somehow she could prove to herself that Tyler was all her heart yearned for him to be . . . .

She looked up into his face, her thoughts plain in her soft and pleading eyes. When he looked at her, did he still wonder if she doubted him? There was a hint of worry in the lines around his eyes. Was he trying to forget that Hank had called her his girl? Was he wondering . . . ?

She moved toward him, and then hesitated. After a second he leaned down, not embracing her but brushing her lips softly with his own as if teasing her.

Then she remembered he was staying the night, camping just outside her door. Suddenly she was tingling and terrified. Drawing away like a coquette, she smiled up through her lashes. "I think I should say goodnight," she breathed, feeling her chest tighten with excitement. Her heart began to race. Here no one could interrupt them or spoil the mood. Her father was probably already asleep.

Still holding her hand, Tyler drew her closer. She found herself rigid as he circled her with his arms. He pressed his cheek against hers, sensing her inexperience.

Then he kissed her, his lips gentle, undemanding. His arms closed around her back as they had the night of the fire, but this time she wore a corset beneath the shirtwaist and skirt. She couldn't feel the warmth of his hands burning through to her skin.

She pressed against him, suddenly unafraid. She wanted him and all he could give her. It was proof of her trust. If there had been others before her, she would make him forget them all. If he had ever been with Amelia he would never want to again.

Panting, he tore his lips from her mouth and buried his face in her neck, kissing her, sending shivers of excitement through her body. When one of his hands closed over her breast, pressed up eagerly by the squeezing corset, her entire body suddenly felt electrified. She was molten inside, weak and mindless. Nothing mattered except that he was touching her. Tightening her arms around his neck, clutching his silky hair, she sought his lips, wanting his hands on her, and he obeyed her silent demand, grasping both breasts possessively. Then with a groan he kissed her deeply, tasting her mouth, circling her back with his arms, crushing her to him as if to make her part of him.

Without a word, they parted and stood trembling, lost in the pulsing sensations flooding them, fighting for control, trying to remember that Daisie's father was only a few feet away in the cabin.

Tyler's voice came out thickly. "I'll get my bedroll."

"Will you be safe by the fire?" she asked, watching his shadow move away in the darkness.

"Sure," he said, his voice unaccustomedly husky.

She followed him as though in a trance, and when they reached the creek, she slipped her hand into his. There the firelight was weak, illuminating only half of Tyler's face, faintly gilding his lazy-lidded eyes, the sweep of his lashes, the curve of his brow and the delicate way his hair grew away in a soft wave from his temples.

His breath brushed her face, warming her cheeks and teasing the tendrils of her hair. She strained upwards and he kissed her, his lips at first cooled by the night air and then suddenly warmed by hers, warmed by their desire for each other. His hands were urgent against her back as he pressed her to his chest and then arched her waist tightly against his so that she touched him from breast to thigh.

"Daisie," he whispered against her lips. "Go away from me now, Daisie. Please, before — "

She silenced his caution, telling him with her lips that she was not going to go away from him. His hands closed over her breasts again, and then suddenly, gently, she drew away and moved upstream into the darkness where the firelight barely reached.

There she unbuttoned her shirtwaist and tugged it from the waistband of the skirt. She parted the front of her blouse, aware that just the top of her white lawn corset cover and the delicate soft skin swelling above it were visible in the frail light. She began pulling the ribbons, heart hammering, cheeks blazing. Her body yearned for the man in the shadows.

Tyler came to her, moving her deeper still into the darkness, well past where his mount still stood tethered. His breath was quick on her face as he helped her undo the top of her corset and spread it back to expose the creamy softness of her breasts. The corset was still tight and confining from her ribs to her hips, but her breasts were freed, and his hands were very warm, very soft, very gentle.

He kissed her between her soft exposed breasts, then pressed his lips against first one and then the other. His mouth was warm and teasing, his breath hot and exciting. Then he straightened, holding her close, protecting her from the chilled night air. He laid his cheek against hers. "Your face is so hot, Daisie. Are you all right?"

She nodded, not trusting her voice, wanting only more, more, more. He stooped and put his hand in the creek, and brought back his cold wet fingers to cool her cheeks. The cold wetness tingled, sending shivers up her spine. Little drops fell on the swells of her breasts, and she took a step back, slipping an inch or two into the icy water.

Laughing, she grabbed up her hem, and held her breath as he tried to help her keep her skirts dry. She felt naughty and bold, and stepped into the numbing water. It rushed around her ankles. Tyler put his hand on her calf, chill drops trailing tantalizingly from his fingers. He looked up at her. His eyes were shadowed, but she could feel the fire in his touch. As he straightened, his hand slid up her leg, lifting the skirt and petticoats, allowing the night air to caress her as she wanted Tyler to caress her.

Then he was lifting her, carrying her across the creek and through the meadow to the aspen grove. Where the rocks were wide and flat, the moonlight shone and there was a hollow she had noticed before but never thought about. "Tell me now if I want too much from you," he whispered as he set her down.

She slipped out of her skirt quickly and handed it to him. He spread it out on the pine needles to make a bed for them, and sat down on it. Dropping to her knees beside him, she reached for his shirt buttons, and opened his shirt, spreading back the soft linen to expose the curved muscles of his chest. She ran her palm lightly over the dusting of dark curls between his nipples.

She leaned toward him, brushing her nipples just a little against his chest until he could stand no more and seized her, turning her back to lie on the skirt and feel his hands take possession of her, uncover her to the cool night air and the warm urgency of his kisses. She accepted him there, quickly, explosively, and deep in herself found the place of her womanhood that Tyler commanded.

The night was suddenly very still. They lay as one beneath the canopy of moonlit aspen leaves. Then he was covering her, pressing kisses into her hair, nudging her with his face, holding her so close she still felt she was a part of him.

At length, he stood and began to pull on his trousers. In the moonlight he looked like a statue, his shoulders broad, the skin finely textured and rippling across his back, narrowing to his lean, muscled waist. He turned and looked back at her. No words were necessary between them. He helped her up, his eyes dreamy, tender. He kissed her softly. "Good night, Daisie," he said at last.

He turned away to stand looking out over the moonlit stones. She pulled her skirt quickly on and buttoned her shirtwaist, still tingling, satisfied but awakened now, a woman in love.

"Good night, Tyler," she whispered to his back. She didn't know what he was thinking. She had no regrets. She felt a shimmering link with him now that through all the rest of her life would never be broken. Even if this was all they ever had, she would never forget him.

She moved down through the grasses and crossed the creek, quivering with weakness but relaxed and at peace. When she slipped inside the cabin, her father was curled in the makeshift new bed, snoring, the worn planes of his face touched by the light from the smoky fire nearby.

Climbing into her bed of pine boughs, she lay still. The air was warm inside and the night noises deadened by the thick wall of earth and logs around them, but her heightened senses picked out the sounds of Tyler spreading out his bedroll, stoking the fire, bringing the horse in closer, uttering low, crooning words to it.

She loved Tyler. She sensed that he loved her, too. But he had not *said* he loved her. He had touched her as if he did; but even so, would that be enough? Could this feeling he gave her overcome the things that would loom so real and important in the morning?

Chapter Twelve

"I was listening last night," her father said softly the next morning, before Daisie was fully awake. "I heard you ask Tyler for work."

Daisie lay still as her father rose from his pallet near the fire. When she opened her eyes, her face blazing and her heart racing with the fear that he had heard more than that simple request, she saw he looked old, worn out. She was afraid of the chill he might take from lying on the ground, of the sickness a harsh winter might bring.

"I'm only going to say this once, Daisie," her father said, looking down on her, his voice low and even, leaving no doubt that what he was going to say could not be challenged. "I told you I've found peace here, and I have. But what I need for myself and what I need to provide for your mother are two very different things. I'm not going back for her until I've found the gold I told her I came to get. I'm a foolish old man now. I see the utter folly of my ways, but I must have my wife looking up to me. I don't mind charity nearly as much as I mind my own daughter thinking I'm so helpless she must find work to support me. You may sew if you wish, but the earnings will be yours. I'll take home gold to your mother to prove I'm still a man."

He might never go home if that was his intention, she thought, stunned.

Tyler had already made coffee by the time she came out of the cabin. Though he was cordial, he seemed withdrawn. She thought at first that he was being circumspect around her father, but as he prepared to leave, she knew it was something more.

Only once was she able to catch his eye. She sensed that he was trying to read her mind, perhaps even her heart. He looked at her so intently, his own emotions so very close to the surface, that Daisie shivered, wishing she could be sure of what she saw. She wanted to believe that their night together had been far more than he anticipated, that the moments they had spent in each other's arms had made her special to him. She hoped that last night she had become more important to him. Possibly, he did not know how he felt about that.

Though Tyler was an attentive as ever, from that day on she sensed he was holding himself away from her. He averted his eyes whenever she saw him looking at her and never stayed long enough or late enough for the overwhelming attraction still burning between them to lead to another night of passion.

Daisie didn't regret what she had allowed to happen, but as the last days of July slipped away in a pleasant, repetitive simplicity, she began to feel almost as though that night had been a dream. Surely Tyler sensed the intensity of her love and desire for him? But perhaps he didn't feel the same way toward her. She had hoped to erase all other women from his mind. Now she feared she might be just another of his many conquests, as Hank had so vulgarly hinted.

Oddly, she continued to look back on that night not with regret or sorrow but with wonder. The beauty of it numbed her. Tyler might be all the disreputable things Hank and Amelia claimed, but she didn't care. She watched him, feeling he was beyond her grasp. For one impossible moment he had wanted her enough to sweep her into the darkness. And that was all that mattered to her.

She cooked and tended the cabin. Her father went over both claims as thoroughly as he was able, and when Tyler came again with supplies, Daisie treated him as a friend, holding herself aloof as well. When she did catch him watching her it was with a secret sense of victory. It meant that he was fighting a need for her that was still alive and compelling within his heart.

The surrounding claims that had been bought so quickly after the discovery of the float proved to have no gold, and so were sold back, mostly to Tyler. He reported one strike on a claim he'd staked north of town, and in short order a mining company sank a shaft there. With the profits Tyler bought a new pair of boots and brought Daisie wine and flowers to celebrate. They laughed a good deal that night, and secretly Daisie's heart ached for his touch. But Tyler returned to town long before her father went to bed, obviously not wanting to be tempted. With a private smile and amazing calm, Daisie began to wonder just which of them was the expert at seduction!

Tyler brought dress goods and an order for two dresses which she stitched together from a list of measurements. She finished so quickly he brought orders for two more and said the ladies she was sewing for were very pleased. Daisie was delighted with the first money she had ever earned.

When at last Tyler brought a letter from her mother, Daisie felt as if England, home and their life there were very far away. She could understand how her father had lost the desire to write. Because the letters took so long to reach England and the replies to return, reading them was like slipping backwards a month or more.

My very dearest Gregory and Daisie,
Pammie and I hardly know what to do with ourselves with both of you away. How happy and relieved we were to get your letters. Just knowing you are together helps the days pass. My new garden is coming along marvelously. The roses are in bloom. I'm thinking of entering the garden club competition. We saw Norwood and he was most curious about you, Daisie . . . .

Inwardly, Daisie groaned to think they'd soon receive her mother's reply to the letter telling her of the robbery. And when she read about the fire, she'd be frantic.

In August the daily cloudbursts became more threatening, and the chill that descended every afternoon sometimes didn't wear off. When the orders for dresses fell off, Tyler suggested taking Daisie's sunbonnet to town as a sample, and the next day brought enough calico to make a dozen. Surprised that so many ladies wanted sunbonnets this late in the season, Daisie set to work, dreaming of all she'd soon buy with her own money.

One day Tyler brought an especially large load of supplies. "I have to be away for a few weeks," he told Gregory Browning.

Daisie said nothing. She knew she had no rights over him, but she ached to think she wouldn't see him for so long. They said a wary goodbye without so much as a handshake. Each seemed fearful of igniting the passion that had once flared between them.

Increasingly, Daisie considered the possibility that once she was conquered, he had simply lost interest in her. She was thankful that she wasn't pregnant and would not be forced to go to him on that account.

Her dreams, however, gave her no rest. She yearned for Tyler's embrace. She busied herself with sewing and cooking. And she nursed her father through a cold that left him weak and cabin-bound.

Inevitably, their supplies dwindled and Daisie's thoughts grew fearful. Perhaps Tyler had come to harm. Perhaps he had met someone new. Perhaps he was back in Cripple Creek with Carla on his knee, laughing . . . or with Amelia clinging to his arm, simpering and gloating.

As Daisie lay awake wondering if Amelia had won him somehow, she suddenly recalled that first day, when Amelia had claimed she scarcely knew Tyler. Had Amelia lied then to cover an affair with Tyler, or later to keep Daisie from wanting him?

In September, the aspen leaves turned a rich, sunlit gold. When Tyler had not come after a month, Daisie and her father were down to a few cans of food and half a bag of meal. Daisie was just thinking about walking to town when Hank and Amelia stopped a shiny new buggy at the edge of the aspen grove one sunny, cool afternoon.

Daisie's first reaction was to reach for the rifle, but she needed supplies more than she needed the satisfaction of insulting the Salters. She wanted a ride into town. Lifting her chin, she welcomed them to camp.

Bobbing and swishing through the meadow in an elegantly styled rose muslin dress, Amelia called hello, refrained from mentioning Daisie's "squatter" appearance, and began to admire the bonnets hanging just inside the cabin door. "I must have some for the new store!" she cried.

Hank bowed hello. His fair hair gleamed with pomade. His black tie was knotted tightly and his new black frockcoat looked tailored and expensive.

"When we realized no one had heard from you since last month — and of course we knew Tyler had gone — we thought we'd better check on you," Amelia said, her eyes not missing a detail of Daisie's appearance.

"How nice," Daisie replied politely. She itched to ask *where* Tyler had gone.

Daisie's father sat near the fire, his lap covered with a blanket, and said little. Daisie poured coffee all round while Amelia chattered happily, describing the hundreds of new people in town, the grand new hotel, and their new store. Hank just grinned at Daisie like an infatuated schoolboy until Daisie was forced to respond.

"You look as if you've got a special reason for coming all this way," Daisie said.

Hank puffed pridefully. "We've come to invite you to see our new store."

Just what she wanted to see, she thought, forcing a smile to her lips. She was thinking only of delivering the ordered bonnets and buying supplies with her own money when she said, "I'd love to see it. I'll get my shawl now and we can go. I don't want to leave Papa alone overnight. He's been ill."

"But you can't get back so quickly. It's already late. We want you to stay. We have new rooms. Nice rooms, Daisie. Surely your father can get along by himself for one night."

Daisie sighed.

"I'll be fine," Daisie's father interrupted.

"I want you to pick out anything you like from our store, Daisie," Amelia went on. "Naturally, we won't charge you. When Hank said you refused our settlement, I was horrified! You lost those wonderful Paris gowns and all that money." She shook her head, "You *must* let us make up for it all."

For an instant Daisie was tempted, but finally she shook her head. "I'll pay cash, thank you."

Amelia's eyes rounded, and she smiled with warmth and surprise. "I see. Of course. I hadn't realized you'd been in touch with your friends in New York. And how is your mother getting along?"

Hank broke in. "We know of a small house in town you can rent for the winter, too. I'd like to show it to you."

"We can't leave this claim," Daisie's father said with quiet firmness. "We're staying here the winter," he finished, as a fit of coughing shook him.

"But Lord Browning — " Hank looked truly concerned.

"Papa knows what he wants, Hank," Daisie said. "And I intend to stay with him."

She slipped into the cabin to tidy her hair, hoping no one in town would recognize her. As she left she admonished her father to take care. "If I don't come back tonight, I'll be here early tomorrow."

"Be careful yourself," her papa said, casting a knowing look Hank's way.

Amelia chattered all the way to town, discussing the various circumstances of a number of residents. Her descriptions of their clothes, buggies and personal habits were astonishingly detailed. Daisie could imagine Amelia discussing her, too . . . living in a muddy cabin and wearing cast-off clothes, her hair uncurled, her nails broken, her cheeks darkened by the sun. . . .

In only two months the town had changed substantially. It was now twice its former size, and the number of respectable, permanent brick structures had almost doubled. The carriage and wagon traffic was as mad as ever, the train as loud. And the stamp mills that pounded the ore brought up from the shafts still filled the air with smoke.

The Salters' store had an elaborate false front and a huge sign. Across the front were windows filled with merchandise. Inside, Hank showed off glass cases filled with expensive finery. Mazes of shelves held everything from boots to dusting powder to canned goods. A rack of ready-to-wear dresses hung nearby, and stacks of shirts stood white and starched on a counter. There was even a French china-head doll.

"Pick whatever you'd like," Hank said, going to the back to consult the hired man who'd been tending the counter.

Shaking her head, Daisie clutched her sunbonnets, hoping she didn't look as much the country bumpkin as she felt. "It's not that your merchandise isn't to my liking," she said to Amelia in embarrassment. "It's that I can't afford anything just at the moment. After I deliver these bonnets I'll have a little something to spend on a few necessities."

Amelia's mouth was still open to protest as Daisie ducked out. Daisie didn't intend to stay in town over night, but if she had to she'd sleep in a ditch rather than risk herself with the Salters again.

At last she found the street listed on the bonnet order and realized it was the same street the Gaslight Saloon was on. She intended to stop there later and ask after Tyler. She felt, too, as though she'd almost earned another whiskey!

When she found it, the address Tyler'd given her turned out to be a plain house wedged between a warehouse and some shacks. She climbed the steps and knocked. Through the oval of beveled glass set in the door she saw a sumptuous entrance hall. A chorus of giggles set Daisie's heart leaping. Suddenly, without knowing how she knew, she realized the sort of place it was. But before she could turn away, the door swung wide. A bosomy blonde woman in pink and orange disarray regarded Daisie doubtfully. "I don't know, honey. You're kind of skinny, but come on in."

Speechless, Daisie felt herself drawn into the gleaming paneled entrance hall.

"You got anything better to wear than that rag? Them your bosoms? Or are you wearing falsies?"

Incredulous, Daisie coughed a nervous laugh. "I beg your pardon!"

"Oh, say, you're good with that accent. That'll help."

"I'm looking for . . . . " Her mind went blank. Unknotting her bundle of bonnets, she found the order. "Casey Malone. These are for her."

The blonde woman started to laugh. "You ain't here to work?" She laughed even louder. Some of her sisters, all equally negligent about keeping their wrappers closed, gathered in the archway leading into the parlor. "She's got some goddamned sunbonnets for us, girls! Now, ain't that nice?" Turning back to Daisie, chuckling until tears gathered in her eyes, she said, "Honey, whoever gave you that order must've been drunk. Casey ain't worked here in three years. Can't say as we can use sunbonnets much, but come on in anyhow. We'll pay you for all your hard work. Looks like you could use the money. Here, rest yourself while we settle on a price."

The girls in the archway were a blur of dangling curls, lacy underthings, dark stockings, and casually exposed thighs. The rooms reeked of perfume and brandy. Heavy blood-red drapes covered the windows, so that even in mid-afternoon the lamps were lit.

Smiling to cover her embarrassment, Daisie backed toward the door.

The blonde woman pulled a lace purse from the red ruffled garter around her left thigh. She yanked out several dollars. "Here, honey. If you ever need real work, real *easy* work, come on back. We could fix you up pretty. I know a lot of gents who'd empty their pockets for you."

Ladies of the night! Daisie went weak with amazement gawking at them. She saw the money in the smooth pale hand and thought of her own rough, red, long-neglected hands. She thought of the hours she'd sewn, working proudly, thinking Tyler admired her industry.

Indignation welled up in her. There had never been any real orders for sewing! Tyler had made them up and paid her from his own pocket! She wasn't earning her own way. She was being taken for a fool. Most likely, Tyler continued to bring her father supplies only out of guilt for salting the claim. And now he had left them. Oh, wouldn't he love the message she left him this time! She'd drink a toast to his everlasting damnation!

Snatching the money, she turned and, all her dignity gone, marched down the stairs. In the street she kept her head high, but she saw men watching her, and knew what they were thinking. They were thinking she was one of those women!

And they weren't that far wrong! Tyler had prevented her from earning money honestly, in effect keeping her as his plaything. That beautiful wonderful night when she undid her clothes and displayed herself she had thrown away everything. She had fallen into his trap, letting him make her his woman, making her no different from those creatures in that awful house!

Without thought or reason, she stormed down the street toward the Gaslight Saloon. Bursting through the swinging doors, she paused a moment to let her eyes adjust to the dim light coming from the gas lamps shrouded in eddies of rising cigar smoke.

As if frightened by her furious entrance, the mechanical music machine ended a crashing, twangy song and stood silent. Men seated around the tables turned. The two bartenders in their purple silk vests regarded her.

As she marched across the room, skirts swishing reproachfully, muddy heels clacking on the gritty floor, she saw herself reflected in a long mirror behind the bar. A fraction of her fury waned. She did look an outlandish creature. Her hair had come loose and tumbled about her shoulders, her cheeks, dark as a farmer's, were studded with freckles as large as snowflakes.

Her eyes blazed. Her parted lips were drawn back in a grimace of determination.

She looked thin, but lean and strong, not delicate as she had once been. Mrs. Darnel's lace blouse fairly hung from her shoulders. The forest-green skirt, properly altered now, accentuated her tiny, work-whittled waist.

Restraining the urge to smash the mirror, Daisie scowled at the bartender, whom she recognized from her previous visit. "Where's Tyler?" she demanded.

Without a word, he nodded toward the same corner where she'd seen Tyler that first day. Shocked, she whirled, around. So he was in town! And he hadn't come with supplies. That proved he had finished with her and her father. Her rage building, she advanced on Tyler, where he sat conferring with a groups of well-dressed men. They were discussing something in hushed tones, pouring over a sheaf of important-looking papers scattered across the table. One man was signing something.

She was almost upon Tyler when he looked up. His expression mirrored first shock, then dawning delight . . . and then he saw her eyes and his face closed down as though a door had been slammed.

Before him on the table were several shot glasses of whiskey. Taking the full one she believed to be Tyler's, she downed it in a single gulp, relishing the astonished faces at the table and the warmth immediately flowing through her veins.

"Tyler," she hissed. She shook the money at him — the money she'd snatched from the woman in the bawdy house. "How very delightful to see you back from your extended trip," she said icily. "I just delivered those sunbonnets your friend Casey ordered. Casey — who has not been seen in this town for three years!"

As she spoke, Tyler settled back, puffing on a long narrow cigar, and regarded her calmly. His face was more darkly marked by the sun. He looked tired. His eyes were not so bright as in the past. The black frockcoat and ruffled shirt accentuated his tan, and a new gauntness in his face gave him a sinister air.

She steeled herself against the emotions raging in her heart, the inner voice that told her she loved this man, wanted this man. She reminded herself that all the accusations made against this man were true! She flung the money down in a gesture of contempt. Her voice was quiet, icy, hard. "I wanted honest work, not charity. I'm glad you've got tired of helping us because we've certainly grown tired of you coming around keeping us dependent."

Hearing faint murmurs of amusement behind her, she whirled and stormed toward the door.

"Who's the wildcat, Tyler?"

"Tsk, tsk, tsk. Hell hath no fury, Tyler."

"Excuse me, gentlemen," she heard him say as she swung out into the dusk. Crashing head-on into someone just entering the saloon, she plowed past the tall dark blur, her cheeks chilled with unbidden tears.

"Daisie, wait," Tyler called. Unheeding, she marched up the street, blind to where she was going.

She had let him make love to her! Of course he didn't want her again! He had what he wanted — money from salting her father's claim, and an evening's entertainment from her. Those trips afterwards were his way of easing off; the last delivery of supplies had been his goodbye.

Choking back a sob, Daisie rounded a corner. She couldn't let Tyler see her tears.

"Daisie! Wait. . . ."

She couldn't wait. And apparently he didn't care enough to chase after her. Now that she knew the kind of man he really was, he might be obliged to "explain himself." Her anger didn't cool as she marched, and Tyler didn't follow. The fact that he was robbing her of the opportunity to reject him again made her even angrier.

After a few minutes, she found herself standing on the train platform, looking longingly up the tracks that snaked out of town, back to England and home and her mother. All she could do was keep walking, blinking and turning her mind from the image that would be etched in her memory forever, of Tyler's face, first startled, then pleased, and then closed and cold.

She was hungry and exhausted. Composing herself as well as she could, she went into the nearest store that advertised groceries. She must get the supplies quickly now — Suddenly, she remembered the money she'd thrown in Tyler's face.

Fool! Her father needed a coat. They had to have food. She took up a can, trembling with a feeling of cold dread that her foolish, female pride might have ruined them. She stared at the price marked on the can in grease pencil.

"Can I help you, ma'am?" a tall, thin, middle-aged man said from behind her.

Daisie didn't look up. "This price — "

"As reasonable as I can make it, ma'am."

"It's lower than at Salter's."

"By a long sight, ma'am." He rocked on his heels, thumbs hooked into his apron strings.

She looked up into a face she would later be unable to recall. At these prices she could stock up with the money Tyler had given her for making the dresses so many weeks ago! She'd been able to eat Hank Salter's roasting chicken; and now she was able to spend Tyler's charity with relish. She began listing all the goods she and her father needed.

"Where can I hire a wagon to take these things out to my camp?"

"My wife and I can drive you after I close up," the man said, taking pity on an obviously indigent greenhorn.

Promising to return in an hour, Daisie went to the nearest dry goods store where she was able to buy a secondhand wool coat for her father. Putting it on herself, she was just going out the door when she turned back to the portly proprietor. "How much would you charge for a prospecting outfit, including a tent and a mule?"

He quoted a price roughly a third of what her father had paid.

"Why would someone charge more than twice that?" she asked, trembling with silent rage.

"I don't know, ma'am. I only know I am an honest man. I charge what I will in this wild camp, but I remember my customers are my neighbors and friends."

* * *

"And so, what did Tyler say?" Daisie's father asked, after the storekeeper and his wife had left Daisie and her supplies. He frowned as Daisie related the events of the day.

"I didn't stay long enough to hear more of his lies. What could he have siad? He invented all those commissions. My work was for nothing. There he sat in his lacy shirt and silver-tipped boots, Papa, while we waited for him, nearly starving. He made us depend on him, and then abandoned us."

Her father looked away. Smoke rolled from the hearth, slipping upward and out through holes he had made in the roof. "You're so quick to judge, my girl," he said softly.

"I was seeing things as they really are!"

"Or, perhaps, as you want them to be. Why are you so afraid of Tyler?"

Daisie couldn't get out a coherent word.

"No matter what you think, Tyler was our very good friend — he has been inordinately kind to us. I think there's more to this than the business with the sunbonnets."

Fearing her father knew or suspected that she and Tyler had been lovers, Daisie veiled her indignation and backed down from the argument.

"You might have let him explain," her father went on. "Who will supply us now?"

"I shall walk into town each week and . . . and I shall hunt!" Daisie grabbed the rifle, squared her shoulders and set her mouth in a resolute line. She imagined herself stalking game, a cunning, capable huntress, fearing nothing and no one.

Sighing, her father went on staring into the fire. "You could be very wrong about Tyler, Daisie."

"I don't think so! You said yourself you expected one day to learn he'd cheated you. Have you forgotten he probably salted — "

"There are some things a man knows. I know Tyler did not salt the claim! He couldn't look me in the eye afterwards if he had."

Daisie shivered. She knew of one man not so far away who could practically rape a girl and then look her in the eye so that she even doubted the evidence of her own senses!

"Papa, we must go home!"

She watched him make a fist. "You go — if you can," he whispered, as near to anger as she'd ever seen him.

One morning in late September they woke to frost glittering thickly on all the sage and scrub oak. Each blade of meadow grass was furred with white, the pines and bare aspens completely coated in fairyland crystals.

"Did you sleep well, daughter?"

"I was cold," she said, shivering as she gazed across the gurgling creek to the beautiful, eerily white meadow. "Who would think frost would come this early?"

He reached into his trouser pocket and brought out his gold watch. "This is still running well. If you took it into town you'd get a good price for it."

He looked frailer than when she'd arrived three months before. His sunken eyes caressed the meadow and rocky ledge with affection. "The gold's here, if only I had the strength left to look."

A deer bounded away into the aspen grove, startling them. Wind rushed in the treetops, biting, warning, malicious, cold. The distant mountain peaks shone with gleaming, sun-glittering white. Daisie's heart grew still with alarm. Snow? In September? She had thought Tyler was joking when he warned them of it.

"I want you to get a good supply of shells," her father said, scanning the aloof white peaks. "Animals will be driven from the higher elevations. And be sure to write to your mother and warn her we may not be able to send letters very often. Buy all the supplies you can. . . ." He took her small, work-hardened hand and placed the gold watch into it, closing her fingers around the cold metal just as her mother had closed her fingers around the red purse. "Daughter, I insulted you not long ago by saying I wouldn't let you take care of me. I see now that I would have perished without you. You know, I haven't once thanked you for coming after me. It meant the world to me. . . ."

She didn't like his tone. She especially didn't like the wistful expression in his eyes. She wished she could refuse to sell the watch, but she knew only too well that their lives depended on it. She was overjoyed that they still had something of value to sell. It would buy them a little more time.

She began the long walk into town the next morning just after dawn. Wearing her only stockings and an extra pair of her papa's to fill out the too-large shoes, Daisie set out with a cheery goodbye. She wore the woolen coat she'd bought her papa. It made her look like a peasant.

The sun warmed the deep beds of pine needles on the forest floor, bringing up the warm, dusty smell of pine and red earth. She savored each breathtaking vista of high peaks, now white in the distance. In her pocket was a long letter to her mother explaining all they were doing to live "comfortably" in a cabin that sounded bigger, cleaner and airier in her description than it really was. She didn't mention that she was about to sell her father's watch. Her mother was probably searching for trinkets to sell as well.

Daisie arrived in town late that afternoon. She was footsore and weary, but she didn't pause. She went to the shopkeeper she'd met on her last trip, and after they'd agreed on a price for her father's solid gold watch, engraved with the date of his marriage to her mother, she descended upon the nearest restaurant where she devoured a meal heavily seasoned with guilty thoughts of her papa finishing the last of their beans. She ordered cake and nearly cried with the pleasure of eating something sweet.

Mrs. Darnel took her in for the night and seemed pleasant enough until she began asking Daisie about what she called "certain rumors."

"I didn't believe them when I first heard them. Why some-one said they saw you coming out of one of those . . . unmentionable places! And then they said you went into a saloon and started downing whiskey and finally got into a row. . . ." She clucked her tongue, and was clearly all agog to hear Daisie's explanation.

Daisie looked amused, but refused to satisfy the woman's curiosity. She was only too glad to leave early the next morning to assemble a winter's worth of supplies. Just as she was coming out of a gun shop carrying boxes of shells, Tyler rode by in his blue-trimmed top-buggy.

He looked better than when she had seen him at the Gaslight. His hat was still the whitest of whites, his leather coat ostentatiously fringed. His trousers seemed molded to his powerful thighs, his silver-tipped black boots seemed to gleam mockingly at her. When he caught sight of her, she turned away, her heart twisting. How could feelings linger so long? she wondered, forcing herself on.

She was on her way to hire a wagon to carry the goods back to camp when Tyler slowed the buggy beside her. He eased to a stop and climbed down. She kept walking.

He fell into step alongside her. "If you'll apologize for causing such a scene in front of my business associates, I'll apologize for leading you to believe you were sewing for — "

"I owe you no apologies!" She turned a corner, heedless of where she was going.

"Do you still want me to stay away, Daisie? Because if you do, I will. Aren't you low on supplies?"

"We're getting on perfectly well without you! I have a dozen men in town at my beck and call. Stay away from me and my father! We don't need the likes of you."

Passersby paused, eyeing them.

Tyler took her arm. "We need to talk."

"The time for talking was several weeks ago, Tyler Reede. I might have been foolish enough to listen to you then. Not now."

He looked bewildered. Daisie was acutely conscious of the current of desire that still flowed between them. But she was also furious.

"Daisie, I don't think you know how hard it has been for me

being away the past several weeks. When you came into the saloon I had just — ''

"Don't you see, it doesn't matter, Tyler? Whatever we had — '' Her voice broke. She jerked away. Amelia's words echoed in her memory. Everything was just as Hank and Amelia had said it would be. Daisie flinched as Tyler reached for her.

"It's over!" she hissed, fighting the tears that rose in her throat. "It never even began!" She fled then, far away from Tyler and his tormented cornflower blue eyes.

A hired wagon took her back to camp. She never once spoke to the driver, except to thank him as he drove away. She and her father packed the cabin with bulging sacks of flour, sugar, meal, and coffee. She had bought two more blankets, a decent pair of boots for her father and some soft gray wool to make herself a warm dress. And there was fingerling yarn for mittens and socks. In her pocket were two letters from her mother — unopened — which she presented to her father after supper that night. Both were a response to the news of the robbery, which was so far in the past that Daisie felt almost as though it had never really happened.

When her father was asleep she lay watching the leaping flames in the hearth, remembering the warmth of Tyler's hands on her, as if by doing so she could cleanse her wounded heart of him. If he came to her now she could drive him from the camp with the rifle . . . but he was not there. He was not at her feet explaining, begging, cajoling, the way someone like Hank might be. Surely, if Tyler had ever loved her, even a little, he would not be able to stay away.

"Where is the Tyler I love?" she whispered to the flames. She burrowed her face beneath the blankets and listened to the wind that had begun to moan outside.

Chapter Thirteen

"Howdy, folks. Say, I didn't mean to startle you!"

Daisie lowered the rifle, stepped out from the protective droop of the roof and stared at the apparition moving along the far side of the creek. It was someone wearing a long brown fur coat. Moments before, Daisie had been convinced the bear was back . . . leading a mule!

The person lifted a battered, shapeless hat from a head of short pale gray hair and grinned. It was a woman, her weathered face round and surprisingly fine-boned. Gingerly, jerking the neck rope of a shaggy pack mule loaded with bundles, she moved across the makeshift bridge Daisie and her father had fashioned over the creek.

Flashing them an infectious smile, her bright, lively blue eyes twinkling, she dashed her hat against her side and then swiped with a laugh at the dust she had raised. Shrugging off the fur robe to reveal a dusty wool jacket and trousers pouched out at the knees and stuffed into a pair of scarred, muddy miner's boots, she bellowed hello again.

"I took you for a bear," Daisie said, amazed.

The woman nodded. "That's what I figured, girlie. Where's Lord Browning?"

"Lord — ?"

Daisie's father rose from the bed inside the cabin and came to the door. His eyes widened. He went out and extended his hand. "Grace! How did you find me?"

"Ain't afraid to ask questions about folks I'm interested in. How ya doin'?" She jerked off a pair of fingerless gloves and shook his hand, then clapped him on the back. "Who's this crazy female with the rifle?" She offered her small, hardened hand to Daisie, and Daisie felt her fingers being amiably crushed.

"This is Daisie," Gregory Browning said, as if the woman should recognize the name. He showed her to a choice seat on a smooth piece of deadwood beside the outdoor fire. "Daisie, may I present Grace Roswell, mountain woman."

Grace colored a rosy pink. "Drifter's more like it," she scoffed.

"Pleased to me you, M-Mrs. Roswell," Daisie said, turning to stare in amazement at her father. Could this be the woman Hank and Amelia had mentioned seeing her father with in the spring? Why had they led her to believe the woman was.

Daisie suddenly laughed at her own assumptions. She had been an easy target for Hank and Amelia's insinuations.

The woman roared. "Just call me Grace. Ain't never both ered gettin' married. So, how're you doin' anyhow? I expected folks to tell me you'd got rich and gone home."

Daisie moved quickly to serve coffee and slices of fresh cornbread.

Her father smiled, shaking his head. "Daisie has found a single float, but I haven't been able to locate the source yet. It's all we can do now to keep ourselves in supplies."

The woman looked the camp over, nodding her head at the storage tent near the ridge, the bear alarm in the meadow, the pile of firewood that had grown higher every day as Daisie worked to drag in fallen logs from the pine forest. "Real nice camp, Gregory. You ain't fixin' to stay the winter?" At their nod she made a short laugh. "You're crazier than me. First sign of snow, I find a town, even though I can't abide towns. Varmints live there. Pure and simple. Mind if I set a spell and talk with you? Haven't seen a female girl in a year or so. Lots of miners to talk to — a dumb bunch. What brings you all the way to America, girlie? Seems you paw told me you was back in England lookin' after your maw."

"I came to fetch Papa," Daisie said, giving her father a knowing smile. "You didn't tell me about Grace," she said.

"Why, we met when your paw here was first out lookin' around in the gravel for gold. I seen this scrawny old fella lookin' at the ground like he'd dropped his watch . . . or his teeth. . . ."

Gregory chuckled.

"And here he says — straight-faced, too — he's lookin' for some gold to take home to his wife and daughters. I says to myself, Grace, this is one *green* greenhorn!"

Eyes twinkling, her father broke in. "She took me into town to buy the right equipment. . . ."

"But I didn't think to hold his hand while he was doin' it, so here he comes out of some jackass store with enough stuff to fit up the whole Ohio 53rd regiment, and carryin' that there rifle like it was a rattler gettin' ready to bite him. That so-called storekeeper wouldn't take back a stick of what he sold your paw, neither, and he sure charged a helluva lot, too. Was your paw ever mad when I told him all he needed was a frypan, a bedroll and a pistol."

They both laughed.

"She taught me to pan," Daisie's father said.

"And then I went off about my business. I just got in for the winter a couple of days ago, and I says to myself, I wonder if that ol' coot found his gold. Sorry to see you ain't."

"What have you been doing with yourself all summer?" her father asked. This was the most animated Daisie had seen him in months.

"Not much, that's for sure. Just goin' from one place to another. I'm no-account, that's nothin' to debate about. And I like it that way!

"I like livin' in these mountains," she explained to Daisie. "They don't change on you. They're dangerous, sure, but they're predictable. I go from one side of a mountain to another, it don't change. People do. People is one kind of varmint one day and a worse kind the next. No offense intended, of course, just talkin' in general terms. Even so, I get an itch to see folks now and again. Helps remind me why I'm out here wearin' my legs out for no good reason except I like movin' around. I was a school teacher back East. One year I came out here to work. Did some teachin' here in the mountains, got to takin' the young uns out for field trips and such. One day I says to myself, Grace, the schoolhouse ain't no place for you. Young uns get on my nerves, you see, all the time wigglin' and wantin' out of their work. So I came into these mountains, and I ain't been out since.''

Grace settled herself in front of the fire and slurped at the coffee Daisie offered. ''Um. Good. Got anythin' nippy to put in it? No? Too bad.'' She shrugged toward the rifle. ''Can you shoot that thing, girlie?''

''Not too well,'' Daisie said. ''Not at all, really.''

''Didn't think so. You would've shot off my foot the way you was aimin'. While I wouldn't have thanked you for that, if I'd a been a bear I would've charged at you, and had you for breakfast. You folks must be doin' okay if you've got coffee.''

Daisie chuckled. ''This came out of my dressmaking money.''

Her father set his cup down. ''Daisie has no confidence in my expert opinion that there is gold on this claim.''

''Sure there's gold! Ain't Crazy Bob, the critter who caused this boom, believed it all these years? Hell, there's gold, all right. Only most of it's underground. If you don't mind me sayin', you two don't look like you could dig up a potato much less sink a mine shaft. Got any blasting powder? Well, never mind. If you still believe you'll find gold after all this time, you'll find it. I got no use for gold myself, except it'd be nice to drink coffee like this more often.''

''How do you survive alone in the mountains?'' Daisie asked. ''What do you eat?''

''Well, folks share with me. In return I help out, or I teach 'em things. For instance, I can read. Some miners can't, so I read things to 'em, like letters or claim deeds or newspaper sheets. I write letters, too, and I'm a fair shot, so I bring down a pheasant or deer now and again.''

"Could you shoot us a deer?" Daisie's father asked, perking up. "One thing we miss is fresh meat."

"Plannin' to keep the carcass here? It'll draw bear and wolves."

Daisie's father looked disappointed.

"'Course, I can shoot you anythin' you want. You like rabbit stew? Bear meat ain't bad, either, once you develop a taste for it. If you're goin' to store fresh meat before a good freeze you're sure to attract somethin' hungry. Might be better if I taught you to aim that rifle good. Then you can bring down your own game all winter long whenever you need it."

Daisie brightened. "Would you? I'd be so grateful. We couldn't eat a whole deer before it'd spoil, though."

"Hell, sell the rest in town! Good business in fresh game. Folks'll buy the antlers, the hide. . . . Shoot, yes, sell what you don't need. I'll help you. I could stay around a day or so, but not much longer 'cause it's not in my nature to stay put long. Nice camp you got here, though, Gregory. Real nice."

After lunch Grace examined the rifle and pistol. While making disgusted, disapproving noises, she cleaned them both, scolding at regular intervals. Afterwards, she showed Daisie how to do it.

Then she took up her own Henry rifle and set out with Daisie to a clearing some distance south around the knoll from the cabin. When she had settled on an area she liked, she ordered Daisie to pace off lengths of fifty yards, one hundred yards and so on, until Daisie was annoyed with so much marching back and forth.

"Got to learn your distances, young woman," Grace boomed. "Ain't goin' to do you no good to shoot at somethin' if you can't guess how far it is from you. It affects the aim, you know. Surely does."

Daisie learned to aim high, heard about bullet trajectory and wind speed and direction and finally hunkered down beside Grace, bracing the rifle on a large smooth boulder.

"Lay your pack under it like so," Grace said, explaining that

Daisie mustn't place the rifle directly onto whatever she was using as a brace.

When Daisie finally squeezed off her first shot she did far better than she expected. Thinking she was ready to go hunting, she got up to leave.

"You're one impatient little lady," Grace said, shaking her cropped gray head. "Git down here. There's plenty more to learn."

"I can't waste all these shells," Daisie said as the lesson continued for over an hour.

"Better to use up a few now then go hungry later," Grace said. "Rifle practice is like catchin' a man. You go through a lot of pain and hard work before you squeeze off the right one." She thought a moment about what she'd just said and then roared until her little blue eyes watered.

Daisie's cheeks flushed. "Have you ever . . . wanted to get married, Grace?"

"Hell, yes. Twenty times at least, but I don't need it — marriage, I mean. It's a lot of trouble hangin' onto a good man. You got them she-wolves at your heels all the time. No, I just take men as I find them, and then go on about my business."

"But doesn't that . . . go against everything we women are taught . . . about fidelity and chastity?"

"Oh, such words! Ain't heard 'em since I was a girl in pigtails. Ain't nothin' more natural than a man and woman comin' together in lovemakin'. Fidelity and chastity's words people made up to cover what they're doin' on the side. You watch sometime. The ones cryin' sin the loudest . . . they know whereof they speak!" She roared, delighted with herself. "Damn, it's good to talk to another woman for a change. Men talk of nothin' but money and gold. Boringest subject in the world."

Daisie kept her eyes averted. "But what about love? Isn't it hard to give love and risk getting hurt?"

Grace elbowed Daisie's ribs. "Love ain't the same business as sin. A man's like a good oaken bucket. Either your bucket's got a hole in it or it don't. See what I mean?"

"No."

"Well, it don't matter to an innocent young thing like you. You'll run across some upstandin' young fella and your paw will say you should marry, and you will."

"What if you were in love . . . and the man wasn't faithful?"

"Girlie, then your bucket's got a hole ain't nothin' goin' to plug it up. I got no use for a bucket with a hole that big." She laughed. "You're mighty curious about men and love for a young girl. I suspect you got some fella on your mind."

Daisie quickly shook her head.

"You could always get this fella of yours in your sights . . ." — Grace aimed the rifle — "and bring him down like so many females do nowadays."

"How?"

"Well, there are ways. You don't look so dumb that you couldn't figure it out."

"And if I couldn't bring myself to do . . . something like that?" Daisie asked, believing Grace was referring to entrapment and pregnancy.

"Then you stand up and say, hey, tall, dumb and ugly, my heart's got a pain in it. Fix it or get on about your business!"

Daisie dissolved in laughter. "Grace, you are a rare creature!"

"Why, thank you. I always did think I was smarter than most."

After another hour a chilly wind came up. Grace decided Daisie had learned all she was going to that day, and ordered them both back to camp for coffee. She spent the remainder of the day telling harrowing stories of hunting adventures and accidents she'd either witnessed or heard about.

Two days later Grace and Daisie went out at dawn to bring down their first deer. Within the first hour Daisie spotted several, but most were out of range. Grace didn't want to scare them off with a shot she knew her rifle and eye couldn't handle.

Half an hour later, when they were more than a mile from camp, they spotted a majestic stag standing alone at the edge of a clearing.

"Oh, not him," Daisie said, feeling suddenly sick at heart.

"He's too fine."

"You just ain't hungry enough yet," Grace said, taking aim.

Daisie's heart twisted as Grace talked to herself, making fine adjustments to the angle of her rifle. A second later she squeezed off a shot that reverberated through the foothills. The stag dropped. Daisie turned away.

"Come on, young woman," Grace said. "One more lesson. Dressin' the kill. Think of it as that man who's got you tense as a rattler."

"That's all right. You go on and do it. I'll wait here. I feel faint."

"I ain't stayin' around to hold your hand forever, you know. I'm about ready to be off. Seems to me if you and your paw are goin' to stay in these hills over the winter you'd better harden up right this minute. Ain't no room for faintin' females around here. Faintin' is for the ones that die. You think you'll survive in that little mud cabin of yours without killin' a few things and dressin' them, you've got some surprises comin'."

Grace moved off, grumbling something about silly females always giving a stout-hearted woman like herself a bad name. Daisie dragged herself to her feet and started resolutely after the old woman, but the rifle in her hand felt like her enemy.

Dressing a deer proved to be a revolting chore that brought up Daisie's breakfast and lunch shortly after Grace opened the carcass and dumped the entrails in the brush.

"Ordinarily I'd have made you do that for practice, but seein' as how you're actin' so female on me. . . ."

Daisie staggered back moments later, feeling drained and weak, and helped tie the carcass, feet first, to a long pole. They braced the pole on their shoulders and lifted. Daisie found out then that killing and dressing a deer was easy compared to carrying it back to camp.

That night they feasted on roast venison. Daisie had to admit it was fine eating.

"A kill like this'll keep you for two or three weeks durin' the winter," Grace nodded. "Cut up the steaks and roasts before it all freezes, though. Else you'll have one stiff slab of meat on your hands. I'd keep what you're not goin' to use right away in that tent yonder. That's far enough away that if bears or wolves come around they'll attack that and stay clear of you.''

Daisie felt ill suddenly. Wolves?

''They'll tear through four feet of snow to get at food,'' Grace was saying. ''Great noses, wolves. Why, I remember just a few years back we had snow from October to May, and in some places the snow was ten feet deep. Most awful feelin' you can imagine sinkin' into a ravine with five feet of snow over your head. Makes you appreciate walkin' on mother earth.''

''It couldn't have been that deep,'' Daisie objected.

''Next time you're on a road around here, ask yourself what the tall poles along the edges are for,'' Grace said.

Daisie frowned. ''I never noticed.''

''Mighty hard to follow a road if it's five feet beneath your feet. Most poles are six or seven feet high. If the snow gets deeper than that nobody's goin' to be movin' about. Now remember, don't let your chimney get covered. During storms you'll have to go out every so often to clear it and dig your tunnel out up to the surface. Don't wait to do it all at once. You might get buried, or kill yourself. You think I'm carryin' on? Just you wait! Come spring you'll get water if that creek swells, but otherwise this is a decent location, back to the wind, face to the winter sun. Not bad at all. I'd say with enough provisions, the two of you might make it.''

Daisie's father looked glum. ''We're grateful for your advice, Grace.''

''Don't mind helpin' folks when they're as nice as you. Truth is, I'm takin' leave of you tomorrow. Got to be on my way. Tell you what I'm goin' to do, though. I'm goin' to leave that mule behind for a few weeks. Then I'll be back for him.''

''That's not necessary,'' Daisie's father said, sorry to hear she was leaving.

''You folks need a sight more wood than you got stockpiled so far,'' Grace said, her tone always brisk and matter of fact. ''That mule can help you drag in a few trees. I don't know that Daisie is handy with a hammer and wedge to split 'em into kindlin', but it's got to be done. That pile of twigs and branches you got outside isn't goin' to keep you more than a week. You'll need twenty, thirty times that."

Daisie already felt cold.

"I'll send someone from town to go after your trees with a crosscut saw. He can split up a mess of it for you. Can't be done all in one day, of course, but it'll get you started. First snow, I bet you'll be headed into town anyway."

Daisie's father's chin went up.

Grace just chuckled. "What's all that goldurned pride got you? Never mind. Don't want to hear it. Another thing you should be thinkin' on is gettin' a supply of water into this cabin. I might could send out a barrel for you. Ain't nothin' worse than hackin' through the creek ice every mornin'."

"Can't we melt snow?" Daisie asked.

"That's a thought," Grace said. "Get your washin' done now, though, before the weather gets any colder. I'd be willin' to bet in a couple of weeks you won't be able to touch creek water it'll hurt so bad. Numbs you better'n whiskey!"

Daisie lowered her narrowed eyes. "If you're trying to scare us. . . ."

Grace chuckled. "I learned a long time ago not to reason with mules. Just hit 'em hard. They'll see the right of things eventually. I'll be back for that animal in a couple weeks. Meantime, I'll see about that hired man. Feed him good, and bring down a deer or two for him to take back for his pay."

"Ask Tyler Reede to come out," Daisie's father said.

"You folks know Tyler? Mercy, ain't he the best lookin' thing this side of the divide? And a nice man, too. There's one worth gettin' a bead on, Daisie!"

"Tell us about him," Daisie's father said, leaning forward, his eyes bright.

"Tyler's a fine specimen, that's for sure, but he ain't nobody's hired man. He's helped more than one man make his fortune in gold, and kept more than one from starvin', too. Hell, I've known him for years!"

"Does he speculate in land?" Daisie asked.

"Of course. Who doesn't if he's got a couple extra dollars? This here claim's a speculation. That boy's made himself a good livin' up in these hills, and he doesn't have to live like a mole to do it, either. If I see him I'll tell him I saw you both." She looked hard at Daisie and then smiled a little to herself.

Though Daisie was sorry to see Grace hobble away the following morning, she was glad to return to her fantasy that their winter in the cabin would be like those in England, rainy with light snows.

The day was so warm and bright, Daisie believed they had a long while to wait before another spell of bad weather set in. Her father dressed warmly that afternoon and attempted to make friends with Grace's mule, Homer, by taking him to a meadow downstream where several dead trees lay about.

Over the next several days Daisie and her father slaved at chopping branches from the dead, easily splintered trunks before they learned that Homer had no intention of dragging the wood back to camp without a hawing, kicking fuss.

Daisie was planning her first hunt alone when they woke to a sugar dusting of snow one morning. Shivering, Daisie brought water into the cabin and reported dozens of tracks, some looking suspiciously like bear, along the bank of the creek.

She delayed until the next day when the weather was mild again. Shortly after dawn she set out, wearing her father's coat and with her heart in her throat.

A mile from camp, she encountered a young buck and hastily dropped behind some trees to take aim. Her first shot went wild, and the buck bounded away indignantly. Daisie sat for several minutes recovering from a fit of trembling and berating herself for forgetting all that Grace had so patiently taught her. The thought of going back empty-handed to a camp where nothing but beans and tinned food awaited her kept her eye keen.

A little further on she spotted another group of deer. Coolly, she selected her victim, aimed — remembering to lift the tip of her rifle — and squeezed off a shot that caught the buck unawares.

He dropped, and the others scattered. Her heart full of anguish, Daisie tiptoed up to the suffering beast. Weeping, she loaded the pistol, aimed at the buck's head and then turned her face away. The shot numbed her stiffened arm, but the beast was dead.

After a brief cry, Daisie set her teeth and opened the carcass. She worked fast and was soon done. As she wiped the tears from her cheeks, she realized she would have to drag the carcass back to camp alone.

Throwing the knife down, she dropped to a boulder and sobbed. She sobbed over her long list of follies, from rejecting Norwood's affection and security to losing her heart to Tyler. She cried for her lost innocence. She cried for her broken heart, and because she was so afraid to trust the man she loved — afraid to make another mistake, afraid of being tricked and used.

At last the sound of approaching footsteps brought Daisie's head up. She reached automatically for the rifle. If it was not her father. . . .

Tyler's voice called frantically from the trees behind her. "Daisie, where are you?"

Her heart leaped. Her tears vanished. Her blood was suddenly on fire. Tyler! Tyler, had come!

She grabbed the hem of her skirt and wiped her face. Oh, for a mirror! A comb! "I'm here," she called, forgetting that she had said she hated him, forgetting that he had humiliated her, taken her and abandoned her. Her mind was filling instead with joy that he had finally, finally come!

He tramped toward her through the trees, his Stetson bobbing as he ducked beneath banches. He'd changed his fringed coat for one with a fleece lining. When he saw her, relief flooded his face and his tight lips relaxed, opening to call hello as if he didn't want her to see that he had been alarmed. "Your father said you'd gone hunting. Alone! I thought he had lost his mind!" He looked angry, then amazed, then alarmed all over again as he grabbed her by her shoulders and stared into her eyes.

Then he was kissing her, his mouth demanding, warm,

commanding, devouring, setting her mind ablaze with that seething desire she had banked for a month. She molded herself to him, relishing the feel of her body pressed against his, savoring the solidity of his hard, strong arms encircling her back, his thighs hugging her own. She felt weak and giddy.

Tearing himself from her, he searched her face, trying to understand what it was between them that had not gone out while they were apart, but now only burned more brightly, consuming them. Blinking, he looked away, down, staring at the dead buck.

"You've brought down a beauty! And dressed it, too. When I heard a rifle shot — " He tore off his hat and pushed back his hair with his forearm.

She fell against him, too weak to battle her emotions. He drew her to him again, holding her tightly, silently, for a long time. At last he pulled a kerchief from his pocket and wiped her face. "You're covered with blood. You haven't hurt yourself?"

She shook her head. Her heart was pounding. Her head reeled. She was blind to reason, deaf to her own warnings, unable to do anything but lift her face and kiss him. His response was instant, enveloping, powerfully urgent, overwhelming, just as it had been that night by the creek. He kissed her with all the passion and depth of that first time beneath the overhang when the attraction had sparked between them. When they were kissing like this, Daisie trusted him unquestioningly.

She stroked his neck, feeling the soft warmth of his skin beneath her fingertips and his silky hair against her palm. "Oh, Tyler," she sighed, so happy to be in his arms. "Why are you here?"

"Grace Roswell left me a peculiar message. Something about coming out here to split firewood . . . and that there was a beauty waiting for me ripe for the kill."

Daisie laughed as she nuzzled Tyler's cheek. "I have been waiting and didn't know it."

"Can we forget all the trouble over the sunbonnets?" he asked softly.

"Yes, please," Daisie whispered. "It was stupid of me to be

so angry. I feel weak. Can we sit down? How does my papa look to you.''

''A little tired.''

Daisie drew away as they sank to a fallen log. ''Lately, I've been so afraid that he has decided to die here. I can't get him to move into town. I can't get him to do anything! If he catches his death I'll never forgive myself. It would kill Mama.''

Suddenly she was back in Tyler's arms, clinging to him. She'd tried to be strong for so long and now she yearned to indulge her weaknesses, heap all her troubles and heartaches on Tyler's broad shoulders. Tyler's mouth closed over hers, warm, urgent, possessive. She knew nothing but the delicious feeling of surrender, the feeling that he would take care of her and make everything right again.

The fire in her blood rose. She pressed against him, heedless to all but the warmth of his lips and his hands caressing her beneath the woolen coat.

Almost without realizing it, they had both slipped to the ground. Tyler pressed against her, brushing back her tangled hair, gazing into her eyes, kissing her cheeks and the tip of her nose and then holding his cheek against hers as he kissed her earlobe.

His fingers made quick work of the coat buttons and then the bodice buttons, freeing her breasts to the faint glimmer of sunlight filtering down through the pines.

His face grew slack and tender, his lazy-lidded eyes sultry as he kissed first one soft eager breast and then the other. Her skin looked so frail, so pale, so soft as his fingers claimed her breasts, caressing her so that the pleasure radiated throughout her body. She had left her corset off that morning, and so her body was bared to his touch and quivered as he trailed his fingers over her skin. He loosened her skirt and tugged the fabric down to press one burning kiss on her navel.

Gasping with desire, Daisie pulled his face to hers and kissed him, her need for him making her strong. He was there for her, suddenly, settling with a tight, restrained sigh into the cradle of her legs, moving slowly, exquisitely against her with a groan of need that warmed her and kept her clinging to him as she plummeted into her own inner, swirling, panting darkness, experiencing with Tyler the crescendo of their passion.

His grip grew rigid. He paused, kissing her with his entire being, pouring his passion into her soul until there was nothing but incandescence. She made a little cry against his cheek, felt as if she was splitting apart and whirling into a knot of flame. He seized her, possessing her mouth, wringing from her all she had to give, blinding her with the explosive awareness that this was her love for him and it was everything.

They lay still together for so long that Daisie began to drift, dreaming of soft fluffy pillows and cool fresh sheets beneath her skin . . . and of Tyler at her side. For the first time in weeks she felt safe. There, lying on the forest floor, with pine needles laced in her hair, she felt happy.

Finally Tyler rolled away and sat elbow on knee watching her. She covered herself then and sat, too. "I have loved you," she whispered, getting to her feet. "And I have hated you." She looked down on him, wonderstruck that he had become so much a part of her. "And now I have loved you again. And I'm still not sorry."

He climbed to his feet and stood with her in the loose circle of his arms. "All it took was one word to bring me back to you — that you needed me."

Then they were clinging to each other, thinking of all that still held them apart, the camp, the lure of gold and Daisie's stubborn, prideful father.

She looked up into his eyes and knew it didn't matter if a thousand women had loved him before her. She loved him, and he had come to her. Tyler was the lion she had dreamed of. He was the one she wanted to capture and tame.

He turned and put his hand on her cheek. "When will you be sure of me, Daisie? When will you know the answers to your questions?"

"There aren't any more questions in my mind, Tyler," she whispered. "None that matter."

She might have asked him things then, but there was really only one important matter on her mind. Did he love her? And if he did, why didn't he tell her so? Why didn't he put her fears to rest? Why didn't he look happy?

They lashed the buck's legs to a long branch and went back to camp. A dozen pack mules stood across the creek, their backs laden with firewood.

"Tyler!" Daisie laughed. "Are you crazy? You want us to leave the camp and provide us with everything necessary to stay!"

"I have to know you're safe and comfortable here. Will you please accept this as my gift? Lord Browning," he called, ducking into the cabin. "I found her. Look what this vixen of yours has brought down."

Daisie glanced at the deer. She'd known she could bring it down. She wished she was as certain she could bring down Tyler.

After a moment, Daisie wondered why they weren't coming out. She slipped into the cabin and found her father seated, his bad ankle propped.

"Dash it all, Daisie. I've gone and twisted it again. Tyler tells me you've shot a deer. He didn't do it for you, did he?"

"Oh, Papa," she sighed, examining the swollen area. "How often have I told you to stay out of that ravine? Why did you have to go in there again? Tyler, will you stay for supper and help me convince — ?"

"I have to unload the mules and get them back before dark."

She sighed, disappointed. Her only thought was to be near him, to feel the sense of rightness he gave her just by being close by.

Unloading the mules took less than an hour. By then Daisie's father had fallen asleep. When Tyler was ready to go, he pulled on his coat, puffing and red-faced. "Every time I ride away from here without you, I wonder if I'll see you again. If something happened to you or your father. . . . I could force him, you know. I could carry him to a wagon."

She shook her head, "We can't do that. His dignity is painfully fragile now. We're all right here, really, except that —] Oh, Tyler, there's so much I want to say and don't know how."

A smile flickered at the corner of his mouth. "It's like torture. . . ."

She wanted to ask what he meant. Was his love for her torture? Why couldn't he just let go and love her as she yearned to be loved? What stood in his way? Only her father's dream? Or was he readying himself for the day she would go back to England, leaving him behind, perhaps forever?

Her heart twisted. "Tyler — "

"Don't go out again alone like that. It's too dangerous! We'll go hunting together next time." The smile flickered again and his eyes brightened.

Daisie tingled. If nothing else, they had had those wonderful moments of love together— and perhaps they could steal a few moments more.

"Thank you for the wood, Tyler," Daisie whispered. "Thank you for . . . everything."

He touched her cheek. "Stay close to the cabin and don't shoot me when I ride in tomorrow. Grace said you had her worried."

"She was wearing a bear hide. I wish you could stay."

He brushed her lips with his. "Tell me what you're thinking, Daisie Browning. Why do you want me to stay?" His eyes danced.

She wanted to say because she loved him, but he already knew that. "I'm thinking that I've never seen eyes the color of yours. I'm thinking that your brows lay so neatly against your forehead, that your hair is such a wonderful, rich shade of brown."

He wrenched her close, kissing her fiercely, and then he was jerking away, dragging the lead mule into the aspens where they had first made love. Then, without a goodbye, he left her standing there with her heart in her eyes.

Chapter Fourteen

The doctor came and went with Tyler the next day, adding the stern warning, "Stay off that leg, Lord Browning!" While the doctor was there, Daisie and Tyler could only look at each other longingly. Tyler left before they could manage any time alone together.

The days remained mild and the nights cold. To soothe her father's irritation and boredom, Daisie wandered near the camp each day scanning the ground for rocks. If she could find even one more containing gold he might consent to spend the winter in town.

Against Tyler's instructions, Daisie went hunting again and brought down another deer, dragging it back to camp herself. When Grace returned for the mule, she traded goods and shells for the meat and took all Daisie and her father couldn't use into town.

In October the weather ceased to smile. Menacing clouds sank, covering the distant white peaks, blanketing the cabin with stunning, numbing cold. Each day they used so much wood Daisie shuddered — and winter had hardly begun.

Following three days of steady snowfall, a foot of the pristine white stuff covered everything. Rounded bonnets of white lay on the cold campfire stones, on the logs laid across the creek, on the tent and woodpile. The creek gurgled between sunlit edges of clear, sparkling ice, and all around the dark pines bore loads of white on every branch.

At dawn the following day, as the sun peeked provocatively from behind heavy banks of clouds to the west, deer ventured to the creek and drank, ears and tails twitching, as though they sensed the menace of Daisie and her rifle. Their store of meat was enough to last several more days so Daisie could enjoy just watching the deer.

Later, as she carried wood into the cabin, she thought of the armloads she'd brought in the day before and the day before that, worried that even all Tyler had brought wouldn't last through November. The wall of firewood had seemed endless the day they unloaded the pack mules and stacked it along the bluff. Tyler had advised her to use wood starting farthest from the door. "It'll save you going so far later on."

She'd been taking the rifle since seeing bear tracks twice by the creek. It was such a terrible chore juggling it when her arms were loaded to her chin with wood. She thought of leaving it behind, but decided perhaps she should behave like a responsible pioneer. Tyler would surely ask if she was being careful. She wanted to answer a confident, honest yes!

Hefting the rifle, she trudged once again into the snow, feeling its weight gather on her hem, making the heavy green wool like lead. Squinting against the glare of sun on snow, she rounded the cabin to the south to check on the tent. Most of the frozen meat was inside, along with the boxed goods, safely packed to stay dry, and the tools.

Finding everything in order, she looked out over the wide white vista to the south and east where, several miles away, the town lay. Everywhere were meandering deer trails. If the wood only held out, it'd be easy to hunt, she thought, turning back.

With its foot-deep hood of white, the cabin looked liked a cave, the doorway like a shadowed cave mouth. A feeble ribbon of gray smoke lifted from the tilting chimney.

At the long woodpile north of the cabin doorway, she set the rifle across the top layer of logs and began to arrange what logs she could manage in the cradle of her left arm. The pine sap smelled strong and sharp. It got all over her hands and coat sleeves. She was fretting about that when she heard a snort.

Hair prickled on the back of Daisie's neck. A thrill of terror shot through her blood, and it felt as though her heart had stopped. At first the bear looked like little more than a hulking shadow beyond the upper edge of the tent. She tried to speak, to call out "Papa!", but her throat closed.

Foraging closer to the tent, the bear lifted his small dark head and regarded her. From that distance she could see his intelligent yellow eyes. He grunted again, taking a heavy step closer. Where had he been when she stood there moments before?

"Papa." Her lips formed the words, but her voice was barely a croak. "Papa. . . ."

Sniffing the ground, plodding several steps closer, the bear reached the tent, swiped at it casually and brought it down in a heap.

Daisie wanted to slip into the cabin, but the bear was actually closer to the door now than she. Any movement she made would draw his attention. Her heart was pounding like a drum, hard and painful, against her chest wall.

The bear caught her scent then and stared at her, nostrils flaring, a low, menacing sound coming from his throat.

Sinking to her haunches, Daisie let the load of firewood roll from her arms into the snow. Then she rose again, as slowly as possible, and lifted the rifle from the woodpile. It was already loaded, but she had nothing to prop it on, nothing to steady her aim. She crouched again.

"Go away," she whispered. She wouldn't have to shoot at him if he wandered away. She should have strung another alarm system behind and beyond the cabin. Each second with the bear's cunning eyes on her seemed like an eternity. She forced herself to take a breath, and the cold air helped clear her head.

Sniffing the air, the bear turned back, crushing the tent again, growling, and causing a great commotion as the pick, shovel and panning tin clattered together. Then, unexpectedly, he turned and looked directly at her again. He sniffed.

Charged with terror, Daisie dropped back and sat heavily in the snow. She couldn't swallow. Her lungs felt frozen, and her heart was fluttering, giving her a queer pain, making her believe suddenly in death by fright.

When she raised the rifle and aimed, she was suddenly amazed by its weight. Her muscles were almost too watery to support it. The tip kept dipping too low. If she missed, the bear would charge.

"What are you doing out there, Daisie?" her father called, then, his voice muffled by the thick cabin walls.

The door jerked open a little. Gregory Browning stuck out his balding head and saw her sitting terror-stricken in the snow fifteen feet from the cabin.

"Stay inside!" Her voice was harsh, strangled. "The bear!"

The bear ripped the tent from the stakes and flung everything aside. Clawing at the hard meat, he turned suddenly. Then he was moving steadily, heavily, toward the cabin, down the hill toard the dooryard. Her father stepped out almost into the bear's path then jerked back, startled. He bared his teeth, putting up his arm.

Daisie strained to level the rifle. It recoiled with a deafening explosion. The shot ricocheted off the ledge behind the tent. Daisie coughed out a cry. She had missed completely!

Panicked, she scrambled up, snow flying. She emptied the chamber, and when she looked up saw that the bear had stopped, momentarily stunned.

"Throw me some shells!"

Her father gaped, blinked, disappeared inside, and returned, looking befuddled. He started out the door toward her.

"No! Throw them!"

He flung her a handful that sailed into the air all around her, dropping silently into the thick layer of snow in front of her.

Wailing, Daisie stood to see where the nearest one had landed. A tiny hole showed where the shell had dropped in. Lunging, she fumbled, dashed away the snow, caught up the shell and wiped it on her coat front.

Holding her breath, she loaded, took aim . . . and screamed! The bear was heading directly for her father, who still stood in the cabin doorway. "Get inside! Close the door!"

Her father held the pistol straight out before him, his arm extended rigidly like a duellist's. He fired, groaned at the powerful recoil, and staggered backward two steps.

Daisie had no time to wonder if he had missed. The bear hesitated just long enough for her to lift the heavy rifle again, get the animal in her sights, and pull the trigger. The force of the blast flung her onto her back.

Pulling herself to her feet, she saw the bear falter. Her shot had gone low, catching him in the lower portion of his body, perhaps in his leg. She had one last chance.

She scrambled in the snow for another shell, sobbing a little when she couldn't find one. Forcing herself to stand, she scanned the snow, saw another small hole, dipped her hand into the stinging cold crystals and plucked out the shell. She cleaned it and again loaded the rifle.

The bear was less than twenty yeards from her now. She knew just where to point the rifle so that the shot would take him between the eyes.

Dropping flat, she propped the rifle on the armload of firewood she'd dropped. She aimed high and waited . . . waited until her hands had stopped quaking . . . waited until her heart had stopped leaping.

One step after another, the lumbering bear closed in on her. She saw yellow eyes . . . ruffled fur . . . pellets of hard dirty snow clinging to his belly and leg fur. . . .

He was at point-blank range. She squeezed off a shot that slammed against her shoulder. Then, scrambling to her feet, she found another shell.

"He's down!" her father yelped, cheering, venturing beyond the door a few more steps. "Excellent shot, Daisie! Excellent!"

Coughing for breath, pressing her fist against her lunging heart, dashing tears from her eyes, Daisie at first refused to believe it. She wanted another shell in the chamber just to be safe. Finding another, loading, panting, sobbing, she looked up to see her father's beaming face. The bear lay motionless at his feet, a spray of red all across the snow.

Raggedly, she began to laugh. She dropped into the snow and went on laughing, but it was not a pleasant sound. It was the sound of a broken-hearted child, terrified, exhausted, drained.

When her father helped her to her feet a few moments later, Daisie felt weak and ill. Clinging to his arm, she plodded toward the bear and stood over it, both sickened and relieved. Then she turned away. "I'll clean it later, Papa. I can't do anything more right now. I need to sit down."

She handed him the rifle and went into the cabin. She fell onto the cot, stared at the glowing yellow coals in the hearth and shuddered. How much more would they have to endure?

Emerging from the cabin an hour later Daisie found that her father had cleaned the bear and begun skinning it. Smiling with gratitude, she went to see what could be done about the crushed tent.

Scattered on the flattened, tangled canvas lay a jumble of jagged rocks and stones that had been dislodged when her first shot went awry. Brushing away most of the rubble, she picked up several of the larger pieces and examined them: The rocks were a strange gray with tiny veins running through, veins flecked with dull gold.

Her heart leaped! Grabbing up all the pieces on the canvas, she took a larger rock and bashed it against the ledge, trying to find the place where her shot had struck. Though she couldn't be certain, it appeared that the chips she held had broken away from the ledge directly behind where the tent had stood, exposing now a dark metallic vein, tantalizingly like the rock Tyler had claimed contained high-grade ore.

Filling both hands, she climbed over the battered tent and scrambled through the snow, her feet slipping. She felt giddy, light-headed, and yet afraid to hope. Her father looked so frail bent over the carcass as he separated the bearskin from the flesh.

She paused, sad suddenly that finding gold should have been his dream, and that she was stealing his moment of triumph. He had risked everything for this. Her heart was suddenly full of love for him as she came up from behind, eyes brimming with happy tears. She didn't have to wait for the assayer's report. She knew what she held in her cold, trembling hands.

"Papa," she said gently. "Look what I've found."

He straightened from the backbreaking job, looking as if he was enjoying himself. "I'm a mess, my dear. What is it?"

She held out her handful of rocks. "Could you come and look behind the tent, please? And tell me what you think?"

Their eyes met. Her heart shivered to see her father's eyes widen, the light dawning in them a bright and eager glow of wonder, hope and victory!

Breathing faster with excitement, he looked where she was pointing and then followed her.

"Isn't this where the former owners did some blasting, Papa?" Daisie asked, showing him the broken rocks scattered on the canvas.

He took the rocks from her and scowled at them. "I've got snow in my shoes and blood on my hands," he said as if they had not suddenly become rich. A rebellious smile broke his scowl. He knew they had succeeded, too! Crouching, he trailed a bloodied finger along the traces of ore. "I knew it," he whispered. "I was practically sleeping on the bloody stuff all along!"

Without a word, he sprang up and seized the pick hidden beneath the tangled tent. Taking a mighty swing at the rocky ledge, he sank the iron into the exposed vein and wrenched out chunks of rock. More ore lay exposed, making him crow with delight. "I knew it!" he shouted.

"You'll hurt yourself, Papa!" Daisie said, laughing and weeping at the same time. "Be careful!"

He paid her no heed. In a few moments he had battered a sizeable hollow and freed enough rock to show that the vein only got bigger. "Gather it all up," he said breathlessly. "Take it into the cabin. I'll get this tent back up. We don't want anyone to see this."

His eyes were wide, his cheeks red, his bloody fingerprints

were all along the pick handle. Daisie let him dump handfuls of ore into her skirt. As she staggered and slipped back into the cabin, her father righted the tattered tent and heaped snow around it to mask the freshly broken rock with its tantalizing gray-and-gold markings.

Once inside the cabin, her father forgot the skinning job and began battering the ore to bits, separating out tiny nuggets and minute beads of gold.

"We've done it," he kept whispering, his eyes ablaze. "We've done it! We're going to be all right. Didn't I tell you there was gold here? Didn't I, Daisie? I knew Tyler wouldn't steer me wrong!"

Jumping up, he crowed and danced Daisie in awkward circles.

"You brought me luck, Daisie, my sweet child! Wait until Tyler sees this. I'll pay for this claim, and the other, and the months of food, and the doctor's calls and the firewood and the pistol. And I'll make him rich, too. Daisie, smile for me!"

"We don't dare tell anyone!" she hissed, suddenly terrified. "Claim jumpers will hear about out strike and swarm over us and take the gold! They'll rob us, maybe shoot us. I know, Papa! I've had money slip through my fingers twice!"

"Tyler won't tell anyone. We'll have the ore assayed in Denver. Tyler can take it. We'll go back to your mother in a golden carriage!"

Daisie pulled away. "How will we get out of these mountains with a fortune in gold? If there is a fortune behind that tent."

"Don't be such a sourpuss. We'll hide it! No one but Tyler will know we've got it. Perk up, Daisie. We're rich!"

Two days later, with another foot of snow on the ground, Tyler came, leading two saddled but riderless horses with him. Daisie saw him coming as she huddled before a huge fire where she was roasting a slab of bear meat.

Looking stunned, he stared at the hide laid out to dry and the pieces of meat already frozen. "You've been busy," he said, looking at Daisie in wonder.

Her father came out, grinning. "Hello, Tyler!"

"You look unusually well, Lord Browning. I expected to find you both frozen and more than ready to desert this land of snow."

"Daisie brought down this beast singlehanded," Daisie's father said, grasping and hugging her shoulders. His eyes glittered with secret excitement. "A handy girl to have around in a pinch. How are you, Tyler?"

"Fine, sir," Tyler said, grinning. "Cold, though. Enough snow for you yet?" His eyes fell admiringly on Daisie.

She looked at the two riderless horses. "Did you lose someone along the way?"

"I've come to urge you both to return with me to town. Warnings have been telegraphed about severe snowstorms to the west. Come into town just for a day or so. I'll sleep better."

Daisie's father shook his head with grin. "This isn't the time for retreat, Tyler, my boy. Come inside. I have something to show you."

Wringing her hands, Daisie began praying. Tyler had said the land was theirs. Now that it had gold on it, would he refuse to accept payment, keeping the gold for himself? Staying outside, she checked the roast, too nervous to do much more than listen to the deep, hushed murmur of Tyler's voice coming from inside the cabin.

Heavy clouds edged in from the west, black and malevolent, and a cutting wind sliced across the dooryard, piercing through her coat and skirts and long underwear. Hard, icy flakes slanted down, stinging her eyes and cheeks. The wind howled around the roof, snatching away the smoke that leaked from the roof vent and chimney.

She crept close to the cabin door. The smoky warmth from inside beckoned.

"We never would have found this particular rock if Daisie's first shot hadn't gone wild. What do you think, Tyler?" Her father's voice was breathless.

Tyler bent over a cloth her father had spread on the cot. On it lay the glittering collection of flakes, beads and dust he had been breaking from the rock for the past two days. "If it's fool's gold, Tyler, I don't want to know! Let me go on believing a little longer," her father said. "Oh, to be in England, now that winter is here."

Daisie slipped inside, pulling the door tightly closed against the rising wind. Tyler ran his finger through the glittering pile. Then he looked up at her father. "I can't be sure without an assayer's report, but yes, I think this is gold." He didn't sound happy.

Daisie clapped her hands over her mouth. Her father sagged onto the cot beside his little fortune, absently massaging his bothersome ankle. "I knew it," he whispered, his voice tight. "I knew it. Take this, Tyler, and see what it's worth. Take it to Denver, and keep mum, mind you. No one must know of our find. Not a single soul. We'll try to gather more."

"But the storm — "

"Dash it all, Tyler, I'm not leaving now!"

Outside, the wind moaned and wailed through the trees, whistling through cracks around the makeshift door, backing up the chimney smoke. Daisie peeked out to see flakes so large and thick the air was white. Already the horses were coated on one side. All footprints were obliterated, and visibility was less than ten feet. At that rate the snow would put out the fire.

Tyler stood, his movements sharp, his face like the stormy dark sky. "I've never known anyone as hard to convince as you, Lord Browning. If I didn't like you so much I'd say it was your stubbornness that cost you your factory. If you intend to stay, I'm staying, too." He glanced at Daisie, bringing a fiery blush of awareness to her cheeks. Together, all night, under the same roof. . . . "Is there enough food inside the cabin to last for three or four days?"

"I think so," Daisie nodded, struck by the seriousness in his eyes.

He turned up his collar and surged past her out the door. "I'll start carting in wood. Daisie, I'll need you to take up the tent so I can use the canvas to shield the horses from the wind. Can you spare three blankets for them? I hate to see good horses freeze to death."

Chapter Fifteen

By the time it was dark, Tyler had erected a canvas windbreak to shield the horses. Several inches of new snow had fallen, and the screaming wind swept it into great peaked drifts five feet high. "If the temperature doesn't drop too much," he said, coming in and beating the snow from his hair and coat, "the horses may survive."

Daisie kept the fire blazing just enough to offset the cold that seeped in. When the snow piled up against the door, less air from outside came through the cracks.

Tyler watched the roof for signs of strain from the gathering weight of snow on it. They ate and talked, and all the while, Daisie was conscious of Tyler's nearness. Any time she wanted, she could touch his arm. When her father grew weary, she bundled him in blankets and saw that he got comfortably snug in the cot against the wall. He fell instantly to snoring.

"He's worn himself out breaking up his rocks," she said, moving back close to the fire.

Tyler circled her shoulders with his arm.

"You were good to warn us about the storm. Though we may not seem to, we truly appreciate all you've done for us." Daisie's gratitude was sincere. Finding the gold had erased all suspicion that Tyler had salted the claim. She was certain he had never been interested in Amelia, either, and that he was simply a shrewd, respected businessman.

"You've forgiven me, then, for all my shortcomings?" Tyler asked, a teasing light in his eyes.

"Whatever you are, Tyler, you have been a true friend. If it were not for you, Papa and I would have starved."

He shook his head and chucked her chin. "You wouldn't have let that happen. You're too stubborn."

Huddling within the homely woolen coat, she shivered. "Here in America, I've done more than I ever thought possible. I'm changed from an ignorant, spoiled English girl not long out of school to an American pioneer, a mountain woman! Mother won't know me."

For a long moment Tyler was silent, gazing into the fire, a line cutting between his brows. "I hate the thought of you going. Until seeing your father's gold, I thought I'd come up with a solution to keep the two of you safe for the winter."

"But I *must* get Papa home. He's so frail."

Tyler nodded.

"And I hate the thought of going, too — except that I miss Mother, and need her. Papa has spoken of coming back," she added, hope rising in her breast.

Tyler brightened. "I didn't know that." He hugged her. "That'll make it easier to say goodbye."

Daisie leaned against him, her cheeks blazing with heat. "Papa talks of getting just enough gold so we can go home. If we keep the strike secret, no one will come here while we're gone and take what rightfully belongs to us. That reminds me, I have a letter for you to take to town. Mama will want to know we're coming. She'll be terribly relieved. I can just see the look on her face. . . . You'd like my mother."

Tyler said nothing.

Daisie looked up. "What plan had you worked out for us?"

"I was going to ask you and your father to live in my cabin. It's larger than this, far cleaner . . . and the fireplace draws." He coughed and wiped his eyes. "How do you stand this smoke?"

"I don't know how I've stood it. I've just had to, for Papa's sake. Are you asleep, Papa?" she whispered.

There was no response.

"Staying in your cabin might have worked well," she said, pleased. "Where is it?"

"I have several hundred acres near here. In the summer I raise beef cattle. A friend works looking after them for me, but sometimes I have to be there myself, like this fall when we drove them down the pass to the Springs and Denver. Cattle droving is tiresome business. The cows stampeded three times the first week. I was tired when I got back." He rubbed his eyes. "I go to Denver several times a year. I buy land for a man I know there — I was with him and his friends the night you and I met. And I buy and sell all the claims that have made me infamous, at a profit, too, thanks to the boom. I make loans to men a sane banker would refuse. I'm not so well off I can afford to throw a lot of cash around, but I'm not much for champagne dinners or diamond stickpins, anyway. I don't own a fancy carriage or a private railroad car. I could invest in mines and hotels, I suppose, but I was brought up to look at material possessions with a skeptic's eye. Maybe some of that Kansas soddy mud is still in my hair. My mother saw to it that I never developed an unnatural love for expensive trappings. She'd frown at my boots." He regarded the dirtied silver tips. "I only know I couldn't sleep at night, keeping my money in my pocket, knowing someone was sleeping in the cold for want of it. I've watched your father grow closer to a similar ideal over the past months, and I hoped he'd give up his quest for riches. . . ."

"But he has Mother and Pammie and me to support," Daisie broke in.

Tyler nodded. "That is what I've had to understand. As a man alone I can afford to give away what I have. If I was your father, and had far less, perhaps I'd hold my possessions a little more tightly. Wanting you and your father to live at my cabin wasn't especially generous, either. It was my way of drawing you closer. You've been very right about one thing concerning the forward Tyler Reede. I have tried to make you need me." He looked intently at her and spoke in a whisper. "The only other value of leaving you here was that it kept you out of the hands of Hank Salter and all the other . . . . ."

Glancing up, she smiled demurely. "You know there was never anything about Hank Salter that interested me."

"I *don't* know that. Every time I turn around I find him with you, doing for you what I wanted to do myself."

"He hasn't been around lately."

"I'm glad. There's something about Hank and his sister I don't trust. I can't put my finger on it. Hank was after you, I know that. If he wasn't so busy now raking in money, he'd still be after you. I think he's waiting for you to come crawling into town half-starved. That's the way a man of his kind works. He'll close in when you're too weak and vulnerable to think straight."

"I could be near death and never go to that repulsive man for help! He and Amelia were expert at making the least little thing sound suspicious, and they drew me right in. Amelia even claimed you two were lovers."

Tyler stifled an incredulous laugh. "She has quite an imagination! I like the way you speak of them in the past tense." Then he looked startled. "You thought — ?"

Daisie nodded. "And then there was Carla. *Should* I say 'Was'?"

"My sweet Miss Browning," he whispered, taking her chin and turning her face toward his. "You'd be amazed to learn the vast number of women in my life."

"And I had a dozen men in town at my beck and call," she quipped wryly.

He grazed her lips with his own. "I think you want me to kiss you."

"Sh-h-h! Papa will hear you!"

"Over those snores?"

Then his lips pressed against hers and her heart was leaping. She slid her hand across his cheek and felt the faint growth of beard tickle her palm. She touched his mouth with her finger-tips, and felt him press his soft, smooth lips against hers.

After a moment, she pulled away, rose and went to a box

stored near the hearth. From it she took a small paper package, which she unwrapped. Before him in the firelight she displayed a bundle of dry, brittle wildflowers. . . and an arrowhead.

"These aren't the ones I. . .?"

Daisie nodded. "You brought these to Colonel Darnel's house the morning after the fire. I would like you to notice that *these* are the flowers I preserved, not the ones delivered in Hank Salter's name." She wanted to add that the arrowhead had come from Cupid's bow, but stopped herself. Tyler knew she loved him. It was now up to him to carry their love into the future. If he didn't, she felt she must not ask why, or take the initiative. A woman could take only so much into her own hands.

She rewrapped the package. Having made her feelings known, she was now vulnerable, open to rejection. When Tyler did not declare his love, or ask for her hand, she added, throat tight, "And so, Mr. Reede, in another week or so Papa and I will return to England."

Tyler drew her back to his side. His face was so near that she could feel his breath on her cheek. She heard him swallow. His gaze was dark, unreadable. "Will you come back?"

"Papa has said we will. How he'll feel once we're home, I don't know."

"I mean you. Will you come back?"

"If Papa and Mama decide — " She flushed.

"Would you come back without them?" he asked.

"I might. I've thought of it, but . . . I wasn't sure how you felt." She could hardly breathe. *Now* he would ask her to marry him. All her worries were over!

He was grinning. "You weren't sure how I felt?"

She shook her head.

"I thought it was written in red wherever I went! After you threw that money at me, I thought you'd never speak to me again. I left Cripple Creek. I was never coming back. I went to Denver. I. . . ."

She silenced him. "Don't tell me what happened there."

"Are you afraid I tried to blot you from my mind with other women? Do you know how hard it's been since I realized all the women I've known until now were . . . were like fool's gold? Pretty, shiny, but not real gold. Not . . . *you*."

Her heart soared. She pressed her face into his neck, overcome with joy.

"I haven't been able to stay away from you! Even when you were here and I was in town, I felt close to you. I wanted you to belong to me, and yet I kept bringing you things to keep you away."

"Why?"

He searched her face and then hugged her. "What good will I be when my heart's in England?"

The rafters creaked. Some melted snow began trickling down the upper edges of the rocks forming the chimney. The fire had burned down while they talked. Abruptly, Tyler rose to put more logs on. He turned. He looked angry.

"I want you to come back even if your parents decide to stay in England, but I know how you'll look getting off the train. You'll be wearing a big hat with feathers and a veil and artificial birds on it. Your traveling suit will be pink or yellow and very clean with no wrinkles. Lots of lace at the throat will make your face look even softer and more beautiful than it already is. You'll have on gloves and white kid shoes and lacy petticoats that will pick up the red dust, but you'll lift them just a little, making me want to — "

He glanced irritably at her sleeping father.

"If you come back to me you'll discover I'm not a fancy rich man in silver-tiped boots, but just a Kansas farm boy who likes his log cabin better than his fancy room at the saloon. He likes his cows better than cards and deeds. This farm boy plays at being a businessman, but all he really wants is the ranch, and a loving woman to share his dreams, and little replicas of himself playing on the corral fence. If you came back, you'd be forced back to calico and boots. You'd dress game with a hunting knife, do laundry in an outdoor tub, cook over an open hearth. That's no life for an English young lady!"

He pressed a hand to his forehead. "I should check on the horses. Go to sleep while I'm outside. It'll be easier on us that way." He grabbed his hat. As he buttoned his coat and turned up his collar to protect his ears, he muttered, "I wish you hadn't found more gold."

Daisie's first instinct was to reassure Tyler. She was no highborn lady! She liked a calico dress just as much as a satin one. But he disappeared out the door in a swirl of snow.

She hugged herself tightly. Her primary duty was to see her father safely home. All else came second. She couldn't promise Tyler she'd come back any more than he could promise to be waiting.

Her head spun. Yes, indeed, damn the gold! What did gold matter next to such a wonderful man? If her parents wanted to live in America, everything would work out. But if they couldn't leave England — if Papa forgot his ideal and took up his yoke again — could she leave them to live with Tyler? Forever?

Burying her face, she felt a niggling fear. Were her feelings for Tyler like those she'd had for Norwood, changeable? Perhaps after returning to England her desire for this rugged man of the wilderness would fade. If her feelings were that weak and unworthy, going home was doubly important.

When Tyler hadn't returned after several minutes, Daisie grew alarmed. Perhaps, after all, he had decided to take the horses to town. Jumping up, she grabbed open the door and slipped out, tugging it shut. Stinging snow whipped across her face. There was no sky, no earth, only a screaming white hell.

"What are you doing?" Tyler shouted, seeing her pressed against the door. "It's stupid to get wet and cold when you don't have to."

"I've never seen a storm like this!"

Tyler had brushed off the horses and adjusted the buffeting canvas lean-to. His face was nipped red, his hair a windblown tangle thick with snowflakes. "Go back in."

"I was afaid you might leave."

He came to her then, his eyes heavy with longing. He threw his arms around her, crushing her to his chest. Then his mouth took hers, warm, urgent, hungry, making her forget that they were standing in a stinging, icy whirlwind, making her forget her father and England and the uncertain future.

She molded herself to the strong, solid curve of Tyler's body, letting his lips move across hers, yearning and straining, wanting him, though the cold was stabbing and cruel and her father was just inside. . . .

She wanted Tyler to hold her forever. For an instant she wondered if her father could get back to England alone. Clinging to Tyler, she blotted the hopeless, selfish idea from her mind. "Tyler," she whispered, feeling her soul wrenched with confusion. "Oh, Tyler, I can't bear this!"

They forgot the snow, the cold, the wind. All they knew was the feel of each other, the warmth, the knowing that they belonged together. "Let's get inside," he whispered suddenly, hoarsely.

When he had closed the door behind them, he turned to brush the snow out of her hair. She was shivering now. They settled before the fire, wrapped in a single blanket. When his hand stole inside her coat, she leaned against him, moaning softly, wishing there could be more, frightened they would have no privacy before it was time to get on that train. She turned so he could caress her breast beneath the layers of warm, rough cloth. She put her hand over his hand, to memorize what it felt like to be touched this way.

"I love you," he whispered, kissing her when she arched against him, her heart leaping.

He loved her! Fighting a knot of joyous tears, she kissed his cheek, his neck, pressing tightly against the caressing warmth of his hand, daring to wonder if they could steal a moment of love with her father only a foot away.

Hissing clumps of soggy debris dropped into the fire from the upper portion of the chimney. Mud began running down the chimney from the roof.

"What's happening?" Daisie murmured as Tyler withdrew his hand and sprang quickly to investigate. One look at the sod sagging and dripping against the chimney and he was out the door. Moments later he stuck his head back in. "Hand me the bucket! The chimney's on fire!"

She handed it out. Seconds later splashes of water fell into the fire from above. Smoke surged into the cabin, bringing her father abruptly awake with a coughing fit. A rafter shifted, and an ominous sifting of fine red dirt rained onto Daisie's head.

Tyler burst back inside, his eyes trained on the ceiling.

"Will it cave in?" Daisie asked, grabbing at the nearest thing in preparation for abandoning the cabin, a crate of canned beans.

Tyler studied the ceiling, then reached up to poke and prod. A little more dirt sifted into their hair, but the rafters appeared secure. "Let the fire burn down. It can't be so hot. Most of the chimney is gone." He glared at Lord Browning, still groggy and confused. "Your days in this cabin, Lord Browning, are numbered!"

He kissed Daisie's cheek. "It's all right. Didn't I tell you a little dirt in your hair is a sign of good character?" He brushed at the top of her head. "The cabin will last the night, I think,"

"Oh, Tyler!" she cried, laying her head on his chest. His heart was hammering. "Do you never stop teasing?"

"No," he said, but he wasn't smiling.

By noon the next day the sky was a clear brilliant turquoise. The sun shone down on the rounded, dazzling white mountains. Tyler dug a path from the door, fetched water and foraged across the creek for grass for the horses.

"I've got to get them back," he said. "The gold here will keep all winter. You've got enough to buy clothes. I'll take you out to my — "

Looking invigorated by the brisk air, Daisie's father clutched his blanket tightly around his shoulders, smiling up at Tyler in a most tolerant manner. "My dear boy, I cannot come into town carrying a fortune in a little bag. Do I look strong enough to hold off an army of thieves?"

Tyler mounted his horse, his mouth tight.

Daisie pressed her mother's letter into his hands. "We'll be all right."

Tyler squeezed her hand. "I'm coming with a wagon next time. Watch that chimney, sir. If the rafters shift again, don't wait for anything. Get out. I don't want to have to dig you out."

"Don't be such a fusspot. And don't hurry on our account. This dratted snow looks very deep. Be careful."

Throwing her father a seething look of impatience, Tyler led the horses loaded with frozen bear meat across the ice-edged creek and through the knee-deep meadow. At the trees he twisted around in the saddle, looking long and hard at Daisie.

She waved. When he was out of sight she went to her father. "Back inside. While the sun's warm I'll bring in more of those rocks. It's no use arguing. We're on our way home and this is what will take us there."

When Daisie had enough ore-bearing rock to fill her skirt, she lugged it into the cabin where her father sat happily before a low fire, bashing the rocks to bits and sifting out the gold. At noon he called to her from the doorway. "Look at this Daisie! Nuggets the size of peas!"

Inside, she gaped at the dull metallic lumps. Numb and weary, she warmed some bear stew and thought of the cash Tyler would get from selling the extra meat. Enough for train fare to Denver, she hoped.

"I think we should ask Tyler to go with us to Denver," she said suddenly, thrilled with her own cleverness. "We'll need protection."

Her father cocked his brow. "You've recently changed your mind about that young man, then?"

"Finding the gold proved I'd been wrong all along," she said, trying not to squirm.

Her father frowned. "And if we hadn't found such proof? What then? Would you have gone on hating an honest man?"

Contrite, she couldn't answer that. "Supposing Tyler went to England with us. He might help you get the business back in order."

"I'm bringing your mother and Pammie here! I thought I made that clear!"

"And if Mother refuses to come?"

Her father paused, considering that possibility and then sighing as though the weight of the world had just resettled itself on his shoulders.

"And *you* might decide after all to stay."

"Do you think Tyler wants to leave his land for you, daughter?"

"Oh, not for me, Papa! To help you—" She blushed. "You . . . know about us?"

"It's been obvious from the first, my dear! I was not born yesterday, I assure you! I recognize the madness of love." He chuckled to himself. "A blind man could've seen it," he added.

"And do you think I should consider leaving my family and country for him?"

Thoughtfully, he regarded his little pile of gold. "That's for you to decide. But you must believe in Tyler and not just wait for circumstances to prove he is good."

"You've been here all this time proving yourself to Mama!"

He chuckled. "Ah, but that's where I've been wrong, you see. As I have sat here gloating over my treasure, which you found for me, suddenly it has occurred to me — I really came away from all I knew and loved to prove myself to myself."

She hugged him. "You've grown very wise, Papa."

"And you, my dear, have grown into a beautiful, strong, sensitive young woman. In regard to Tyler, do what you think is right. He has yet to speak to me of his intentions."

It's true, she thought. He still hasn't mentioned marriage. "He wants us to stay at his cabin. Can we, if this roof caves in before we have enough gold to go home?"

"Nonsense. The roof is as sound as I am."

Daisie found that no comfort.

"I have it in my mind to hire Tyler to guard our claim. Twenty per cent sounds reasonable," he went on.

That did seem like a depressingly good idea. Daisie bundled up again and went back out to exhaust her frustrations on the damnable rocky ledge. By nightfall Tyler hadn't returned. She had blisters to shout about. They ate stew again and Daisie listened to her father spin his dreams of a triumphant return to his wife.

Snow fell again that night. Daisie was so tired she didn't hear the howling wind. The following morning everything glistened white. Waking early, her father hummed as he battered his rocks. By noon she began sewing little pockets and rolls of gold into her father's coat lining. He decided it was safer for him to carry it, and she humored him as though he were child.

When she grew too tired and irritable to sew any longer, she tossed down the coat, flexing warmth back into her icy fingers. "I don't see any use in this," she snapped, her patience exhausted. "I can sew until spring and still you'll keep us here."

"Nonsense. I have everything planned down to the last detail. If we get through town acting the part of defeat, no one will suspect we found gold or bother our claim." He tried on the weighty coat, chuckling as he patted the faint bulges beneath his arms and hidden in the lining. The coat looked weathered and worn, dirty, spotted, and bagging with age. "I think this will do nicely. It's time we were on our way."

Daisie dropped onto the bench. "You're serious?"

"When have I not been serious in this venture, child?"

"Why couldn't you have spared Tyler the worry then?"

"Even Tyler must not know how much gold we have. Someone might ask him about us, and I wouldn't want him to have to lie, or to make an unintentional but fatal slip of the tongue. Come, come, Daisie. Smile! If Tyler loves you, he'll wait until the end of time for you."

Daisie's heart did not feel as certain of Tyler as that.

Far into the night they talked and worked, happy as pirates. The temperature dropped alarmingly, and half way through the night they burned the last of the firewood Daisie had brought in that afternoon. Frost began forming on the inside of the walls.

Daisie went out for more wood. The sky was a dead black,

with stars like chips of ice. Her face ached with cold that was so penetrating it made the very air she breathed hard and savage in her lungs.

In the morning the sun dazzled them. Tyler arrived in the wagon again, his face covered with a black woolen scarf. Frost clung to the fabric where his breath came through and froze. Breathing hard, he stood in the doorway ready to drag Daisie and her father away with him, too cold, furious and determined to tolerate another refusal.

Bundled in every bit of clothing they had, wrapped in blankets, their voices muffled by scarves, they welcomed him with relief. "We're ready," Daisie said.

Tyler blinked in surprise. Then he snapped, "And about time."

His teeth chattering (the temperature inside the cabin was scarcely above freezing), Gregory Browning showed a pair of twinkling eyes, then, docile as a lamb, followed Tyler out to the wagon. They climbed beneath the heap of fur lap robes, too cold even to think about giving the camp a farewell look.

"Are the trains still running?" Daisie asked once they had safely reached the road.

"When they can," Tyler said curtly. He was still too angry, and baffled by their sudden capitulation to be civil.

Their time together was nearly at an end, Daisie thought. All three were quiet, lost in their private thoughts.

Chapter Sixteen

"We can't stay the night here, Tyler," Daisie gasped, looking up at the grand new Stanton Hotel, finished while she and her father had been living at their camp.

"I don't see why not. You look like you need a nice hot bath and clean —"

"Thank you very much," Daisie said pretending to be offended. She smiled, though. "No, Tyler. This hotel would cost too much. Carry on. Take us to the Colorado Hotel."

Grinning for the first time, Tyler clicked his tongue in his teeth and turned the wagon. "You're determined to play the part, aren't you? Destitute English lord and his fragile, plucky daughter exit Colorado boom town remembering happier days."

Disapprovingly, Daisie's father cleared his throat. "You would not make a newspaperman, Tyler."

Daisie sniffed. "I'm not likely to be careless at this late date. Cold, Papa?"

"Something in my coat is keeping me warm as toast."

At the Colorado Hotel, Tyler helped Daisie to the shoveled walkway and then gave her father a hand. Inside, a knot of miners huddled around a potbellied stove in the middle of the lobby. Her father haggled over the price of the room, looking convincingly like a defeated prospector. Daisie ignored the miners staring at her, reminding herself that it didn't matter if she looked as though she'd just crawled out of a hole. She had, and it was something to be proud of.

"What more can I do for you both?" Tyler asked, looking in a better humor now that he was warm and they were safely in town at last.

"Will you find out about the trains?"

Tyler nodded, tipping his Stetson. "And then as soon as I get the wagon back, I'll take you out to dinner. The Stanton has a fine dining room."

Daisie edged closer to him. "Tyler, no! We haven't the right clothes."

"I thought I'd bring — "

"No!" she whispered, glancing about at all the men listening.

"Let me do something special for you before you go," Tyler said. His eyes showed his desire to be alone with her.

"Let us rest for tonight. Tomorrow is soon enough to toast this old man's failure. All I want to do now is sleep," her father said.

He did look alarmingly weary. Daisie patted Tyler's hand, then hurried to help her father up the stairway. The extra weight in his coat made walking difficult.

"You're weak, Papa," Daisie scolded, helping him up the last few steps.

"Don't fuss. Does anyone suspect?"

"Let them," she grumbled. "*I* know how to gun down a bear." She hefted the rifle Tyler had brought in from the wagon.

After settling her father in his room and feeling relieved to see that it was decently furnished, she watched him lie back on the mattress with a sigh of appreciation. "Ah, the comforts of civilization." In moments he was snoring.

While he slept she tried to arrange for a tub and bath water to be brought up, but learned that no such luxuries were available. She hated to leave her father alone, but she couldn't stand being dirty another instant. She hurried out to see where the nearest bathhouse was, and as she was crossing the muddy street, heard someone call her name.

"I can't believe my eyes," Amelia Salter gasped as she stood safely on the shoveled walkway in front of a barbershop. "We haven't seen you in weeks! Wait! Hank's just inside. Let me call him.''

Amelia was wearing a fine wool cape over a brown worsted skirt. Though her jaunty hat was obviously new, her blonde curls were the same dull shade.

"Don't disturb him on my account," Daisie called. Amelia was beckoning frantically at Hank through the window. "I'll stop by to say goodbye later. I'm in a hurry — "

"Are you leaving us? But you can't — Hank, hurry!" Stepping into the street, Amelia made her way closer, her eyes keen and quick. "Dear me, your hair . . ." She forced back a superior smile. "Where have you come from? Have you been in town long? Is your father well?"

"So nice to see you again, Amelia, but I must be getting back to him."

Hank appeared in the barbershop doorway, half his face still lathered. His hair was brushed and sleek. His vest, shirt and trousers looked straight from Denver. "*Dear* Miss Browning." He started toward her, his eyes reminding her of the bear's.

"I'll call after I've cleaned up," Daisie said, backing away.

"You're not leaving Cripple Creek?" Hank exclaimed. "Let us take you and your father to dinner first!"

"Of course you must stay with us," Amelia cut in, blocking Daisie's escape. "We'd be so hurt if you didn't."

Daisie edged around her. "Are you still taking in boarders? You don't look as if you need the money so badly. Besides, we can only pay with frozen bear meat now. We haven't a penny." She hurried away, not waiting for a reply.

"Bear meat?"

Back at the Colorado Hotel, she found Tyler just starting up the stairs. "Oh, I'm glad you're here!" she panted, joining him. "I was checking on bathhouses and ran into the Salters. I'd sooner face the bear again! Do I look so very terrible, Tyler?" she whispered, showing him up to her father's room.

He put his arm around her shoulder. "I think you look wonderful. Please let me take you out tonight."

"We'll see how Papa's feeling," she said, hurrying into the room to see her father, pat the lumpy places in his coat, and reassure herself that he hadn't been robbed.

Her father woke briefly, grumbled at being disturbed, rolled over and went back to sleep. Trembling, she sank to the edge of the mattress. "I'm so nervous!"

"I'll stay with him," Tyler said, understanding how afraid she was of losing what little they had. "No one will be suspicious if you buy a dress or coat. You mustn't start jumping at shadows. That will make people think you've got something to hide."

"You're right, as always," she said, sighing, trying to relax as she stood and drew a ragged breath.

He followed her to the hallway and waited while she inspected her own room across the hall. She longed to fall across the bed and sleep for a week. In the hall, Tyler steadied her. "Forget the Salters. You're so much better than both of them. I don't understand why you worry about what they think."

Embarrassed, she looked away. "You won't leave Papa?"

He shook his head.

She took the money Tyler had gotten for their bear meat and her spirits soared at the thought of being clean again.

Acting worried about every cent she spent, Daisie selected a dress at Mueller's Dry Goods and then decided she must have new shoes and underthings, a woolen cape and a bonnet. Taking her parcels to the bathhouse, she hired hot water and privacy in one of several soggy, bare cubicles. The room next to hers resounded with coarse male singing. She slipped into the steaming tub and lathered, thinking this was the most enjoyable moment she had known since Tyler last kissed her.

She scrubbed her hair with new scented soap and rinsed the last of the grit from her scalp. When she stood raw and dripping an hour later, she felt like a woman again.

Dressing in new clothes from the skin out raised her confidence another notch. She knew she did not look the picture of fashion, but her hair squeaked, her nails were clean and she smelled faintly of lavender. She twisted her hair into a knot and secured it with new hairpins. Then she washed her old clothes in the bathwater — she had learned that water was precious — and rolled them into a bundle. She would happily burn them . . . when they were safely away from Cripple Creek.

She hurried back to the hotel, to find Tyler waiting in her father's room, gazing out of the window. He turned when she came in.

"I didn't recognize you when you came out of the bathhouse," he said, letting his eyes roam over her face. Desire was naked in his eyes. "You look brand spanking new."

"I feel such a lot better! Why were you watching me?"

"I hate to let you out of my sight."

They slipped from the room and stood in the hallway. "I want to kiss you," Tyler whispered. "Where can we go?"

"Don't torment me! What about the trains?"

"One leaves in an hour. Another leaves tomorrow about the same time if the weather holds. Stay a few days and rest. Unless we have more snow, you can go any time. Why hurry away?"

"Every moment in town is a risk." She kept her voice low in case anyone in the nearby rooms was trying to listen.

"Let's walk a while. I don't want to leave your side when we have so little time left."

"I would have liked to go walking," she sighed, pulling away, her heart paining her. How could she leave him? She felt a physical wrenching, as if to leave Tyler would split her body in two.

She could think of little else to say. She was obsessed with the fear that if she let her father and the gold out of her sight for even an hour, the gold would vanish.

Tyler turned toward the stairs. Wanting to run after him, feeling a knot of tears form in her throat, Daisie merely waved and gave him a little smile as he went down, the light gone from his eyes.

Her father slept soundly until Daisie got so hungry she had to wake him. He seemed confused at first, but then smiled as he recalled that they were in town and nearly on their way. Daisie explained the train schedule.

"We'll have dinner with Tyler tomorrow night then, and leave the day after," Gregory Browning said. Daisie's obvious delight at having two more days near Tyler brought a smile to his face.

Only two short days, Daisie thought with an aching heart.

They ate box suppers, fetched by Daisie, in their rooms before retiring for the night. Daisie lay awake for hours, yearning for Tyler. She wept to think of leaving him until she could weep no more.

Tyler arrived early to take them to breakfast. He seemed cheerful, but Daisie sensed his depression.

"Would you like to ride out to my ranch today?" he asked. "The weather's holding."

Gregory Browning smiled agreeably. "Of course, my boy, but let me have that bath I need so desperately. Then we'll be off."

At noon they hired a wagon and set out. Riding north fifteen miles, they came to picturesque valley opening to a vista of gleaming white peaks beyond a small isolated cabin.

"Now, *that* is a cabin," her father said. "I don't imagine you threw that together in a few weeks . . . on a bad ankle."

"No, sir. It took most of my first summer here. I stay part of each winter and find it warm and secure. In the spring I'll buy more cattle from Texas and graze them here. I plan to put up a barn over there next year." Tyler surveyed the scene before them with a sparkle of pride in his eyes. "I wish my parents had lived to see this valley. Compared to our flat, barren homestead, this looks like paradise."

Inside, everything was neat and comfortable, though at the moment covered with frost. The single room was large. The rafters were closed off by a loft floor. The massive flagstone fireplace was properly constructed and took up half the north wall.

In mid-afternoon they returned to town, rested and then went to dinner. Many miners had left for milder elevations, so the street traffic was light. The lively saloon music sounded forlorn in the chilled darkness. Heaps of snow lay about everywhere, and the streets were rutted and muddy. Everything was muffled, giving a feeling of stillness, of waiting.

They kept to neutral subjects as they picked their way toward the hotel. Tyler wore his black frockcoat and Daisie her sober blue dress from the dry goods store. Her father looked proud but destitute in his baggy coat.

The hotel had sprung up on the same street as the Colorado's raw pine frame. Inside the grand lobby were glittering chandeliers, thick carpets, imported walnut furniture, rich brocade wallpapers and large, rather ugly potted ferns.

"Where did all these elegant people come from?" Daisie whispered, startled to see so many wearing evening clothes.

"They've just come from the opera house. They're mostly managers for the mining companies, and their wives."

In the dining room, everything that Daisie had left behind in England came rushing back; the faint tinkling of crystal goblets, the silent waiters, the sparkling tableware. Her eyes feasted on the neatly arranged tables, the lush velvet draperies drawn back to reveal a view of the sparkling, scattered town and the white mountains beyond. And the room was so warm! "Isn't it grand, Papa!"

Tyler escorted them to a table where Daisie and her father, in their dowdy clothes, were the center of attention. They had just ordered wine when Daisie looked up, laughing, and saw Amelia Salter glaring at her from across the room. Her laughter ceased abruptly.

"Oh, dear," she mumured. "I suppose they'll insist on speaking to us."

Tyler followed the direction of her eyes. Now Hank was scowling across at them.

"They invited us to dinner, too," Daisie whispered. "I was so intent on getting away from them I didn't clearly decline. Should I go over and speak to them?"

Tyler's shrug implied that it was not for him to say.

"I'd like to give that young bloodsucker a piece of my mind before we go," Daisie's father muttered.

Tyler cleared his throat. "Looks like you'll get your wish. . They're coming over."

Daisie steeled herself.

"Oh, but you *do* look so much better, Daisie!" Amelia said, extending her gloved hand.

Instead of shaking it, Daisie nodded.

Amelia's satin evening gown was a gaudy combination of orange and pink, with enough ruffles, pleats, frills and trim for three gowns. It positively reeked of bad taste and cheap toilet water. She wore all the jewelry her neck, ears, wrists and fingers could accommodate.

"What an enchanting gown," Daise said, with false politeness. "Did you have it made specially?"

"It's all the way from Chicago, designed by one of the best dressmakers in that city. Let's join them, Hank. Hello, again, Lord Browning. You're looking . . . pretty good." Uninvited, Amelia took a seat next to Tyler. Hank dragged over a chair from a nearby table and wedged himself in between Daisie and her father.

"I suppose in no time you'll be in lace and ruffles again," Amelia said to Daisie. "Everything she owned came from Paris and was made of hand-stitched, embroidered silk," she added, for Hank's benefit.

Daisie thought of the lovely things she had lost in the fire. Why had Amelia assumed that all Daisie's things came from Paris? Had she gone through Daisie's belongings?

Now, her eyes fixed on Tyler, Amelia said, "And when will you be seeing the Brownings off, Tyler?" Daisie thought she looked at him as hungrily as one of Grace Roswell's she-wolves.

"Tomorrow," Daisie's father answered for Tyler. "How's the new store?"

"I wish you'd take a moment to stop by, Lord Browning," Hank said. "We have more rooms than before. I suppose it was lucky for us the old one burned."

"The other owners whose buildings burned that night haven't been so fortunate, have they?" Tyler said, his voice light. "None of them had as much fire insurance as you."

Hank drew himself up, but his sister's calming hand on his arm kept him from replying.

"We're doing all we can for those unfortunate people," Amelia said. Glancing around, she noticed two of those very gentlemen dining nearby. Her face flushed scarlet.

"Have you already ordered?" Daisie asked, hoping they would take the hint and go back to their own table.

"We'll eat with you, since you're here," Amelia said quickly. "Tell us every single thing you've been doing up at your camp. Have you found any more gold?"

Gregory Browning's look of defeat was so convincing Daisie felt like applauding.

"I am *so* sorry." Amelia said. "Isn't that a shame, Hank?" But she looked as though she didn't believe a word.

Hank looked at Daisie. "May I see you outside, alone?"

Tyler had been leaning back in his chair. The legs thumped loudly to the carpet as he straightened.

Surprise made Daisie unusually blunt. "No, I don't think so, Hank," she said flatly.

"Say what you have to say right here, Hank," Amelia said, her dark eyes wide and innocent.

He shook his head blushing a little, like an embarrassed schoolboy.

Amelia sighed. "Did you say something about a bear, Daisie?"

Daisie's father brightened. "My girl here brought down a four-hundred-pound bear in two shots, single-handed."

"I didn't," Daisie laughed. "You helped."

"I skinned the beast. And I found only two wounds, both from the rifle you fired. It was a remarkable feat of bravery. Remarkable."

Amelia looked skeptical. "Fancy that! Shooting a bear. What luck," she cooed. She had edged quite close to Tyler, by now.

"Papa's exaggerating, of course," Daisie said, smiling. "It was really quite a small bear."

Tyler's eyes danced with amusement. "Tell Amelia about the deer you hunted alone."

Amelia pouted. "Really, Tyler, you mustn't make fun of her. Hunting alone, my eye."

Daisie shivered at the barely concealed malice in Amelia's tone. Why had she never noticed it before? "What are your plans for the winter? she asked.

With a saucy, suggestive smile Amelia strained toward Tyler. "We're building a very nice house, and I'm planning to give wonderful parties. I'll invite Tyler to every one."

Gregory Browning looked as if he was having difficulty restraining himself from making a caustic remark.

As if he hadn't heard Amelia, Tyler said idly, "I think I'll be building a barn in the spring."

The waiter took their order and, after more strained politeness, the food came. Daisie's mouth watered over the roast beef and vegetables. Amelia ate with her pinkie fingers curled, and her mouth pursed.

When they had almost finished the dessert course Hank once again turned tortured eyes on Daisie. "*Please*, may I speak to you in private? It's urgent."

"It's no use!" Amelia snapped, jabbing her brother's side with a look of anoyance. "If you ask her to marry you again, she'll only put you off longer. She just can't make up her mind about anything."

Choking with shock, Daisie wondered if Tyler would believe that Amelia's lying insinuations were completely unfounded.

Tyler was looking thunderstruck.

Hank threw down his napkin. "Amelia, I told you to keep out of this. Now you've ruined my last chance to win Daisie. Let's go." He rose from the table, nearly knocking over his chair.

"But I'm not — "

"Let's go!" he hissed. His eyes were suddenly hard. He no longer looked like a schoolboy. Without his solicitous mask, Daisie recognized him as the man who had forced himself on her the night of the fire.

Tense with irritation and anger, Daisie said softly, "Goodbye, Hank. Amelia."

Amelia's lips pinched together. She stood and lifted her head, surveying the diners who were watching them. Her expression haughty, she withdrew a small red leather purse from her beaded reticule. Extracting a twenty-dollar gold piece, she tossed the coin onto her half-finished plate of cake. "That should take care of our bill."

Her heart leaping wildly, Daisie stood up. Swallowing hard, she put her hand on Amelia's arm. For a moment she couldn't think. "Don't go away angry," she said, gently, her voice low and sugarsweet.

"I'm tired of the way you've led Hank on and toyed with his affections," Amelia retorted.

Someone nearby chuckled.

Daisie felt Amelia trembling. "Hank," she said, turning to where he was edging toward the exit. She gave him an imploring, tender smile. "Do come back for just a moment. I don't wish us to part this way."

Hank's face went slack. His hot gaze locked with Daisie's. He came toward her like a man who thought a dream was about to come true. She could feel him touching her with those probing, repulsive eyes.

Tyler pushed his chair from the table, his face hardened with anger, his hands curled into fists.

Daisie's father sputtered in amazement.

"We're going!" Amelia snapped. She made to shove the red purse back into her reticule, but Daisie's grip prevented her. She bit her lower lip, as she tugged to be free of Daisie's tightening grasp.

Relentlessly, Daisie turned Amelia's arm, twisting the palm upward to expose the purse again.

Her heart thudding, for a moment Daisie couldn't think what to say. She just stared at the purse. The silence lengthened awkwardly. Hank tore his eyes from Daisie's face long enough to notice that everyone in the room was watching them.

Just as he was about to put a triumphantly possessive arm around Daisie, he became aware that Daisie was shaking with anger, and that the knuckles were white on the hand that gripped his sister's arm.

Amelia jerked to be free, but Daisie held her tightly, anger lending her strength. Her mind raced as she considered how to confront Amelia with the truth.

Unable to see Daisie's fierce grip on Amelia's arm, Tyler rose behind Amelia and moved listlessly toward the exit, just behind Hank. But something of the tension in their silent struggle must have reached him, for he turned suddenly, to see them glaring at each other with burning hatred. "What's wrong?"

Daisie was panting with suppressed rage. "Tell Tyler where you first saw this little purse, Amelia," she said through clenched teeth.

Amelia's eyes narrowed to dark ugly slits. "I *found* this, you high and mighty English bitch. I found it! I'm not going to stand here and listen to your accusations."

Hank's face was suddenly ashen. He backed away, but Tyler blocked his exit. Several men nearby stood up.

"Where did you first see this little purse, Amelia?" Daisie's voice was almost a snarl.

"You had one like it," Amelia hissed. "But this one is mine!"

Again Hank tried for the door, but Tyler stood ready. Hank shrank back, his eyes darting nervously about the room in search of an escape route.

Totally unnerved by the rage burning in Daisie's eyes, and perhaps by her own guilty conscience, Amelia cracked. "I *found* it!" She shrieked. "You said yourself you dropped it."

Daisie released Amelia's hand. Her eyes were suddenly cold, blank and utterly merciless.

"Take the damn thing then, if it means that much to you!" Amelia choked, dashing the purse at Daisie's feet. "This whole business about you and your father being rich English aristocrats is a pack of lies. A pack of *lies*!" she shouted, looking around. "I didn't do anything wrong! I helped her, and look what she says about me."

Daisie's father rose from his chair. "I haven't heard one word of accusation against you, young woman. Daisie merely asked where you first saw the purse. She didn't ask where you obtained it. I happen to know that little purse belonged to my wife. For years she carried pin money in it."

"And Mother gave it to me the day I set sail for America," Daisie said softly. "It had enough money in it to get Papa and me back to England. That was the money stolen from me the first night I stayed upstairs in your store."

"I found it, I tell you!" Amelia snapped. Her face twisted into ugly lines as she backed away.

"It hardly matters now," Daisie said, her voice trembling. "Tyler has loaned us enough money to go home" — she glanced toward him — "because the other money I got to take us home perished in that fire."

Hank couldn't get past Tyler. He flexed his hands nervously, his expression hunted.

"The money did perish in the fire, didn't it, Amelia?" Daisie pursued. "Or was it just conincidence that the store burned down the very night I had something more for you to steal?"

Amelia swung so quickly that Daisie couldn't avoid being slapped. Her cheek stung and tears sprang to her eyes. She raised her own hand, and with power welling from the depth of her anger, she struck Amelia's cheek with all her might.

Staggering, squealing with rage, Amelia swung again. Her hand smarting, Daisie caught Amelia's arm, dashed it away and waited, claws ready. "*Don't* try that again, Amelia!"

Hank leaped to his sister's side, throwing his arms around her. "Do you want to get us arrested? Stop it!"

"How dare you accuse me of setting that fire! I was upstairs with you. I could have been killed!" Amelia screamed.

Daisie stumbled backwards into her father's arms. "But your precious brother Hank wasn't upstairs that night. You locked him out, remember? Because — "

"No! It's not true! She's lying. She's trying to make us look bad!"

Everyone in the room was standing.

"What about that, Salter?" someone shouted. "Where were you when the fire started?"

"And how come you had so much fire insurance? Did you plan to burn the place down from the start?"

"That fire cost my store!"

"When are you planning to pay what you owe me, Salter? Have you paid anybody lately, or are we going to get more excuses?"

The voices rose. The questions multiplied. The other diners began to close in.

Hank looked like a cornered animal. His eyes accused and reproached Daisie, as if she had betrayed him. Then his lip curled back and his eyes scorched through her plain blue dress, telling her in one ugly look what he would've done to her if he'd gotten the chance. "I would have married you," he sneered, eyes ugly and hard. He flung his sister against the table and lunged for the exit. Throwing himself against Tyler, Hank sunk his fist deep into Tyler's stomach and launched himself toward the door. But curious people gathered there from the lobby delayed him.

Tyler grabbed the tail of Hank's coat, swinging him around and, landing a punch to Hank's jaw that momentarily stunned him. Blood welled on Hank's swelling lips.

With a squawk, Amelia sprawled into the table, sending dishes shattering to the floor. One of her bracelets caught on the table-cloth. Trying to free it, with a frustrated wail of anger she whipped the cloth from the table, raining the last dishes onto herself as she fell to the floor. A corner of the heavy cloth caught on a jeweled pin in her curls, pulling her curls down over her right ear.

"It's a wig!" Daisie cried, laughing.

Her wails of anger turning to tears of humiliation, Amelia tried to straighten the dull curls, yanking long hairpins from the tangled mass of hair.

Tyler jerked Hank to his feet and held him with one arm twisted behind his back. "Somebody want to fetch the sheriff?'' he said, marching Hank into the hotel's lobby. "Let's go answer some questions about that fire, shall we?''

"It was her idea to rob Daisie!'' Hank shouted. "I didn't want to. *She* planned everything. Make *her* pay the bills.''

"*You* set the fire!'' Amelia screamed after him. "*You* ran up afterwards to get Daisie's money!'' Amelia cast a look of pure hate at Daisie. "Did you have to tie the money to the god-damned bed?''

Daisie stared in disbelief.

"He never did get the damned money,'' Amelia muttered. "You tied the money up too good and the fire burned too fast. We burned down the whole stupid store for nothing. For nothing! And I was going to let him marry you! *Marry* you! That's the biggest laugh of all!''

She plucked several more pins from her curls and tore off the wig to reveal a head of flattened, matted, light-brown hair. "God I've hated wearing this damned thing every day.'' She got to her feet and threw down the wig. "You want to know why he was going to marry you, Daisie la-dee-da Browning? To get that damned claim! He figured a few more months out there and your father'd kick off. You'd inherit. He'd mine it and we'd take the gold. We were going to be millionaires! Then we'd dump you.'' She shook her head. "What I don't do for that damn fool.'' Then she roared with laughter. "Tyler never salted your claim, you little idiot! You've really got gold up there, and I bet you never find it. You're too stupid. I'll bet Tyler's still got the deed in his name, too! Good riddance, Daisie Browning! I wish to hell I'd never met you!''

Daisie sank to the nearest chair. Amelia let the disgruntled townsmen lead her away without a struggle.

Someone patted Daisie's father. "Don't listen to her, old fella. If anybody salted your claim, it was probably them. Never did like or trust them. Looks like they cheated everybody in town.''

Daisie's eyes shot to her father. His expression mirrored panic.

"Papa, don't worry!" she whispered. "We're going home to Mama. And we can't stop now. She's expecting us."

Trembling, he found his way back to his chair and sat down. He was still holding his napkin in a shaking fist, and everywhere he looked, she knew he was seeing thieves.

Chapter Seventeen

Glancing up at the heavy gray sky, Daisie looked back at Tyler's somber face and squeezed his hands. "Well, it's goodbye then."

For a moment a fugitive ray of sunlight streaked from behind a cloud, blinding Daisie and making her eyes sting. Tyler's face glowed. He had taken off his hat and the sun caught the gold lights in his warm brown hair.

He was squinting against the glare and the clear cornflower blue of his eyes paled in the strong light. He looked remote, as if he was already a memory.

Squeezing his hands even harder, she tried to engrave his face in her mind's eye so that she could call up the image in the weeks and months ahead. She ached at the thought of leaving his teasing grin, the happy look in his eyes, the way his cheeks rounded when he was feeling most playful. The wind came up, stirring his hair and whipping strong color into his checks. His lips looked so soft, so generous and tender. She wanted to kiss him — had wanted to ever since they'd left her father's camp — but they hadn't had a moment alone. She kissed him, instead, with her eyes.

The cutting wind increased. They were engulfed in a swirl of hard little flakes, and then suddenly the air was thick with snow. She worried that they wouldn't get out of the mountains if it snowed too hard.

"I'm going mad, Tyler! I want so much to be with you."

Tyler brushed a tendril of her hair away. "It looks like gold, Daisie," he whispered, slipping his hand to her cheek. "If I had a million dollars in gold I'd trade it for you as you look at this moment."

Ask me! her mind cried. Ask me! Ask me!

He must have some reason for not asking, she thought tormentedly.

His eyes softened, growing sad. She longed to ease the look, but her own eyes reflected the pain of this moment.

"Take care of yourself," he whispered. "I want to kiss you goodbye. I don't care what your father thinks."

"And I don't care what the people of Cripple Creek think, either."

"What can they think, except that you're the most beautiful girl ever to come here. Daisie, I — " He seized her, crushing her against him.

She pressed her cheek hard against his heavy coat, wishing she was closer to him, wishing she could feel the heat of his bare skin on her hands, the warmth of his hands on her breasts.

Her throat closed. She didn't want to cry and spoil everything. She wanted to be brave and leave him remembering her happy and beautiful. She lifted her face and found his lips. If anyone was watching, she didn't care. She loved Tyler and wanted to stay!

From somewhere behind her, her father cleared his throat. "I say. You've got quite an audience."

Reluctantly, Daisie pulled away, keeping her face turned while her cheeks cooled and her brimming eyes cleared. Adjusting her bonnet and cape, she peeked at Tyler, and saw that he was looking all around, especially at the darkening sky in the west.

"I wish you could have left while the weather was still good. Now I'll worry," he said as the snow fell harder.

"Making our statements to your sheriff certainly did take a long while. I don't like having those two hooligans extradited out of state, though. Will justice be done? Why couldn't they stand trial right here?" her father asked.

"Seems somebody in Denver connected them with a scheme involving murder back in St. Louis. I think Daisie was very lucky to survive her relationship with them."

They were silent for a long while. The train stood huffing behind them, as though impatient to be gone. A shriek of warning came from the steam whistle. Daisie's heart began to pound hurtfully, and she felt afraid. She was getting on that train — no question of that. And she might never see Tyler again! Tyler said nothing and wouldn't look at her. She touched his sleeve. "Tyler? Goodbye."

He shook his head. "Not goodbye, Daisie."

Her father chuckled. He shook Tyler's hand, an unspoken question in his eye. "She's a treasure, isn't she, my boy? Perhaps I can convince my wife to come to America."

"I'll see you then, sir." He looked at her father to confirm he would guard the camp. Daisie found herself being drawn away. Her father's grip was firm, pulling her toward the train.

The conductor yelled "'Board!'", and the chugging, hissing black steam engine made serious noises of departure. The whistle shrieked again. Daisie helped her father up the first step. When she looked back, Tyler was brushing the snow from his hair. He clapped his hat on and jammed his reddened hands into his coat pockets.

Suddenly she felt unbearably cold, and not just because the wind cut under her cape and swirled beneath her skirts, or because the snow had dampened her new black shoes and was numbing her toes. She dashed away a flood of tears and forced a smile.

She climbed onto the platform after her father. The train lurched and then began rolling. She whimpered, feeling sobs of protest clutching at her stomach. Goodbye. Oh, God, goodbye. . . . The train slipped between the raw pine buildings and great new snow-covered mining installations. Tyler called something to her, but the wind whipped his words away.

"What?" she shouted, holding the handrail and leaning out.

Her father snatched at her cape. "Careful, Daisie!"

Tyler loped to the edge of the platform and cupped his hands around his mouth. Then he lost his balance and had to leap to the snow at the edge of the platform. Catching himself, looking as if he was laughing, he cupped his hands again. "Don't talk to strangers!"

Daisie laughed, but there were tears on her cheeks, tears that the wind soon turned to icy rivulets. When the train rounded a curve and they lost sight of the depot, Daisie turned away, gasping. She buried her face in her father's coat front.

"Tut, tut, Daisie," he crooned, patting her back. "Get hold of yourself." He held the door to the coach car for her. "Come inside."

"Didn't he say *anything*, Papa? Not even a hint?"

He shook his head, his eyes regretful. "He had two extra days to speak to me, and he never approached the subject of marriage once. I gave him every opportunity, but I was not going to bring it up and put him on the spot. Some men are simply not of a mind to marry, my dear, and if he wanted you under any other circumstances, well, I wasn't about to sanction that!"

Daisie shrank into herself, stung by the thought that Tyler might want her, but not for marriage.

Her father went on. "This way, perhaps, we can imagine that he . . . has some impediment. It was best you both parted amiably." He fell silent. "It's plain how he felt, though. Take comfort in that, my dear."

She could not! She sank into a seat, limp and desolate. The ride was going to be long and cold. As they chugged away, the snow swirled outside, settling thickly on everything, insulating her against the great beauty of the land she had grown to love and feared she'd never see again.

Listening with half her mind as her father described his stage-coach ride into the mountains the previous spring, she dozed, remembering her own ride into Cripple Creek and the "forward" Mr. Reede who had introduced himself.

"It was snowing like this," he went on, hoping to amuse and distract Daisie.

She would not be distracted. She wondered what Tyler was doing. Was he wandering the streets, berating himself for not asking for her hand? Or had he gone to the Gaslight Saloon where Carla would amuse him?

Not knowing why he had not asked haunted her. With her father still talking, she let her weary eyes roam over the jostling heads of the passengers. All were men except for two highly painted women toward the rear, who were laughing over something. How could anyone laugh when Daisie Browning's heart was broken?

Her eyes fell on a pair of men watching her from across the aisle. They looked as if they knew her, and all about her. One glanced at her father, looking him over with interest. Daisie's skin prickled.

She hugged her father's arm. "Are you tired, Papa?"

"Nonsense, never felt better."

Leaning close, she whispered, "Those two men are staring at you."

Appearing wonderfully casual, he gazed around the entire car before glancing at the curious men. He coughed as if weak and tightened his coat with a shiver. It would not do for anyone to think his coat looked strangely heavy. She wondered if her father should pretend to be so feeble. It might invite greedy men to accost them.

Surely no one suspected they had anything of value. They were dressed like beggars. She was tempted to say something confirming they were penniless, but at the last minute tightened her lips. If she *had* been penniless, she would have been ashamed and pretended to have plenty of money.

In places the train moved plainfully slowly. The wind increased, drifting snow across the tracks. The engine was equipped with a monstrously large plowing wedge that sliced through the drifts, but even so, their descent was cautious. Twice the train slowed to a crawl, taking a particularly nerve-racking, ice-covered curve with care. Then twenty miles from town the train plowed through a small avalanche and jolted to a halt.

One of the men across the aisle leaned closer. "Want to help dig, ol' timer?"

Daisie's father started to stand.

"Naw, never mind! Just joshing. We'll do it!"

Several men got off, and Daisie watched them struggle forward through the deep snow piled along the tracks to where the engineer was conferring with the brakeman and firemen. Snow began falling so heavily that the nearby rock walls were blotted out. She wondered if they'd be stuck overnight.

After an hour she got out to watch the digging ahead. Men scrambled over the heaps of snow, looking like ants.

"We may have to go back," she said, going back to her father, her heart fluttering. "I'll have to say goodbye all over again!"

"This simply won't do," her father grumbled. "Now that I can go, I want to go."

A short time later the engine fired up another head of steam. The whistle shrieked. The cars lurched backward. None of the men digging had returned to the car. The engine strained to back away from the snow, but there was no progress. When the men came inside to warm themselves, Daisie heard that help had been sent for and was on its way.

Hours passed as the passengers dug in shifts. Just before dark a train stopped a mile behind and men tramped along the track, swarming over the blockade of snow, digging, shouting, hauling.

They had had nothing to eat or drink for hours, and it was still snowing. One of the women made coffee from melted snow, and Daisie drank it, though it was worse than Amelia's famous tar. The engine went on hissing. The snow fell, capping the tops of the cars with six fresh inches of white.

When Daisie saw Tyler yank himself up to the first step and come in the door at the end of the coach, her heart leaped with the sweet torture of seeing him again.

"Are you digging, too?" she cried, standing to take his icy wet hands. She rubbed them, longing to kiss warmth back into them, but it was only slightly less cold inside the coach than out. This time she would not be able to let him go! "Come with us to Denver! Just for the ride."

"No, Daisie," he laughed, looking as if his heart was twisting as painfully as hers. "It's better this way. Really."

Ask me now! her heart screamed. When he looked as though he had no intention of proposing in front of the tired, hungry passengers, she asked, "How does it look in front?" The hope was gone from her voice.

"They're almost through." He slipped his arm around her shoulder and hugged her. "You'll be all right without me."

She was going to cry.

The whistle shrieked. Tyler straightened. "Goodbye again, Lord Browning. Daisie. . . ." He started down the aisle and didn't look back.

Daisie held herself rigid. She felt fastened to him with invisible bonds that were stretching now, tearing her in half, leaving her bleeding. . . .

She clamped her eyes shut. It wasn't right for him not to want to marry her! She couldn't come back to be his mistress, could she? She wanted a future with him. She wanted those children he'd spoken of! And yet . . . what did propriety matter in the face of this overwhelming love?

He stood outside, watching from the embankment. The weary, snow-shrouded passengers tramped back in. The two sharp-eyed men returned to their seats across from Daisie and her father, taking in every detail of his appearance.

"Got the snow all cleared away," one said, winking at Daisie. "You can sleep easy now."

She wouldn't close her eyes!

The train lurched forward. The whistle blew again, muted, sad. This was the end. She pressed her nose against the cold window. Her breath fogged the glass, obscuring Tyler's dark silhouette against the blue-shadowed snow.

With torturous, slow, grinding screeches, the train inched through the narrow, snow-choked gorge and down through the mountains, leaving Tyler far behind.

The storm settled deep in her heart, cold and aching. Her thoughts swirled like the flakes outside, and finally she rested her forehead against the glass. She had come to bring her father home, and home they would go. Together.

She had not meant to sleep, but near dawn her head was nodding onto her chest. Hearing whispers, she opened her eyes slightly to see the man across the aisle bending close, putting his hands on her father, patting the coat. His accomplice was leaning over his shoulder, whispering, "It's under his arms. Get your hand in there and rip it out."

In a low hiss, Daisie whispered, "Take your hand away." From the carpetbag her father had brought from England, she pulled the loaded pistol and brandished it in the general direction of the two men. Just for a moment, as she steadied her aim, she felt that the two men were personally responsible for taking her away from Cripple Creek — and Tyler.

Gaping, smiling silent apologies, they edged back, raising their hands in amiable surrender.

Snorting, her papa came awake. "What is it? Here, daughter! Let me have that. Are these gents bothering you?"

In the darkness she watched the men's uneasy smiles. "No harm done, folks. No need to get fired up."

"I'll have you know, my good man, that my daughter and I just sent two murdering thieves on their way to prison. I assure you, if we had anything of value worth stealing, we most certainly would not give it up to the likes of you."

Several uneventful hours later they made their connection to Denver and shortly after dawn they stopped for breakfast at an isolated station on the snowy flats. They kept careful watch all the remainder of the way, and when they pulled into the depot at Denver late that afternoon, a great sense of relief settled over Daisie.

She remembered the day she had stood on the busy platform alone so long ago when she had been just a girl in a fancy pink suit, brimming with audacity and naiveté. "Shall we go to the Brown Palace, Papa?"

"To the assayer's office, my girl!" he whispered, taking on an air of dignity she had not seen him wear for many years. She hurried along beside him, dodging the travelers crowding the platforms. Several trains stood in the station, their massive black engines belching puffs of smoke high into the sky, steam hissing in voluminous white clouds into the icy air.

Ahead, she thought she saw two familiar figures crossing some tracks to reach a far platform. A train beside them shrieked and hissed, huffing and screeching as it lurched backward and then forward, heading south.

Daisie's heart did a queer leap. "Look over there, Papa!"

The locomotive's great snow wedge stabbed ahead, blocking their view.

"You're dawdling like a schoolgirl, Daisie."

"I saw someone, Papa. Look there! Look between the cars. It looks so like — '' She pointed, afraid to say.

Her father sighed. "Whom do we know in Denver that we might see here?"

"Look, Papa! It's Mama and Pammie! Look! There they are!"

"That's impossible," he said, chuckling, stopping and scowling as the cars passed slowly in front of them.

When the last one rocked away, passengers began crossing the tracks from both sides.

"We have to be sure, Papa. If they get on that train over there — '' Daisie grabbed his arm. "I'll help you across."

"I tell you, it's not possible! Whatever would possess them to come so far?"

"The same thing that prompted me, Papa. Come on!"

He stood a moment, first scowling, then smiling a bit hopefully, and then shaking his head and scowling again. "Impossible."

Daisie went to the edge of the platform and waved. "Mama! Look this way! Mama!" She turned to see her father looking down at himself in dismay. "Hurry! She doesn't see us. See the way she's clinging to Pammie's arm? She's worried about missing her connection. She'll never notice us — not the way we look."

He joined her and they stepped down into the icy cinders among the rails and ties. He could hardly make it back up the foot-high step to the opposite platform his coat was so weighted with gold.

Daisie's legs were strong enough to manage the step easily. "Mama! Pammie! Over here!" she shouted, waving and pulling her father along.

Another train was pulling in. They had to watch carefully to avoid others. It looked as if her mother and Pammie were planning to board the one pulling in, and then they were blocked from view as the engine puffed past and screeched to a halt. The whistle blew and the engine gave off white clouds of steam

Her father couldn't keep up. At last Daisie released him, lifted her skirts and trotted across two more lines to come around the rear of the train.

"Mama! Mama, whatever are you doing here? Mama, look! It's me! Daisie!"

The two standing ahead were intent on discussing something with the conductor who was just stepping down. He shook his head and pointed back in the direction Daisie and her father had just come from.

Gasping, Daisie broke into a run as her mother and Pammie moved off apparently to round the train at the front. She panted up behind the two, closing the gap. "Mama! Do stop and let me get my breath! Don't you know me?"

The woman and girl turned.

Daisie's mother blinked, her eyes narrow with worry and confusion. She was wearing a wonderful dark traveling bonnet tightly knotted beneath her chin with royal blue ribbons, and the wind ruffled the glossy brown fur of her muff. Her navy-blue coat tugged in the icy wind.

Pammie whirled, her face bright and eager with excitement. She looked wonderfully prim in a gray hat and traveling coat trimmed neatly with dark-gray braid. Her boots were trimmed in fur. They made a delightful pair, hooked together at the elbows, their faces round with wonder.

"Daisie?" her mother whispered, opening her eyes in astonishment. "Daisie, my darling! Is it you?" Her eyes swept over Daisie's garb in disbelieving horror.

Then they flew together in a chorus of squeals. Her mother kept patting Daisie's face to assure herself that her daughter was real. "Whatever are you doing here in Denver? I expected to find you in the mountains. Where is your father? Oh, Lord, where is he *now*?"

Daisie laughed. She was weeping, but she felt wonderful. "What are you doing here yourself? Didn't you get our letter—?"

But of course they wouldn't have if they had been traveling.

Drawing a breath to calm her racing heart, Daisie peeked through the nearest gap between the cars and saw her father waiting in bewilderment just where she had left him.

"Come on," she said, seizing her mother's and sister's sleeves.

She dragged them along to the head of the train and carefully guided them across the tracks. When she pointed out her father standing forlornly on a deserted platform, Daisie imagined the picture her mother must see. The man who had left her so plump and proud now stood in a ragged, spotted brown woolen coat and baggy trousers still muddy at the cuff.

The boots she had bought him had never been shined. His hat was weathered and battered into a shapeless lump. Around his neck he wore a muffler that Daisie had cut from Mrs. Darnel's ugly green skirt, and his face had so changed from plump and spoiled to lean and worn that he looked at once far younger and far older.

Daisie's mother gasped softly. "Gregory, darling? Daisie, that can't be your father. He looks like the man who delivers our coal. Pammie, don't say a word. Let him think. . . . Gregory, my dear. . . ." Suddenly she was weeping, almost screaming with shock and joy, rushing ahead unassisted, leaving Daisie to hold back her sister and her squeals and questions.

"Let them be together for a moment," Daisie said, her heart warmed by the great love between her parents. She envied their good fortune, their years together, their enduring love.

Pammie looked frightened. "Is Papa all right, Daisie? He looks different."

Daisie blinked away stinging tears. "He's wonderful," she said. "And he has some happy surprises for you and Mama." She looked down into her sister's face and then hugged her. "What brought you all this way? How could you afford it?"

"Mr. Bedlow forced a loan on us. When he learned you had lost the second fare in a fire, . . . Daisie, was it terribly awful in the mountains?"

Daisie laughed, thinking of the cot in the Salter's store, the dirt sifting into her hair in the cabin, the bear sprawled and bloody in the snow dooryard. And Tyler's ready laugh, his hands, his kisses. Her eyes grew moist and she shook her head. "You'll see for yourself!"

Her parents turned back toward her. They all moved together across the tracks to the protection of the depot's eaves. Snow was falling. The sky looked heavy and gray. A brisk wind stung Daisie's flushed cheeks.

She looked into the comforting sameness of her mother's face and sighed. "I am so very glad to see you, Mama!"

"Why are you crying?" her mother asked, gathering Daisie close. "You look charming in that . . . outfit. And I know just the thing to bleach those freckles. Really, Gregory, you should have made Daisie wear a hat if she was going out in the sun."

Daisie turned to her father, and suddenly they were laughing, remembering the hours they had spent working together in camp, and those last exhausting, freezing days when she had mined the gold-bearing rock from the ground with a pickax. Going out in the sun? If her mother only knew. Daisie wondered what she'd say when she saw her daughter's hands.

"Yes, dear, I should have made Daisie wear a hat. But come along. I think this calls for a carriage ride and then Brown Palace Hotel. I have business to attend to, but it can wait one more night. I have something to show you. Pammie, my pet, I suppose this surprise trip to America was partly your doing."

Pammie threw her arms around her papa's neck and clung to him. "Did Daisie tell you she broke off with Norwood, and he broke off with her on the same day? Did Mama tell you" — she looked back at Daisie with a little-sisterly gleam in her eye — "that because Daisie left so suddenly everyone is saying Norwood broke her heart? Well it's true, Mama. They are!"

As they went around to the line of waiting carriages for hire Daisie relished the feel of her mother's hand in hers.

"Now tell me everything from the very beginning," her mother said, as they climbed in beneath the fur lap robes. "What about that young man you mentioned in your letters Daisie?"

"Ah," her father interrupted, putting his finger alongside his nose. "Let me tell you about *Tyler*. And when do you want to see our land in the mountains, my dear?" He pulled a folded paper from his breast pocket. He unrolled it just enough for Daisie to see the signatures and dates at the bottom of the deed to their claims. The date for the first was from March, the second from August. The claims had been theirs all along. Daisie's heart caught in a moment of regret for all her suspicions, for all the time she had wasted. She missed Tyler not just with her heart and body; she missed him with her being, her soul.

"Really, Gregory," her mother was saying. "We're here to take you home to England. You needn't keep up the pretence any longer. We understand that things went badly, but we'll manage. The main thing is that we're together again."

"You'd come this far and miss seeing the finest piece of land on this earth? Bought and paid for, as they say in these hills? Well, let me tell you what we found there."

"Sh-h-h, Papa," Daisie said, tapping his shoulder. She glanced back at the driver.

Her father pursed his lips, eyes dancing. "Quite right, my dear."

As they rode into town, Daisie watched her father hug and pat his wife and smile like the proud, stubborn, dignified man that he was. She smiled for herself, too, for to do her duty had brought happiness to the people she had loved all her life. But now she was free. Her thoughts reached back into the mountains. *Tyler, wait for me.*

Chapter Eighteen

". . . and then Hilary wrote that you hadn't written to say the passage money she sent arrived. The next thing I knew, I had a letter from you about a fire, saying that you hadn't anything left to wear and were moving out to the camp indefinitely!

"I was horrified. I asked myself, what is happening in that wild place? How can I sleep knowing Daisie has no clothes or money, and that she'll be away all winter? I was beside myself. And then dear Mr. Bedlow came one afternoon with this wonderfully mad idea that Pammie and I should come to America. . . ."

Pammie squirmed with excitement. "Mama didn't want to come at first."

"But of course by then we were all doing such mad things. I took myself firmly in hand and said, Cynthia Browning, you shall take yourself to America, too."

Smiling to think her mother had grown so bold, Daisie made sure the door to their two-room suite was securely locked. Then she stood holding the carpetbag in her trembling hands. Her father cleared his throat, looked appropriately official and grave, and gazed at his wife expectantly.

She grew flustered and stopped speaking. "What is it, Gregory? Are you terribly upset with me for coming after you?"

"My dear, I have something to show you." With great ceremony, he removed his coat and spread it out on the wide inviting bed. He took from its sleeve the hunting knife he had carried with him and began stabbing at the queer bulging lumps along the inner seams of his coat.

"Gregory, whatever are you doing to your coat?" Cynthia Browning cried, looking as if she thought he had taken leave of the very last of his senses.

Daisie had sewn the gold into tiny cloth bundles shaped roughly like cartridges. As her father began cutting the rolls of calico from the seams and underarms of his coat, he laid them out in rows. When he had removed all from one seam, he began tearing excitedly at the inner lining where the heaviest bundles were concealed.

Then he stood, grinning. Spying a small tray meant for tips lying on the dresser, he brought it to the bed. Fingers trembling, he cut open one bundle and dumped the golden lumps and powder onto the tray.

"Don't open them all, Papa," Daisie said. "We must still see the assayer."

"Ah, yes, you're always right, Daisie." He lifted his eyes, smiling, as his wife gaped down at the tray. "All these bundles contain this same stuff, my love," he said. He patted all the places in his coat that were padded with gold.

Pammie began to squeal. "You've found —?"

Daisie grabbed her. "Don't say it! With the luck Papa and I have had here, this gold is likely to sprout legs and walk away tonight. We must get it to the assayer first thing in the morning and then change it into cash."

Her father sank into a chair and gazed at the tiny golden pile on the tray. "We don't know how much it's worth, my dear," he said to his wife, his eyes betraying mixture of hope and uncertainty. "We mined as much as we could before starting home. We might have frozen in our cabin, and we didn't dare travel with anything more than this. The bandits here are exceedingly clever. Our young friend Tyler gave me a rather generous rate of exchange for the gold I gave him for our train tickets and the settlement for the mortgage on our claims."

A mortgage, Daisie thought, chuckling. Her father still liked to protect his image. Perhaps men really were the frail creatures Tyler had claimed they were.

"Now we can go back to Cripple Creek and protect the claim ourselves — and none too soon after what those bloodsucking Salters said. I have not been sleeping well knowing it is unguarded, I can assure you."

"We'll see about that," his wife said, finally tearing her eyes away from the gold. "I should think you'd benefit from several week's rest. You look like a refugee. Daisie, dear, clear off this bed so your papa can sleep. You girls go into your room now and let Papa and I have some time alone."

Daisie felt peculiar being ordered about. She had grown far from childhood in the past months. Gathering the coat, bundles, carpetbag and tray, however, she left the room as ordered.

"What does he look like, your new young man?" Pammie asked, flopping onto the bed in the next room and bouncing. Her mischievous young eyes glittered.

Embarrassed, Daisie tucked the bundles of gold into her father's coat pocket and settled herself in a chair facing the door. She took the pistol form the carpetbag and relished her sister's amazed gasp as she checked to see that it was properly loaded.

"Put that down! I'll tell Papa!"

"Hush," Daisie said, placing the pistol on the table beside the chair. She reached twice to be sure she could grasp it without awkwardness. Then she wedged the lumpy coat behind her and sagged back with exhaustion.

Pammie frowned. "You're not coming to bed?"

Daisie rested her hand on the pistol grip. "No, darling Pammie. I shall sit up all night, and I shall be ready for anything and anyone."

Pammie's eyes flashed. "I like this country!"

Daisie felt as coltish as her little sister the following morning when they all emerged beaming and filled with joy from the assayer's office. They exchanged the gold for American currency and trooped to the nearest dry goods store, outfitting themselves in the finest ready-to-wear clothes available. Piling their parcels into a hired carriage, they rode to the hotel in triumph and dined in the dining room on the most expensive items on the menu.

They treated themselves to dancing at the amusement garden Tyler had taken Daisie to on her first night in Denver. It was there that the celebrating grew wearisome for her. With her thoughts constantly on Tyler, she found little else amusing. Having strange young gentlemen flock about her, angling for attention, introductions and dances seemed little more than a childish game of tag she should have put away along with her pigtails and short skirts.

"I've been watching you, Daisie," her father said as they arrived back at the hotel late that evening. "You've got something on your mind. Or someone."

As her mother and Pammie proceeded them down the corridor Daisie dropped back and looked into her father's eyes. "I can't stop thinking about Tyler."

"On Monday I'll try to contact him. I want him to know we haven't gone far. It won't take much to convince Mother to—"

Daisie's mother peered from the suite's doorway. "What are you two whispering about? Of what must I be convinced?"

"Ears like a cat," he chuckled, turning and smiling. "My love, I see no reason to go back to England when we have land here and a fortune to protect. If I did not remember so clearly how much snow is in those mountains, I'd drag you there this very day. I suppose, though, spring will be soon enough. I lived in this hotel quite comfortably last winter. I will enjoy it again, especially with my family at my side."

Daisie's mother's face closed into a stubborn frown. "I won't hear of it. Don't think Pammie hasn't informed me that Daisie sat up all last night with a loaded pistol!"

Daisie glanced at her father and shrugged. "It seemed the only way to be safe, Papa."

"My dear, you don't know the half of what Daisie and I have

been through,'' he said, hugging Daisie approvingly. ''We have here, my dear, a true pioneer woman.''

''Then you won't mind if I go back to Cripple Creek,'' Daisie said, knowing she had trapped her father.

''Tut, tut, Daisie. You mustn't run after Tyler. If he wants you, he'll do the right thing.''

''Not if he thinks I'm leaving for England and may never come back. I can check on the claim for you.'' Her heart began to lift.

''It's not seemly for a young girl to go chasing — ''

His wife put her hand on his arm. ''Daisie will listen to reason, Gregory. I'll speak to her.''

He regarded his wife. ''You don't know our Daisie very well.''

Smiling into her mother's sweet face, Daisie said with perfect calmness, ''I am going back to Tyler.''

Her father looked anxious. ''But in what capacity, Daisie? In what capacity?''

The weather kept Daisie waiting nearly three weeks, but at last the sun prevailed. From a high, clear early December sky the sun poured down its warmth, melting the snow on the plains and in the foothills. Once again trains ran on time, and Daisie kissed her parents goodbye.

They had called, written and wired Tyler in Cripple Creek, but no answers had come. Daisie bought what she hoped would be a suitable dress for returning to life in the mountains and, with her hopes and uncertainties tucked in a corner of her mind, boarded the train south where it would connect to the mountain-line.

In spite of several minor delays, she made good time and found herself three days later standing on the bleak platform at the Cripple Creek depot where she had first stepped down six months earlier.

Wagons slogged through the red mud. Most of the stamp mills were silent. Residents went about their daily business at an easy pace. When the train whistle whooped, sending the cry to the still white slopes all around, Daisie jumped.

Not waiting for a hired wagon, she crossed the slush to the nearest boardwalk and strolled, thinking the town had come to belong to her. She was home.

A few stores were boarded up for the winter, but surprisingly, despite the bleak cold, the town lived on. At a corner, she turned to see half-finished, snow-covered structures replacing those lost in the fire. The Salter's Emporium sign had been taken down. In its place flapped a hastily painted canvas sign advertising Dansen's General Merchandise.

Turning away, Daisie headed directly for the Gaslight Saloon. The bar was practically deserted, with most of the chairs up-ended on the tables. A man was sweeping up as if he never intended to finish.

"I'm back," she said to the bartender. "Is Tyler here?"

"Ain't seen him."

"Do you mean today, or this week, or for how long?"

"I mean, I ain't seen him since you left town. I've rented out his room."

Uneasily, Daisie went out and stood in the cold, feeling empty and afraid. When she crossed to the livery, she found Tyler's top-buggy there; but his horse had been taken away about the time she and her father left town.

"Can I hire a wagon to take me into the mountains?" she asked the tall, gangling livery boy.

He squinted. "I wouldn't recommend it. Snow's too deep. Sleighs are all out right now."

"Then do you have a saddle-horse for hire?" She added quickly, "An extremely tame one?"

He shrugged.

Making an appointment for two hours later, Daisie hurried through the drifts and shoveled piles of snow to every restaurant, asking after Tyler.

No one had seen him. No one knew where he might have gone. At one rustic eating place Daisie found Grace Roswell. The woman looked up from her plate of beans and laughed.

"Blast my hide, would you look at that! It's little Daisie. How are you, girlie? Done well for yourself by the looks of you. How's your paw?"

"He's fine. I left him in Denver with my mother. Have you seen Tyler?" She sat and ordered coffee. She felt as if she had lived in this raw town all her life.

"We were just talking about you. And about them two Salters you got hauled off to St. Louis for trial! Ain't that a story! Let me shake your hand."

Daisie laughed. "It was purely accidental, I assure you."

"Have you heard who they really were?" Grace asked, her eyes merry.

"There's more to the story?"

"Hell, yes! Turns out Hank Salter is Henry Suthers, or something like that. Not only are they wanted in Missouri for swindling a widow and causing her death, they been in prison more times than most can count, and that's where they met! Most amazing of all, that little butter-wouldn't-melt-in-her-mouth Amelia wasn't Hank Salter's sister at all, but his wife!"

Daisie blanched. "But he asked me to marry him! Even Amelia talked of it — " Then she remembered Amelia's bitter laugh that last day in the hotel dining room.

"I think you're damn lucky you didn't get burnt up in that fire he set," Grace said. "They could've got rid of you just as easy as look at you."

Shivering, Daisie turned the subject to pleasanter things, describing how she and her father had found her mother and sister in the Denver depot. Then the hour grew late and Daisie said her goodbyes, promising to come back if she was unable to find Tyler.

"Where do you suppose he would go if he isn't around here?" Daisie asked.

"Doesn't he have a brother back East?" Grace asked.

A cold knot of dread formed in Daisie's stomach. Suppose she was too late?

"Take care of yourself riding in the snow," Grace called as Daisie opened the door. "Trust the horse."

Daisie tried to smile. "Did you hear I gunned down a bear with that rifle you taught me to shoot?"

Grace leaned back in her chair and hooked her thumbs in her trouser pockets. "Ain't I the teacher though?" she said, grinning. "But I'll bet you shot low the first time."

Daisie smiled and nodded. And that's how I found gold, she thought. "Goodbye."

As she rounded the corner toward the livery stable, the sky began to darken and sink with the threat of more snow. The livery boy was waiting for her. Beside him stood an absolutely enormous chestnut gelding with slow, patient eyes. The boy led the massive beast out where Daisie could look up at the saddle and wonder how others mounted so easily.

"One foot in the stirrup, straighten, swing the other over. Nothing to it, ma'am. Just pull up when you want to stop."

She wasn't listening. Contorting to get her foot into the stirrup without getting tangled in her skirts or showing off every inch of her petticoats and long woolen undies to the onlookers, Daisie straightened her leg and swung. Seconds later she wobbled in the saddle, gripping with her thighs and thinking she had reached the height of her folly and madness. The snowy ground looked very far away. She was sure she would pitch forward onto her head at the horse's first step.

Unable to recall a single word of what the stable boy had said, she urged the horse, which was called Blaze, along the street toward the edge of town. She thought surely she'd topple off at any moment. However, by the time she was ambling along the road that had taken so long to walk in the hot summer sun, she was feeling a little more secure.

When Blaze stumbled, she settled her weight deep into the stirrups and discovered suddenly that she was finally riding rather than pitching. From then on she and the big horse were comfortable friends. She could balance, and he seemed to know the way, so she trusted him as Grace had suggested. Suddenly she was enjoying herself.

She found the aspen glen changed from the month before. The aspen trunks were blotched and gray against the perfect fall of snow. She ventured as far as the meadow and then halted, remembering how treacherous the footing was there.

The creek still gurgled softly beneath heaps of ice and snow. Across it was a hump in the embankment where a burnt upper edge of what had once been a chimney stuck up. Below that was a hint of the doorway hollow.

Near the rocky ridge was a faintly pointed drift that was probably the tent covering their hard-won treaure. If Tyler had checked on the camp within the last three weeks, his tracks had long since been covered by snow.

Reassured that their claim was safe, Daisie turned back toward town. The sky sank lower still, and the wind lifted, moaning softly in the treetops, whispering that she had waited too long to start back.

Almost without thinking, she turned and headed north into the darkness of the late afternoon. If Tyler wasn't at his cabin, perhaps she could stay there until the storm passed.

Her backside ached by the time the cabin came into sight. If any smoke lifted from the stone chimney it was too dark to see it. There was some evidence of tracks but a light sifting of snow had covered them.

Tying the horse where he would be out of the wind, she tapped at the rough-hewn door, but got no answer. Peeking inside, she was suddenly hungering for the rustic warmth within.

Inside, she removed her cape and built up the fire. Compared to what she had seen when Tyler brought her to visit the month before, the cabin now looked as if a dozen men were living there, all sloppy ones.

Muddy clothes were heaped on a table. Several boxes of provisions were just inside the door, broken open but not unpacked. The pine frame bed was slept in, the quilts thrown about. A book lay face open on the floor nearby.

She brewed coffee and went on snooping. Utensils cluttered a dry sink. A red union suit was hung up to dry in a corner. A calendar was tacked to the wall, each day marked off with a vehement black X.

On the table were several tin plates in need of washing, a

mug, some businesslike bundles of papers and a half-empty tin of beans.

She shuddered. What if Tyler had sold the cabin?

She was just pouring herself some coffee when she heard the soft snort of a horse outside. She was going to have to see to her own horse for the night, she thought, feeling suddenly, inexplicably uneasy.

The door wrenched open and a man stood there. Outside, snow drifted down from the sky. It was almost dusk and everything was an eerie, dreamlike, faint blue-lavender.

He was wearing a fur hat. His beard was reddish and wiry. The great leather coat with the fleece lining made him appear as large as a bear.

Daisie had put her carpetbag on the floor near the hearth, and now stood more than ten feet from it. The pistol was in it. Her heart felt as if it had stopped.

He closed the door, wiped his face with his sleeve and grinned. His teeth flashed. Then his cornflower blue eyes were shining. ''What's for supper, Daisie?''

Chapter Nineteen

Crossing the cabin, Daisie threw herself into Tyler's arms. "I didn't recognize you!"

His arms closed around her, strong and warm. She lifted her face and, before she could say another word, his lips were on hers warm, urgent, searching as he crushed her tightly against his body.

She grabbed off his hat and tossed it aside. He chuckled and pulled away to look down at her. "What happened? Why are you here? Is your father all right?"

"He's fine. Everything's very, very fine." She gazed into his eyes, trying to believe she was there, that he wanted her and looked glad to see her.

His lips felt wonderfully warm. His teasing whiskers tickled her cheeks. Then he was nuzzling her neck, sending shivery thrills through her.

"You look so different," she said, laughing, panting. She released him, watching him take off his coat, hugging herself with delight. "I've been looking everywhere for you!"

"I've been here all along. Did you see it's snowing again?" he added. "Have you been here long? I was hunting, but didn't have your luck."

"Not long. I'm glad it's snowing. Let it snow forever!"

His eyes darkened. He paused in the act of pulling off his snowy boots. "Can you stay a while?"

She smiled with a flash of devilment in her eyes. "Yes!"

Straightening, he came to her, gathering her up. "I didn't know if I'd ever see you again." He pressed against her, speaking a language of warmth, of desire.

His eyes grew heavy, his lips soft. He kissed her with a tender passion, as if he didn't want to wait for explanations of why she was there so much sooner than he might have expected.

"When Papa and I reached Denver," she began, and launched into the story.

Tyler listened, grinning when she described finding her mother and sister, raising an eyebrow to think they had come so far.

"We should all have guessed that's what she would do." He led Daisie to the bed and sat on the edge with her. "I felt desolate after you left," he confessed. "I couldn't stand to stay in town where I'd expect to see you around every corner. I came here to be alone, to hold your memory close — to wait. I didn't know if you would come back to me. I had to leave it completely up to you, and I couldn't keep you with me and let your father go back alone. I had to let you go. I knew you might never come back. . . ."

"None of that matters now. I'm here, and Papa is safe."

He crossed to the fireplace and laid several more logs on. Outside, the wind rose. He cocked his head, listening. "I should see to the horses. Are you hungry?"

As the fire leaped and snapped, filling the room with piney warmth, Tyler went out again to put the horses in a small lean-to against the back of the cabin. Daisie stood just outside the door watching him move in the frigid darkness, knowing that the entire night ahead belonged to them. .

The pines leaned with the wind. The distant peaks under the forbidding black sky gleamed a frigid blue-white. He drew her back inside and bolted the door. "Now, tell me why you're here."

She laughed. "To be with you, of course!" She came eagerly into his arms. "I came because I love you. I'm free to begin my own life. I want to live here in the mountains with you."

Tyler's lips curve into a tender smile. "And to think I was

afraid you needed fashionable gowns and fancy high-buttoned shoes to make you happy."

Laughing, she kissed his nose. They stood by the fireplace, watching the flames leap like their hearts, feeling how the heat on their faces matched the heat blazing between them.

Suddenly she turned to him, murmering on a caught breath, "Love me, Tyler. Love me!"

His arms went around her, enveloping her in a warmth far more comforting than any fire's. His lips closed over her, parting them, driving his urgency and commanding passion deep into her being. She slid her hands to his neck and felt his blood pulsing, felt the corded strength, thrilled to think he had wanted her before and now wanted her again. She slid her hands across the width of his shoulders, sensing their iron-hard solid power, then down over his arms feeling the muscles swelling as he held her, as he molded his hands over her shoulders, as he slid his hands to her waist and hips. She trailed her fingertips across the fullness of his chest, feeling the quick rising and falling, knowing he wanted her touching him, wanted her wanting him, wanted her surrendering to him.

She plucked at the first shirt button, then the second. Quickly she was at the buttons of his union suit, exposing more and more of his chest where the provocative red-gold curls grew. She ran her palm over them, shivering with excitement.

Tyler cupped her cheek with a trembling palm, turned her face and kissed her eyes. "I love you," he whispered. "God, how I love you." He pulled her toward the bed.

He drew her down beside him and pushed her back, opening her bodice, pulling the frail, narrow pink ribbons of her corset cover, discovering again the ripe swells of her breasts. He kissed her with warm lips, moaning softly as his hand strayed, first to her throat, then to trace the delicate bones of her shoulders, then to push back the fabric and free her skin to his eyes and fingertips. Her thoughts were as leaping and hot as the fire, driving her up and up in red and orange waves that engulfed everything.

"Love me, Tyler! I want to be your wife," she whispered,

pulling him close, feeling the wonderful, delicious comfort as he loomed over her, his face shadowed, his broad shoulders so wide, so strong. . . .

He closed his eyes and kissed her, melting her into that rare, sweet dream where her love for Tyler beat with demanding strength. She clasped him to her breast and became part of him, one with him, moving with him to the song of their love.

"I like the night," Daisie whispered. She snuggled close and rested her head on Tyler's bare shoulder. "I can't tell if an hour has passed, or three."

He tangled his fingers in the soft, wheat-gold waves of her hair. "Your hair is so beautiful, Daisie. Have I told you I love you?"

"Do you?" she asked softly.

"You're a tease," he chuckled, throwing off the covers and climbing from the bed. "And yes, I love you."

She watched him carry two logs to the fire. He moved with grace, his body finely muscled, young and supple, his chest full and deep, his back rippling with strength, his waist taut, his hips lean. His powerful thighs swelled and corded as he crouched to stoke the fire.

She belonged to him. Something in her trembled to think she had found her great love, and that he was so beautiful to her eyes and heart. "What time is it, do you suppose?"

He shook his head. "The storm's eased off. We can go back in the morning. Your parents will want to know you're safe."

A stone of shock and desolation settled in her heart. Go back? But why?

She couldn't speak! He expected her to go back. She had told him she wanted to stay.

Why? What wasn't right between them?

She covered herself and lay back down, blinking, flinging her whirling thoughts to inane things so she wouldn't begin begging to know why.

"If you're in a terrible hurry to be off tomorrow," she said softly. "We'd better sleep."

Tyler came to the bed and stared down at her. Heavy thoughts darkened his eyes, but he said nothing. He climbed back into the bed beside her. He pressed the edges of the quilt away from her breasts, beginning to kiss them, making her feel the exquisite agony of knowing this was all she'd ever have of him. This was the end. If he wanted her to go, and so quickly, with no explanation to ease the pain in her heart, then she would go. Forever! She'd never come back to this sweet torture!

She gave herself to him again, clinging to him, soaring and plummeting, her body afire, her heart shrinking in a far corner, screaming why, why?

Afterwards, she slept a little, but when the first rays of dawn filled the window, she woke feeling empty, drained, numb. Tyler lay curled tightly against the cold, facing away as if he hadn't been aware of her beside him all night.

She warmed coffee, pretending they were long married, that a baby slept in a cradle by the hearth, that it was a holiday, or perhaps her birthday, and they would soon drive into town to see her parents. . . .

What would she do if Papa insisted on moving to Cripple Creek, building there, living there, keeping her there where she might see Tyler?

She looked back at Tyler and realized he was awake, watching her.

Quickly she erased the pain she knew must be twisting her face and forced a smile. "I thought you were still sleeping. It's a lovely morning. Do you want to get started right away? If not, I'll put on another log."

For a long moment he was silent. Then he sprang up and into his clothes. "Let's get going right away."

Ice flooded her veins. "You haven't said what you think of us staying in Colorado — Papa and all of us, I mean," she said. "Mama isn't used to the idea yet, but by now Papa will have convinced her. You won't have to trouble yourself looking in on the claim when you're busy here. I was there yesterday. It looked . . . lonely."

Tyler didn't answer. She finished dressing after he threw on his clothes and went out to ready the horses. Somehow she'd endure this, she thought. Perhaps she wouldn't stay with her parents if they moved here. She couldn't bear to be near Tyler, knowing he loved her, but wouldn't marry her. Somehow she had to ask him why. But she was afraid to!

They had scarcely finished eating when he pulled on his coat and reached for the gloves she'd hung by the fire to dry.

Bundling into her cape, bonnet and mittens, she turned her back on the untidy cabin and went out into the lung-stinging cold.

Tyler brought her horse to the door.

"What will you be doing while I send a message to my parents?" she asked.

"I'll see if the train's going to be on time today."

She stepped back, stung that he would treat her so indifferently. Then, hating her own weakness but unable to stop herself, she blurted out, "I didn't think I would have to go back so soon. Not when I came so far to find you. I thought it would mean something to you, Tyler, that I've come so far, and . . . . Oh! My poor aching bones. I don't think I can sit this horse today. I have the worst backache."

She glanced up to see his mouth twitch in a smile.

"My sore bones are nothing for you to smile at!" She turned away, her heart numb. He wanted her on the train! "Tyler, I'd like to make my own decisions about if and when I intend to return to Denver. I don't like the way you're rushing me off! And I don't understand. . . why." Her last words came out in a small, unhappy whisper.

His smile grew a little wider.

She stamped her foot. "I don't want to go!"

"Then stay in Cripple Creek if you like, Daisie. I just thought it would be a good idea to get back to Denver as soon as possible. I don't want to leave your parents out of this, not when we're lucky enough to have them both together now."

"Leave them out of what?"

He shrugged and turned away, his face assuming a serious look. "It's up to you, Daisie, but I think you might want them with us when we're married. Of course, if you want to get married here — "

She whirled so fast her horse shied. "Married? Who said anything about. . . ?" Understanding dawned. "You've been teasing me!"

His eyes twinkled. His face broke into a broad grin.

"You heartless man!" she cried, laughing suddenly, almost weeping. "How could you let me think you didn't want me? All night I've been. . . . How could you do that to me? Are you telling me we'll go back to Denver today, together?"

"Of course," he said, coming toward her.

"To get married?"

"Of course! I didn't exactly reject you last night, did I? I thought I made my acceptance very clear."

She squealed with frustration. Stooping to gather a double handful of snow, she flung it up into his face. Then she was flailing his chest with her fists, but only in play, for he was gathering her up in his arms, laughing, and shaking the snow from his eyes.

"Daisie, Daisie, don't you know how much I want and need you? I've never doubted I wanted to marry you. Since that very first day on the train — no, before that, in Denver — I've wanted you to belong to me. I've been waiting for you to be sure you would be happy here with me. This is very different from England! Yesterday I knew you were sure."

"But you never asked!"

"No, I guess I never did, but I didn't think I had to. You did the asking for me. Miss Browning, I officially accept your proposal of marriage with my humblest apologies for toying with your. . . " — he paused and looked down, his eyes resting on the ripe swell of her bosom as his hands reached to press against her — "your very beautiful affections."

Daisie grabbed his whiskers and tugged his face closer.

"Is that what you call them, Mr. Reede? You nearly broke my heart last night!"

"Gently, gently, Daisie. Remember, I love you." His voice was deep, husky, suggestive. "We should be going now."

She threw her arms around his neck. "You're not getting off so lightly, Mr. Reede. I'm not quite ready to leave yet." He feigned astonishment. "Why, Miss Browning. . . ."

Taking his hand, she led him back toward the door. "Come along, Mr. Reede. No one gets away with teasing me, not for very long."

"And what would you like me to do to make up for teasing you?" he whispered.

Inside, the cabin was still warm and sweet with the fragrance of the night. As she closed the door and began burrowing into Tyler's clothes, freeing his skin to her touch, she lifted her laughing face to be kissed. His warm lips found hers and held her spellbound while her trembling body responded, molding to his, arching up to be caressed as only he could caress her. She belonged to him. And now he belonged to her.

She was forever changed. She had taken matters into her own hands, crossed to a raw, bright world to find her father, wrestled treasure from the wilderness and tamed the lion of her dreams.

SWEET WILD WIND

Joyce Verrette

In the primeval forests of Canada, passion was born in the mystery of a stolen kiss.

A high-spirited beauty, daughter of the furrier to the French king, Aimée Dessaline had led a sheltered life. But on one fateful afternoon her fate was sealed with a burning embrace . . .

Vale – his sun-bronzed face and buckskins proclaimed his Indian upbringing, but his words betrayed another heritage. Convinced that he was a spy, she vowed to forget him – this man they also called Valjean Etienne, Comte de la Tour, Marquis d'Auvergne.

But not even the glittering court at Versailles where King Louis XV himself courted her favours, not even the perils of the war-torn wilderness, could still her impetuous heart. For no other man could stir in her soul this gentle madness, this SWEET WILD WIND.

Futura Publications
Fiction/Historical Romance
A Troubadour Book
0 7088 2931 7

TO LOVE AND TO CONQUER

Joyce Verrette

SHE WAS MORE REAL TO HIM THAN LIFE ITSELF

They were born worlds apart but destined to a passion that would survive the Inquisition that ravaged her country and the conquistadors who enslaved his. Rianna Alava of Madrid was driven from Spain to discover a great civilization in the Inca kingdom of Peru . . . and to find her refuge in Shalikuchima, a fabled warrior fighting to save his people. She first appeared to him in a blazing vision. Then she appeared in the flesh – the woman meant to ignite his spirit, to capture his heart and soul.

Futura Publications
Fiction/Historical Romance
A Troubadour Book
0 7088 2929 5

A REBEL'S LOVE

Joyce Verrette

Raised a loyalist on a luxurious Virginia plantation, golden-haired Venetia Fleming had been sent to England away from the fires of the American revolution. But from the moment she met Joaquin St Cloud, her sheltered world became no more than a memory.

Spirited aboard his swift war frigate bound for New Orleans, she became a prisoner of love unable to resist the notorious rebel and privateer. Venetia herself would become a rebel spy, but not until she faced almost certain death did she realize that she would sooner give up home and country than betray the man who had pirated her away from all safety, won her to his cause and taken possession of her heart forever.

Futura Publications
Fiction/Historical Romance
A Troubadour Book
0 7088 2932 5

LOVE'S TENDER FURY

Jennifer Wilde

'My kind of book – bold, racy, exciting!
I couldn't put it down.' Rosemary Rogers

The turbulent story of an English beauty, sold at
auction as a slave, who scandalised and captivated
the New World in her fight to conquer her masters.

Marietta Danvers was a woman wronged – seduced
by her employer, charged with theft by her jealous
mistress and shipped to the Colonies to serve
fourteen years in bondage to the man who bid
highest. But Marietta was also beautiful, educated
and resilient and she was determined to prevail
over the handsome, silent planter who bought her
to be his housekeeper; over the dashing
entrepreneur who supplied girls to the New Orleans
red light district and over the wealthy sadist who
used her in his madness.

Futura Publications
A Troubadour Book
Fiction/Historical Romance
0 8600 7446 3

CRIMSON CONQUEST

Sandra DuBay

Abused by her brutal husband, lovely Athenais de Montespan yearned for the love of the one man in all France who seemed completely beyond her reach – none other than the handsome, sensual Louis XIV. As Maid of Honour to Queen Marie-Therese, Athenais was constantly in Louis' presence and at last she won the royal heart.

Surrounded by every luxury, envied by every other woman at Versailles, second in power only to the King himself, Athenais at last believed her future secure. But then she was forced to confront a rival for her lover's affections, a woman she herself had raised from poverty and introduced to the Sun King's glittering court.

Futura Publications
Fiction/Historical Romance
A Troubadour Book
0 7088 3049 8

THE DAUGHTERS OF CAMERON

Aleen Malcolm

FIRES OF PASSION RAGED IN THEIR BLOOD . . .

Behind them lay the American wilderness ravaged by war, gripped by savagery. Before them rose Scotland's stormy cliffs and the promise of reclaiming their proud ancestral estate, their bold heritage.

Sultry, sun-kissed Kestrel and the exquisite, raven-haired Rue. Together they had seen what no woman was meant to see and steeled themselves to trust no one. Only men as stong as Nick Mackay, as fearless as the dark pirate Hawk, could hope to penetrate the proud fortress of their hearts.

For in their blood raced the fiery spirit of the Black Cameron, legendary Highland beauty. Like their mother before them, they were untamed, reckless in danger, destined to love one man, and one man only – rapturously, passionately, and forever.

Futura Publications
A Troubadour Book
Fiction/Historical Romance
0 7088 3040 3

CHILDREN OF THE MIST

Aleen Malcolm

When fiery, emerald-eyed Kat MacGregor left France for the mist-mantled shores of her native Scotland one fear haunted her above all other – that she and her family would be discovered by their traditional mortal enemies, the clan of Campbell. At the crumbling grey mansion where unwilling kinsfolk were forced to house them they existed as best they could. Their identity achingly hidden, they seemed to be truly

CHILDREN OF THE MIST.

Dressed as a boy, Wild Kat accompanied her father on his shady card-sharping exploits. Then a shattering twist of fate propelled her into the arms of magnificent hawk-faced Darach Campbell, Lord Rannoch, from whom her true name must forever remain secret.

Out of terror and blood feud would be born, unwillingly, dark irresistible rapture.

Futura Publications
Fiction/Historical Romance
A Troubadour Book
0 7088 3164 8

FIREBIRD

Julia Fitzgerald

Across the barriers of race and tradition, a passion that knows no frontiers.

FIREBIRD

Beautiful Lady Kara Melisande falls hopelessly in love with her dashing Castilian suitor, Sancho Cortez de Rodriguez. Young and inexperienced, she willingly agrees to be his and trustingly sets out across the sea to his Spanish homeland.

But in that savage land the formidable Duque de Braganzia discovers her, recognises her beauty and makes her his captive. Proud bearer of the crest of the legendary Inca firebird, fierce champion of his people, with looks to rival a Greek god's and a temper to match Kara's own, he represents a challenge to her passionate nature . . . which she will find hard to resist . . .

Futura Publications
A Troubadour Book
Fiction/Historical Romance
0 7107 3036 5

WICKED LOVING LIES

Rosemary Rogers

Another epic story of passion and adventure from the bestselling author of SWEET SAVAGE LOVE.

From the innocence of a sheltered Spanish convent to the splendour of a Sultan's harem . . . from the intrigues of Napoleon's court to England on the brink of war . . . and the wilds of Louisiana . . .

The story of two people whose paths were destined to cross and recross through revolution, war and captivity in a saga of intrigue and desire. One was Dominic Challenger, roving sea captain. The other, Marisa de Castellanos, the golden-haired beauty whom he had once captured and ravished . . .

Fiction/Historical Romance
0 8600 7570 2

All Futura Books are available at your bookshop or newsagent, or can be ordered from the following address: Futura Books, Cash Sales Department, P.O. Box 11, Falmouth, Cornwall TR10 9EN.

Please send cheque or postal order (no currency), and allow 60p for postage and packing for the first book plus 25p for the second book and 15p for each additional book ordered up to a maximum charge of £1.90 in U.K.

B.F.P.O. customers please allow 60p for the first book, 25p for the second book plus 15p per copy for the next 7 books, thereafter 9p per book

Overseas customers, including Eire, please allow £1.25 for postage and packing for the first book, 75p for the second book and 28p for each subsequent title ordered.